PENGUIN BOOKS

Dream a Little Dream

Actress and freelance journalist Giovanna is mum to Buzz and married to Tom Fletcher from McBusted. She grew up in Essex with her Italian dad Mario, mum Kim, big sister Giorgina and little brother Mario, and spent most of her childhood talking to herself or reading books.

To see what makes Giovanna smile, view her blog at www.giovannasworld.com or her Twitter page @mrsgifletcher.

by the same author

Billy and Me
You're the One that I Want

Dream a Little Dream

GIOVANNA FLETCHER

PENGUIN BOOKS

PENGUIN BOOKS

UK | USA | Canada | Ireland | Australia
India | New Zealand | South Africa

Penguin Books is part of the Penguin Random House group of companies
whose addresses can be found at global.penguinrandomhouse.com.

First published 2015

001

Copyright © Giovanna Fletcher, 2015

Set in 13/15.5 pt Garamond Mt Std
Typeset by Penguin Books
Printed in Great Britain by Clays Ltd, St Ives plc

A CIP catalogue record for this book is available from the British Library

ISBN: 978–1–405–93125–0

www.greenpenguin.co.uk

MIX
Paper from
responsible sources
FSC® C018179

Penguin Random House is committed to a
sustainable future for our business, our readers
and our planet. This book is made from Forest
Stewardship Council® certified paper.

To my very own Scabby McNabby . . .
I love you nobkey. ;-) xxx

I

*I'm by the canal. I should head straight to work, I'm already late —
I promised I'd be in early today to help my boss Jonathan dye his
hair blue — but I decide to sneak in a trip to The Barge Café first.
Docked on Hertford Union Canal alongside Victoria Park (I assume
it's a permanent location as I haven't seen it move in the eight years
I've lived here), its pop-up white picket fence sits on the canal bed,
with red and green bunting draped between its peaks, enclosing several picnic benches for customers to perch on.*

*On the off chance that passers-by haven't been seduced by the
quaint vibe the floating café offers, a little black chalkboard listing
all the day's specials sits on the pathway — meaning you have to look
at it to sidestep around it. And once you've looked, you're sucked into
its charms. You have to go in.*

*The barge itself is a good size. By that I mean it's not small, but it's
not huge. It's big enough to contain a counter of cakes and treats which
sits snugly across its width, and eight little wooden tables, each accompanied by a pair of cream chairs with red gingham seatpads to match
the tablecloths. I could try spinning off some barge facts and figures here,
but I don't know anything about them . . . nor do I find them interesting. This barge gives me coffee. I like coffee. I like this barge.*

*'Caffeine. Give me caffeine,' the voice in my head always begs at
the mere sight of the bunting flapping in the wind as I hastily make
my way along the canal. Who am I to deny such a simple request?*

*I spend far too long at the counter wondering if I can handle the
guilt that comes along with a slice of Bakewell tart, or whether it's*

best just to leave it be. I decide against it and order a skinny latte from Dermot O'Leary, who's sweating in his trademark suit behind the counter. Once he's finished and handed me my order, I turn to disembark.

I catch sight of something in my peripheral vision, yet I'm already out of the door and on solid ground by the time the image is processed.

Brett Last.

No one special, just a friend of a friend who I hung out with occasionally in my first year of university when we had house parties or whatever. I can't really remember more than his face and name, everything else about him is a blur – facts that have escaped my memory over the last decade spent living as a grown-up.

How funny seeing him there, though – sipping on an espresso with his little finger sticking out as he brings the tiny cup to his pouting lips.

I could turn back.

Go say hi.

I don't.

He wouldn't remember me.

That would be odd.

Awkward.

Time to sort out Jonathan's blue hair I decide, walking with purpose towards the Underground.

My phone blasts out The Killer's 'Mr Brightside', telling me it's time to get up and get ready for work. I could've gone for something jollier, or just one of the standard ringtones on my phone, but being woken by a passive-aggressive tune seems to work wonders for me. It sets me up for the day as it sends fire through my bones and wakens my sleepy head.

I don't jump out of bed in a mad dash to get ready for work. Instead I lie there and take in the morning. My room is awash with sunlight bursting through the curtains – clearly failing in their task of being any sort of light barrier. Not that it matters – I've always had the ability to sleep anywhere. I don't need it to be pitch black or even quiet – I once fell asleep in a busy pub and I wasn't even drunk. Besides, I actually quite like being greeted by the sun when it's time to get out of bed and start another day. I really struggle when it's grey and miserable outside; I'd rather roll back over and write the day off, giving in to the gloom. Yes, the weather plays a big part in my mood – I need a little sunshine in my mornings to get me started on the right foot.

I kick my legs free from under my duvet and have a little stretch – my body debating whether it's ready to leave the warm bed I've been cocooned in for the past nine hours. While it mulls over the notion of a Wednesday morning, I pull my fingers through my dark brown hair, untangling the knots as I go – my wavy barnet was glossy and smooth when I went to bed last night, so God knows what I did in my sleep for it to get into such a frizzy, dishevelled and alarming state. Birds could nest in there and I wouldn't have a clue . . . well, until they started tweeting. Obviously. Then I'd probably have a mad panic and vow to stay on top of having my hair relaxed every few months whilst smacking my head to get them out.

I take my hands to my pale sleepy face to catch a mammoth yawn and leave them there – my fingers pulling at my puffy cheeks and skin – taking note of the spot that seems to have invaded my chin in my sleep. I decided against freeing my face of make-up residue last night and slept in it instead (pure laziness – it was easier to just dive under my warm duvet than spend two minutes wiping it all off with a cold wipe), so no doubt my mascara (I use a crap one that seems incapable of staying on my lashes) is smeared all around my dark brown eyes in a rather un-attractive manner. Thank goodness I'm waking up alone and not having to greet some hunk in this state. Every cloud and all that.

Brett Last, I think to myself as my body reaches out for another stretch – my long limbs sweeping across the dou-ble bed, leaving me in a star shape. How odd that he should make a fleeting cameo appearance in my dream. I haven't seen him for what . . . nine or ten years? And even then, I spent the majority of my first year at university roaring drunk (didn't we all?!) – I'm surprised I didn't kill off all the brain cells holding the details of Brett's scrummy face. Although even in my conscious state I still can't quite place him. Weird.

Dermot's appearance is fairly self-explanatory as I'm an *X-Factor* junky and was up late last night catching up on the previous weekend's show – I'd been staying at my mum and dad's when it was actually on, and they abhor 'reality shows that pull on the heart strings of the public like they're fools'. I'm quite happy to be part of that fool-ish public – long may Simon Cowell reign over us with his genius television shows.

And then there's Jonathan's blue hair – the thought of my straight-laced and miserable-faced boss doing anything of the sort is enough to make me chuckle as I drag my sorry arse from the warmth of my bed and into my bathroom –

finally committing to getting the day underway, ridding my face of the smudged dark make-up and investigating that pesky spot.

There are two ways I can get to Bethnal Green tube station from my flat – I can walk along the canal or I can go via the park. Both offer pretty epic scenery, which I do try to absorb when my mind isn't preoccupied with work or some life-drama, although if I venture through the park I'm more likely to have to pass all the secondary school children hanging around outside the gates once you come out the other side. I'm great with kids – love them in fact, but I was a total moron at school as I longed for guys to find me attractive and girls to like me. I definitely hung out with the less cool kids in my class. This is something I'm fine with now that I'm older, wiser and have realized there's more to life than Richard Tayler's butterfly-inducing smile and Michelle Lewin's approval of my hairstyle. However, there's something about boys and girls of that age that freaks me out and makes me feel vulnerable – it's as though I'm back in school and fourteen years old again, nervous of their attention. I want to turn around and scream at them, 'I went to uni and became popular! I have friends! Plus, loads of guys fancy me!' Slight exaggeration on that front, and not something any of these kids are remotely interested in hearing from a complete stranger, but nonetheless, my unresolved teenage angst makes me walk the ever-so-slightly longer route to the tube. And having dreamt of The Barge Café on the canal last night there was no way I could traipse by without going in and getting myself a little treat. Even if it does mean I'll be a couple of minutes late. Okay, fine – by the time I make it to the tube, stand for seven stops on the Central Line and get to the office in Soho, I'm ten minutes late. But as I wander to my desk with my lukewarm skinny latte in hand (and my Bakewell tart – clearly I have more willpower in my dreams) no one seems to mind.

Even my boss Jonathan seems unbothered.

I spy him in his glass cubicle scoffing down an apricot Danish pastry, something I know his wife Dianne would tell him off for. He's meant to be watching his sugar levels now that he's been diagnosed with diabetes, but the amount of food I know he has stuffed away in his drawers, along with the sight of his burgeoning tummy, suggests he's doing anything but.

He clearly doesn't need my help straight away (unless it's to pick up more sugary treats), so I remove my black coat, unwrap my multi-coloured scarf and peel off my emerald wool jumper. It's freezing outside, meaning I had no alternative this morning but to layer up – however, as soon as I enter work I turn into a furnace and hastily yank at my clothes as though I'm playing a quick game of strip poker for one. Minus the cards or a single ounce of fun.

When I'm finally sat at my desk and painstakingly slow computer, I immediately sign into Facebook whilst simultaneously trying to load Twitter and Mail Online. I find that you can't really kickstart your day without knowing what you've missed in the hours you've been away from your desk. And yes, I could've caught up at home rather than when I got to work – but then I'd have been even later. At least this way my body's in the building, even if

6

my mind is off wondering why my old classmate Claire Snow feels the need to post pictures of her newborn's poop running down her husband's leg, why some pop star's having a public rant about his record label or hearing that heart-throb actor Billy Buskin has been spotted back in LA after taking some time away from the limelight to bake cakes in some quaint little village in Kent. My brain NEEDS to know all this stuff before I can start looking at the mundane diary that belongs to my boss Jonathan – one of the masterminds behind Red Brick Productions, a television production company that specializes in reality TV shows about people relocating abroad.

When I tell people I work here they immediately assume I'm constantly swanning off to various fun locations for work. I'm not. At all. In fact, I've not been on a single trip. Jonathan regularly gets to go on scouting, recce or shooting excursions to gorgeously sunny locations, as does the majority of the office (it's not a particularly large company). But not me. My role at this desk is deemed too important for me to be let loose from the chains that bind me here. At least, I'm sure Jonathan mumbled something along those lines when I dared to mention that I'd love the opportunity to travel to Greece with the team a few months ago. He was munching on an egg mayo sandwich at the time so it was difficult to make out his exact wording while little bits of food were spraying from his mouth, but he definitely said the words 'hold the fort' and 'not a bloody holiday' before shunning me away to make him a cup of coffee.

Perhaps one day I'll find myself on the Research team – they always seem to have fun faffing around in various locations. Or maybe I could work in Development, brain-storming new ideas each day around the boardroom table. I often spy them in there talking away and wonder how much work actually gets done when I can hear them talking about the Kardashians, Miley Cyrus or their weekend plans. Not that I spend the majority of my day earwigging, of course.

While avoiding starting work and having a little stalk on Facebook to see if I can find Brett Last (rarely do I just stick to my newsfeed – it's much more fun rooting through people's profile pages), an event pops up in my notifications.

It's from Dan Tipper.

My ex.

It's an invite to a housewarming party he and his girl-friend are having at the weekend.

I outwardly groan with my head in my hands.

'You all right, Sarah?' asks Julie, PA to Jonathan's business partner Derek – her desk is positioned parallel to mine outside our bosses' office doors.

She's in her late forties, very mumsy and ready to look after anyone in the office if there's the slightest thing wrong with them. I love that about her. Her caring brown eyes look at me with concern as her hands rest upon her heart – making her Mother Teresa tendencies even more sincere. In fact, she's small like her too. Pint sized! Although, she's certainly no saint. You should see Julie at a works do when she's had one Bacardi and coke too many . . . Jeeeeez! She goes from timid nurturer to wild maniac – trying to round everyone up to do shots of tequila.

But here she is in her default mother hen mode – her

dark brown hair cut short below her ears and her outfit an array of pastel shades.

'I'm fine,' I answer, trying to rearrange my face into something that looks like a smile.

'You sure?' she pouts, her chin down and head slightly tilted to the side in the way that mums talk to young children – sympathetic and imploring all at once – the look that makes you want to spill the beans on everything you've ever experienced in your life.

'Yeah,' I mumble, trying not to cave at THAT look.

'Okay, you let me know if you're not feeling great though. Promise?'

'Promise,' I reply, pursing my lips as I turn back to my computer screen, aware that her eyes are still on me – waiting for me to crack.

Luckily, we're interrupted by the arrival of Derek, who nods a quick hello in my direction before turning to Julie.

'Sorry, but could you move next week's flight by twenty-four hours?' he asks with an apologetic smile.

Tall, sporty and in his late fifties, Derek has always seemed much more approachable than Jonathan – his brown eyes are caring and his voice is a tad more inviting than the barking nature of my boss's. He's not a pushover, though. He's still a leader – he's strong and everything you'd expect in a businessman in the city, but there's just a realness to him. I never feel like he thinks his staff are beneath him, unlike Jonathan, who seems to think he's the king and we've all been put on earth to serve him. I'm gutted it wasn't Derek looking for a PA when I applied.

'Of course,' Julie replies, sitting up straight and grabbing her notepad.

'I've got a family meal on and I don't fancy being the brunt of my wife's anger if I miss it.'

'Wouldn't want that,' she giggles, watching him walk away before picking up the phone and calling the company travel agent.

With Julie's mind now occupied elsewhere, I'm free to mull over the sight before me.

For most people an invite to such a cosy little gathering from their ex would be unexpected, uninvited and downright rude – especially when said ex dumped you for said new girlfriend – but for us it's fairly standard behaviour. Sadly, and rather disturbingly.

For me.

Not him.

Dan and I met at university in Leicester. We lived in the same halls, studied the same degree (Media and Communications) and secured the same bunch of friends (enter Natalia, Carly, Alastair and Josh). It wasn't love at first sight, but we haphazardly stumbled into each other's beds one too many times during our first two years and unsurprisingly feelings started to grow. When uni ended, we moved to London with our pretty pointless degrees thinking we'd take over the world of television, but instead I ended up with porky Jonathan (it might be a television production company, but I'm basically just his skivvy) while Dan tried freelancing and temping where he could. Luckily for him, the freelancing eventually led to Dan becoming the Digital Media Executive at a fancy PR company – I've no idea what the role entailed, but it sounded good. It was there, on the first day of his new job, that he met Perfect Lexie (that's the full name I've given her since – others know her simply as

Lexie) and decided that what he felt for her in that single day he'd never felt for me. It was that quick. That cutthroat. That cold.

The worst of it was that we talked about it.

In great depth.

That night.

'So, it was a good first day?' I'd innocently asked while we were sat at the dinner table tucking into the turkey and sweet leek pie I'd spent hours making. It was his favourite – I thought his new job called for a celebration of some sort so had taken the afternoon off to spoil him.

'Yeah . . .' he shrugged, nonchalantly.

'You sure?' I encouraged, finding it strange that he wasn't forthcoming with every detail of his first day in his important-sounding position. I was worried he hated it. 'Is it not what you thought it was going to be? Because everyone feels weird when they start somewhere new – you've just got to get used to it.'

'No, the job's fine . . .'

'Oh. Is it the people? Are they cliquey? You'll charm your way around them in no time. Who wouldn't want to be friends with you?' I babbled with a smile – stuffing a whole floret of broccoli in my mouth and gaily munching away.

Watching me, Dan took a deep breath and delicately lowered his knife and fork on to his plate. Pensively, he lent across the table and grabbed my hand affectionately – his thumb rubbing the back of my hand.

For a moment I thought he was going to propose – and the first thoughts that crossed my mind were that my knife was still lingering awkwardly in my left hand (mid-pie-slicing), and that I possibly had bits of broccoli stuck in my teeth. I quickly manoeuvred the knife with my right hand and swept my tongue along the front of my teeth, before looking up at Dan with a sheepish grin on my face.

Funny that I felt shy in that moment, and acted coy and demure.

Rather shamefully, Dan wasn't smiling back in quite the same way though.

He was smiling, but the smile wasn't one of unconditional love. Instead, it said 'sorry'. It's a look that has haunted me ever since and physically makes me shudder with embarrassment – especially as I'm still able to recall the slowness with which my own loving smile slid from my face as it tried to maintain an element of hope for our situation.

But the fleeting thought of a declaration of never-ending commitment puffed out its last breath as it withered away and died quietly. Instead, Dan enlightened me in unknown matters of the heart. His heart.

'The thing is, Sarah . . .' he began, before proceeding to tell me everything that had been on his mind for the previous few months. He'd started to see me more as a friend, not someone he was hoping to grow old with. He'd apparently felt that way for quite some time, but meeting Perfect Lexie (and fancying the pants off her) had only helped to confirm those thoughts. There's not much you can say when someone is as brutally honest as that. Besides, rather annoyingly, what choice did I have? Screaming at him wasn't going to change his mind. Instead, I chose to nod along to his heart-breaking monologue and flick burnt bits of flaky puff pastry around my plate, all the while biting into my bottom lip to stop myself from crying.

I didn't want to cry and I didn't.

Not in front of him anyway.

I cried bucketloads over the subsequent days and weeks (then months and now nearly two years) – but in that moment, in our little kitchen-diner, I managed to hold them back.

Dan witnessed me being composed and mature in my response.

So at least I managed to keep some dignity.

And that's where our story should've ended. He should've moved out and disappeared into the sunset with Perfect Lexie, leaving me to eat my chicken pie in peace. But that never happened. It was never an option. Even if I'd wanted to (and I did want to), I couldn't just cut him out of my life because of our best mates, who we'd jointly acquired at uni during the best days of our lives.

My rocks were his rocks.

My happy memories with them were his happy memories with them.

Now, that sucked.

My friends – our friends – gathered around me in support, of course they did. They were there to throw away my snotty tissues, to ply me with endless shots to drown my sorrows and then carry me home when the Sambuca had woken the emotional wreck inside me – but I knew they could only be there for me in that capacity for so long before they felt awkward about the situation. I didn't want them looking at me, with my mascara running down my face and my lips puffed out in ugly-girl-crying-horror, and wonder when they'd be able to go hang out with fun-time Dan again. Because you can bet that he wasn't in the same state that I was. Not when, within a week of splitting up with me, he was already out on dates with Perfect Lexie. He'd moved out of our flat pretty sharpish, but that didn't mean I was unaware of his whereabouts . . . thanks to me having access to his email and all of his social media accounts. Yeah, yeah – I'm awful, but he really should've been on top of changing his passwords, seeing as he specialized in all things digital.

With Dan lost – absconded into the arms of Perfect Lexie, I didn't want to lose my friends as well when they got bored of my moping ways. If pushed, they would choose fun-time Dan, of course they would. I would too if the choice was between a sullenly desperate me and a happy him!

Plus, their pity irritated the crap out of me fairly quickly anyway – as did their tiptoeing around me whenever Dan came up in conversation, which invariably he did. Our worlds were so ridiculously entwined it was impossible to know where to start the unravelling and separation of our lives. A task that was made more complicated thanks to our friendship group.

And so, I fought back in the only way I could, making the decision to hide my true feelings and act like I was fine with everything. *Absolutely fine, fine, fine. Breezy, breezy, breezy. My boyfriend might've dumped me after seven years together and jumped all over my heart using a pogo-stick, but hey, we're all alive and life is so hunky-fucking-dory – let's all hold hands and sing* Kumbaya My Lord *around a campfire as we marvel over the wonder that is life.*

I was even the first to suggest Perfect Lexie came along to our weekly Wednesday quiz night at our local pub once they were officially a couple (two weeks post split). God knows why I put myself through the torture, but it felt like the only way to gain a little control of the situation I'd become helpless in, even if it did mean that I stayed up in bed wailing the whole night afterwards.

Seriously, she was so annoyingly perfect with her pretty little face decorated with luscious lips and huge green eyes, silky smooth dark blonde hair and killer boobs. She had the sort of humour that all of our friends appreciated, causing them to wet themselves laughing at various times during the night. I'll admit, it was nervous laughter at first – giving me sideways glances to check I was okay with their treachery, but my goofy smile seemed to put them at ease. In fact, I found the goofier the smile I mustered the more successful I was at keeping up the pretence.

God, it was a tough night.

The only thing that appeased my hurting heart was the fact that Perfect Lexie had the most irritating laugh I'd ever heard. It was nice to find a fault – even if that fault made me want to rip my ears off every time the donkey-on-helium sound ricocheted out of her mouth.

Shaking my head to clear those memories, I scroll over the little Facebook invite in front of me. I'm sure it doesn't mean that Dan has no consideration for my feelings, even though we dated for seven years, planned to buy a little pug puppy together (a girl – we were going to call her Monroe – Monnie for short) and had talked extensively about our future. Surely not. It's just that sometimes I'm sure he's forgotten we even have any sort of extra history outside of our friendship group. Especially when he's there rubbing his hand up and down Perfect Lexie's back and giving her bottom a quick grab when he thinks no one is watching. But I'm watching, of course. And the sight always makes me want to vomit – even though it's been nearly two years (actually, twenty-one months and twenty-five days, but who's counting?) since he dumped me to be with her and her perfect butt.

My phone vibrating along my desk thankfully cuts into my thoughts. I sigh and let the anxiety drain away from me as I look down at my phone and see it's my (our) friend Natalia calling.

Everything's absolutely fine, fine, fine. Breezy, breezy, breezy.

'Hey lover,' she shouts as soon as I pick up – she's clearly power walking somewhere as I can hear wind swooshing past and a babble of people around her.

'All right?' I croon back. 'Where are you?'

'On my way to Harrods to pick up some pieces I've ordered for a client. It's chaos out here – I think everyone's already out doing their Christmas shopping!'

'It's only November,' I moan.

'Not everyone waits until the weekend before and panic buys online.'

'Guilty as charged,' I laugh – although there's no way I'd rather be out in the crowds elbowing people over festive treats when I can do the whole thing from the comfort of my bed in my pyjamas.

'Anyway, you on the book of face?' she asks.

'Where else?'

'Seen the invite?'

'What invite?'

'From Dan? It says you've already accepted. Very prompt of you.'

Bugger – I must've pressed 'Going' by accident. Although, clearly, this 'event' wasn't something I'd be able to dodge too easily.

'Oh that!' I tut as though it's already escaped my mind and isn't burning a weeping hole into my achy breaky heart (thanks Billy Ray Cyrus). 'I didn't realize they'd moved already.'

Another lie. Of course I knew that they'd bought – yes bought, not rented (that showed proper commitment – bet they even have a joint bank account to match), a house together just off Columbia Road – my dream location and, rather annoyingly, within walking distance (it's the other side of the park) from the little rented flat I share with Carly, the third girl from our original university friendship group. The flat is the same one Dan and I shared together. The one he deserted me in. I should've moved, I know that – but it's so close to the park and affordable. Plus, Carly was looking for somewhere to live after coming back from yet another travelling gap year (this time in Thailand, Cambodia and Laos), so it seemed a shame to have all the upheaval of finding somewhere new and then moving when the flat I was already in was actually all right and probably better than anything else we'd be able to find in the area. Sod all the ghostly memories surrounding the place and my weeping whenever I looked at Dan's empty wardrobe space. Well, that void has been filled and it's a girlie pad now. There's even a Ryan Gosling poster hanging in the living room to prove it.

'I think their parents went round to help shift boxes over the weekend,' informs Natalia.

'That's nice.'

'I'm surprised they're doing a party so soon, though – I'd have thought they'd want to settle in first.'

'Any excuse for a drink,' I say dryly.

'Apparently it's a gorgeous place,' Natalia continues to natter on. 'I'm going to get home envy. I know it. Every time I go somewhere new I can't help but plan through everything I'd do with that blank canvas,' she chuckles down the phone, disappearing into a land of interior design and all things decorative. It's no wonder Natalia was snapped up by a huge design house and is given hundreds of thousands of pounds to spend on each new build acquired by the company. So many of their clients have more money than sense, but that's something Natalia doesn't mind. She lives, breathes and dreams soft furnishings and can sniff out a Farrow & Ball wall a mile off – giving you not only the name of a particular paint or wallpaper, but the actual catalogue number too. She's a rare breed. 'Dan will be absolutely taste-less and shoving any old crap from Ikea in there if given half a chance, but I'm sure Lexie is going to do an amazing job on it – she's got a whole scrapbook of plans. She showed it to me the other day.'

'Great!' I interject with more gusto than necessary, not wanting to hear any more about Perfect Lexie. I'd love to say I'm not as bothered by her presence in our lives as I used to be (I'm aware how unhealthy it is to hold a grudge for so long over her perfectness – she can't help it), but she'll always be the girl who I got left for, so I don't really want to sit here hearing my best mate Natalia gas about how fab she is. 'Pub later?'

'Of course,' Natalia responds. 'Where else would I be on a Wednesday night? We've got to win our crown back.'

When we first started pub quizzing we were pretty naff, but somehow over the years we've become semi-decent pub quizzers and (thanks to the world of twitter keeping us all up to date on current affairs – yes, I do use it for more than just stalking Jessica Alba's beautiful Honest Life) we've managed to scrape our way to success. A grand total of thirteen times we've topped the leader board and won a free round of drinks – no drink tastes as good as a free one and the last time we received one of those was two weeks ago. Last week we lost to a team of local performing art students who we'd never even seen in the pub before. Tonight, it was time to reclaim our winner's title.

'Sweet. See you there!' I chirp, putting down my phone, closing my webpages along with the ghastly Facebook invite and immersing myself in my to-do list – a collection of chores that I'm sure aren't worth the time I spent slaving away at university – or the debt it put me in. The first three bulleted tasks are to pick up dry-cleaning (easy and I love an excuse to get out of the office), phone the DVLA to query the three points Jonathan's wife Dianne accrued when speeding up the M6 in their Bentley (not entirely sure what they expect me to do) and look into getting Beyoncé tickets for Jonathan's teenage daughter Harriet and her mates (a gig that has been sold out for at least six months). Not one of those are TV related at all, but I guess that's the life of a PA – it's my job to make Jonathan's life as easy as possible so that he is able to perform to the best of his abilities in his job . . . which includes making his home life easier too. Well, it takes a pretty understanding wife not to mind the many late nights and weekends of unkept plans, a fact she constantly reminds him of.

I'm about to look up the number for the DVLA when Jonathan comes out of his glass cubicle and over to my desk.

'Sarah . . . ?' he starts with a frown as he looks down at his mobile phone, oblivious to the crumbs that have dusted his black sweater vest.

'Yes, Jonathan?' I smile, happy to be distracted, hoping he's got a wonderfully exciting and creative task for me to take on.

'Could you get me a cup of tea? Mine's cold – oh, and two sugars this time, please,' he adds, with what appears to be a conspiratorial wink.

Clearly that's not something to tell his wife about. The extra spoonful of sugar I mean. Not the wink.

Eurgh.

2

After scrambling through rush hour on the tube and heading home to freshen up, Carly and I find Alastair, Josh and Natalia already sat at a table in the corner of our local that we've christened 'our spot'. Surrounded by plum plush cushions and dimly lit in the dingy pub setting, the table is scattered with empty crisp packets and, judging by the empty glasses in front of them, the boys have moved on to their second pints of the night. Having already had a trip to the gym (lads) to play squash (not so laddy), they're both in their comfy clothes, looking rosy-cheeked from the exercise and the gym's piping hot showers – meaning they smell yummy and fresh, too.

Natalia, on the other hand, is still in her smart grey work suit (she loves a fitted jacket/skirt combo) and is perched to the side of Alastair, frowning into her iPhone – no doubt scouring the internet for an antique piece of furniture or discontinued piece of fabric made in the deep dark holes of some faraway place. Her petite frame is hunched over in frustration, but as Alastair nudges her to let her know we've arrived, the worry dissolves and she looks up with a beautiful smile, sweeping her long dark hair away from her tanned face and flicking it elegantly over her shoulder. She jumps up from her seat and wraps her arms around both of us at once.

We sway in our hug, all 'Aahing' at being reunited –

something that never fails to spread a tinkling of happiness through my weary workday bones.

'Hiya,' sings Carly with a grin, breaking away and plonking herself down next to Josh, who instantly pulls her in for a hug and kisses her on the head. My bearded blond friend is unquestionably the best hugger to have ever graced the earth – it's one of his better qualities and makes up for the fact that he's usually late for everything and is the messiest person ever. His hugs really surround you and make you feel safe – it's probably aided by the fact that he's not muscle-ready like Dan, or model-thin like Alastair. He's simply wonderful.

'Beer?' Josh asks, as Carly picks up his pint and takes a swig from his glass. There's no need for polite etiquette here – there never is when you've seen each other in the worst states possible.

'Please,' Carly grins, her freckled face making her look like a naughty child. Even though she returned from travelling a couple of years ago (just in time to witness me get savagely dumped) she's still managed to maintain her bohemian look – her white blonde hair looks continuously windswept no matter what she does with it, and her clothes always have that slight 'rolled out of bed' look about them. A look she manages to pull off effortlessly. If I tried out that style I'd appear ten sizes larger than I am and my mum would be chasing after me with an iron. Oh the shame that's attached to a creased top in my family home!

'That's us, then,' says Alastair in his warm Leeds accent, looking around the table once the drinks and food have been ordered. His thick long hair is pulled up into an effortless man bun, giving me serious hair envy. It seems so unfair that my hair – which, as society has led us to believe, should always be down in lusciously flowing locks – is frizzy and uncontrollable, whereas his – which society denotes should be kept short and boring – is hair I'd sell my left foot for. Alastair really has that trendy East London look perfected with his man bun, tattooed arms (I could sit for hours looking at that inked artwork and still manage to find something new that I hadn't noticed before – angels, aliens, clock faces, pin-up girls – they're all in there), and his ability to pull off the double denim look with ease – I'd just look like I was auditioning to be in a B*witched tribute act if I attempted anything similar.

'What about Dan and Lexie?' asks Carly. 'They not coming?'

Their absence hadn't escaped my notice, obviously – I was busy enjoying my friends without them. Plus, I might put on a front of being okay with everything, but I'd never outright ask a question about them if it can be helped. Even now, after two years. I prefer to have them banished from my thoughts whenever possible.

'Unpacking boxes,' Alastair laughs in reply, his olive-coloured face creasing up around his dark eyes.

Josh and Alastair raise their thumbs in the air before pushing them down into the table and giving them a little twist – causing them to erupt with laughter.

'Under the thumb?' I question with a smile, raising an eyebrow at their charade skills and immature behaviour.

'Totally,' laughs Josh with a wink.

Has been from the day he met her, I think to myself – pleased that I manage to keep bitter or sad thoughts like that to myself. It's somewhat comforting to hear the boys have a little dig at my past love and the dude that left me behind when something better came along.

Relief floods through me knowing the perfect duo won't be joining us tonight. I'm surprised to feel my shoulders noticeably relax at the news and the rest of my body soften – I wasn't consciously aware I was still so tense about the whole thing. Although, perhaps the fact they've moved into their first proper home isn't helping to ease my strained mind.

'We all going on Friday?' asks Natalia.

'Bit soon for a house party,' suggest Josh, opening another bag of salt and vinegar crisps along the seam so that everyone can tuck in – too hungry to wait patiently for the food that's on its way to us.

'That's what I said,' says Natalia, diving in for a crisp while looking at me with a satisfied expression.

'And talk about last minute,' adds Carly with a munch.

'I know, how on earth can I find something to wear in just two days?' Josh gently mocks as he raises his hand to his chest to highlight the 'drama'.

'Oi,' Carly pouts as though insulted, making Josh pop his arm around her again in case he's actually offended her – which, of course, he hasn't.

'He's probably getting us round there under false pretences,' says Alastair. 'He'll be handing out tools at the door and getting us to paint.'

'I'm rubbish at decorating,' I admit, wanting to join in the conversation somehow, even if it is about my ex and the lovely new home he's bought. I've learnt over time that silence is the best way to draw attention to yourself around this bunch. Silence equals unhappiness – voiced thoughts of any kind mean you're fine, which is why I've been known to goofily join in with chatter that outsiders would rightly assume uncomfortable for me to be a part of. 'Although sounds like Natalia's perfect Friday night,' I joke.

'Bagsie the roller!' shouts Carly with one hand in the air. 'What? There's only ever one and I'm not being told off for my shabby edge work. Dan won't care but Lexie will be totally anal about sharp lines.'

'And so she should be,' frowns Natalia, shaking her head as though trying to eradicate the thought of a badly painted wall before it lingers and gives her nightmares. 'We're not going to be painting.'

'Yeah, I was only joking. I'm pretty sure they're getting a team in for that,' says Alastair, sniffing as he pulls his pint to his lips and knocks it back. 'And I don't mean us!'

'Oh shit,' Josh mutters under his breath.

We all follow his gaze and spot the cause for his interruption – it's the winning team from last week, the performing arts bunch. We were hoping their arrival last week was a one-off, but judging by the theatrical way they're pirouetting through the door, it looks like their victory has given them a thirst for more. How annoying.

'Eurgh,' snarls Carly, one side of her upper lip curling up in disgust.

I can't help but laugh at the serious expressions on my mates' faces as their hope of a free drink is put at risk – it's not like we're all students, still living off our student loans like the opposition! We all have actual jobs. We can actually afford to buy them – and generously pay for theirs if we wanted to!

For me, the reason I love quiz nights is not about the free pint or glass of wine (depending on my mood).

It's not about winning.

It's about being here with my best mates, totally united against the rest of the room. Having my friends all in one spot (especially without certain people) pleases and relaxes me. There's nowhere else I'd rather be but in their company with this feeling of unwavering togetherness.

Who would've thought that some crappy questions on naff topics could evoke such a powerful feeling?

3

I'm caught in an unexpected downpour on my way to work. I reach into my bag for my emergency umbrella – always there, just in case (Mum would be proud) – but as I go to put it up I discover the whole thing is made of giant pink feathers. I faff and shake it, trying to get the blooming thing to work and protect me from the rain in some way, but it's no use. Instead I release a puff of fluff into the air as the feathers become loose and eventually fall to the ground.

I squirm and shudder as cold water trickles down my neck and finds its way to the inside of my coat – soaking my work clothes and, more uncomfortably, my knickers.

It's pouring. Like, torrential rain. Big dark clouds have graced the skies from nowhere and I can hear the rumblings of angry thunder in the distance.

Looking up, I spot The Barge Café and decide to take refuge. I don't really have time – I'll definitely be late – but there's no way I'm walking to the station in this weather, I decide. Plus I had my hair sorted at the hairdressers the day before – a new head of caramel highlights and an angular sixties bob that Vidal Sassoon would be proud of – so I'd rather get it out of the wet in the hope that it'll go back to the pristine style it was in when I left the hairdressers and not curl into a frizzy mess. It's unlikely, but it's worth a shot.

At the counter I continue to battle with my useless umbrella while ordering a vanilla latte (full fat, extra syrup). Once the umbrella is finally down (the feathers are all crushed and disfigured, but at least

27

I won – it's now compact, at least) and I'm handed my coffee, I look up and realize there are no free tables, although there are the odd spare seats scattered around. Clearly, I'm not the only one hiding from the awful downpour.

I look around at the other customers and wonder which of them I wouldn't mind sitting next to. Not being snobby, but I don't fancy sitting next to the two schoolboys who are clearly looking at some lad's mag while excitedly munching on their bacon butties.

Then my eyes land on him.

Brett Last, flicking his shaggy blond hair out of his face with a quick movement of his head.

It's quite a beautiful sight.

I'm still ogling his perfectly structured face, his square jawline and thinly formed lips when he looks up with his gorgeously sexy hazelnut-coloured eyes, all stripy and golden brown, and sees me staring.

I'm pretty sure my mouth is open in a gawping fashion.

I might even be dribbling.

Yep.

Just a bit.

Okay, a lot.

'Sarah Thompson?' he calls over in surprise, his face awash with delight.

I nod. It's all I can manage.

'I'm Brett – we met a few years ago? At that party?' he says as though it's a question, perhaps thinking the gawping expression I'm currently wearing means I don't have the foggiest who the Adonis sat in front of me is.

'Yes, yes. I remember,' I reply, brushing my soggy hair away from the side of my face with the back of my wrist while I juggle with my useless umbrella and hot coffee.

'Come sit down,' he insists, pulling out the empty seat next to him and patting it.

Why bloody not, I think to myself as I make my way over — gliding past the other customers — my eyes firmly set on the seat next to Brett . . .

Brandon Flowers has a lot to answer for, I groan, as his rocky crooning takes me away from The Barge Café, away from that seat and away from Brett's unbelievably magical eyes that I was just about to gaze into.

So odd, I think, the thought of the handsome near-stranger making me smile as I cuddle into my pillow dreamily, wishing it could physically morph into the beautiful Brett.

I sigh longingly at the thought.

If only . . .

I wonder if I could actually pull off a bob now that I'm an adult. My mum decided to chop all my hair off when I was nine because I'd been chewing gum at a friend's house (I wasn't allowed it at home) and it somehow ended up tangled in my hair when it fell from my mouth as we were playing (on reflection that's probably why Mum banned gum indoors). Apparently there was no alternative but to lop off my almost-bum-length hair to just below my ears, creating a nasty nest on the top of my head.

I looked like a little boy with a crazy afro . . .

It was tragic.

Would I be tempting fate to repeat itself if I took the plunge and chopped it all off now? Probably. My frizzy, unruly, straw-like mane would enjoy the weightlessness far too much and go crazy.

What a shame.

But Brett . . .

I laugh as I give the pillow another squeeze at the thought of him.

'Sar,' calls Carly, walking through the door without knocking with her phone to her ear – she's wearing off-white cotton knickers and a pink vest top that's struggling to contain her huge boobs. Plus, I can see her nipples through the fabric – not that I've not seen her totally naked on multiple occasions, but it's still a sight first thing in the morning. 'Nat's on the phone. What are you wearing tonight?' she asks, leaning on the doorframe with her hand on her hip.

'God knows,' I frown, a knot forming in my stomach from the thought of having to go to the housewarming.

'Casual though, yeah?'

'Yeah,' I reply, my fingertips digging into the pillow in my arms.

'Told you,' Carly says into the phone before laughing at Natalia's reply. 'Are you coming here to get ready? Oh okay, we'll just meet you there then.'

Carly gives me a wink and then leaves the room, shutting the door behind her as she goes.

Frustrated, I tense my elbows into my ribs, tighten my hands into fists, clench my butt and bring my knees into my chest. Opening my mouth, I give an almighty voiceless scream, my body shaking as I do so.

Once it's out, and my body is no longer scrunched in rage, I take a deep breath and feel my head ringing from the pressure.

I feel sick when we arrive at Dan and Perfect Lexie's house. It's as wonderful as I'd feared and I can't help but feel deflated that it's not mine and that I have to be there to witness the milestone while giving lots of friendly supportive chatter.

I'd already been online and checked out the property on Rightmove as soon as they said they said they'd put in an offer (don't judge me, I'm just a nosy ex with nothing better to do than dream of the house I might've lived in once upon a time) – but this two-bed house is even more beautiful in real life. Don't get me wrong – it's not a mansion or anything grand – but it's homely, snug and theirs. No wonder I'm smacked with jealousy once we land on their 'home sweet home' doormat.

Dan answers the door with a megawatt smile that would make Mickey Mouse proud. His dark hair has been freshly cut – short at the back and sides with a bit of length on the top. It's the same style he's had since I first met him – actually, he did have a skinhead at one point, but that was only because the trainee at the barbers totally messed it up and ran a pair of clippers too far up the back. Dan was mortified and wore a snapback for a whole month. He even tried sleeping in it at first until I managed to persuade him otherwise. Still, I guess it's nice that he cared what I thought.

Back then.

'Ladies,' he grins, moving to one side and welcoming us in. As soon as the door is shut he makes the lunge for a hug – humming as his strong arms really squeeze me into his soft blue jumper and crush my Remembrance Sunday poppy, before finally releasing me and moving on to Carly. It kills me that he still smells of Issey Miyake – a scent that lingers for eternity. I make a mental note to take my coat to the dry cleaners first thing – or to douse it in Febreze before I go to bed. There's nothing worse than getting an unexpected whiff of an ex and being transported back to a time you'd long since forgotten . . . or wish you could forget.

Thankfully Carly and me aren't the first to arrive from our bunch – Natalia and Alastair are already loitering in the kitchen when we get there, talking to a few of Perfect Lexie's best mates – Hannah, Alice and Phoebe.

I smile outwardly, but internally my insides groan.

I'm sure they're all fantastic girls, but they love to get drunk and tell me how weird it is that I can't let go of Dan – especially as he's clearly so happy and well suited to their wonderful friend Perfect Lexie.

Alice in particular freaks me out a little – she's so cute and innocent the majority of the time, but having been jilted by her ex-fiancé a few years ago she's super untrusting and highly suspicious of me – it's a side of her that loves to come out when she's been on the vino, which is a little unnerving as she's currently stood nursing a glass of red as she leans against the kitchen side and talks to Alastair in an animated fashion.

Yes, I understand how strange it must be for them all to have Dan's ex floating around whenever there's a social gathering, but I'm pretty sure I lost my grip of him and any hope of our future together when he dumped my wobbly arse and went off with their mate a couple of years ago.

I seriously hope I'm not cornered by any of them tonight and lumbered in any sort of awkward conversation. Although, like I said, I'm sure they're great when they're not wined up and ready to give a lecture.

By the time Josh joins us an hour later, we've moved into

the living room and the party is in full swing with around thirty of their mutual friends sipping wine and catching up on the dramas life has graced us with since our last social gathering – which I believe was Dan's birthday last month. I'm thankful that our little group has taken ownership of Dan's spanking new bright orange sofa, meaning I've been able to wedge myself in between Alastair and Natalia – making the prospect of having to talk to others outside my friendship group relatively low. Hurrah.

'I can't get over how gorgeous this place looks already,' gushes Natalia to Perfect Lexie, who has been floating around the room serenely since we arrived, like a chuffed little fairy. There's not even a hint of apprehension that someone might mess up her freshly decorated pad with muddy footprints or by clumsily spilling red wine on their newly restored wooden floor. It's almost as though her mind is off somewhere else (albeit a happy place). I'd be having major anxiety if it were me. Especially as they've clearly worked so hard on the place. In just a week, it's already changed drastically from the pictures I saw online during my stalking session. I'm surprised that it's not been decorated in a twee and girlie manner like I had expected with Perfect Lexie in charge – instead it's vibrant, bold and strong. The walls remain neutral with dull greens, greys and creams, letting the furniture and accessories bring the room to life with blocks of colour. I wouldn't have put Dan down as the sort to have bright orange and purple sofas – but in this room it works in a non-feminine way. It's certainly a home for both the sexes.

'It's stunning,' I say honestly, hating myself as the words come out.

33

'Thank you,' giggles Perfect Lexie. 'We've had the week off so have managed to get loads done.'

'Poor Dan,' laughs Alastair, subtly circling his thumb around the tip of his nose. Perfect Lexie is clearly unaware of the gesture, but I've clocked it and, judging from the grin on his face, Josh has too.

'I'm in shock,' smiles Natalia, continuing to look around the room. 'You two could become a decorating master team with this speed. I'd hire you.'

'Well, we wanted to make sure it looked decent before having everyone over – but there's still so much left to do. Especially upstairs – you should see the state of our bedroom!'

While the thought of their bedroom lingers in my mind, bringing on a nauseous feeling, Dan comes over and puts his arm around Perfect Lexie's waist. Running his hand under her cream knitted cardigan and over the flowery fabric of her blouse, he bends to whisper something in her ear.

She looks up at him with the same serene expression she's been wearing all night and then nods with a glowing smile.

I watch as Dan takes her hand and turns to face the room.

'Okay everyone,' he calls above the chatter and the sound of Ke$ha's 'Tik Tok' playing in the background.

It takes a moment for everyone to adhere to his request and for the music to be turned down, during which time Dan turns to our group and grins manically.

'While we're all here and coherent,' Dan starts, looking at Perfect Lexie and flashing her a slight raise of his eyebrows, causing her to giggle into his chest before turning around and smiling at the room. 'We just wanted to thank everyone for coming along tonight. No doubt some of you are just here for a little snoop around, but it means a lot to us to have you here helping to create some new memories in our new home.'

He pauses then and his cheeks begin to flush. If I didn't know Dan I'd think it was the fact that he's decided to wear a jumper even though we're indoors, in a heated home that's filled with people – but I do know him, and I know that flush of colour means that he's about to say something of great importance. Something that means a lot to him.

'Although, I've got to tell you, there have already been some special memories created in our new home.'

'That's my boy!' shouts out Alastair from beside me with a cheeky grin, causing everyone else to erupt with laughter before Dan can continue.

'Thanks, mate,' he laughs, pulling Perfect Lexie into him and kissing the top of her head protectively. 'But on a serious note, what you guys don't know is that once all our boxes had found their way inside last weekend – and once our families had decided they'd had enough of us working them too hard and begged to go home – I asked Lexie to be my wife.'

I'm unaware of anyone else's reactions as I'm too busy trying to control my own.

My face is stuck in a singular smiling expression – unable to take my eyes off the newly engaged couple.

My stomach tightens as I wait to hear more – because there is more, he couldn't possibly just leave it there, could he.

Those knowing instincts are confirmed when Dan waves his hands above his head to shush the babble of excitement from their thrilled loved ones and the squeals of exultation from Alice, Phoebe and Hannah.

'I'm glad you're all happy,' he laughs, licking his lips before continuing. 'From the moment I met Lexie I knew unquestionably that she was the girl of my dreams – the girl I hadn't been aware I was looking for, because I wasn't sure such a mythical human existed. Funny, caring, kind, clever . . . ditzy – I knew I'd do all I could to make her the happiest girl alive.'

Including dumping me and breaking my heart, I think.

Blink back that emotion.

Blink back those tears.

You will not do this.

Not here.

Not in front of your mates.

Not in front of that fucker.

'. . . and now I hope I'm going to be able to make her the happiest *wife* alive,' he scoffs.

'You would not believe how hard it's been keeping this a secret,' squeals Perfect Lexie to much laughter, as her arms flap by her sides with excitement.

'I don't know how she's done it,' muses Dan, shaking his head in mock astonishment before pulling out a bling-ful ring from his pocket and placing it on Lexie's wedding finger.

Their audience erupt once more, the noise startling me and making my head cloudy.

Can this really be happening?

Why am I here?

'So, if you'd all raise a glass and join me in saluting my wonderful wife to be, my dream girl – Alexa Hansford. Soon to be Mrs Tipper.'

'Soon to be Mrs Tipper,' choruses the room.

With my fingernails digging into the palms of my hands to control my emotions, I raise my glass along with everyone else, although I can't quite trust myself to open my mouth and join in with the toast. Instead, I keep my jaw clenched and smile – my eyebrows raised in what I hope looks like happy surprise, rather than something I'm doing to keep control of my devilish tear ducts and my face that wants to screw up in disgust.

It's then that I feel Carly's hand rest on my knee, as the rest of our friends giddily get up from their sitting positions and head to congratulate the newly engaged couple.

'You okay?' she whispers, leaning in to me discreetly.

Before I can answer, my eyes lock with Perfect Lexie's friend Alice's, who's looking at me rather untrustingly, as though she's trying to suss out my reaction.

Grabbing hold of Carly's hand, I lift my face up into a smile. I even manage a laugh – although it's more of the hysterical sort than of the happy variety.

I stand up, with my hand still in Carly's, and step towards the ecstatic crowd that's gathered around the newly engaged couple.

'Congratulations, guys,' I manage, once I'm stood in front of Dan and his Perfect Lexie.

'Cheers, Sar,' Dan beams, pulling me in for another Issey-Miyake-fuelled embrace that near enough chokes the life out of me. In fact, in that moment I wish it was more than just a metaphorical choke – I wish the aftershave would morph into a pair of hands that could throttle me away from this happy scene that I should most certainly *not* be a part of.

'I'm so pleased for you guys,' I muster with a cough, escaping his hold and turning to face the thrilled expression on Perfect Lexie's face.

'That means so much,' she replies, her hug squeezing me just a little too tightly.

4

I have no idea how I made it through the rest of the night, but I knew that I couldn't leave and that I couldn't do anything that would highlight my very existence in any way. I'd never live a dramatic scene down, and staying there whilst blending into the background was my only option.

On reflection, it makes complete sense why exes can't be friends once one of them has shat all over the other's feelings and left them in a brown muddy puddle of despair.

I can't help but wonder why on earth I've made everyone else feel comfortable with our situation. Why didn't I make things more awkward and shout from the rooftops about how unfair the whole betrayal was back when he first dumped me? My thoughts and feelings are completely irrelevant now. Time has moved on – the world is a different place to what it was back then. No one cares what the ex thinks when they assume she's meant it every time she's insisted she was perfectly fine with the awkward scenario of her ex remaining in her life – not when she actively goes out of her way to include said new couple in everything she's arranged for the group since their romantic collaboration – including her intimate birthday celebrations or cosy weekend trips away.

As I lie in bed that night a few thoughts occur to me.

One, that I wasted seven years of my life running around after such a heartless twat. Two, that I then wasted the subsequent two years trying to make life easier amongst our friendship group for such a heartless twat. And three, that I'm still wasting my energy and tears on such a heartless twat. I mean . . . WTF?!

If I were to break my feelings down I'd be able to pinpoint the precise second of the evening that caused me to feel so monumentally crap and discarded – and that would be the declaration of Perfect Lexie being the girl of Dan's dreams. The one he'd always dreamt of meeting. His mythical human.

I mean, seriously?

Who even uses words like that?!

Plus, if that were the case, then what on earth was he doing with me before she came along? Was I just cheaper than hiring a maid or organizing a laundry service? Was I just convenient?

In answer to my earlier thoughts when the Facebook invite pinged into my life, he clearly didn't think anything of me and my feelings.

I meant nothing to him.

To clarify, it's not like I'd want Dan to think of my feelings when proposing to Perfect Lexie – God knows I'm aware I'd be the last thing on his mind in that moment (unless to briefly consider how lucky he was not to have settled with me before meeting her) – but I'd just like him to have had a little bit more sensitivity when dishing out the wonderful news. Was that really too much to ask?

I should've hated Dan years ago for his malevolence towards me. Actually, I did. I hated him then for discarding me so easily, for making my happy life so miserable and for bringing that perfect being into our lives to make me feel so inadequate every time there was a social gathering.

I hated him for not loving me back in the way that I loved him.

And I still hate him for all of that.

But now, I mostly hate him for making me feel so discontented.

And then there's the self-hatred he's awakened. I hate myself for what I've allowed that break-up to turn me into – a grinning psycho, constantly bashing away my true feelings so that I don't make others feel uncomfortable. Regardless of how much pain that inflicts on myself.

What a twat.

Him.

Not me.

Oh, okay.

Fair point.

Me too.

I should've packed up and gone travelling to Australia two years ago. My little brother Max was out there when we initially broke up – I should've joined him. I could've shacked up with some tanned surfer dude and waved goodbye to pasty Dan and Perfect Lexie. What a missed opportunity.

It takes hours of sobbing into my pillow for me to realize the real root of my problem. Ultimately, it's not the engagement, or that I couldn't compete with Perfect Lexie's 'mythical' ways, or the fact that Dan doesn't want me – that's now been true for years and I can honestly say I have no feelings of hankering love towards him at all. His behaviour towards me has shown what a cock he is, so why on earth would I want him back? No, none of those things are what's driving me into a gut-wrenching spiral of lugubrious hell. Rather, it's the fact that NO ONE wants me.

Not a single soul.

Don't get me wrong – I've not regrown my virginity (it's not that bad), there have been a few drunken flings since Dan, especially in the early days when I was grateful for any attention from the opposite sex, but nothing more than that. No romantic dates, no heart-lifting declarations, no flutters of the heart to cause me to smile myself to sleep.

Nothing.

Not that I'm in any denial of it being anything other than my own doing. I know that it's my fault. I've erected barriers to stop anyone getting close and able to make me feel so out of control and vulnerable again. But now I can't help but feel ridiculous for doing that. I've wasted years of potential happiness – blocking anyone who's so much as sniffed around me wanting more than I was willing to give and immersed myself in trying to make my friends think I was some sort of power woman who could forgive and forget unequivocally.

But I'm lonely.

I wish I had *someone*.

Not to validate my existence in some anti-feminist way, but just someone to call when I want to talk about nothing, someone to stay inside and snuggle with when it's raining outside.

Someone to make me feel special.

Like I'm the girl they've been dreaming of – instead of the one they were putting up with until real perfection came along.

5

'If you could have one superpower, what would it be?' he asks, leaning in to me – the feeling of his warm arm against mine causing a tingling sensation to run across my limb, while simultaneously making my breath catch in my throat.

It's night time and dark outside.

We're sat top front of a double-decker bus, surrounded by a bunch of grannies knitting miniature dog outfits, whilst listening to Michael Bublé singing 'Wannabe' by the Spice Girls. It's an obscure version of the 90s pop classic, but somehow Michael makes it work as he sits next to each old dear, feeding them cookies while they bash their needles in time to the music.

I've no idea where we're going or where we've been. Although, judging from the state of my outfit (a pink tight-fitting mini dress that echoes something I'd have worn in my teens – when I didn't have to worry about cellulite) and the fact that I have my shoes perched on my lap (they're the Manolo Blahniks I begged my mum and dad for three years ago but have hardly worn because I can't actually walk in them – I'm pretty chuffed with myself that they're getting some wear) I'd say we've possibly been out dancing. The atmosphere is one that comes with the end of a night – chilled, sleepy and comfortable.

'Hmmm . . .' I ponder, playing with the buckle of my useless suede footwear. 'The ability to scan people's hearts to see whether they're good or not.'

'Wow,' he nods, laughing the air out of his lungs as he looks straight ahead. 'I don't think that's in any of the comics I've read. Usually people just go for the flying thing or being able to see through clothes. They're clearly perverts.'

'What would you choose?'

'Seeing through clothes.'

'Pervert.'

We laugh in unison and his arm rests against mine once more.

'I prefer your superpower . . . although what would you do with all the bad-hearted folk?' he asks seriously, his hazelnut eyes turning to look at me.

I flounder for a moment at the empathetic look in his eyes.

'I'd lock them all up together and let them all break each others' hearts as much as they liked.'

'Leave us good-hearted lot to fall in love with no fear of being mistreated?'

'Something like that,' I mumble, clutching on to my shoes, realizing I've said too much – that I probably sound like some bunny-boiler who's too wounded to move on from her ex.

'I don't know how anyone could ever break your heart.'

I screw up my face and look at him, 'It seems pretty easy for some.'

'Really?' he asks, his hand taking mine. 'Well, I know I never would. I'd want to keep it as safe and treasured as my own . . .'

And with that, Brett disappears along with the bus, grannies and Michael Bublé.

I'm on a beach, on my own, with the warmth of the sun on my back and the sound of waves crashing against each other in the distance.

I see nothing but my feet in the white sand and the shallow foamy water washing over them, repeatedly.

Nothing else exists outside this constant movement.

I'm transfixed.
I'm calm.
I'm happy.

I wake before my alarm and lie there in my crimson-coloured sheets, taking in the new day that's invading my room. I didn't even bother to draw my curtains last night. Instead I chose to sit at my window and howl at the moon like I was in some sort of film – actually, it wasn't as beautifully held together as some romcom featuring Reese Witherspoon. It was more like the ugly-girl-crying horror that comes at the end of *EastEnders* when someone is wailing open-mouthed in the rain before the drums come bashing in – daa-daa-daa-daa-da-da-da-da.

What a loser.

My face feels delicate, puffy and raw from the emotional meltdown. Yet, instead of the lost, vulnerable feeling I've felt in the past after such a depressing outburst – I feel peaceful.

Thankful, even.

Thankful for the ability of my dreams to pick me up from moments of utter shite and propel me somewhere else – somewhere that grannies get serenaded by Michael Bublé and a ridiculously hot, caring and kind man declares that he'll take good care of my heart and never let it get trampled over again. I liked the utopia I dreamt up. And then there's the beach, the waves, the calm – washing away the trauma from the previous night. Erasing the pain.

In my calmer, more accepting state (although God knows how much longer it'll stick with me), part of me feels relieved.

I've always known that Dan and Perfect Lexie were destined for their 'happily ever after', so on some level it's nice to have that over with. I was only ever his girl-friend, but Perfect Lexie? Well, she's his future wife. What we had clearly pales into insignificance and should never be thought or spoken of ever again. Although everyone else has been making a flipping good job of that (with my help), anyway. So it shouldn't make too much of a difference to how we all live our lives from here on in.

I close my eyes and let out a sigh – expelling the leftover tension that's loitering above my serene state and threaten-ing a wobble of emotion. I said I wasn't sure how long it would last, although the breathing helps almost instantly.

I really should take up yoga, I think to myself, I'd be great at the whole breathing out negativity whilst in funny positions thing – I've got a lot of negativity to expel. Maybe I'll book myself into one of those retreats and get away. Oh to get away . . . wouldn't that be lovely!

'Sar?' Carly calls, knocking on my door and interrupting my plans for a whole new me.

'Mmm . . . ?' I answer with another sigh.

'Can I come in?' she asks, already opening the door.

She staggers in sleepily, still in her baggy PJs, and climbs into the empty side of my bed. Funny that. Even though I've been single for longer than I care to remember the left side of my bed is always un-slept-in and crease free . . . what a waste of my gorgeous bed's dream-inducing capa-bilities and springy mattress – I'm surprised it doesn't dip on one side like a well-used chair you'd find in an old per-son's home. Although, on the plus side, sleeping in this way does make it easier to remake the bed each morning when all I have to do is shake and straighten the sheets on one side.

Yet another silver lining to single life.

Carly pulls the pillow down and cuddles it, snuggling into it sleepily.

'You all right?' she asks simply. Not asking much but asking everything in those two words. Subtly giving me the choice to share if I want to.

I close my eyes and nod back. I even manage a smile. Yet, unlike the ones I might've given before – this one I mean. It's not forced or put on for her benefit. It's a natural smile – one that grows simply from having someone care about you. I'm lucky to have such amazingly kind and thoughtful friends – who still look out for me, even though I've told them a million times before that I'm fine. They're not as fooled as I had hoped. But I like that.

'Do you remember Brett Last?' I ask, turning and switching off the alarm on my phone now that we're awake.

'Who?'

It usually takes Carly's brain a whole hour to warm up before she's of any use to anyone so it's silly of me to ask when she's still half asleep.

'He was someone's friend at uni, maybe someone from our halls? Came out with us a few times.'

'Was he the dude that got thrown out of The Basement for throwing up over some girl?' she recalls with a disgusted look on her face.

'No . . . I'm pretty sure that was in the third year and Josh's friend James.'

'Oh. Oh yeah. He was gross.'

'This guy had blond messy hair, brown eyes . . . probably around six foot five? Maybe taller?'

'Not a clue.'

'You must remember,' I say, shaking my hands at the ceiling and asking the universe what my friend took on her travelling hiatus that's dented her memory so badly. 'Brett. Last.'

Carly giggles and shakes her head. 'Honestly, I haven't a clue. I can't even remember what I had for dinner last night, so how could I possibly remember that?'

'I made us shepherd's pie,' I moan, pulling the pillow from under her and bashing her over the head with it. 'I slaved away making that – nice to know you enjoyed it.'

'Oops,' she grins, grabbing the pillow from me and cuddling it once more. 'Why'd you ask, anyway?'

'It's a bit odd,' I exhale.

'Go on . . .'

'He's popped up in my dreams.'

'Weird.'

'Yeah,' I say, screwing my face up into a smile at the thought of us side by side on a night bus.

'Saucy?'

'No!'

'Really?' she asks, her eyebrow lifting in disbelief. 'You're smiling.'

'No, nothing like that. Honestly.'

'What then?' she asks, looking confused.

'First of all it was nothing – he was just someone I noticed in the background. You know how that happens. I woke up thinking it was funny to see him there when I haven't seen or thought of him in so long. Plus, I didn't

49

even know him back then anyway. It's just weird – he seems so familiar and I'm always happy to see him.'

'Yeah, that is odd,' Carly nods, her lower lip pouting out as she ponders what I'm telling her. 'Hold on, you said first of all . . . There's more?'

'Yeah,' I nod, starting to feel uncomfortable now that I'm sharing an insight into the weirdness of my mind. 'He's popped up twice more since.'

'Oh,' she says, taken aback. ' How random.'

'After the first time it made sense for him to at least be floating around in my brain as I'd dreamt of him before and briefly thought about him the following morning, but I've no idea why he popped up in the first place.'

'Maybe you saw someone who looked like him and it made you subconsciously think of him?' she suggests.

'Maybe.'

'Or maybe someone else had his name? That could've sent off a little trigger.'

'I didn't think of that,' I mull – although the thought of it being something so insignificant saddens me a little. After three dream encounters it appears I'm quite attached and smitten.

'This is just like the film *Inception*,' she gasps, pushing her way out of the covers and sitting up.

'I hope not! That was the trippiest thing I've ever watched.'

'Still don't get it?'

'Nope.'

'Me neither,' she admits, flinging herself backwards onto the bed and giving a little squeal as she stretches out her arms. 'I'm so glad it's the weekend.'

'Same.'

'I'm shattered,' she yawns. 'What you doing today?'

'Going to see my parents.'

'Ooh . . .'

'Hmmm . . .'

'Just what you need.'

'Max is going to be there, so I'm hoping it won't be too bad.'

'Ah Max!'

'Yeah – complete with Andrea and bump.'

'Cute,' Carly gushes. 'I bet she looks amazing.'

'Of course she does!'

In the time since my break-up with Dan, my brother Max has returned from travelling, found 'the one' (she was also travelling around Oz), proposed, had a gorgeous little wedding ceremony at the local church where we grew up and is now expecting his first child – who is due next month, showing just how much one's life can change in the space of a couple of years.

Whilst I'm incredibly proud of him and gush over how much I love bump-wearing Andrea and couldn't wish for a better sister-in-law, their blossoming romance and impending offspring have given my parents a huge reason to be concerned over me and just how little my life has moved on when theirs has witnessed so much.

Like many caring parents, they took the break-up as badly (if not worse) as I did. No doubt they were concerned what the little girl they'd brought up and poured morals, manners and intelligence into had done wrong not to secure such a catch into a happily-ever-after fairytale.

I'm in no two minds over whether it's something Mum

still ponders over – I'm one hundred per cent certain that my singleton status is on her mind every time she despairs over my fashion sense ('Short skirts don't secure your own husband, just someone else's, Sarah – likewise, frumpy is too far the other way as no man wants to date his nan'), tuts over one of my friends getting a new job ('Good prospects equal good husband-catching abilities – without a solid career what chance do you have, dear?') and is devastated to hear of others my age who have secured their life partners. It's not good to be left on the shelf so late in my dating life. Even if I'm only twenty-nine . . .

The room is brightly lit and huge – like some sort of sterile experiment lab. Although it's completely empty and I'm alone.

I'm high up.

At first, I think I'm suspended in mid air, or flying, but then I realize I'm actually sat on a giant plank of wood that's suspended from the wall behind me, keeping me miles from the ground.

I'm small, like a little borrower.

I sit there in silence for a moment, listening to the sound of nothing – because nothing does have a sound. A very loud one that is unnervingly full of suspense for something to come along and fill it.

The loud silence is interrupted by the deafening sound of clomping echoing around the empty room, caused by two giant figures walking in through a door to my right.

They stop in front of me, bending over as though inspecting the sight before them.

'I'm not sure . . .' says a male voice – low, grunt-like and displeased. 'She's a bit stale.'

'She's not a loaf of gone-off bread,' chimes a woman's voice, who sounds remarkably like my mother. 'She's a pretty little thing.'

'Would've been thirty years ago,' says the man, although his face is a blur — all I can spot are the frames of his prescription glasses.

'Very capable,' encourages the lady.

'Doesn't look it.'

'She's highly intelligent.'

'I'll have to take your word for it,' says the bemused male.

'Does she talk?'

'Used to.'

This causes the male to exhale gruffly.

'It looks like I don't have much choice, doesn't it. She's the only one left.'

'Exactly.'

As the faceless man leans further forward I catch a glimpse of myself in the reflection of his glasses.

I'm old.

My frizzy hair is grey and manic.

My face is covered in deep wrinkles to match those found in an elephant's leg fold — hard, leathery and crinkled.

My eyes are dark, deep-set and the saddest things I've ever seen as they imploringly gaze at the figures in front of me, begging not to be left behind.

'You know, I think I'd rather just leave it,' he sighs regrettably.

'What?' she shrieks.

'This isn't going to work,' he says with disdain.

'But . . .'

'Being on my own doesn't seem like such a bad thing, considering the alternative,' he interrupts, flicking his head in my direction.

'You can't just leave her here.'

'She's not my responsibility,' he replies flatly.

'But, if you don't take her, who will?' cries the woman in desperation — confirming that she is indeed my mum.

'Not my problem,' he scoffs, walking out of the room — my mum sobbing as she follows, leaving me sat up high on my wooden plank.

Alone.

I wake with a start, realizing that Carly and I are still in my bed – we each must've dozed off. Although the dream has already started fading around the edges and becoming muddied, an empty and unnerving feeling is left behind. 'Being left on the shelf' has always had a metaphorical significance until now, so it's flipping great to have a visualization to go with that horrendous spinster of an outcome. With dreams like that, who needs nightmares? And where the heck was Brett to add a little bit of sweetness? Surely my dream could've engineered a bit of that to give me a little emotional boost before heading over to my mum's.

Shit!

'What's the time?' I ask my sleepy-eyed friend, already reaching over to grab my phone to check.

'Huh?' she murmurs, nuzzling into her own arm.

'Fuck,' I groan, sitting up and looking around the room.

'What?'

'We went back to sleep.'

'And . . . ?'

'I'm meant to be at my mum's in half an hour! What's worse than an unmarried daughter? One that's tardy.'

'Oh the shame,' Carly says laughing, pushing me out of the bed. 'To the shower with you.'

'I don't have time.'

'You stink. Make time. What's worse than an unmarried tardy daughter?'

'What?' I ask, dashing around the room and grabbing clothes that my mum might deem suitable for a single lady hoping to procure a husband – finally fishing out my cleanest pair of black jeans and the maroon blouse with cream hearts all over it she bought me last Christmas.

'One that smells like she's been rolling in dog crap,' Carly says flatly.

'Thanks.'

'You're welcome,' she replies, rolling over and going back to sleep.

6

One hour and fifteen minutes later, I'm in my reliable red Mini Cooper (a present from Mum and Dad for my twenty-first birthday), and pulling onto my parents' driveway. They live in Tunbridge Wells in Kent, a short walk from The Pantiles – in the same house that my brother and I grew up in.

It has gates.

Big, black iron ones.

And everyone knows that a house with its own set of gates (complete with a buzzer system for security) is above the norm and a bit posh. Yes, my parents are well off. Not rich, just better than comfortable. Not that they've helped me and my brother out that much (other than to surprise us with our first cars, both Mini Coopers, which we were obviously both sincerely thankful for) – but beyond those, Mum and Dad took on the tough love approach and sent us out into the world with next to nothing in the hope that it would make us strive for more, seeing as we grew up with a taste for 'the good life'. My brother did more than okay with this method of parenting – he's a marketing manager for TechWays Corporation in Covent Garden. Not bad for someone who spent a whole year smoking spliffs in the Australian sun when he was twenty-five.

However, I work for Jonathan as his slave. Therefore,

my parents – my mum in particular – feel that the only chance I have of sampling 'the good life' once more is to marry up. But seeing as I'm single and living in a rented flat with my best mate, I think I'm failing in that department, too. Still, at least they have had a fifty per cent success rate with their parenting techniques so far.

Jumping out of the car I grab my bag and coat and am greeted by a waft of self-pity as the smell of Dan's lingering aftershave drifts up my nostrils and makes me feel nauseous. I forgot to Febreze my coat last night and mentally bash myself over the head as I make my way to the front door. We're meant to be going out later for a family walk. So unless I want the embarrassment of asking to borrow something from Mum's wardrobe I'll have to make do and take Dan along with me. How irritating.

'All right,' Max smiles as he opens the door. He has the same small mouth and cushiony lips as me, but he clearly takes more after Mum and her French roots – my granddad was born in France but moved here during the Second World War. He fell in love with my gorgeous Nana and never moved back, although we still head over there every other Christmas. We both have the dark hair and dark eyes, but he has the olive skin colouring to accompany it – I still burn like crazy if I'm in the sun for too long, no matter what factor protection I use, whereas he goes a gorgeous golden brown colour. It's highly frustrating. 'Thank God you're here – she's going off on one already,' he says with an eye-roll before his bulky frame leans in for a hug, no doubt relieved that his older, less-achieving sister is here to take the brunt of Mum's insults while he sits back and watches.

'Better not let her hear you saying things like that, Max,' Dad whispers with his eyebrows raised before sweeping past him and giving me a hug – reminding me that their views on my failures in life don't necessarily overshadow their love for me.

Not all the time anyway.

'Hello, Dad.'

'Lots of traffic?' he asks with a wink, his blue eyes lighting up mischievously as he places his hands on his hips and sticks out his little pot belly (something Mum is continuously moaning at him for).

'Hmmm . . .' I murmur noncommittally.

'That's what I thought,' he nods. 'Told your mother how bad traffic can be in London of the weekend – especially so close to Christmas.'

It's only early November, but I decide to go along with his lie.

'Sarah. Finally,' my Mum smiles, when I'm in the hallway – looking my outfit choice up and down approvingly, before placing her hand on the sides of my head. 'Did you leave the house with wet hair?'

Well, I can't give her the satisfaction of me getting *everything* right, can I? I came clean and in an outfit I knew she'd like – I did try. Worryingly I notice we're actually matching in our outfit choices – trousers and blouses – although my take is, thankfully, a little younger and current than hers with her crease-free white blouse, mustard-coloured chinos and a pearl necklace to accompany the look . . . now, that is posh! Plus, whereas my hair is wet and pulled up into a messy top bun, her short dark mane is set to perfection in very precise waves.

She draws me in for a brief hug, the smell of her heavy perfume riling and calming me all at once.

'Where's Andrea?' I ask Max, longing to rub that deliciously shaped bump of hers which has no doubt grown a crazy amount since I saw it a month ago.

'Asleep upstairs – she didn't get much sleep last night so she's having a rest,' my brother says.

With her hands still on my shoulders and her face out of Max's view, I spot Mum rolling her eyes before releasing me and returning to the kitchen. Whoever heard of a heavily pregnant lady needing a lie down . . .

Just as we start to follow Dad into the lounge, Max puts his arm across my shoulder and leans in with a whisper.

'I heard about Dan and Lexie.'

'Yeeeeah . . .' I say slowly; there's nothing I really want to say on the matter.

As soon as we all left their house last night, Dan and Perfect Lexie went on to Facebook and shared their joyous news with their friends online by changing their relationship status' to 'engaged' and their profile pictures to one of them both looking offensively happy with Perfect Lexie's mighty diamond on show.

My mum has Facebook.

Of course she does.

I had to get my nosy stalking tendencies from somewhere. Actually, seeing drunken photos of me emerge most Sunday mornings during my early twenties is probably what's led her to be so despairing of me.

'You okay?'

'Of course,' I shrug, nodding towards the kitchen. 'Does she know yet?'

'I don't think so. You going to tell her?'

'And see the look of disappointment on her face? I mean, I know it's been a while, but I think she's still holding on to some miracle of a reunion. God knows why. He was a cock to me.'

'We'll just keep her away from her computer all day – let her find out when you're not here,' he says, squeezing my shoulder.

'She's bound to flipping ask after him today, anyway. She always does.'

'Don't worry, I'll get Andrea to fake some contractions to take the focus off you.'

'If she could do that all day, that would be fab,' I smile, rubbing his back as he pulls me in tighter then lets me go.

I fling myself onto the sofa next to Dad before leaning over and placing my head on his shoulder.

In response, Dad kisses the top of my head.

I'm such a daddy's girl.

'Do you want a tea, Sarah?' Mum asks, wandering in.

'Any peppermint?'

'Yes,' she says, smiling as she turns to leave the room, clearly happy that I've gone for the healthier option. 'Warm you up before we go out.'

'I'm wondering if we should just stay in today actually, Mum,' Max suggests – instantly looking sheepish when Mum turns back to look at him with a face of stone.

'Why's that?' Mum asks, frowning. She likes our family walks, and she also loves sticking to whatever's been planned. She's never been one for spontaneity.

'Well, Andrea could probably do with a rest. It's not easy

for her travelling around all week for work. She just needs to chill out,' squirms Max.

'Today? But she starts her maternity leave in a week's time. She can rest then.'

'Maybe a day on the sofa would do her good,' nods Dad.

Mum huffs at him. 'But what about our walk?'

'My knee's still playing up a little anyway,' Dad shrugs.

'What's wrong with your knee?' I ask.

'Nothing much. Just twinging every now and then. Nothing to worry about,' he says to me before turning back to Mum. 'Why don't you and Sarah go into town and have a walk around instead?'

'Oh . . .' I start, but before I can come up with a reasonable excuse as to why I couldn't possibly go out for a walk on my own with Mum, the phone rings – the shrill tone breaking into our plans.

'Hellooo,' Mum answers with her posh telephone voice, causing me and Max to stifle giggles. I don't know what it is about being with Max, but as soon as he's around I feel like a child again with my maturity level crashing to the ground and shattering into a multi-coloured mess all over Mum and Dad's nice cream carpets. It's a wonderful feeling.

'Oh, Pat – how are you?'

My stomach hits the floor with a wallop as my head whips back around to Mum, who's evidently on the phone to DAN'S MUM.

I think about diving across the room and grabbing the phone from her, or faking a clumsy trip and whipping the telephone cable out of the wall, but instead I sit there and watch the one-sided conversation happening before me. I'm helpless.

'Did you look into those Zumba classes I told you about? Find any local ones for you..? Oh that's good – honestly, it's so much fun.'

I'd no idea our two mums had even kept in touch beyond a polite Christmas card exchange, so this friendly conversation is completely mind-boggling for me – so is the fact that my mum's started going to Zumba. It's far too young, hip and wild for her.

'Oh yes. Well, Sarah's here today actually – come to spend some time with her old mum and dad,' she chirps with a measured chuckle, before listening to whatever Pat is saying. 'She's only just arrived actually – we've not had a chance to chat yet.'

I look at Max and see that he's hiding under a sofa cushion with just his eye peering over the top. Dad is obliviously watching Formula One racing on the TV in front of us – doing a great job at blocking us all out.

'Oh . . . ?'

The silence from her is deafening as she listens to Pat.

'Well, that is lovely news. You must be so thrilled . . . when did this all happen?' she asks, swallowing hard as Pat replies. 'Please pass on our best wishes. What a happy time for you all.'

Once goodbyes have been exchanged (fairly swiftly) and the phone replaced on to its base, Mum stays rooted to the spot, looking out the front window with her back to us.

She stays like this for what must easily be a whole minute.

I look at Max in confusion.

He shrugs.

I know my mum extremely well, but even I find it difficult to read her thoughts just by looking at her little (surprisingly pert) behind.

Dad, without even looking up from his programme, intervenes. 'Everything okay, love?' He's been married to mum for thirty-six years, and he must sense when there's something brewing.

'Yes,' Mum coughs, clearing her throat.

Has she been crying?

Surely not.

'Just noticed that those ivy bushes have become a little unruly out front. I'd better make a note for Simon to trim them back when he comes next week.'

And with that she turns on to the heels of her slippers and stalks into the kitchen with a task for the gardener.

I look at Max once more and see him mouth the word 'Shit'.

Quite right.

Her reaction was worse than I'd feared.

We always knew growing up that a silent reaction was far worse than a voiced one.

Silence meant Mum and Dad were really angry at our behaviour.

Silent rage meant we'd been extremely disappointing.

What a shame that at twenty-nine years old I'm still extremely disappointing.

How tragic.

'Shall we go then?' Mum asks without looking at me, as she comes back into the room ten minutes later wearing her coat and putting on her leather gloves.

'You haven't given her a tea yet,' Dad says, breaking out of the hypnosis of his programme and becoming confused at what's happening around him.

'She can get one in town,' she says flatly.

I don't bother looking at Max, who's still hiding behind his pillow. Instead, I give Dad a kiss and mutter that we won't be long, before skulking off into the hallway and grabbing my shoes and Dan-fumed coat.

I expect an ear bashing of some sort from Mum as soon as we turn out of the black gates of our family home, but she stays silent.

She stays tight-lipped for the whole walk down to the High Street and as we mooch around several shops. We wander into Cath Kidston (I have a vision of Max and Andrea's baby being dressed like something from *Little House on the Prairie* in all these gorgeous prints), where her behaviour becomes unbearable. She doesn't once cave in to the pointless small talk that I'm trying to lighten the mood with. It's excruciatingly painful – to the point where I can't take her silence any longer and have to address the elephant dancing around in front of us.

'I only found out last night, Mum,' I blurt.

'What, dear?' She says, her eyes wide and innocent as though she hasn't the foggiest idea of what I'm talking about.

'That Dan and Lexie got engaged.'

'Oh that. It's nothing to do with me . . . I don't need to hear anything about it,' she says curtly, before continuing to screen the rail of floral baby clothes in front of us with great interest. 'I don't think we can buy any of this stuff for the baby until we know the sex, Sarah. It's all so gender specific.'

A change of subject means she no longer wants to talk about the topic that we didn't just talk about. Odd, seeing as it's a topic I shouldn't have to talk to her about anyway – or rather, it should be her trying to offer me some comfort over the fact that my ex is still very much in my world and rubbing his wonderful life in my face while I plod through mine with no direction or purpose. Simply going through the monotonously repetitive cycle at work with no passion or drive while having a 'living for the weekend' mentality, where I simply work to fund my rent and nights out with friends.

There's no excitement.

Nothing new.

Something needs to change, I realize.

'I'm going to ask Jonathan for a promotion.'

The words are out of my mouth before I've really given them much thought, but once they are out I wonder why I've never thought of them before.

Mum's face lights up instantly as she throws her arms around me and gives me a hug – a real one.

I'm pretty sure I hear a sob, she's clearly in an emotional mood today, but once she lets me go she's back to being composed. 'I think that's the best thing I've heard you say in a while.'

'Thanks Mum.'

'And I always thought you were too good for Daniel anyway,' she glowers authoritatively, before threading her arm through mine and leading us out of the shop.

Right.
Now I've just got to get myself a promotion then.
How hard can that be?

7

I'm neck deep in water, in a warm indoor swimming pool, with the sound of voices, splashing and whistling bouncing and echoing around me. It's bright with sunshine spreading its rays through the glass walls that surround us on all sides.

Several other women are also in the pool, wearing matching red swimsuits, head caps and goggles. Only one wears something different — she's in an all-black outfit from head to toe.

'Right,' someone barks in a broad Italian accent to get our attention.

I look to the side of the pool to see Strictly Come Dancing's *judge Bruno Tonioli, strutting up and down with his hands on his hips, in the smallest black speedos ever created.*

'I want to see that again,' he orders with a click of his fingers and a dangerous sparkle in his eye.

The girls in the pool instantly flap to move into an arranged formation.

I manoeuvre myself into an empty spot — guessing that it's where I'm meant to go.

Classical music starts blaring out across the room.

The girls around me slowly kick out their arms and legs in unison, their bodies swirling around elegantly to the music with passion and a dramatic flare.

I follow their lead. Trying to be as composed and graceful as I can manage — truth is, I've never really been the strongest swimmer, but I try my best to keep up with what is clearly a synchronized swimming team.

A circle is formed — us girls in red surround the one person in black before she curls up into a ball. In response we all flip around and float on our backs, each holding out the red oval shapes that have appeared in our hands.

Everyone else is still and composed, but my oval shape won't behave. It's causing me to wobble around uncontrollably — and my bottom to swerve from left to right, and up and down, beneath me.

Unable to steady the oval or myself, the red material slips from my hands and flies off into the distance.

Forgetting how to swim, I grab the girl to my left — my bingo-winged arm flying out of the water and taking hold of her strong swimmer's shoulder.

Catching her unawares, she goes under the water and panics, grabbing the girl to her left who does the same and grabs the girl to her left, who grabs the girl to her left . . . and so on, until Bruno blows his whistle and screams for the music to be cut.

'What was that?!' he shrieks.

I'm not in the pool any more. Instead, I'm stood next to him and am the target of his rage . . . rightly so. Looking into the pool I see the girls are formed in a misshaped flower, with a black centre and red petals — a poppy.

'You were swinging your arms around like a lost primate running through the Amazon jungle looking for her mother,' he shouts. 'You had no clue of the moves and your placement was appalling. Where was the passion? Where was the need? Where was the want? And elegance, my dear? I'd have seen more elegance on a dinosaur wearing stilettos walking along the cobbled streets of Amsterdam.'

'But . . .' I try.

'Yes, let's talk about butts. Yours is too big. It stuck out like that of a mandrill monkey — big and colourful.'

68

'Bruno,' I try again, but he starts dancing to his rant – blocking me out further with every twirl and jump – shouting, twirling and jumping, shouting, twirling and jumping.

Eventually he twirls so fast that his feet leave the ground and he flies above my head. His ranting becomes high-pitched singing as his spins accelerate. His body becoming a mini cyclone of colours whizzing through the air, before it explodes.

Millions of paper poppies float from the sky – their sharp edges hitting me on the head on their way to the ground.

I look to the pool to see the other girls in red have disappeared – yet the one all in black remains. Only the centre of our Poppy was not a girl as I thought I'd seen. It was Brett.

He looks pleased to see me at first, then, spotting something to the right of me, he shouts out.

'He's back!'

I turn to see Bruno has morphed into a giant speedo-wearing lizard. His tongue hissing and gobbling up all the floats as he makes his way to us.

Suddenly a hand grabs mine and pulls me.

'Quick!'

Brett drags me through the forest that we're now in and we run savagely – like wild urchins – trying our best to escape the demented reptile that's coming for us.

We hold hands, our clasp strong and unyielding as we focus on what's ahead of us. Jumping over bushes, ducking under branches and swerving pink flamingos, we never falter – we can't with Bruno so close behind us.

My heart is thumping as the adrenaline pumps through my body, making me more agile, supple and fit than ever before.

When we come to a rock formation that we need to climb, Brett wraps his strong arms around my waist and draws me up to him, our *bodies grazing each other's momentarily before we have to continue with our flight.*

Although, when we run again, my mind is clouded by the thought of having him so near. I'm not as quick as before – I'm clumsy. I trip over small stones on the ground, I misjudge distances between us and the surrounding forest, I slow us down and allow Bruno to catch up.

Just as I'm about to dive through an abandoned aeroplane to take refuge, Bruno the lizard grabs me by the ankle and throws me in the air.

I'm flying up, up, up, up into the sky.

I keep my eyes closed, too scared to look down below – too scared of falling back into Bruno's waiting mouth and not into Brett's arms.

I wake up to find I'm holding my breath and have my eyes scrunched up in suspense. Wandering into the bathroom, I find a frown line has become indented into my forehead from my night of active dreams – Bruno from *Strictly* in little pants before turning into a lizard and chasing me and my dream lover into the wilderness ... I wonder over its significance as I get into the shower and start washing my hair. Today's the day I ask Jonathan for a promotion and I've just been ear-bashed over my ineptness ... brilliant timing.

Absolutely perfect.

I get into work early, ready to start the first day of the rest of my life as someone who is determined, passionate and driven (I am those things – piss off, Bruno). I'm full of gusto and it feels as though I'm on the brink of something wonderful and life-changing. If I can manage to better myself in the career department, that would be one area of my life in a decent state of affairs – and one is better than none.

I smile to everyone as they walk into the office a little after me, asking how their weekends were and seeing what they got up to – but mostly I get my head down and get on with some work to show that I'm super dedicated to the company and take my role here seriously. I don't even go on Twitter, Facebook or the Mail Online – except for a quick peek at that just to make sure nothing major has happened like a huge celebrity fracas or another boyband member dramatically quitting my favourite band, but I'm on there a mere thirty seconds maximum before closing the webpage, satisfied that all is well with the world (apart from the awful sight of that reality star in a teeny tiny bikini in Dubai – set-up shots if ever I saw them).

Jonathan arrives half an hour later and in a foul mood – grunting at me for a coffee before slamming his office door shut behind him.

This isn't part of the great plan I'd envisaged.

Thanks to getting mentally bashed in my dream by Bruno (I'll never be able to watch *Strictly* in the same way ever again) and the fact that Jonathan is clearly in the grumpiest mood I've ever seen (and that's saying something because I've seen him have some stonkers), my nerve wavers. In fact, I delay my vision of storming into Jonathan's office and demanding the career advancement he'd promised in the initial advertisement I replied to for my job all those years ago and potter around, ticking off my meaningless list of tasks instead – after I've delivered him the best coffee he's ever had at super speedy speed, naturally.

A few hours later, I'm in the ladies', sat on the loo, when I overhear Dominique and Louisa from Development talking at the basins in front of the mirrors.

They both joined the company a few months before I did, but by the time I arrived they'd already formed a clique that I am only privy to at certain times, when they allow it. Usually when they want to do some digging around things concerning Jonathan, the business or office gossip that I might have inside knowledge on; like the time Penny from Accounts was fired for coming into work off her face on pills before going into a presentation meeting. She told Jonathan he could 'Go fuck himself' once he'd suggested she stick to her original brief rather than talking about a fairy in the sky called Twinkle-Minkle who wanted to come and feed them all chocolate. It was pretty exciting stuff, especially when she started screaming and the police had to be called, so it's no wonder Louisa and Dominique wanted to dig for info in that case. Obviously, I always tell them all I know, and then they go back to being a duo once I'm no longer of use to them. Office politics and class-room behaviour seem to go hand in hand.

Blurgh!

'There's not much he can do – his visa has run out,' Louisa moans – I can tell she's sticking her lips out into a pout. She loves a good pout. The number of photos she posts on Facebook with that poutmouth is ridiculous. Many different locations, thanks to her job, but one stupid poutmouth expression.

'So he's got to go home?'

'Exactly.' Pout.

'When?'

'Next month!' Pout.

'But where does that leave your relationship?' asks Dominique, clearly sad for her friend.

'God knows, I mean we knew this would always be the case but it seems to have crept up on us so quickly.'

'Yeah . . .'

'I'm gutted. We know a long-distance thing isn't going to work out – I mean, it's fucking Australia.'

'It's not that far.'

'It's the other side of the shitting world,' says Louisa, exasperatedly.

'Oh, Lou.'

'Yeah, I know! And if that wasn't bad enough, you're leaving.'

'Shh!' Dominique fires quickly – but my ears are already pricked and ready to hear more.

'It's not official yet.'

'But with that offer I'd have thought it was a foregone conclusion. I'd have grabbed my coat and run out the door straight away. Fuck this place.'

From what I can hear, Dominique has turned to sign language rather than verbalizing her response to her loose-tongued friend, as I can hear lots of fabric swishing and hands smacking in the air.

'Whatever,' Louisa replies sulkily, clearly annoyed that she's been shushed mid-strop. 'Life is going to suck, anyway. Maybe I should just go with him – better than being left here on my own.'

'I don't see why you don't . . .'

The conversation is dropped and the pair continue whatever they're doing in silence.

By this point I've been in the loo longer than socially appropriate. They'll definitely think I've been going for a number two (which I haven't, FYI), so I decide to wait it out a little longer to save any awkwardness. Nothing like catching those sideways glances as though pooping in a public toilet is something to be scoffed at.

Not that I did, anyway.

No really.

I didn't.

There's going to be a position free on the Development team, my head sings that afternoon, distracting me from the arduous task of writing out the company's Christmas cards – a job that I seem to do earlier and earlier each year.

Scribbling out the same thing again and again seems to numb my brain enough to knock the fear out of me. I find myself walking over to Jonathan's office door and giving it a purposeful knock – now's the time to strike!

'Sarah?' He booms, lifting his arm in the air and waving his hand in a regal fashion to beckon me in quickly.

'Jonathan,' I reply confidently, walking into his office.

He seems in a jollier mood after a working lunch out at STK. Clearly a good steak and some red wine (no doubt followed by a calorific dessert) is just what he needed.

'What can I do for you, Sarah?' he asks, leaning back into his brown leather chair and swinging around to face me.

Jonathan's office is an eclectic mix of work and home. One wall is lined with books (mostly big, thick, luxurious, travel ones) for research and another is home to an array of shelves, showing off his various awards for past TV productions, pictures of his travels and of his wife and daughter. His office furniture isn't the sort you'd usually see in an office (cold, tasteless and boring like the rest of us use), it's all individual and handmade in Italy, helping to make his office comfortable, unique and oozing charm and warmth ... It's not reflective of his personality in the slightest, if anything it's a representation of the opposite – of the anti-Jonathan.

'Well, Jonathan,' I start, swallowing the lump of nerves in my throat and banishing the thought of mouthy Bruno from my mind. 'You know I love working here –'

'That's good,' he interrupts while nodding.

'And that I've been here for –'

'Years.'

'Yes ...' I frown, his cutting in annoying me. 'Well, as much as I love working as your PA – '

'You're an integral part of our well-run machine.'

Seriously, how much did the man drink at lunch?

'Thank you,' I smile, because even if it is drunken waffle, it's still lovely to hear I'm valued. 'It's just, when I first started here I hoped being your PA would be, like a sort of, er, stepping stone to other positions within the company.'

'Really?'

'It's not that surprising really, Jonathan. I did a degree in Media – '

'You did?'

'Yes. I got a 2:1 ...'

It feels weird being proud of that pointless set of numbers so long after having gained them when they've been of little use to me so far in life. In fact, do they even count any more? Or do they expire after a certain amount of time – expecting its owner to have dulled the need for them thanks to the endless jobs and experience they've surely gained thanks to its existence? I hope not, otherwise I really am stuffed.

'Well done . . .' Jonathan booms, pursing his lips.

'And I remember there being something said about learning the ropes within other departments when I applied.'

'There was?'

'Yes.'

'Interesting. Must've been Julie's input,' he reflects with a pause, looking past me towards my colleague's desk. 'Well, carry on,' he mumbles, turning his hand in a circling motion as if it might help me get to the point quicker – which I would have done if he hadn't kept interrupting me in the first place.

'I know there probably aren't any positions available right this second –'

'No, not right this second,' he says, scratching his forehead whilst frowning.

'But I was hoping that in the future, if a space did become available – either on the Development or Research teams, maybe, well, whether I might be considered . . . ?'

Jonathan looks at me with surprise – his eyebrows raised.

A squeak-like sound escapes his mouth.

I've no idea how to interpret his reaction, so plough on hopefully.

'It'll be a change, but I know how the company works and how you like things done. I'm hard working and dedicated . . . plus, I speak French and Spanish,' I add, in mild panic that I'm not selling myself enough.

'You do? How well?'

'Yep. Good, basic level,' I nod.

Slight exaggeration there – I was pretty good at it back in the days of the classroom (I got a B in both for my GCSEs), but haven't spoken a word of them since. I bet if you asked anyone who took a language at school if they remembered any of it, the answer would be 'no' beyond 'My name is . . .' and 'Where is the swimming pool?' However, it's still proudly sat on my CV – which hasn't been updated since I started working here at Red Brick after I left uni. There's been no need.

'And I would happily train someone up to become your new PA,' I add generously – knowing that it wasn't a term put into my original contract. Yes, surprisingly, I did read it . . . my dad made sure I did.

'Hmm?'

'That way I can show them exactly how you like things done. You probably won't even notice the difference within a day or two.'

'Yeeeees . . .' he says slowly, thinking over my words. I won't lie, even though I do want him to agree with me that it could be a smooth transition, it does sting slightly that he isn't protesting over me being so easily replaceable. Even just to be polite. 'Well, I'll bear this in mind, Sarah.'

'Really?' I ask, confused that this whole conversation has been relatively easy.

'Yes. Something to think about if someone deserts us – although hopefully that won't happen any time soon,' he scoffs.

I smile back in reply, hoping that Dominique takes up whatever amazing offer she's been tempted with elsewhere.

'But it's good to hear you're dedicated to us, Sarah.'

77

'I am,' I confirm with a punch of my fist as though I'm in some black and white musical about to burst into song. My boss thinks I'm dedicated, an integral cog in the running of the company and now my life is set to flourish. I'm practically beaming at him.

'Although, I hope you're not planning on leaving us if this doesn't materialize soon?' he asks, raising his eyebrows at me as though he's concerned I might.

It's a question but not a question ... in fact, it's most definitely a leading question and I fall right into his trap.

'Definitely not,' I answer boldly without blinking. Or thinking.

'Great,' he winks. 'Is that all?'

I nod.

'Lovely,' he claps. 'Cup of coffee when you're ready please, Sarah.'

Never have I been so happy to scurry out of Jonathan's office and make him a brew. I've planted the seed – now I just need those blooming stars to align when Dominique buggers off.

8

I'm walking through the cobbled streets of Covent Garden on a warm, sunny day with Brett by my side – we're holding hands and swinging our arms in unison as we go, looking like your typical smug London couple whose lives have been made all the better from finding someone to share their days with.

'Coffee?' I ask, nodding towards a nearby shop.

He nods.

We go in.

I order two espressos.

Brett casually rests his hand on my hip while we wait. As he watches the female barista bashing around on the machine, my eye wanders around the shop, falling on the dozen pictures of us hanging from the wall behind the counter – all taken of us in the last few minutes as we walked down Monmouth Street.

I smile at the sight of how great we look together and find myself nuzzling into Brett's shoulder happily.

His hand moves from my hip to my head, as he starts to run his fingers through my hair.

God, this feels good, I think to myself – not just the comfort of his touch, but all of it. This.

'Two espressos,' says the barista, sliding two miniature takeaway cups in our direction.

'Thank you,' I say, gliding out of the warmth of Brett's arms and taking them from her – putting a spoonful of sugar in mine before turning to Brett. 'Sugar?'

'One, too,' Brett smiles, making my insides melt.

'You got the time?' asks a squeaking voice behind us.

I turn to see a little boy gazing up at Brett while tapping on his wrist. He's cute. He has short dark hair, bright green eyes and a face full of freckles.

'Er . . .' Brett mumbles as he shakes his wrist, twisting his watch so that the clock face is in view.

Even though the boy looks cute and must be only six years old, I'm cautious and wary – just as I am every time someone approaches me in London, even if they're just asking for directions. You never know who's going to try and mug you in broad daylight – it doesn't help that this little scamp reminds me of the Artful Dodger in Oliver.

But it's not the boy I should be cautious of.

Beyond him I see Brett's and my bags by the front door of the shop (why we left them there in such an exposed place in the middle of London, I don't know), and notice the figure of a burly man in a red suit rifling through them whilst tugging on his white beard.

I panic.

My laptop is in there – and my purse and phone.

No sound comes out of my mouth to warn Brett that the little shit in front of him has obviously been sent to distract us, so instead I leap around them both and dive towards the robber.

I manage to grab hold of a piece of fabric on his red jacket, but it tears as he darts away from me, hobbles out of the shop and on to the back of a lone reindeer which darts up the road.

It's then that I see it.

He's left my laptop, purse and phone behind.

But he's taken my chocolate bar.

A very expensive and delicious-looking chocolate bar.

I cry out in despair as the gold of its wrapper glimmers out of sight in the old man's hands.

I weep into the tiny square of material from the robber's clothes.

I wake up with a frown on my face, clutching hold of my duvet cover.

Did Santa actually just rob me in the middle of Covent Garden? And did he really steal just a bar of chocolate? There's clearly a simple moral to this dream and that is not to take chocolate for granted.

Or to ever trust Santa.

Oh, but Brett, I sigh with a smile. There he was again – literally the man of my dreams. He's becoming quite the recurring character now, always slotting into my dreams somewhere, bringing with him the feeling of togetherness and warmth.

That feeling sticks in my mind and lingers in my heart. A gorgeous sensation that I'm glad to hold on to through-out the working day. In fact, it's still with me when I walk into the pub, ready for another Wednesday night group quiz night.

This time, the whole team are planning on being in attendance, something I'm grateful for. Even though I know it means I'm going to have to hear wedding chat from Dan and Perfect Lexie all night, I'm glad no one's going to be missing. Because we have to win. Last week we lost out once again to the performing arts group. It's a loss that hit us badly, so we're planning on coming back fight-ing with all guns blazing . . . or multiple packets of crisps and assorted nuts at the ready.

It's funny, I don't usually care too much whether we win

or lose, but sometimes I think it's nice to have a distraction in life to keep you moving forward and help block out things that might irk you. Like wedding chat. The pub quiz is my very welcome distraction from something I shouldn't have to hear anything about. Ever.

'All right, Josh?' I ask, spotting him looking into the distance, lost in a trance, daydreaming. So far only me, Josh and Alastair are here – the boys having come straight from the gym again. Dan was with them but opted to go home to pick up Perfect Lexie on the way, Carly had a last-minute fashion disaster (she managed to split the side seam of her skirt as she was bending over in the street to do up her shoelaces) so has quickly gone home to change, and Natalia is on her way after getting stuck in Harrods with an indecisive client – it's the story of her life.

'Yeah, yeah,' Josh nods, his usually cheerful face seeming pensive as his lips purse together.

'Worried?'

For a second he looks perplexed, as though he hasn't the foggiest idea what I'm on about, but then he twigs and laughs, before looking stern and serious – a look I'm not used to seeing on his lovely, bearded, cherub-like face.

'Well, I'm certainly not up for letting those high-kicking theatre lovies get a hat-trick,' he says, bashing his fist down on the table in defiance and showing me his warrior face.

'Grr . . .' I reply, baring my teeth and letting him know I mean business too.

'How's work?' Alastair asks, his shoulder nudging mine. It's not usually a question that's asked, seeing as I've been doing the same job and same routine for donkey's years, but my guess is that Carly has mentioned my new promotion-grabbing mission to the others.

'Good, I think.'

'Sounds promising,' he smiles.

'We'll see,' I wink, not mentioning that I'm waiting for Dominique to quit before I can move up the office ranks (I mean, seriously, what is she waiting for?). 'What about you guys? What's new? Wait – Alastair, did you have a date last week?'

'Guilty as charged!' he grins cheekily, as he rubs his hands on his chest.

'And . . . ?'

He screws up his face.

'What a shame.'

'Yeah – I thought she looked nice,' sighs Josh.

'When'd you meet her?' I ask Josh – sure that Alastair met his date through someone at work.

'He bumped into her the next morning,' Alastair laughs.

'In our kitchen,' adds Josh, raising his eyebrows.

'Oh . . .' I chuckle. 'So it did go well.'

'In some ways,' smirks Alastair. 'But I don't think I'll be seeing her again.'

'What? Why?' I ask, floored by his conclusion.

'Just because,' he shrugs.

'You guys are so weird.'

'We are,' nods Josh, smirking.

'Did you realize she had better hair than you? Is that what scared you off?' I joke.

'Hey lovers!' Natalia interrupts, walking up to the table

before sitting next to me with a sigh. 'Wine . . . I need wine!'

'I'll go!' offers Alastair. 'Same again?' he asks me and Josh.

We both nod.

'But hold on – you haven't finished your story . . .' I moan, trying to grab his elbow to sit him back down, but failing – he's up and on his way to the bar quicker than I can react.

'That was the end,' Alastair shrugs cheekily before turning to the bar, pulling his brown leather wallet out of his back pocket and fiddling with his wondrous man bun.

'What's that about?' asks Natalia, shrugging out of her coat.

'Oh, nothing,' I sigh. 'Lads.'

She rolls her eyes and smiles. 'I bet I can guess,' she exhales. 'Well, we've all been there.'

'Nat!' I exclaim. Natalia is probably the quietest of our bunch, meaning that when she comes out with little lines like this they always take me by surprise.

She giggles at my reaction.

'See,' says Alastair from the bar. 'And don't even act like you've not done it, Ms Thompson . . .'

My face reddens at his remark, causing him to howl with laughter.

'Oi!' I call.

'Oh, here they are – the future Mr and Mrs Tipper,' coos Natalia at the sight of Dan and Perfect Lexie walking through the door hand in hand, closely followed by a very red-looking Carly.

I manage not to scowl and concentrate instead on my

beautiful friend behind them, pushing her blonde hair off her face, looking flustered.

'Drink?' asks Alastair, managing to stifle his laughter.

'Beer for me,' winks Dan.

'Lemonade, please,' smiles Perfect Lexie.

'Yeah, I'll have the same,' adds Carly before the three of them wander over to our table.

'You all right?' I ask her, once hellos are dished out (yes, hugs were given) and everyone's sat down with their chosen beverages.

'Yeah – Dad called and held me up so had to run here. Knackered,' she puffs, closing her eyes and taking a deep breath.

'They're heeeeere . . .' whispers Natalia eerily as she slowly turns back to the performing arts group who are walking (just walking this week) through the doors, all wearing their signature lycra – even the guys in the group.

'Eck,' grunts Alastair.

'They're going down!' sings Perfect Lexie, waving a rude girl finger in the air with attitude.

Dan frowns at her in disgust before breaking into a laugh, causing her to let rip with her own donkey laugh. Somehow her laugh seems to have stopped grating on me quite so much – either she's calmed down *or* I'm finally getting used to it after almost two years.

'Come on then,' chirps Natalia, beaming at the pair of them. 'Plans?'

A smile pings on to Perfect Lexie's face.

'I'm so glad we can talk about this now – that's why we couldn't come last week. I'd have burst trying to keep it all in.'

'Not surprised,' Natalia says, 'I'd have been the same.'

'We're thinking February with a nice Valentine's Day themed wedding,' she tells us, nibbling on her bottom lip.

'Ooh, you can have lots of fun creating the biggest love-in of a celebration,' nods Natalia approvingly, the cogs of her brain visibly spinning, deciding what she'd do if it were her. 'February – that gives you a nice leisurely amount of time to plan too.'

'And save,' adds Alastair, nudging Dan's elbow.

'Not really,' smiles Perfect Lexie. 'I mean February next year. As in three months away.'

'Whoa . . .' exhales Alastair.

'Why the rush?' I ask, stuffing a salt and vinegar crisp into my mouth to stop myself from saying any more – I hate Valentine's Day anyway, but it's great to know that the commercially special day is going to be properly crapped on, and stripped of any sort of beauty it might've possessed for me now and for the rest of my life.

'You're not . . . are you?' asks Natalia, her eyes wide.

'What? Pregnant?' laughs Dan with a squeak in his voice.

'Do I look it?' asks Perfect Lexie, looking more amused than offended.

'Well, you are drinking lemonade,' notes Alastair.

'So is Carly,' she giggles, raising her hands to cover her eyes before continuing. 'No, I'm not up the duff – but it's good to hear that thought is going to be the first thing people wonder when they receive our lovingly thought through wedding invites and spot the date.'

'So romantic,' nods Dan with a smile, nudging her shoulder with his.

'My parents would kill me,' Perfect Lexie states, her eyebrows raised to prove that she really means it. 'They're quite traditional.'

Nice to know Dan's gone from one set of crazy in-laws to another, then.

'Ladies and gents, if you'd like to get seated, we'll be kicking off in about five minutes,' says Ian the pub landlord into a microphone that's set up, alongside a giant speaker and stand, right between the gents' and ladies' toilets. Such a beautiful backdrop.

'Just gonna go for a pee,' whispers Carly before tiptoeing off.

'Be quick!' Alastair calls after her.

She waves her hands in the air in reply.

'Time to get serious,' mutters Josh, almost to himself.

And so, for the next hour, a sombre atmosphere takes over our usual jolly mood as we work together to complete what has to be the toughest quiz we've done in a while.

'Okay teams,' Ian says into the microphone an hour and a half later. 'Bex has gone through your entries and, not for the first time ever, we have a tie situation.'

'Ooooh . . .' says everyone in the pub. Everyone, that is, except the hardcore locals who couldn't care less about the stupid quiz – they'd rather just sit at the bar in their usual spots, slurping down their pints without all our commotion going on around them.

'The two teams who will be battling it out to be crowned the winners are . . . "Rehomed from Leicester" and "The High-kick-flyers".'

More 'Ooohs' from the crowd.

It's us against the theatre lovies.

'Shit just got real,' says Dan, roughly shaking each of us on the shoulder in the way I've seen sport players do.

I don't like it and have no control over my nostrils as they flare at him in revulsion.

'Okay – so just write down your answers to this question. The winners get the crown and that free round of drinks for their team,' Ian says joyously, clearly loving the dramatics of it all.

'God, I hate this bit,' moans Natalia into her hands.

'Concentrate,' I whisper.

'Here it is,' Ian starts, rolling his shoulders, puffing out air and shaking his bald head from side to side like a sportsman getting ready to compete.

'Get on with it,' someone shouts impatiently.

'All right, Dave,' Ian calls off mic to a beefy-looking man with tattoos sat at the bar. He exhales one last time before delivering the important question. 'What date did *Countdown* first air on Channel 4?'

'I know it!' squeals Perfect Lexie, grabbing the pen from Josh and writing down November the 2nd, 1983. 'I know it!'

'You sure?' queries Dan.

'Definitely – it's the same day my sister was born. I know it.'

'I don't think it was that long ago,' he replies, shaking his head.

'Are you calling my sister old?'

'No . . .'

'Because I'll tell her you said that,' she smiles cheekily.

Dan puckers up his mouth and gives her an Eskimo kiss before planting his lips on hers. They linger there then move back into the Eskimo – their noses rubbing gently.

My heart aches at the sight, yet I can't seem to tear my eyes away at the tenderness being exchanged.

'Lex – you sure that's the right answer?' asks Alastair, cutting in on their 'moment', looking dubious and a bit annoyed that the two are losing focus at this crucial part of the game.

'Definitely,' she says, straight-faced, turning back to the rest of us.

As Dan tears his eyes away from Perfect Lexie, they land on mine. His cheeks turning pink when he realizes I've been watching their intimate moment – I could hardly miss it, we were having a group discussion at the time.

Embarrassment floods through me as I find myself wondering what face I was pulling when he looked over. I'm hoping it wasn't one of utter disgust and disbelief – because that's what I was feeling inside. Although I'd probably be the same if I was in their shoes – take me and Brett and our total smugness in our coupledom when walking through Covent Garden . . . oh wait, I could get away with that sort of crap then because I was in a dream and Brett doesn't actually exist in my real life.

What a wonderful way to make myself see sense – to highlight the fact that I'm all on my own and ridiculously far away from having what Dan and Perfect Lexie have.

'It's one of those once-heard-never-forgotten facts,' Lexie continues adamantly with the tie-breaker answer, looking very pleased with herself.

Dan picks up his beer and takes a sip.

I pick up my wine and do the same, trying to take charge of the breath that has gathered in my throat, causing me to feel uneasy.

The team's answer is written down and taken up to Ian by Alastair, who fist pumps the air as he walks back to us.

The table smile manically at each other in suspense. I join in, remembering how much I wanted to win and trying to throw off my inner turmoil from sabotaging the jubilant feeling that'll come along with the impending victory.

'Right, well, that's interesting. Both teams have the right day and month, but only one team has the correct year.'

'Us,' whispers Perfect Lexie with a giggle.

Our team is a mess; Carly is watching through her hands with her face screwed up, Alastair has his fist in his mouth, Josh and Dan share a similar stance with their arms crossed over their chests and their chins tucked down, and Natalia and Perfect Lexie are holding hands looking like they're ready to cheer in celebration.

'There's only a year in the two answers, but only one is correct,' Ian continues, shaking his head. 'I can tell you that *Countdown* was first aired November 2nd, 1982.'

All our heads whip around to Perfect Lexie as her face drops.

'But . . .' she says weakly, her cheeks becoming flushed.

'This week's winners are,' continues Ian, dramatically, '"The High-kick-flyers".'

A cheer erupts followed by a mini stampede as the performing group races to the bar.

'Oh crap,' I mutter.

'I'm so sorry . . . I was convinced that was right,' says Perfect Lexie, looking like she's on the verge of tears.

Dan puts his arm around her shoulder protectively, and pulls her petite frame into his, although I notice his cheeks are still pink now that he's finally become properly aware of me (his ex) sat at the table.

'We'd have got nowhere near the right answer without you,' soothes Josh, managing very successfully to hide his own disappointment.

'It's a game,' shrugs Natalia, picking up her phone.

'Who cares,' says Carly, leaning over and squeezing her hand.

'You're fine,' winks Alastair, standing up with purpose as he retrieves his wallet from the back pocket of his jeans. 'Drink, anyone?'

'Not for me,' I reply, also getting to my feet. 'I'm going to head.'

'Yeah, me too,' adds Carly, scrambling together her belongings, which she seems to have scattered everywhere since arriving.

'You're not going to stay?' asks Josh, sadly.

His question is directed at both of us, but I can tell he's really asking Carly – she's his usual partner in crime.

'Not tonight,' she says, shaking her head apologetically to the rest of the group.

'Bye, guys,' I say, giving each of them a hug – clenching my jaw as Dan squeezes me tighter than necessary and holds me longer than I feel comfortable with. I'm surprised he isn't aware of how tense my body becomes in his grip, or the fact that I hold my breath during the whole encounter.

'I'm so sorry,' Perfect Lexie says again before we leave.

'Seriously, there are worse things to worry about,' mutters Carly as we walk out of the pub doors and into the cold wintry air.

We link arms and wander home in silence, each lost in our own thoughts.

9

A party is taking place around a pool with all my closest friends. And Dan and Perfect Lexie.

It's afternoon.

The space around us seems limitless, with no walls or boundaries to cage us in — although there's nothing other than a kidney-shaped swimming pool, three chunky green velvet sofas and a huge tree next to the sofa on which I'm sat, alone.

No one is in the water.

Carly and Josh are snuggled in their normal manner on the sofa next to mine and Dan, Alastair and Natalia are sat on the furthest sofa across the pool.

Unlike the others, who have comfortably got their feet tucked up underneath their bottoms, Dan is in a sitting position with his feet on the ground and his legs wide apart, his body facing mine.

He's staring at me.

Really staring.

Suggestively staring.

Like he wants me.

I'm surprised at the stirrings it causes within me as I feel a fire growing from between my thighs and creeping all the way up my body and down to my toes.

His look makes me tingle.

His look makes me warm.

His look makes me want him, too.

The intensity of his stare makes me look away and feel uncomfortable.

I know they're bad feelings to have and I know that I don't want to feel them. I must block him out and not encourage him.

Suddenly Perfect Lexie is by my side — although not on the sofa. She's on a rope swing at the bottom of the tree, swinging back and forth in a serene manner while singing to herself.

She's in a world of her own.

Her eyes flick up to meet mine. Without warning, she jumps off the wooden swing seat with ease.

'I've arranged a little surprise,' she whispers to me with a smile.

And, in a flash, I understand what's happening — it's Carly's birthday and we're all here to celebrate. Perfect Lexie is about to perform.

'Hold this,' Lexie whispers, handing me a wooden baton, before pulling herself up the rope of the swing like a monkey and sitting on the branches above.

It's then that I see the scaffolding she's erected. A big structure mingled in with the tree's leafy branches, and towering high above it in a rickety way that seems unsteady and handmade.

That's what she's been doing, I realize. That's what she used the baton for.

Perfect Lexie, perched on a branch, looks at us all with a glowing smile before leaping up further through the trees.

I'm watching, impressed and moved by the fluidity in her moves — the gracefulness and the beauty. Having never really stopped to appreciate her in this way before (I usually blank it all out or turn everything positive about her into something negative about me), I'm floored by her brilliance, and the way a sweet vulnerability and innocence shines through.

A movement next to me catches my eye. Part of the wooden frame she's swinging from is starting to buckle.

She notices it, too. She looks at me imploringly as a flicker of panic crosses her face.

It's not safe.

She should come down.

But she looks so wonderfully magical up there, *my mind tells me.* She can't stop now.

I jump up from my seat and sprint over to the wood that's threatening to give way. Instinctively, I throw my weight against it to steady it. It's painful to do, and hard — but I can't call out to the others. They need to watch her. Need to see her majestic qualities.

The structure is bigger and stronger than I am. I know I won't be able to last much longer against its willpower to drop. I grit my teeth and tense my body, willing it to stay in place — knowing that if I were to move and let it crumble, not only would Lexie stop dancing, but she'd fall.

I don't want Lexie to fall from that great height.

I want her to continue in her serene state.

I want to keep her safe.

I look up to see Lexie reaching the very peak of the frame. She stops and grins down to us all before jumping in the air with a twirl and nose-diving towards the ground.

That's it, she's safe, *I realize, stopping my fight and running away from the structure.*

Above me, Lexie grabs hold of ropes, making her way back down to us — beautifully and effortlessly swinging through the air with unbelievable strength and control, as planks of wood tumble and collapse behind her.

It's like something from an action film.

When she hits the ground gracefully my friends gather to congratulate her, completely oblivious to the destruction going on right next to them — and what I helped to prevent.

I don't mind. As I look at Lexie I feel a sense of awe and pride. But mostly, I feel protective.

*

95

Some dreams you'd rather wake up and forget — and that was one of them, I sleepily realize as I curl into my duvet covers. Reawakening sexual feelings for Dan and fangirling over Perfect Lexie are not my idea of a fairytale dream . . . but part of it sticks with me as I get ready for work.

Lexie.

Not Perfect Lexie, just Lexie — an innocent and sweet girl who isn't really to blame for Dan ditching me so unceremoniously. Not really. I mean, it's possible that if she hadn't entered our lives at that point, me and Dan would still be together — but it's clear that I didn't make him happy and that he felt something was lacking between us, even if that fact wasn't verbalized or shown to me in any way before it was too late. If I'd have had a heads-up, perhaps I'd have been able to change something — put in more effort or something — but we'll never know. He clearly didn't want to work at things, he wanted a fresh start with someone new.

I shouldn't have held Lexie *so* accountable for the problems in our relationship, I think she was just an easy target for my loathing. I wonder what I would've done in her position, and I wonder how much Dan would've bent the truth to make himself look like less of a dick in the scenario we'd found ourselves in.

Lexie is just a girl who had a guy fall in love with her; perhaps I should stop being so hard on her in my head, because even though I never act on those thoughts or find myself being rude to her, those negative feelings are still there. Still underlying every encounter we have. I'm aware that if I don't make a conscious effort to pause and reflect, they might linger on forever and snowball into something unmanageable.

Lexie didn't break my heart – she just caught hold of someone else's when they were in the midst of doing the smashing.

Dan is an entirely different matter, though. I still think he's a twat, but for the moment, my heart is telling me to pop a lid on my attitude towards Lexie. She's not perfect, she's as flawed and vulnerable as the rest of us and, ridiculously, I now find myself feeling maternal towards her.

It's a notion that sticks with me throughout the morning as I sit quietly at my desk at work getting on with my daily chores like Cinderella, wondering if I'm ever going to be allowed to the ball – or, in this case, the boardroom where all the dreaming happens.

'Sarah, could you come in here for a minute?' Jonathan asks, popping his head around his office door, then giving Julie a little wink before heading back inside.

It took precisely seventy-one hours and eight minutes for Dominique to further mull over her offer (from when I'd overheard of its existence while sat on the loo – not doing a number two) before handing in her notice to Jonathan and Derek. Which happened one hour and twenty-three minutes ago.

Since then I've been daydreaming about Jonathan dancing over to my desk, with a big fat cheque, taking me by the hand and guiding me through the office to my new spot on the Development team . . . but so far that hasn't materialized. In fact, this is the first time Jonathan has spoken to me since Dominique walked out of his office with a smug look on her face, now one hour and twenty-four minutes ago.

'Coming,' I breathe, pushing out my chair and skipping

in with speed, wondering if this is the moment I've been hoping for – the big promotion.

'I've been thinking about what you said the other day,' he says slowly, getting back into his chair.

It is!

It's THE big moment!

I'm about to WIN at life!

'Oh?' I say coyly, trying to suppress my excitement.

'Yes. Obviously you've heard that Dominique handed in her notice this morning?'

'Yes, I did,' I say, trying to squish my excitement and sound sad about her departure.

'A total surprise,' Jonathan says, shaking his head in confusion. 'Didn't see that one coming.'

'No. Me neither,' I lie.

'So, as luck would have it – I'm now looking at replacing her when she leaves next month,' he continues with a frown, looking at me from underneath his bushy eyebrows.

'Right,' I say, my eyes widening as a grin pings on to my face. I can't help it.

I am.

I'm about to WIN at life!

'I have to follow normal procedures and interview you, of course,' he grumbles in a formal manner before picking bits of sugar and crumbs off his sweater vest and flicking them on the floor.

'Yes, of course – that's what I thought. I never assumed you'd just hand me the –'

'And in the interest of fairness and out of respect to how it's always been done,' he cuts in (naturally), 'I'll also have to open the door to other candidates.'

'Oh.'

Well, that stops my excitement with a punch.

'Nothing to worry about, I'm sure.'

'No . . . ?'

'Just routine,' he says flatly.

'Really?'

'Good business, that's all, and hiring has to be something Derek and I both agree on.'

'Of course.'

'Interviews will be held here next Monday.'

'Great.'

'But I'll get Julie to sort all that out and give you a time,' he says, waving his hand around flippantly at the detail.

'Julie?'

'Well, you don't want to be dealing with the enemy,' he scoffs. 'I've asked Julie to deal with setting up interviews for potential candidates.'

'Oh, right,' I say, wondering how much I could persuade Julie to stuff up all the timings so that no one turns up, or to only pick really crap applicants for me to go up against.

'Like I said, nothing to worry about,' he winks. 'In fact, as a goodwill gesture, why don't you take the rest of your interview day off. On us.'

'But won't you need me to – '

'I'm sure Julie will manage,' he says firmly.

'If you're sure,' I reply, feeling weird about the idea. To my knowledge there hasn't been a single arrangement in Jonathan's life that I haven't had some part in organizing since I started at Red Brick eight years ago. However, if I'm about to move up the office ranks, I'll have to get used

99

to leaving Jonathan's affairs up to someone else to organize and worry about.

'Very sure,' Jonathan says with a final wink before walking around me and opening his office door – letting me know he's finished with me and that I can leave.

'Thank you,' I mutter, leaving the room feeling confused, excited and extremely nervous.

Julie greets me with a manic grin and a celebratory dance of the arms:

'So exciting,' she mouths.

I'm in a dingy hotel reception, waiting for the concierge to get off the phone so that he can hand me my room key. While standing there, I look around the small lobby. It feels more like a doctor's waiting room than part of a guesthouse – chaotic from the toddlers and children running around, but with the thick lull that accompanies the sick, as strangers flick through out-of-date magazines, mindlessly hoping to be seen quickly.

There are several babies crying – full-on crying like they're mid-meltdown. I look at their mothers but they aren't doing anything, instead they sit with their eyes closed and arms folded, blocking out the relentless squawking coming from their young offspring.

'Here you go, darling,' says the concierge, pulling my focus back around to him. Although now the hotel staff member has been replaced with TV chef Jamie Oliver, who's dressed in a lime green vest top, pink tutu, cream tights and brown cowboy boots with a Christmas hat on his head. He cheerily holds out a piece of celery for me to take. 'I think this is what you're after.'

'Oh . . .' I say, inspecting the celery stick with confusion.

'Room 456,' he nods with his famous cheeky grin as he flicks the white bobble of his red hat over his shoulder. 'One of our best. Brilliant, brilliant, brilliant.'

Now, I don't want to offend Jamie (it's Jamie Oliver, no one would want to upset that lovely man), so I take the celery stick from his hand and start walking towards the lift, dubious that this stringy vegetable is going to help me get into my room, but willing to give it a try.

When the lift door opens there's a black buggy inside, but no adult around to push or look after its occupant. I look back, but everyone has frozen into a tableau of what was there before: children mid-run, toys mid-movement, Jamie Oliver mid-making a cheese and truffle omelette. So I turn back to the buggy in the lift and get in with it, pressing the button to my floor.

At first I do my best to ignore the abandoned buggy – after all, if I don't look then it's not my responsibility – however, seeing as I'm in the slowest elevator ever, curiosity takes hold of me and I find myself side stepping over to it. It looks like a nice buggy – one of those posh designer types that all the mums use around the park while they jog or lunge along. Although this buggy hasn't been any-where – the wheels, bars, foot muff and carrycot are all pristine as though it's never been used. Running my hands along the smooth metal handlebar, I feel my fingers graze over something rough.

It's a word, written in a tiny font.

I bend over and squint my eyes to see it clearer.

Brett.

Now I'm really curious.

I'm about to push up its hood when the lift stops and the doors fly open – dozens of other women come streaming in, each pushing iden-tical prams to mine. It's a squeeze fitting everyone in but finally the doors close and we start moving again.

The other mums all gaze at the little babies sleeping peacefully as though nothing else exists – not this lift, not the other mums or babies, not me.

I look down at the pram I've now claimed as my own.

I wonder what's in there.

I crouch down and lift the hood a fraction, peering into the dark space beneath, and see the silhouette of a baby. Relief floods through *me, as I was sure it was going to be something sinister — a manky cat or rabid dog that would jump out and attack me.*

The lift stops once more, this time it's my floor. After some bashing of wheels and worried looks from the serene mums who fear I'll wake their babies, I eventually exit the lift along with my buggy.

With the celery stick still in my hand I walk up to my hotel room door — which looks suspiciously like my bedroom door in the flat — and hold my vegetable key up to the lock. The door springs open and inside is my room — my actual bedroom, although slightly tidier.

I carefully manoeuvre the wheels through the doorframe and park the buggy in front of my window in the sunlight. Perching on the end of the bed, with my new four-wheeled carriage by my side, I take a deep breath.

Reaching out with inquisitiveness, I lift the hood all the way back — so that a face is visible.

I gasp.

The face is adorable and gorgeous and soft and innocent and cute and beautiful.

The face is his.

I can't contain my desire to hold him — even though I know I shouldn't, even though I know he isn't mine. Slowly, I pick him up, surprised by his lightness, and cradle him into me. It feels natural — natural to be spellbound by the stillness of his perfect face and the unevenness of his chest as it rises and falls.

I have no desire to be anywhere else, but in my room watching him, and hearing the squeak of his nose as he breathes in and out, in and out.

I close my eyes and enjoy the sensation of him.

Two dreams on consecutive nights that cause me to wake up with an overriding feeling of being maternal — if that's not my body and subconscious telling me that my bio-logical clock is ticking and to get a move on with finding my baby daddy sharpish, then I don't know how else to interpret them.

It's all very well my body having broody outbursts in my sleep state – but if the universe would like to take it upon itself to dish out the guy before hammering home my bur-ied longing, that would be fab.

I decide not to focus on the fact that I'm twenty-nine and still trying to get a grip on life, and instead focus on the possible stepping stone at work which could be the start of a better me/future, dragging myself get out of bed and into the shower.

I leave the house nice and early again, as I have all week. The cold is really starting to set in now that it's November, but thankfully the last few days have been full of sunshine first thing – I can cope with the frost that comes with winter, but not the rain. Therefore, hav-ing the sun grace me each day has been much appreciated. There's nothing like waking up and getting out of the house early on a sunny day when the rest of Victoria Park is still fairly quiet and tranquil. Everything seems a little more magical – as though you're on the cusp of something new and exciting . . . or maybe that's just me this week now that I've started thinking about my career and what I want for myself.

Thanks to my being super organized, with plenty of time to get into work, I stop in on The Barge Café on the way. I'm just stepping back on to dry land with a green tea (super good) when my mum calls.

'Hi, Mum,' I answer chirpily. Clearly the early morning

Vitamin D intake is working wonders and boosting my spirits.

'Hello, darling. Any news?' she asks, getting straight to the point without any trivial niceties.

It's the first time she's been in touch since the weekend. I'm surprised she's managed to restrain herself from calling me every two seconds to see what progress I've made in bettering my prospects at husband catching – because everything in life is based on bagging yourself a man to take care of you. Clearly.

'Not yet,' I sigh.

'Oh, didn't you ask?' she asks sadly, after a huge tut. Not sounding at all shocked at the little scenario she's made up in her head where I disappoint her once more by failing to follow through on my words.

'No, I did,' I say, proudly.

'Oh.'

Now she's really surprised.

'And . . . ?' she prompts.

'And, well, Jonathan said he'll think of me when the time comes to replace someone – but now one of the girls in Development has handed in her notice, so it looks like I'm in with a chance.'

'That's fantastic,' she squeals.

Actually squeals.

I don't think I've heard her squeal like that since I was a child and taking part in the egg and spoon race at school.

'Yes. All I've got to do is go for an interview,' I say enthusiastically, knowing that this is the real sting in the tail.

'What?'

'An interview,' I confirm – knowing she heard me the first time.

'But they know you, Sarah. What could they possibly find out from you in a ten-minute business interview that they don't already know? You've granted them the longest-ever interview by staying there in such a low position for so long when you could've been snapped up by various other companies over the years.'

She doesn't usually say nice things about me – and I'm sure I heard a few kind words in my favour within her rant, so I choose to focus on those and not let her panic worry me.

'Mum, it's just a formality,' I sing, repeating the words Jonathan said to me while hoping I sound light and optimistic.

'Really?'

'Yeah – you know how PC everything is these days. Got to be seen giving everyone a fair chance.'

'Sounds ridiculous to me.'

'Yeah . . .' I agree, trying not to let my mum rile me into a flap about the whole thing.

'When will they be giving you this "interview"?' she asks, really punching out each syllable as though the word disgusts her. I mean, how dare they subject her daughter to something as barbaric as an interview?! It's clearly one step away from torture.

'Next Monday.'

'Hmmm . . . well, hopefully you'll be fine.'

Hopefully.

Don't most mums cheer on their kids and offer them unwavering support even if they don't have the slightest chance of getting what they're reaching for in life? Take all those nutters on *The X Factor* and their mums who storm in to the audition rooms to tell Simon Cowell that he's making the biggest mistake of his life by not taking their tone-deaf child through to boot camp, before hurling a load of abuse at him when their passionate plea doesn't work. Not that I'm suggesting for a second that that's good parenting – it's simply embarrassing and I would be mortified if my mum were to do something like that – but just a little bit of belief in me and encouragement without any cynicism would be amazing. I bet it would feel incredible.

Instead, I get 'hopefully'.

Her tone doesn't quite fill me with confidence and once the call ends I'm left feeling bemused and miffed.

Taking a sip of my hot drink, I spot the café's logo on the polystyrene cup and breathe a little sigh.

I block out my mum and all uncertain work issues for a moment and instead console myself with thoughts of Brett and wonder when our next dream date is going to be. Is it slightly worrying to admit that I've been looking forward to going to sleep at night? I mean, there's been some quirky shit going on in some of my dreams, but amongst that – there's been enough to make me wake with a smile. I've no doubt he's part of the reason I've got such a spring in my step . . .

With my eyes closed, I sway to the most beautiful and heartfelt jazz music I've ever heard. The raspiness grips me, carrying me by the throat on a journey of grit and truth.

I'm lost in it.

Nothing else exists.

Just me and the music.

My eyes open and I see the saxophone in my hands. It's me delivering those licks, that soul. My body ducks and swoops as I hit the top notes and shimmies down for the low ones — an extension of the instrument I'm holding.

The brassy sound echoes down the tiled tunnel, giving commuters a beat to walk to as they invariably avoid eye contact with me, even if I've seen them clicking their fingers along to the soulful melodies I'm creating as they power walk past like a herd of cattle.

Trains to catch, people to see.

No time to stop.

No time to enjoy.

They can't free themselves until they reach their destinations, no matter how much their fingers and toes want them to get lost in my delectable tones. They do not want to live in the present, even though the music coming from my hands and body excites and tempts them.

Those feelings must be oppressed.

They must keep their stony faces looking forward and not deviate from their normal routine.

What a shame, *I think*, that this freedom of expression is only being enjoyed by me . . .

I close my eyes and swing to the beat for another moment, getting lost in the world of the music.

When I open my eyes again, he's there. Standing across from me in the tunnel, while commuters continue to stream between us in their lifeless fashion.

Brett has arrived.

He stands still, legs apart, arms by his side, and watches me.

My fingers dance around quicker and slicker than before now that I have an audience to impress — now that he's here. I riff and lick up and down the instrument with speed and ease — going wherever the music wants me to with no limitations or restrictions. I'm free and calm.

I'm pretty brilliant.

I really am.

He thinks so too.

I can tell by the way his eyes flicker as they watch me, the way his mouth twinges, wanting to smile, and the way his muscular chest is moving up and down more than ever as his breathing quickens.

He is frozen to the spot.

He's fascinated by me.

I am fascinated by him.

He wants me.

I want him.

I look to the ground to see his toe starting to tap to the rhythm I'm creating. Gently at first, as though it's not even moving, but then the music takes over his being and he's full on stomping the ground with his foot. His shoulder gets involved then, popping forwards — the force driving him to pivot round in a circle. His arms rising up and joining the rest of his body in its carefree abandon.

In a place full of people adhering to the monotonous drone of rush hour on the tube, he is free. He is alive. Unashamedly enjoying me in the moment without a care for who is watching or what they might be thinking.

The energy pouring out of him is exciting and intoxicating.

I want him.

He wants me.

A brutal honking sound blasts along the tunnel as a huge red cross lights up above my head.

Looking back to where Brett was dancing seconds before, I find he's disappeared and been replaced with Simon Cowell and David Walliams — sat behind a desk, in front of a scary-looking studio audience.

I'm auditioning for them.

Crap.

I continue playing, willing my fingers to cooperate and continue with their fluid movements, but it's no use. I can't play. Not just because Simon makes me feel nervous, but because I can't actually play. I've never had a saxophone lesson in my life. I can't even blow into the fucking thing.

And so I pretend I'm playing along to the backing track, hoping they won't notice.

They do.

I hear laughter from the crowd as Simon buries his head in his hands in despair, but David loves it. David is up on his feet dancing, willing the crowd to clap and sway along.

They do.

Still no sound comes out of my brass instrument, but it's a euphoric feeling to have thousands of people cheering me on.

When the song comes to an end the room erupts in support.

'That was, without question, the best audition we've seen this

year,' says David in his usual flamboyant manner. 'I'm glad I was here to witness what was undoubtedly a huge moment in British history. You're a star.'

'You know what?' Simon says, looking pensive as he taps his fingers on the desk in front of him, squints his eyes and purses his lips.

I've no idea what his verdict is going to be so I stand there staring at him open-mouthed like a pathetic child hoping to be praised.

'I like you,' he states, remaining measured as he nods his head.

I'm frozen with my heart in my mouth, waiting for him to say more.

He raises his eyebrows at me playfully.

'And I've got an apology to make – I think I pressed my buzzer too early,' he smiles, giving me one of his cheeky little winks. 'So you don't actually play or know what you're doing. Whatever. I think this competition needs someone like you. I think David's right. You're a star in the making.'

Cheers.

Grins.

Happiness.

Success.

I spot Mum and Dad sitting in the front row of the audience, both wearing t-shirts with my face on them, weeping with joy and pride for their daughter – the phantom saxophone player.

I wake up laughing – actually cackle laughing while crying with happiness all at once, feeling utterly foolish and weirded out when I realize it was just a dream. Not that I'd want to be a *Britain's Got Talent* success story (even though it was lovely to be praised, valued and bizarrely respected momentarily), of course – I'm just overwhelmed with how those emotions can be carried through from one state to the next, leaving me in limbo until the worlds separate and things become clearer and I remember who I am, what I am and where I am.

Ah . . .

It's Monday.

Today is the day where life gets real and I'm about to be given the opportunity of actual furtherance.

Holy crap.

Needless to say, I'm a nervous wreck as I get ready for my interview with Jonathan and Derek.

Poor Carly sat on my bed for hours the previous night watching me try on everything in my wardrobe a million times – at one point she even fell asleep. Anything suit-like felt ridiculous, like I'm making too much of an effort to be taken seriously, and my normal work attire suddenly seemed old and ragged. It was a tough task having to pick something that screams 'employ me', but before we both crept off to our beds, we agreed on a loose blue swing dress with a pattern of dark blue broderie detailing on the front, tights and low heels. It's smarter than what I'd wear to the office every day, but I don't feel as though I'm pretending to be someone else who's far more intelligent than I am. It just looks like I've made a bit more effort than usual.

I'm wearing that lovely dress, and feeling utterly employable, when I get to the office entrance four hours later than normal (but fifteen minutes earlier than my interview time), although I'm flummoxed when faced with the front door and the buzzer.

I'm stumped.

What do I do?

Do I punch in the security code and wander in to the place that I've spent more time in over the last eight years than I have my own flat or, seeing as I'm there under a different guise, do I buzz and get welcomed properly?

I buzz.

A confused Shirley on reception answers and lets me in before offering me a coffee and asking me to wait on the sofa near her desk.

It's awkward.

It's so strange being here in this capacity and I feel as though all eyes are on me, judging by the fact that I'm sat there and not at my desk – I wonder if they all realize I'm here for the job interview and not just skiving at reception.

I know it's my nerves that are making me feel so exposed. In reality, no one has really stared – they've merely glanced to see who's walking through the door as they do every time someone enters. Aware that fresh meat is on the horizon and wondering if the next candidate is male or female. Everyone loves a bit of totty in the office to ogle at, don't they? Or is it bad to admit that I've spent interview days in the past checking out the talent as it walks through the door, wondering if I'm about to bump into my Mr Right?

Yeah . . . totally unprofessional.

What a pervert.

'Sarah,' giggles Julie, tiptoeing over after saying goodbye to a younger girl (fresh out of uni by the looks of it) who's clearly just come out of her interview with the bosses. She's smiling sweetly and seems totally relaxed, so I imagine it went well.

Balls!

'How you feeling?' Julie whispers, refocusing me as she grips on to my arm.

'I'm all right,' I sigh, feeling the nerves punch around in my stomach, making me wish I'd been to the loo one more time when I arrived.

'You'll be absolutely fine,' she coos, taking hold of my hands and squeezing them. 'Just be you.'

'Thanks Julie.'

I'm truly grateful that she has a little more faith in me than my own mother does.

'Come on then, bring your coffee with you,' she says, turning to walk back into the main area of the office. 'You're going into Jonathan's room.'

Nice, I think. Another place that I'm supposedly comfortable in.

'What's everyone else been like?' I whisper to her as we walk.

'Not a patch on you,' she smiles, which is exactly what I need to hear.

And with that another voice rings out in my head – this time it's Simon Cowell telling me I'm 'a star in the making'.

I walk into Jonathan's office with a huge grin on my face.

I'm a hoot. Literally, a laugh a minute. I have Jonathan and Derek in stitches as I answer their questions on why I'm right for the role with ease and humour, intelligence and passion. When Derek hands me his pen and asks me to sell it to him (it's all very *Wolf of Wall Street* – why on earth would I ever need to sell them a pen?), I chuckle before replying, 'Has Julie been stealing office supplies again? I swear I saw her walk out of here with a box of twenty BICs the other day.'

I might've swerved around their ridiculous question, but their reaction to Julie being the reason they've been left in a pen-less position and having to buy the one in my hand is a positive one. I'm left in no doubt that they like me – which is pretty good going, seeing as I've worked for them for so long.

I walk out feeling confident and happy, knowing I've presented myself in the best possible way. I've even managed to impress myself – what a pity my mum wasn't in there to watch too. Actually, it's a shame they don't film these things – I would've asked for a copy as evidence that I didn't balls it up. It would've curbed her doubt over my capabilities and let her see I'm not totally useless.

'How was it?' whispers Julie, sprinting around her desk to escort me back out to reception – as if I don't know my own way.

'Really good,' I grin, unable to control myself.

'Aaaah!' Julie sings quietly, grabbing my arm and rubbing her hands along it. 'I'm so pleased.'

As I leave, I spot the back of the next candidate's head at reception.

He's male and greying ever so slightly – that's all I can see from the angle at which he's sat as I walk past.

No point, granddad, I mutter quietly to myself with a chuckle, *vacancy's been filled.*

Clearly the high I'm feeling from the adrenaline pumping around my body has gone to my head.

I think I need to lie down before the unnecessary cocky

attitude takes over and I allow myself to become a total twat.

As more time passes that afternoon I start to feel unsure whether I've gauged the interview correctly. I'm not sure what I expected to happen next, but not hearing from the office for the rest of the day makes me worry and over-think everything.

Maybe I wasn't as charming as I thought.

Was I over-familiar?

Maybe I said something stupid.

Was saying Julie stole pens offensive?

Maybe I wasn't funny.

Were they giving me pity laughs?

Oh, the shame I'd feel if that turns out to be the case.

I'd had a vision of Jonathan calling me straight after leaving the office to tell me that they're so impressed they'd love to hire me immediately, but, as the afternoon rolls by and it starts to get dark outside, I realize that's not going to be the case.

It takes a serious amount of self-control not to ring into the office myself and see what's going on . . . I don't want to appear too needy, or undo all the great work I did in my interview.

How frustrating.

Instead, I sit in bed, scrolling through the TV channels, flicking between films and reruns of *Keeping Up with the Kardashians*.

If push comes to shove, I start reasoning with myself, I could always audition for *Britain's Got Talent* with my non-existent saxophone skills. It seemed to go down pretty well in my dream – and that look of pride on Mum and Dad's faces . . .

Eurgh!

Ring, phone, you little fucker.

12

'You know the best thing about you?' he asks, rubbing his nose against my cheek in a playful manner that tickles.

'No . . .' I reply girlishly with a sheepish grin, closing my eyes and enjoying his nuzzling.

We're in a bedroom I vaguely recognize but don't place straight away – but it's not mine. Looking around the oval space, I see wooden floors beneath us, and big wooden chests personalized with the initials H.P. and R.W. resting against the castle-stoned walls, filled with funny-looking sports gear. We're lying on a wooden four-poster bed that's adorned with plenty of red starry fabric either side for privacy. Looking around the room I notice there are three other identical beds in the room and that, actually, they're all a little smaller than normal – that's when I realize where we are. We're in a very abstract version of Harry Potter's Gryffindor dorm at Hogwarts. A wizard's boarding school for children. A fact I'm totally blasé about as we cuddle up in the four-poster bed.

A child's bed.

Above us the roof is missing – instead I look up to see millions of stars, magically twinkling above us next to a C-shaped moon.

Brett's arms are wrapped around me.

We are fully clothed in his and hers stripy pyjamas. Mine pink, his blue.

'It's the way your cheeks smell,' he says softly.

'My cheeks?'

It's quite a surprise. No one's ever commented on my cheeks before

– either in appearance or smell. They're just so nondescript. They're just cheeks – not chubby or sculpted or rosy or pale. Just cheeks. Nonetheless, I feel a sense of pride for them now.

'Yeah . . . they smell of toasted marshmallows,' he chuckles as he takes a big breath and breathes me in, humming in delight as he does so – a smile springing to his face. 'I could sniff them up all day long and never be satisfied.'

I giggle in response like a little girl, becoming bashful but loving the affection all at once.

'I wish your cheeks and I could stay here forever,' he whispers, before placing his lips on them and gently kissing them repeatedly.

The whole thing takes my breath away as my head spins into a nice and light dizziness, my eyes crinkling up as my smile grows even further. I keep them closed and enjoy the feeling of being there with Brett – and the sensation of having his lips on my skin and his fingertips wandering up and down my bare arms, making my skin shiver euphorically.

How great it is to be held and worshipped.

How gorgeous it is to be appreciated.

How lovely it is to be admired.

When I wake up I feel warm, fuzzy and loved. The feeling you sometimes get when you've spent a whole night snuggled in the arms of someone amazing – who makes *you* feel amazing too.

With my eyes still closed, I nuzzle into my duvet and breathe out a contented sigh.

As the air releases from my lungs, the realization hits me.

It was just a dream.

Again.

An utterly romantic dream about someone I don't really know. Seeing as I've found it so difficult to place him, I clearly never knew Brett very well back when he was fleetingly in my actual real life.

But then, why have my dreams decided to feature him so heavily? What could my subconscious possibly be trying to tell me?

Please don't tell me I met my soulmate (and destined love of my life) ten years ago and missed my chance of a never-ending love story? That would majorly suck.

Perhaps there's another reason for his repeated presence – I bet those little dream fairies started feeling sorry for me having a lack of male company in real life and decided to give me a boyfriend in the land of nod instead . . .

Highly likely.

He's my pity boyfriend from the sleep fairies.

In that case, they're certainly working hard – he's actually in more dreams than not. In fact, it's starting to feel strange when I wake up in the morning and I haven't had another encounter with Brett Last. It might've only been a couple of weeks since he entered my life but bizarrely it's beginning to feel like quite a natural occurrence to have him there with me in my dream state. I feel deflated when I wake up and he hasn't been in them – or worse, if I haven't dreamed at all.

How odd.

I wonder why my brain has picked him to play the leading man of my sleep-filled hours over all the other guys in my life – eligible or otherwise. Not that I'm complaining, it would be awful if I was having continuous dreams like this about Dan – or even Jonathan. I'd totally freak out if I'd dreamt of a night lying in his arms. That would be far worse than someone who might as well be a fictional character. Can you imagine? I think I'd have to quit my job.

My job.

My tummy tightens and a feeling of dread crumbles down on me at the thought of what does or doesn't lie ahead.

Why can't I go back to sleep and back to Brett's warm embrace instead? Why isn't that actually an option?

I scramble out of bed, trying to remain positive – after all, I know the interview went well. It's not as though I was lost for words or that I collapsed under the pressure of having my two bosses grill me as to why I deserved the new position on the team. What a shame that confidence I was so full of yesterday didn't fancy lingering around just a little longer. Instead I'm this annoying, self-doubting mess.

If I felt weird the day before when I went into the office as an outsider to be interviewed, today feels even stranger because everything is exactly as it was before. Which is to be expected, but it's depressing, nonetheless. In my mind I've made a huge leap forward, but in reality nothing has changed. Yet. It's important to retain a little bit of hope in all situations . . . until the fat lady sings and all that.

I go about my morning routine as normal and try not to stare at Jonathan with huge, imploring, puppy dog eyes when he comes in a short while later.

He flashes a smile at both me and Julie, but, infuriatingly heads straight to his office without talking.

I exhale loudly and throw my head into my arms on the desk.

'You okay, Sarah?' asks Julie with concern.

'Yeah . . .' I grumble.

For once she doesn't try to get more out of me; instead she trots off before coming back with a tray of teas and coffees.

'Tea for you,' she says with a smile, placing a mug in front of me.

'Thank you,' I manage, continuing with my work.

'Got you one of these too,' she says, handing me a plate with a big pink sugary doughnut on it – like the ones you see Homer Simpson scoffing down.

'That's so lovely of you,' I smile, genuinely touched – although I'm so nervous there's no way I could eat it now.

Julie then takes one coffee in to Derek and another in to Jonathan.

She's in with Jonathan for a while, as happens every so often – she does like to natter and she seems to be the only one who can keep Jonathan quiet for long enough without him interrupting them. Others might find it strange that she goes into him considering I'm his PA and she's Derek's, but, actually, I quite like it. Plus, it's not as if Julie's after my job. I'm pretty safe there.

I cover up my doughnut to save it for later, sip on my tea and monotonously continue to work through Jonathan's pile of receipts, seeing what can be put through as expenses. It's a mind-numbing task, but exactly what I need – even if it does make me sick to see the amount Jonathan spends on his wife each month. Well, I hope she enjoys her two-thousand pound necklace from Tiffany & Co. – I mean, that's more than my monthly wages, and you can bet that it wasn't even a present for a special occasion.

She probably just moaned at him greedily until he caved in and bought it – just to keep her quiet.

Clearly anticipation makes me grouchy.

And bitchy.

The rest of the morning passes by in a blur of receipts and I'm thankful for the distraction, until twenty-three hours and twelve minutes after my interview the previous day, when Jonathan sticks his head out of his doorway.

'Sarah, can I have a word?' he calls, gravely glancing at Julie whilst pursing his lips.

I spot her bow her head sadly in reply.

Oh crap.

I shuffle my way into his office with dread, already knowing that the outcome is going to be a negative one. How could it possibly be anything else following those expressions of doom and gloom? I should never have joked about Julie stealing from the office – she really is an important member of the team. Maybe Jonathan's told her and she's made a formal complaint. Maybe I'm here to get told off. Maybe I'm getting sacked and Julie was just giving me that doughnut to stop me from feeling bad.

Oh double crap . . .

'Well done for yesterday, Sarah.' Jonathan says with a nod, thankfully cutting into my thoughts that have decided to go for a cheeky little run around Hyde Park and leave me in blind panic. 'You really did an excellent job.'

'Thanks,' I mumble as we both sit down.

I'd really love for him to get straight to the point today . . . and quickly.

'I've said this before, I'm sure, but I want you to know

how much we value you in your current role and how important you are to the company.'

This time I say nothing in the hope that he'll speed things along. I don't want my ego rubbed in consolation for my failure, I'd rather be told 'no' straight away so that I can get back to my crappy little desk outside his office and pretend this never happened – or go to the toilets and have a wail in private while stuffing the big pink sugary doughnut in my gob. That option is very appealing, too.

'The thing is, you were up against people who've had a lot of experience working in Dominique's role. A couple have even worked solidly in Development since graduating some years ago,' he says, as though he is genuinely sad to tell me that I'm not good enough and have been beaten to the role.

'I tried, but I ended up here . . .'

'Exactly,' he agrees, thankfully cutting me off before I manage to start whining. 'And I think a large part of this is our fault – we should've realized you wanted to spread your wings here,' he sighs, shaking his head.

His reaction is so sincere that it makes me want to giggle nervously in response.

Thankfully I don't.

'I'm sad to say that your lack of experience means you're not quite ready to be promoted just yet,' he puffs, looking at me for some sort of a reaction.

'Right . . .' I nod, bashing my thighs with my hands as I attempt to get out of my chair and return to my desk (or to the toilets with my new best friend The Doughnut).

'However . . .'

There's a 'However'!

I sit back down and wait for him to finish, pushing thoughts of the doughnut from my mind while I wait to hear more.

'I've been talking to Derek and Julie, and between us we've come up with a plan for you to become a bigger part of the team. Dip your toes in as it were,' he adds, waving his fingers in the air so they resemble a deformed spider.

'Oh?'

Light.

End.

Of.

Tunnel.

Yes!

'I'd like you to be present in brainstorming meetings – get out there with the teams and then see what goes on . . . learn on the job. You'll still be working for me, of course – but Julie has agreed to cover both desks while you're on other jobs – as long as you continue with the main bulk of your workload too.'

'That sounds great,' I blurt – it might not be exactly what I wanted, but at least 'it's a shoe in' as my dad would say.

'Really?' Jonathan asks, surprised by the grin on my face.

'Absolutely,' I laugh, relieved to be given the chance and already wondering if I'm going to be allowed on any trips abroad.

'There's no pay rise yet, of course.'

Oh . . .

'You're not actually taking on a new role. But I'm certain that it won't be long until you can get yourself in a good enough position to be promoted properly,' he adds.

I don't care.

I'm thrilled to have succeeded on some level – and, yes, more money would've been nice, but it's not the end of the world. Is it?

I spend the rest of the afternoon at work grinning wildly . . . while eating my big pink sugary doughnut at my desk without a hint of guilt or shame.

I'm so chuffing happy that I decide to call my mum on the walk home to give her the good news. Yes. I call her.

'So you got it?' she shrieks before I can tell her the full story. 'Oh darling, I'm so thrilled for you – I always knew you were a clever little thing. They'd be stupid not to promote you.'

I think about correcting her.

I think about straightening up our wires so that they run alongside each other in unison rather than being horribly crossed like some crazy spaghetti junction on the motorway, but then I think against it.

There's no need for her to hear the ins and outs of how I've not actually been promoted. Or to learn that, instead, I've been given the chance to take on far more work *for free*, in the hope that I'll be promoted properly at some unspecific point in the future . . . possibly when someone else leaves and frees up a position. Possibly. Although there's no guarantee.

There's no point bothering her with any of that.

Just let her think I'm a genius for a little longer while I guiltily enjoy her warmth.

13

I'm on the opposite side of the road from my childhood home, but instead of a road between us, there's a river winding its way around the houses. I'm sat on its riverbank, surrounded by weeds and stinging nettles, unable to move.

Not that I seem too bothered about being stuck somewhere. I'm extremely content as I sit eating chunky chips in curry sauce from the local chippie. This masterpiece of the food world was a regular during my school days and eaten during most lunchtimes — nothing can beat the soggy chips and the spicy sauce as they warm your throat and tummy.

Mum would die if she saw me eating this, *I think guiltily, looking up at the house.*

A lump of sauce drops down on to my puffy white dress.

I pull the fabric up to my mouth and suck on it, hoping it won't leave a stain. It's not mine. I borrowed it from Julie for the weekend.

Further up the river I spot Carly, Josh, Alastair, Natalia, Dan and Lexie, along with what looks like Tom from McFly through the trees. They're all in yellow canoes, paddling quickly in my direction as though they're having a race. There's lots of shrieking, shouting and laughter as they go.

I stand up and wave, being careful of the nettles around my ankles.

'Oi,' *I call, cupping one hand to the side of my mouth.*

There's no reaction. They can't hear me over the fun they're having.

'Hey!' *I call again, this time waving my free hand in the air while the other continues to cradle my precious chips.*

Nothing.

I huff and sit back down, deciding to wait for them there instead. They're obviously coming to see me in the house, I reason. I'll just wait.

Turning back to my childhood home, I notice it's on fire. Smoke and flames are ferociously blowing out of every window, singeing Mum's delicate lace curtains into nothing.

I get up to run to it but find that my ankles are clamped in iron clasps, meaning I can't move from the spot I'm in at all. I can't get there.

'Mum! Dad!' I yell, hoping the house is empty. Hoping they're not in danger.

I feel helpless and confused as panic mounts within me.

I manically call out to my friends down the river. They have to hear me. They have to help.

Nothing.

In my hysteria I start waving my arms. Chips and curry sauce fly in the air and land all over Julie's special white dress. I scream. Scream until my throat burns — but still nothing, they can't hear me. They're having too much fun.

My panic turns into anger, turns into rage.

I'm so angry that I yell to the heavens like Hulk, letting rip as my body is overcome with seething.

'Raaaaaaaaaaaaaaaaaaaaawh!' I yell, my raspy voice visibly booming through the trees around me like a soundwave punching out through the atmosphere.

Suddenly I'm free from the bank and storming towards my friends, my newfound physical strength pushing me towards them, even though I know I should be going towards my home and putting out the fire.

My blood boils further as I spot them all messing around — no longer racing, but playing with their oars and knocking each other's canoes to make them wobble, or childishly splashing water – leaving them all soaked through. Their clothes cling to their bodies, hair hangs droopily about their faces and Tom's round-rimmed glasses are steamed up with condensation from all their adventurous fun.

Their laughter is so loud it reverberates around my brain and makes my head pound, as though their jolliness is a physical being that's come at my brain with an army of miniature hammers.

Their carefree fun mocks me in my time of need.

My feet find the water.

I wade through with purpose and an unquenchable anger.

I get to Alastair's canoe first. Grabbing it by the nose, I pick the whole thing up – Alastair included – and throw him up in the air and down the river like a discarded toy I no longer want to play with.

The girls scream, scared of the monster in front of them.

'Quick,' Tom shouts, turning his canoe and paddling speedily in the opposite direction. The others do the same.

I'm about to go after them but one stays behind.

Natalia. Her boat gets stuck on weeds – meaning she is unable to row to freedom with the others. She's trapped. She's mine, I realize, reaching for her canoe.

'Why did you ruin her dress?' she shouts sobbing, stopping me mid-grab. 'You know how important that was to her. Why are you such a bitch?'

'What?' I start. The anger sliding away, leaving me feeling fragile and confused.

'I can't believe you'd do that to her . . . to us. After everything we've all done for you. You're not the best friend I thought you were. You're nothing to us.'

She breaks free from the weeds that were holding her there with me, turns and heads after the others.

I look down at the dress covered in lumpy brown sauce and I weep.

I've ruined it.

I've ruined everything.

I'm left on my own, wearing a curry-stained wedding dress, with my childhood home burning behind me.

'We've booked a venue!' shrieks Lexie before I've had a chance to take my coat off and sit down.

It's pub quiz night yet again, and this week I've come alone because Carly's managed to catch a tummy bug from someone at work. Natalia isn't coming because she's got a meeting with her boss about potential new clients and Josh has had to go back home to see his mum and dad for someone's birthday. Therefore, for tonight's pub quiz it's only me, Alastair, Dan and Lexie.

While the boys chew each other's ears off with some football chat, I'm paired with Lexie for a confab. While I'm glad to be given the chance to get to know her a bit more, I can't help but think it's a shame she has a wedding to my ex to talk about.

It requires a great deal of effort to suppress the feelings that I've promised myself I'd put to one side – especially as last night's angry dream has put me in the strangest and weirdest mood. I've been a woman on the verge of exploding all day, something that's not helped by this scenario.

'That's great!' I smile, although aware that the expression hasn't quite reached my eyes. 'Where? Did you get Valentine's Day?'

Thankfully, having been through the whole wedding process with Andrea and Max a couple of years ago, I know the standard questions to ask and, like most girls, I'm truly fascinated by weddings – although maybe not by this one.

'Well, originally I wanted to go to the church that I went to growing up, but they're fully booked – seems quite a few people shared my idea of using February the 14th, but were far more organized about it.'

'Or gave themselves more time,' I offer.

'And that,' she laughs hysterically, before continuing excitedly with her plans. 'We've decided to go to the church near Dan's parents instead. They got married there, so did his mum's parents and Dan's sister – plus, Dan and the others got Christened there when they were babies, so it's pretty special anyway.'

'I know the one,' I say flippantly, wanting to rush her through the conversation that she's obviously so desperate to have.

'Oh?'

'I've been there,' I shrug, thinking back to Dan's sister's wedding and the few times we went Christmas carolling there.

Lexie's face drops.

Oh fuck.

I'd been there as Dan's girlfriend, and not as part of our friendship group. I mentally lift my foot and kick myself in the face. I didn't need to say that and remind her that I've been there as Dan's girlfriend in the past – before she knew him or the pretty little church even existed. It's a shitty thing to do and I know it, so immediately feel bad.

'Beautiful building. It'll be absolutely perfect,' I nod manically, feeling myself go a little pink and goofily back into my old ways as I try to dig myself out of the hole that I've collapsed into – or to at least make her feel better and buoy her back to talking fun wedding chat. Because, oddly, now I really do want to hear it – she deserves to talk about it as much as she wants to after me being such a twat . . . and because it's her wedding day, a day every girl has licence to talk about it as much as they like. It's a fact. Even if said chat is with your partner's ex who's in a foul mood.

If Lexie is at all perturbed or taken aback by my familiarity with her special wedding venue in the remote village in Essex, she manages to pick herself back up very quickly.

'It will,' she smiles, regaining her excitement. 'We've then opted to have a little marquee in Dan's parents' garden. Chilled and relaxed.'

'Sounds great,' I say, able to picture the entire scene and feeling sick at the thought of it all taking place in a spot I know so well – although at least I'll have no reason to go back afterwards. 'Now you have a venue and a date you can really get planning.'

'Yes – I've got a huge checklist that I have to start making my way through.'

'Lots to organize,' I nod.

'Yeah,' she shrugs. 'But I'm on top of it all. I have this huge folder to fill,' she giggles, tapping a bag on the floor that has a pink folder sticking out of it, something Natalia would be extremely interested in – she's insanely impressed by anyone's ability to organize as efficiently as her. 'I've just been emailing this company about invites. I guessed they should be one of the first things I think about, seeing as it's so close. I'd love them to be personal to us, but they take a while to make and as the wedding isn't ages away I'm worried about leaving it too late to tell people and then finding out they can't come because they've just booked holidays or something. So, it seems like a bit of a mad dash to get them out, you know?'

'Yeah . . . you could do quick "Save the date" cards?' I suggest. 'They probably aren't too expensive and it'll give you some more time to sort out your real ones.'

'You don't think it's too late for them already?'

'No! Plus, if you were to send the real invites before the end of the year they'll get muddled in with Christmas cards and possibly overlooked anyway.'

'True . . .' Lexie says with a smile. 'I don't know why I didn't think of that.'

'Ah, you've got lots to think about,' I say, brushing it off.

'Ooh, I have something for you!' Lexie says, reaching into her bag.

'Oh?'

'It's nothing major, but . . .' she stops as she hands me two wrapped presents.

'What's this for?' I ask, looking at the gifts in my hands.

'To say well done for . . . well, now that you're going to be taking on so much more at work, I thought it might be good to keep all the new stuff and ideas in something nice,' she says as I unwrap them to find a personalized red moleskin notebook and a beautiful gold pen.

'That is so thoughtful of you,' I say, genuinely touched, surprised and feeling like a total fraud. 'I'm really going to look the part when I turn up to my first brainstorming session.'

'You are,' she smiles.

'Right, I have one chicken salad, one bangers and mash and two prawn curries,' says Bex the barmaid, juggling our dinner plates in her hands before putting them down in front of us.

I went for a prawn curry. It's a sorry state of affairs when your cravings are led by your dreams, isn't it?

We're tucking into our meals when our pub quiz nemeses arrive.

It barely causes a stir – just a group sigh.

'I don't know why we're even bothering tonight,' I mumble, munching on a prawn. 'There's no chance we're going to win with half our team missing.'

Alastair grunts into his chicken salad with a shrug.

'When did you become so pessimistic?' Dan asks.

It's a question I'd rather not answer – because he definitely wouldn't like my response and I definitely wouldn't like the ginormous atmosphere it would place in the room for evermore.

'Let's just have a laugh with it,' suggests Lexie with a shrug.

And that's exactly what we do. Once the game gets underway we laugh at the questions we don't know and make up the most ridiculous answers we can think of.

It's lots of fun, but obviously we don't win. In fact, we actually manage to attain the worst score in our group's pub quiz history – an epic fail. However, I did manage to relax and actually enjoy myself in Lexie's company . . . something I didn't think would ever happen.

14

The space around me would be pitch black if it weren't for the millions of bright glistening dots dancing and occasionally whizzing around me. Little balls of light that magically glow and sparkle, radiating warmth.

My feet are treading air, yet I'm fine – not fazed by the fact there's nothing solid to grip hold of. Instead I revel in the lightness of my body as I take in the breathtaking view around me. The vastness of it is something to be marvelled at. The vibrant silence is something full to listen to.

I feel fingertips placed on my shoulder and turn to be greeted by a familiar face, with two huge hazelnut eyes staring at me.

I stare back – his eyes sucking me in like a big pool of chocolate, or like a newly opened jar of Nutella, so gorgeous that you can't wait to grab your spoon and dive in.

I watch as his eyes move over every part of my face. Every detail is absorbed – his gaze lingers on every crack, blemish and mark witnessed. His expression is forever changing at what he finds; my dark eyebrows, the mole on my left cheek, the little red mark under my eye that springs up in winter (something I notice but no one else ever does, even when I point it out), the scar on my forehead from being hit by a rounders bat in junior school (I needed stitches), the wrinkles around my eyes that are increasing daily as I edge closer to my thirtieth, my frizzy brown hair that's currently floating around uncontrollably, my own dark brown eyes, my ski-slope nose, my peachy pink lips. All of it.

He sees me in a way that doesn't make me feel exposed or want to hide.

He accepts it all as a part of me as we float there, gazing at each other, the space around us continuing to dance with the little balls of light oozing wonderment.

The tip of his tongue pokes out of his mouth briefly and licks his top lip.

I wish that were my lip, *I think, looking longingly at him.*

Our eyes lock and we just hold each other's gaze — plenty being communicated through our unspeaking lips.

He reaches out and gently puts a hand on my waist.

I'm naked.

He's naked.

Something I hadn't noticed before.

His hand nudges me slightly and guides my body to his, our bare flesh meeting in the air. My knees knock against his before sliding through to let our thighs and calves meet, the tops of our free feet glide along each others' before hooking hold, my breasts bouncing on his toned chest . . . I'm aware of every part of his body as it comes into contact with mine, and the weight of his warm piece as it rests against my pubic bone.

I wrap my arms around his tanned body and pull him close, drawing him in so that more and more of our bodies are touching as we float around in circles.

His stubbly cheek is rough against the side of my face — I nuzzle it, my cheek, lips and nose tingling as they explore his beautiful face.

I feel his heavy breath in my ear and it makes my heartbeat quicken.

He wants me.

I want him.

Suddenly his lips are on mine, giving me quick, hard kisses.

Kisses of desire, kisses of passion, kisses that say more than words ever could. His tongue is in my mouth probing, licking, roaming — exploring, before his teeth find my lips and nibble gently.

He pulls away but continues to kiss and lick his way to my ears — gently sucking my earlobes before finding my neck.

Oh my neck.

My body sings and sighs in wanton need.

I run my fingers through his blonde hair, pulling at it as I enjoy the sensations firing through my body.

He moans, swallowing hard, spurring me on.

Slowly my fingertips swirl down the back of his neck, over his torso and lower to what I want.

I find it.

Find him.

Sliding my legs up around his waist, I rotate my hips so that we meet — the tip of him circling me slowly. Teasing us both.

I look at him.

He wants me.

I want him.

I make us wait a little longer, despite the pleading his eyes give me. Willing me to let him in.

Not yet.

Round and round and round I go, enjoying the need in his eyes. Loving the power he's given me.

I give in just a little, his eyes widening with pleasure as I do so. He places his hands on my bare bottom and tries to speed me up and pull me in further. I push him out and away — going back to how it was before, round and round and round . . . my hips rotating, my body alive with sexual need — enjoying this feeling of liberty as we float around entwined.

Then I'm done. I can no longer wait.

He's in me and we both gasp for air from the mounting desire that's been eating away at us – relieved to give into its cries.

We're fast and desperate, quick and wild – throbbing, pulsing, thumping. His arms are around me, on me – grabbing my breasts, groping my thighs, caressing my bum. I marvel at the whole thing, how crazy it makes me feel – how primitive and free. This is heaven.

This is everything.

And then he stops and pulls me away, his hands cradling my face, his thumbs rubbing against my cheeks. Then he leans in and kisses me gently on the lips – soft and loving, a stark contrast to the frantic behaviour of moments before.

It makes my heart melt and my body ache.

I'm confused when I open my eyes and look around the room. What just happened? Or didn't just happen? Did I really have the best sex of my life while floating around in space, with some guy I knew almost a decade ago – in my sleep? Why would the world be so cruel?

I let out a moan, a big fat groan of dissatisfaction.

I must be really sexually frustrated, I reason, realizing that my last sexual encounter was over eleven months ago, at Alastair and Josh's New Year's Eve party – with one of Alastair's old school friends. He only lived down the road so I stumbled back to his after the big countdown and had to do the walk of shame the next morning ... Highly embarrassing, seeing as Alastair was aware of the situation, but thankfully I haven't seen his friend since. I think he has a girlfriend now. Lucky him.

I can't believe I haven't had sex since then, though. How utterly depressing. Because it was really rubbish – and I don't mean that he was bad necessarily, I wasn't on top form either. It was all too drunken and sloppy for it to be anything great. It certainly was nothing to write home about . . . unlike that little cosmically orgasmic dream I've just had about Brett.

'Argh!' I moan again, bashing my pillows in protest at life's unfairness.

'You okay?' Carly shouts, banging on the door.

'Yeah . . .' I call back with a sigh.

The door opens and Carly pops her pasty little face around the doorframe.

'Still feeling rough?' I ask.

She nods with a pout. She really does look the worst I've ever seen her. And that's saying something.

'Poor love,' I say, pulling back the duvet cover on her side of the bed. 'What time is it?'

'Six-thirty,' she replies, accepting my invite and scrambling into the bed.

'That is early . . .'

'Very.'

I realize my alarm clock is set to go off in thirty minutes for work, and as soon as work and the office enter my thoughts a swarm of butterflies takes hold of my tummy. Today is a very important day at Red Brick Productions. Following Dominique's departure last Friday (we all went to the local pub and got hammered together) it's time for her replacement to join the team – and for me to meet whoever it was that beat me to her position. But, even more fun than that – I'm hoping it's also the day that I step away from my desk and into the boardroom of meetings, ideas and magic. Jonathan did say something about having me learn the ropes and the Red Brick way of doing things at the same time as the newcomer (to save him going over everything twice). Fingers crossed he follows through with that plan, but, either way, Dominique's out and I'm one step closer to promotion myself. What an exciting day.

'What's wrong with you?' she asks, cutting into my vision of the perfect work day.

'Huh?'

'I was just about to vom again and I heard you having a right strop.'

'Oh . . . dreams,' I say, suddenly remembering where I spent last night and feeling giddy as the image of Brett nibbling on my earlobe flashes in front of me and sends a shiver through my body.

'With Brett still?'

'You don't want to know,' I laugh wildly.

'Yeah I do! Go on.'

'Carly, I love you dearly – but seriously . . .'

She leans over and looks and me, her eyes inspecting mine for clues.

I can't help but blush.

'Nooooo! You had a sex dream!'

I cackle into my pillow hysterically.

'What was it like? Was it all *Fifty Shades* with bondage and whips? Is that why you're blushing so much?'

'No!' I scream, wondering how to explain that I had the best sex in the world whilst suspended in air, surrounded by millions of stars. It's a tad more soppy and romantic than the hardcore porn she's expecting.

'Hmmm . . . I'll get it out of you eventually,' she laughs before adding, 'You filthy bitch.'

We both crack up then. We laugh until our eyes start to

stream with tears and we're sighing with the exhaustion that too much giggling gives you.

'You going into work today?' I ask, still sniffling as I climb out of bed and go to my wardrobe to check on the outfit I've already pre-picked – a black shift dress with gold detailing that I'll pair with a chunky mustard knit, some tights and ankle boots. The dress and cardigan are new. Having looked in my wardrobe on Saturday morning (Yes, I planned my outfit today two days ago – that's how important it is), I was still majorly underwhelmed by its offerings so decided to go on a mini shop. Totally justified seeing as today isn't just a normal working day . . . it's the start of my future.

'Nah, think I'll be able to wrangle another day,' says Carly with a sigh.

'Bet they're going nuts with the amount of people off with this.'

'Yeah . . .' she exhales quietly, cuddling into my pillows.

'I hope you don't give it to me,' I say, turning to her in mock distress as though she has the lurgies.

'Doubt I will.'

She closes her eyes as though she's about to go off to sleep again, but they close just a smidgen tighter than normal and cause her forehead to crease into a frown. When she bites the corner of her bottom lip, I know for certain that she's trying her hardest not to cry.

'Oh chick, you okay?' I ask, going over and putting my arms around her.

She stops fighting it then and lets the tears flow freely as she sobs.

Carly never cries. Ever. Even when she was left stranded

in Thailand with no purse or phone, after being mugged outside a temple, she remained calm and collected.

'Oh, I'm sorry . . .' she cries, flapping her arms in front of her eyes to stop herself from crying. It doesn't work.

'You don't have to be sorry, Carly!'

She takes a deep breath and exhales loudly, lifting her hands over her face.

'What's up?'

'Nothing,' she sobs.

'Seriously? You're going to try and tell me that nothing has made you bawl your eyes out?'

'I'm just feeling emotional.'

'Yeah, I gathered that . . .'

'Argh,' she moans, pulling the duvet cover up over her head and hiding her face. 'I just don't know what to do.'

'Carly, I might be the dumbest person in the world right now – but what's going on?'

I'm greeted with silence as her body shakes along to her quietening sobs.

'Please tell me,' I ask softly, realizing she needs a softer approach than normal. 'Maybe I can help.'

'You can't.'

'You don't know that.'

She brings down the duvet cover so I can see her face again. Scrap what I said earlier – now she *really* does look the worst I've ever seen her. Not only does she look sick and tired, her face is now red and bloated from her meltdown.

'Come on,' I encourage, sweeping her blonde hair off of her face. 'You can tell me. Promise I won't judge . . . in fact, I can't judge – I'm just a dirty slutbag who has sex dreams about strangers. I'm disgusting.'

'You are,' she nods with a pout, managing a slight smile.

I grab hold of her hand and pull her into my arms for a hug, meaning her head is resting just above my boobs – bad time not to be wearing a bra, but I'm guessing my free boobs are the last things on her mind right now.

'I'm so stupid,' she exhales.

'You are,' I agree, hoping to make her laugh.

'Thanks,' she says, squeezing into me.

We don't talk for a few minutes. Instead, I let her lie there while I play with her hair – even though I know this delay means that I'm eating into my preparation time. However, thanks to us getting up so early I'm sure I won't be late – it might just mean I have to chuck my hair up in a messy up-do rather than blowdry it . . . which is totally fine because my friend clearly needs me.

I hear Carly lick her lips like she's about to speak, but still there's a moment before any sound actually makes it out, as though she's really weighing up whether she should share whatever is troubling her.

She sighs heavily.

'I'm pregnant,' she says flatly.

We both stop breathing as those words are released into the room.

I can't see her face because her head is still resting above my boobs, and I'm really glad she can't see mine, because as soon as those words are released into the room my jaw drops in shock. That's not what I was expecting. At all.

'What? You sure?'

'That's what the tests say,' she squeaks, as she sits up and turns to look at me.

I rearrange my face into something that seems a little

less horrified – which is good as I'm sure she's looking at me so closely to gauge my reaction.

'And you've double-checked?' I ask.

'Yep. Peed on a stick fourteen times – I'm one hundred per cent up the duff . . . there's a bun cooking in my oven.'

'Whoa.'

'Whoa?' She exclaims. 'Sarah, what am I going to do? Me, with a baby? That's crazy.'

My mind wanders back to the dream I had with the dozens of serene mothers and the abandoned baby in the empty lift – I wonder if some part of me had picked up on what was going on with Carly without me realizing. Perhaps it wasn't my own maternal instincts I've been picking up on . . . Or is that loading too much significance on the crazy world of sleep? Possibly. Although the fun I've been having in them lately – there's no way I want to brush them off as a collection of leftover thoughts waiting to be discarded by a busy brain. No, no, no . . . crazy space sex is the way forward, even if my dreams do leave me gagging for it and highly frustrated when I wake up.

'Who's the dad?' I ask, refocusing on the conversation in hand and trying to remember whether Carly's been on any dates in the last month or so. I'm pretty sure she's not brought anyone back here (not that I know of anyway), but has she stayed out at all?

'I can't say right now,' she frowns, biting her lip.

'Does he know?'

'Yeah,' she nods. 'I told him straight away.'

'And?'

'I think he needs some time to think . . .' her voice peters out, so she shrugs instead and fiddles with her hands in her lap. 'What a mess.'

'How long have you known?'

'A week. Slightly longer. It was fine at first. I didn't feel any different. I only did the test because I was a bit late – I didn't actually expect it to come back positive. And these tests – they actually say the word pregnant. There's no faffing around or getting it wrong – it's there for you in bold writing for you to cry over.' She shakes her head manically as the tears threaten to spill once more. 'God, I've been so emotional!'

'I can see that.'

'Seriously, I've been feeling so sick. It's awful. And the bloating? I feel like I'm six months gone already.'

'You don't look it.'

'I ripped my skirt!'

'Oh God!' I laugh, remembering the night she had to come back to the house to change.

'My body just changed overnight. It's bonkers.' She pauses and looks at me with a bewildered half-smile, her eyes sad and worried. 'There's just so much to think about, you know?'

I nod, but the truth is I can't even begin to imagine the thoughts that are going through my best friend's head.

'I don't know how you've kept this to yourself.'

'It wasn't easy, in fact that's been one of the hardest things.'

'So none of our group know?'

She shakes her head.

'Shit . . . this is massive.'

'Life changing.'

'Yeah . . .'

'No more wild nights out, no more going travelling with just my backpack for company . . . that's it. Still, I guess I always knew I'd have to settle down and grow up some time.'

'How will your parents take it?'

'Oh, they'll be fine – delighted even. I'm not worried about them at all.'

Carly's parents met working on a cruise ship. She was the result of a quick bonk on her dad's last day on board. He didn't even know about Carly until he heard through someone at work that her mum had given birth. In what then became one of the most romantic stories of all time, he hunted her down and proposed to her on her front doorstep. Twenty-eight years and two more children later they're still going strong despite the unconventional start, and now run a guesthouse in the Lake District. So it's not too surprising to think they'd deal with the situation with compassion and love – unlike my own mother, who'd probably disown me.

'Do you want me to stay home today?' I offer, knowing that the suggestion is far from ideal, but something I would do without question if she wanted me to. 'You know me – I'd do anything for a day on the sofa,' I shrug.

'No, you're all right.'

'You sure?'

'Yeah. Besides, isn't today an important one for you?'

'Slightly,' I smile, pursing my lips at the thought of leaving her like this. 'Are you sure you'll be okay?'

'Yeah . . . I'm just not ready to go to work yet. I'd rather immerse myself in crappy TV and live in denial a little longer.'

'You take your time.'

Carly nods in agreement, breathes in deeply and exhales with force.

'You'll get through this. You've got all us guys around you.'

She breaks down into sobs once more.

It's heartbreaking to see my strong, funny and carefree friend in such a vulnerable, frightened and sickly state.

I throw my arms around her shaking shoulders and hold her.

15

I'm a mixture of emotions when I finally leave the house — I'm worried about Carly and all of the life-changing decisions that must be clogging up her brain right now, but I'm also still giddy from last night's dream and excitedly nervous for the day ahead.

With the sun shining as I make my way to the tube, I can't help but feel positive about what's in store. I feel like skipping along the canal, sliding down the escalators on the Underground, spinning around the poles on the trains and clicking my heels all the way up to the office front door.

Today is going to be a good day, I tell myself as I arrive at my desk fifteen minutes early.

With a grin I grab the notebook and pen from my bag and pop them to the side of my computer before heading to the loo to ensure I'm one hundred per cent ready when Jonathan and the newbie walk through the door. Unfortunately, I never did get time for that blowdry this morning so had to opt for plan B and a high bun instead — it's not one to rival the awesomeness of Alastair's man bun, but at least my hair isn't all frizzy and in my face.

'Is he here yet?' Julie asks as she speed-walks in the door ten minutes after me, looking flushed from her commute.

'Who?'

'Brett.'

148

'Brett?' I ask. I know there is more than one Brett in the world, but even so – given my crazy nightly escapades with Brett Last the name still catches me by surprise and makes me wonder if I'm actually still dreaming.

'Yes, Brett. Dominique's replacement – is he here yet?' Julie asks again, looking around the empty office. 'I'm guessing not,' she concludes, taking her bag off her shoulder and hastily placing it underneath her desk.

'No, he's not.'

'He struck me as someone who'd be early to everything,' she continues, removing her camel trench coat and wool scarf and hanging them on the hook outside Derek's door. 'No doubt he's waiting up the road, having a coffee – not wanting to be first into the office.'

'Maybe,' I reply.

'Hopefully not the last in, though,' she chuckles to herself.

Clearly I'm not the only person excited about today.

'What's he like then?' I ask, realizing that I've been so consumed in myself over the last week that I haven't actually asked much about the new member of the team. Probably because I haven't wanted to hear all the great things that bagged him the job – and, in turn, realize the qualities that I clearly lack.

'Oh he's lovely. Really handsome, too,' winks Julie.

'Really?' I ask, raising my eyebrows at her in disbelief.

'Really,' she laughs.

Julie's taste is somewhat questionable – a fact I usually tease her over, so I decide to wait and see for myself.

In the distance I hear the buzzer go off and Shirley welcoming someone in.

149

'There he is,' chimes Julie, beginning to totter over to reception excitedly. 'Told you he wouldn't be last.'

I glance over at reception to watch Julie greet the man who squandered my chances of promotion, and my heart stops.

Surely not.

How?

I must still be dreaming.

This can't be happening.

This has to be some sort of weird dream within a dream – I've had them before and it's incredibly freaky when you think you're awake but you're not. Surely that's what's occurring now, because the truth is too baffling to comprehend.

Brett Last is standing in the reception of Red Brick – in the office, where I work – and is shaking my colleague Julie's hand.

Actual.

Brett.

Last.

'This is Sarah,' I hear Julie say as she turns back to me with Brett's hand still in hers.

I've no choice but to walk over to them.

'Hi,' I say, my voice shaking slightly as I animatedly wave my hands in the air like an early-morning CBBC presenter.

I immediately hate myself.

And there he is . . . Brett Last, Real Brett, looking over at me and holding out a hand for me to shake.

I put my hand in his and offer the flimsiest of handshakes – it's appalling and droopy – but my mind is elsewhere, trying to absorb him and make sense of the situation I've somehow found myself in and trying not to hyperventilate over the fact that I'm having actually physical contact with Brett Last. My subconscious mind has turned him into a celebrity – I might as well be stood in front of the god that is Ryan Gosling and having him recite lines from *The Notebook* to me, I'd be just as gormless and awestruck.

Although this Brett is different. Not hugely, but there are tiny differences that I can't help but notice – he's a smidge smaller in both height and body-mass, for a start – he's still tall (and taller than me), but as I stand next to him I'm aware that he's not the six-foot-five guy from my dreams. Maybe more six foot one or two ... His blond hair has turned to a mousey brown with age, and there are definite flecks of grey running through it.

And then there are his eyes ...

His hazelnut eyes aren't how I remembered them at all – they're still sparkly and friendly, but they're green. Green. Just Green. Not the stripy pools of golden brown that make my heart skip a beat. And then there are the wrinkles that crease around them, reminding me, along with those grey flecks, that he is ten years older than he appears in my memory and in my dreams ...

He's a man. A really hunky and attractive *real* man that I've been sort of dating during my sleeping hours.

Well, that's a headfuck.

Even though he's not exactly the guy I've been dreaming of, he *is* the guy I've been dreaming of and the expression on his face tells me that I am most definitely looking at him in a way that is peculiar and making him feel uncomfortable.

I collect my jaw from the floor and swallow the saliva that's gathered in my mouth.

'Do we know each other,' he asks slowly whilst squinting at me, waving his finger between us in confusion.

'Erm . . .' I say with a frown and slight shake of the head, trying to buy my discombobulated brain some time.

'Did you go to UCL?'

'No, Sarah went to Leicester, didn't you, dear,' offers Julie with a wink when I'm too baffled to answer.

'Leicester! That's it,' he nods thoughtfully, putting his hands back into the pockets of his suit trousers. 'My mate's brother went there and we trekked up a few times. Ned, you know him – Alastair's brother.'

That's it! Alastair's brother Ned! He used to go up to see Alastair all the time in the first year before Ned got a job abroad – no wonder I thought Brett was a friend of someone's at the university.

'Yes, I know him,' I manage, swallowing again. 'We're still good friends.'

'Ah, do you know how Ned is? I hardly see him any more, I just catch up with him on Facebook every now and then.'

'You're on Facebook?' I ask, startled. Having looked him up several times and found nothing, I was sure he wasn't on there. I'm flummoxed that my natural stalking abilities have missed him.

'Isn't everyone?'

'I am!' Julie interrupts, popping her hand in the air with a smile. 'We can add each other later. Do you want to come with me, Brett? I'll show you to your desk and you can get settled in before Jonathan arrives. He won't be long.'

'Thanks,' he says, taking a hand out of his pocket and picking up the rucksack at his feet, which has a black cycling helmet dangling off it. 'What a small world,' he muses to himself with a smile and a shake of the head.

I go back to my desk in shock. I'm not entirely sure how I pass the time, but ten minutes later Jonathan is shaking Real Brett's hand and showing him to his office.

'Coffee please, Sarah,' he booms to me as he strides passed.

'Certainly,' I say, happy to be walking away from my desk and to have a menial job to occupy my brain with.

It doesn't work.

I daydream while making the coffee and think of all the adventures I've had with Dream Brett over the past few weeks. Worse than falling for a fictional character, because at least then you know you're never going to actually meet them because they don't exist, my subconscious has taken the body of someone I used to know and turned them into my ideal man. Said ideal man is now in my actual life and I have an overwhelming attraction towards him thanks to all these memories of us wandering through Covent Garden hand in hand, or running away from overgrown reptiles . . . but none of it ever happened. I can't actually be attracted and emotionally connected to the man sitting in Jonathan's office because I don't know him.

It's all utterly ridiculous.

My thoughts turn to Carly and I wonder how she's feeling now she's offloaded to someone else. I should've just stayed at home and not bothered coming in today. I wish I had.

After taking a deep breath I wander into Jonathan's office

with my tray of beverages. I hand Jonathan his milky coffee with two sugars, then steel myself as I give Real Brett his.

'What's that?' he asks, frowning at the cup and looking utterly confused.

'Espresso, one sugar,' I mumble, realizing my error too late.

'Oh no – I couldn't drink that,' Real Brett laughs, holding his hands up and refusing to take the drink from me. 'I hate coffee. Sorry, I would've said only you ran off so quickly. Too efficient,' he adds with a pursed smile.

Real Brett doesn't drink coffee . . . well, that's mildly confusing and bizarrely disappointing. But then, he isn't Dream Brett – that really is a fact that I'm struggling to comprehend.

'Oh, silly me!' I flap, putting the drink back on the tray. 'Would you like something else?'

As I catch his eye there's a glimmer of something, a little spark of amusement. For a fleeting moment my heart surges as it occurs to me that I'm possibly living in some twisted universe where dreams and reality collide to make some weird augmented reality – and that Brett is just playing games with me and pretending to be this slightly altered figure of himself who hasn't had those memorable encounters with me in the past few weeks.

'No, I'm good with just water thanks,' he says with a polite shrug, turning back to Jonathan.

Maybe not.

'Sarah,' Jonathan interrupts. 'I know I said about you being in with Development today, but as it's Brett's first day, would you mind if he settled in first?'

'No,' I almost scream, relieved that I won't have to be in

the boardroom with a guy who I've had space sex with – even if he hasn't the foggiest that the event took place.

Space sex.

Oh gosh, my face turns crimson as I think about it with Real Brett stood next to me. My breath gets caught in my throat as my body reacts to the memory.

'Are you okay, Sarah?'

'Huh?' I ask – worried they can read my mind and see all the devilishly horny and naughty things living in there.

'You look like you're burning up,' adds Real Brett with concern.

'Oh, my flatmate – she's been ill. Probably caught something off her,' I blurt.

Not bloody likely – unless it's possible to get pregnant from dream sex, which I highly doubt.

'Oh dear,' frowns Jonathan, looking from me to Real Brett. 'If it gets worse just let Julie know and head home – we can't have everyone catching it.'

I'm not sure whether his offer is because he genuinely cares for my wellbeing, because he really doesn't want to catch my faux bug, or because he's just hoping to look good in front of Real Brett. Whatever it is, I'm thankful for the offer and smile feebly at him as I exit the room.

I manage a further forty-three minutes and seventeen seconds of clock watching before leaving to head home, promising to do some work from there instead.

Well, this little turn of events will certainly make Carly laugh.

When I get back to the flat I hear muffled voices coming from Carly's bedroom.

'I'm home,' I shout, not wanting to hear anything I shouldn't. Any other time I'd be all up for earwigging, but not today. Not with the bombshell she's dropped.

Josh comes out of Carly's bedroom looking sheepish with his head bowed.

'Josh?'

'Hey . . .'

'What are you doing here?'

'I just came to talk to Carly.'

'Oh . . .' I think before saying this, but am pretty certain I'm okay in doing so – especially if he's been looking after her. 'So you know?'

'Yeah . . .' he sighs.

'Massive,' I reply.

'Yep.'

'Huge.'

'Ah-ha . . .'

'Sarah,' Carly shouts before joining us in the hallway. 'Stop being so stupid.'

Now I'm thrown – how did her being up the duff become about my intelligence?

'What?'

'Josh.'

'Yes.'

'Josh?'

'What?' I frown, getting annoyed – it's already felt like an extremely stressful day and my brain can't cope with being ridiculed.

'It's Josh!'

'What is?'

'Josh is the dad.'

Now I'm floored.

'What? How?' I stammer. 'I mean, I get the how part . . . but, how?'

'We've been getting closer for a while,' starts Josh.

'But you've always been close,' I blurt, remembering the amount of time the two have spent together over the years. There's been nothing to suggest that anything had happened between them or that their relationship had advanced beyond just friends.

'Yes, but . . . it became more,' says Josh.

'Since when?' I squeal, still trying to make sense of what is happening.

'It started about a year or so ago.'

'What? Why didn't you say anything? Why keep this from all of your friends? From your *best* friends?'

'We didn't want things being awkward if it all went wrong,' says Carly, as Josh takes her by the hand and pulls her into him. 'We've all been there before and it's horrible – we thought if we could contain it then – I don't know . . .'

'We just thought this would be easier, at least until we worked out what this actually is and where it's going.'

'It's really not a big deal,' adds Carly.

'Not a big deal? You two have been off having sex in secret and making babies! That's a fucking huge deal.'

'We realize that . . .' sighs Josh. 'It's not been easy – any of it. Hiding that we're a couple – or figuring out what to do now. This is the kind of stuff we go to you guys for.'

'This morning you said the dad needed some time to think,' I say to Carly.

'I did,' nods Josh. 'I went home for a few days to clear my head. I've been a bit of a shit, to be honest.'

'I'd say,' I reply flatly. I can't help but be pissed at him for not being by Carly's side supporting her, regardless of his own inner turmoil.

I look at the two of them – two of the greatest people I know – and shake my head in disbelief.

'Fuck,' I whisper forcefully.

They look at me expectantly.

'Fuck!' I shout, starting to laugh, my hands slapping against my face. 'This is bonkers!'

'Yes,' nods Carly, on the verge of tears again.

'Are you really going to be crying for the next nine months? Because I think we should put out some sort of flood warning.'

Josh squeezes her closer and kisses the top of her head. It's the cutest darn thing I've ever seen.

'Oh you guys . . .' I weep, walking over to them and muscling in on their hug, overcome with emotion as our arms hold on to each other. 'I love you three so much.'

It's then that Josh's body begins to shake.

'Oh shit – that stuff's contagious,' I joke, holding them both a little tighter. 'Wait, what about the others? When are you going to tell them?'

'I think Alastair suspects already,' says Josh.

'Really?' asks Carly, looking up at him.

'Well, we've had some heated discussions on the phone,' he shrugs.

'True.'

'Actually, I think he knows I've got *someone* pregnant, he's got no idea it's you though . . . I think that'll be the shock.'

'I think that'll be a shock for everyone,' I say. 'When are you going to tell them?'

'Soon, I guess. We haven't really thought about it,' frowns Josh.

'We've been so consumed with working out what to do and then, before that, hiding what's been happening, that actually telling everyone seems a bit daunting,' says Carly, biting her lip.

'Yeah . . . they're a vicious bunch, our mates,' I wink. 'They'll never understand something like this.' Pause. 'Bunch of wankers.'

Carly laughs.

Once Josh has headed back to work we throw on our PJs and snuggle up under the duvet in my bedroom with bacon sandwiches and some salt and vinegar crisps while we watch back-to-back episodes of *The Real Desperate Housewives of Beverly Hills* – reality shows, aka zombie TV, are the cure to all ills. It's a fact.

We're always in my bedroom. Firstly, because it's the brightest room in the house thanks to the large windows, but secondly, Carly's room is an absolute dump. You literally have to wade through piles of discarded clothes to get to the bed. Plus, I have a TV in my room and she doesn't, so it makes more sense for an afternoon of lounging and telly watching if we want to be in bed rather than on the sofa in the living room. This is more comfortable and it's been a tradition to get through stressful times and hungover days in this manner ever since Carly moved in two years ago. The only thing missing from this little scene is lovely Natalia, although I guess we can't all skive off work.

'Why are you home anyway?' Carly asks, munching away.

'Argh,' I groan, rolling my eyes.

With all the drama here with Carly, Josh and their baby-making, I'd totally forgotten the horrors of this morning.

'Sounds interesting,' she says, turning to me while continuing to stuff food in her gob. 'What's happened?'

'The new person started today.'

'Yeah . . . and?'

'Well, guess who it is.'

'No idea,' she shrugs, not even attempting to guess.

'Brett Last.'

Carly's jaw drops so dramatically that a piece of her semi-chewed sandwich comes rolling out of her mouth and on to the bed in front of us.

'As in the one you've been dreaming of?' she whispers dramatically, popping the lost food back where it came from, unashamedly.

'Yes,' I nod. 'That's the one. Although he's not quite the same, I guess.'

'Dreams do that,' she nods sadly. 'I once only dated a guy because I dreamt he was good in bed . . . he wasn't.'

'Tragic.'

'I know,' she sighs, shaking her head free of the memory. 'So what's he like?'

'I don't know. I freaked out and left.'

'Not surprised.'

'I was shell-shocked but dealing with it at first, praying that I wasn't going to have to spend too much time with him, and then last night's dream and space sex flashed before my eyes and –'

'What was that?' Carly asks with a smirk on her face.

'Oh crap, I didn't tell you that bit, did I?' I blush.

'No, you didn't,' she cackles.

'I just don't know how I'm going to face him.'

'Don't be silly.'

'No, seriously, I know things about him, but I don't. For instance, I went to make him a coffee – Dream Brett always has an espresso with one sugar – then gave it to Real Brett and he doesn't even like coffee. In fact, he was quite disgusted that I'd put one in front of him.'

'What a mindfuck.'

'Exactly. His accent's different too – it's got an ever-so-slight cockney twang.'

'Ooh, like Tom Hardy or Jude Law,' she asks giddily, seeming to enjoy my woeful tale. 'That's nice. So manly and sexy.'

'It's not quite as prominent . . . but yeah – like that and a bit deeper than I thought it would be. It's just not how I'm used to hearing him talk. Well, hearing Dream Brett talk, I mean.'

'Oh, I see what you mean,' she nods. 'So odd.'

'And I found out how we know him – Ned. Alastair's brother.'

'Really?' she asks with a frown, clearly working her way through her memory bank of names and faces. 'Ohhhh . . . *That* Brett Last. Now I know who you mean. Oh, he was well fit,' she nods while pouting her lips. 'So he hasn't aged well then?'

'It's not that, he's just . . . not Dream Brett,' I sigh, hitting the palm of my hand into my forehead at the absurdity of the whole thing.

'Are you really going to compartmentalize them like that – Dream Brett and Real Brett?' she asks, moving her hands from left to right as though I'm storing each of them in tiny boxes. 'It's going to get really confusing.'

'Get? Get? It already is,' I squeal, rolling my head back on to the pillows in despair. 'Are you sure I'm not dreaming still?'

'Definitely not, but I can pinch you to prove it if you like,' she offers, crabbing her little fingers towards my arms.

'No thanks,' I grumble sadly. 'What am I going to do? I'm meant to be learning the ropes from him at work. I can't do that now.'

'Of course you can. You've just got to stop thinking of Dream Brett. It's probably because you've thought of him so much that this infatuation has grown so huge.'

'I'm not infatuated,' I stammer, hating how utterly bonkers that sounds out loud, but unable to stop my cheeks from blushing and contradicting the words I've spoken.

'Yeah ...' Carly nods, raising an eyebrow in my direction. 'Clearly. In that case, stop thinking of the dream version of the guy and he might disappear.'

'But I like him,' I moan, puffing my lips out as I think of all the fun we've had together.

'And I'd really like not to be on the cusp of parenthood, but these things happen and we need to roll with them,' Carly says sardonically. 'It's time to say goodbye to Mr Dreamboy and start living in reality.'

Talk about tough love.

A little whine of sorrow comes from my soul as I pick up my sandwich and continue to nibble on it, pretending to be immersed in whether Brandi Glanville and Lisa

Vanderpump will ever patch up their troubled friendship while actually thinking about Dream Brett.

What's worse than a real-life problem? One that exists totally in your mind and is therefore out of your control to put an end to.

I can't guarantee that I'll stop thinking of him.

I can't even guarantee that I want to.

And I certainly can't guarantee that I'll stop dreaming of him.

I just have to try my best to see Real Brett as a totally different person altogether, but then, let's face it – he is!

16

The ground beneath my bare feet is dry and earthy as I walk along the path set out before me — one single straight line placed in the centre of a never-ending rapeseed field, continuing on for as far as I can see. With the hot sun warming my shoulders, I hold out my hands and touch the tips of the yellow flowers as I go, enjoying the sounds of the birds in the trees and smiling to myself every time a rabbit or fox makes its way across the opening of my countryside haven.

I walk and walk, taking in the blue skies and the strong smell of the fields — feeling calmer with each step I take. I know that, by remaining on this path, I will be led somewhere safe, happy and content — I will be led home.

Far in the distance, a head pops up above the yellow flowers. Two eyes watch me for all of a second before falling back down and disappearing.

I stop and stare — willing the face to show itself again, so that I can be sure that it's him.

But there's nothing.

After a few moments, I give up waiting and continue along the path, although this time I feel sadder than I did before. As though I'm missing something. The calmness I held at the start has been disturbed and shaken. Instead, anxiety has taken hold and makes me wary.

I'm nervous as I walk. Even though I know I'm heading somewhere I want to go I now have doubts over my desires.

A head appears again to my left, right on the horizon, and makes me jump. I turn and face it – face him – but just as our eyes lock he's gone again.

I run.

I ignore the path dictated to me by the mud on the ground – even though it's what I think I need and will take me to safety – instead, instinctively, I run into the yellow, trying to reach where he was. Where I know I want to be.

I run and run and run – the crop whipping my hands and legs as I speed past – leaving them stinging, the rabbits scurrying away from the intruder in their peaceful playground, the sun becoming hot and unbearable.

But the blanket of yellow before me never changes. I never get closer to the spot where I thought I saw him. I'm like a hamster on a wheel, running round and round and never reaching my final destination.

I stop, gasping for air. Looking all around me to see if I'll see him again.

There!

Over to the left!

He's gone again, but this time I'm on to him, this time I'll find him.

I run, faster than before and with even more frantic determination. Not caring that my black dress is being torn by the effort or that I'm disappearing into the unknown.

I run for what feels like hours, but find nothing.

Nothing.

I cannot find that face.

It dawns on me that he is an illusion. He isn't there, even though I'd like him to be.

Perhaps the real him is waiting for me back at home, I realize, thankful that all is not lost.

I turn to walk back to where I came from so that I can return to the safe path that was laid out for me, but there's no trace of the route I ran. The flowers have blown back together as though I'd never invaded their serene space.

I'm stranded without a clue of how to get out.

A face to the left.

I gasp with excitement, ready to go again.

A face to the right.

I stare in confusion.

Then another, and another, and another. Dozens of Bretts along the horizon and in the field — those hazelnut eyes all staring, all mocking.

I try to run away from them now, away from their taunting and lies — but it's no use. In every direction I turn there's a new face bursting up through the flowers to surprise me.

I close my eyes and I scream.

I sit up in bed with a jolt, glad to be awake and away from the never-ending rapeseed field, but still feeling unnerved at the chaotic sight of dozens of Dream Bretts ridiculing me so heartlessly. It's the first time Brett has done anything to unnerve me in my dreamland and it leaves me feeling tearful and confused.

Breathing deeply, I regain some calm, remembering that it's only a dream and nothing to be worried about.

Only a dream . . .

To dispel one would be to shrug off the whole lot . . . I'm not sure that's what I want.

I reach under my pillow, find my phone and press the display button. It's three-thirty in the morning.

I roll over, close my eyes and try to get back to sleep,

but all those heads keep bouncing up in jest – hundreds of different versions of Dream Brett pinging into view, but none of them the real him.

The *real* him . . .

How laughable.

Giving up, I grab the remote and put on the TV – hoping late-night reruns of *Countdown* will empty my brain of this torment.

I switch off my alarm when it eventually sounds a few hours later and think about calling in sick. However, Carly comes into my room at seven-thirty and practically forces me out of bed by stripping the duvet off me so that I'm freezing cold and exposed.

'What are you doing?' I shriek, shattered from being up in the night.

'You're going in,' she orders. 'I'm not letting you skive.'

'And what about you? If you're allowed time off to hide away from all your shit then why can't I?'

'Fair dos,' she shrugs, dropping my bedding on the floor. 'I'll go in too.'

'Really?' I ask, shocked that she'd make such a snap decision like that, but then, this is free-thinking Carly – full of spontaneity and Josh's baby.

'Yeah. I'm bored here anyway – there's only so much crap I can watch and eat.'

And with that she storms out of the room and starts getting ready.

Looks like I'm going in, I sigh – really wishing I could roll back over and dream the day away . . . as long as they're good dreams of me and Dream Brett having a whole host of adventures and none of the twisted crap where I can't find him. Last night's dream was just cruel in comparison to the dream the night before.

If I mull over the turn of events any more I'll be forced to change my mind and avoid the office, so I slide off my bed and throw some clothes on – not really giving it much thought or caring what I look like. The office has seen me in far worse than the weekend's worn jeans and my old school Disney jumper with Mickey and Minnie on the front.

The weather outside is abysmally grey and wet so, grabbing my umbrella, I walk through the park feeling sorry for myself, unable to stomach the thought of walking along the canal and past The Barge Café – the place that holds poignant dream memories … I'm in a foul mood and can't wait to go home and back to my bed – providing my dreams have something nicer to offer.

Annoyingly, the short commute into Soho is quicker than normal and I arrive at my desk earlier than ever. More annoyingly, though, the next person to arrive is Real Brett. I notice him walking in and shaking out his umbrella by the front door, but keep my head buried in the diary in front of me – begging that he'll think I'm super busy with something important and leave me alone.

It doesn't work.

'Feeling better?' he asks, striding over with his soggy umbrella still in his hand – he really should've left it by the entrance rather than dripping water all through the office.

I feel a tut brewing and stop myself – I am not my mother.

Real Brett leans on my desk with his free hand, waiting for a response.

I look up at him and, without necessarily meaning to, I frown. Well, my mother would've been far more direct.

'Clearly not,' he concludes from my grumpy expression. Pause. 'Nice jumper.'

I look down and see Mickey and Minnie grinning up at me like two lovesick buffoons and instantly wish I'd worn something else.

'Thanks,' I mumble.

'I'm sure I have one just like it – but perhaps I shouldn't admit to that,' he laughs to himself. 'Fancy a coffee, then?'

'You don't like coffee,' I say bluntly.

'No, but I can still make you one – it's just a little button on the machine, right?' he asks, walking through the empty office towards the kitchen area. 'It can't be that hard.'

I look back down at Jonathan's diary and try to find some little task to do – rather surprisingly, there's not much I can get on with until he gets in.

'So it turns out there's all sort of buttons and crazy contraptions,' Real Brett shouts across the office. 'What sort do you want? Big one, small one? Black? Milky?'

I sigh and lower the organizer on to the table. Uncrossing my legs, I get up and walk over with a bit of a strop.

'A small one . . . an espresso.' I say, peering my head around the door to find him looking perplexed while studying the various buttons in front of him. 'Bottom left.'

'Nice,' he nods, pressing the button on the machine and looking relieved that the ordeal is over.

'Argh,' I yelp, quickly grabbing a cup and popping it underneath the spout just before the boiling hot liquid comes squirting out.

'Well, that could've been a disaster,' he winces.

'Could've,' I puff.

We both stand there in silence, awkwardly watching the coffee slowly fill the cup. I'm completely aware of his breathing and the way he pulls his bottom lip through his teeth with a little squeak.

I try my best to block out the thought of his lips, feeling my cheeks blush slightly and trying to remind myself that this guy in the kitchen is not the one I've had obscene sexual chemistry with.

I don't know this dude.

Not really.

'You know Ned's just got married and that he lives in Dubai now?' offers Real Brett before nodding, as though confirming that what he is telling me is actually true. 'I looked him up last night – funny how friends we were so close to now only exist on our computers as a bunch of photos and status updates.'

Facebook! I'd searched on there again last night but was still unable to find anything. Not that it's something I can ask about – I can't exactly admit that I've been stalking him, can I? Plus, I'm not even sure I want to find out more about Real Brett – it was Dream Brett's profile I was looking for and that obviously doesn't exist.

'It's the world we live in,' I shrug.

'I guess. Sad though,' he sighs. 'Hey, so how are the rest of your mates? Josh, Dan, Carly and that.'

'They're all really good,' I nod, not really having the enthusiasm to expand my response.

'Didn't you and Dan hook up at one point?' he asks, deep in thought. 'I'm sure Ned told me that.'

'At one point,' I say with a frown, miffed at Dan's mention but interested to hear the two had once been talking about me – that we weren't just some kids at his friend's brother's uni. 'That ended.'

'Ah, I see. Say no more. Guess you guys don't see much of him, then.'

'No, we do.'

'Oh.' He frowns and purses his lips, his confusion at my revelation thankfully stopping him from asking further irritating questions.

'Right, thanks for this,' I half-smile, grabbing the coffee from the machine and holding it up. 'I'd better get on before Jonathan gets in.'

'Of course,' he says, pouring himself a glass of cold milk.

'Milk?' I ask, stopping before I get to the door.

'Yeah, I know – my mates all rib me for it. Say I've never really grown out of the baby stage. What can I say? I just like milk,' he admits, before taking the glass to his lips with a grin.

'Right, well . . .' I leave the room, unable to stop a smile cracking on to my lips at the sight of his sheer delight over his guilty pleasure.

'Sarah, nice to have you back,' booms Jonathan as he walks passed. 'All better I trust?'

'I hope so,' I say with a slightly uncomfortable-looking face – best to give myself a bit of leeway in case I feel the need to escape later on.

'Good,' he booms. 'We need to carry on sorting out the Christmas party plans, but first, I want you in the boardroom at ten.'

'Eeek!' I hear Julie squeak at me when Jonathan's out of earshot. 'Here we go – your first time contributing.'

Suddenly I feel very nervous as I straighten up my new notebook and pen on my desk, my grumpy mood being replaced with anxiety.

The Development team is made up of three official members of staff: Damian, a skinny redhead with a lisp who's the head of the department, trout-mouth Louisa and Real Brett. It's a small bunch, but relatively big compared to other production companies out there who did away with their Development departments years ago to cut back costs – preferring instead to pool ideas from the rest of the eager staff in the office to save money. Which could probably be the more realistic reason why I've been asked to contribute any ideas I might have without any increase in salary.

Even though I've worked in this office for eight years and am as comfortable here as I am at home, I feel stupidly nervous when, at nine fifty-eight, I walk the measly sixteen steps from my desk to the boardroom. Suddenly it feels small and exposing – and nothing like the comfy room I've wandered into countless times for a gossip out of earshot.

Jonathan doesn't come along to formally welcome me to the team as there's been some problem with a director on a show being made in Turkey (he shouted obscenities at one of the couples relocating for some unknown reason and they are now refusing to film with him), so instead he sends me in alone.

Real Brett is already sat at the eight-seater table when I walk in, so I have a sticky moment deciding where I want to sit – anywhere opposite will mean I have to look at him (and I can't trust myself not to ogle his beautiful face or frown at it), next to him means I won't have to see him but we might have some fleeting bodily contact (and I certainly can't predict what crazy reaction would come out if our knees brushed under the table). By a quick elimination process I whittle the chair options down to two – both on corners, but one where Real Brett would be looking more at me and the other where I'd be looking more at him. It's a tough decision to make when trying to think through every possibility.

I'm hurried along by Damian.

'In we go,' he says in a slightly irritated tone before whizzing round and sitting directly opposite Real Brett.

I decide to go for the spot where I'm looking towards Real Brett, but he's facing elsewhere – I don't think I'd handle having his eyes on me during this whole meeting, and at least this way I can busy myself in my notepad if necessary.

'Hi folks,' Louisa pouts, sauntering in carrying her iPad and iPhone, permanently looking as though she's about to take the perfect selfie.

'Nice to have you here with us, Sarah,' she says with an insincere smile as she sits in the spot I dismissed, right in Real Brett's eyeline.

'Thanks,' I mutter, surprised that she's not being overly welcoming, especially as we've never been on bad terms.

'Almost feels as though Jonathan's sneaking his spies in to check up on us,' she laughs – although it's not a real laugh, it's faked so that she could get the comment out without looking like a bitch.

'Spy?' repeats Real Brett, raising his eyebrows. 'Really?'

'To get you up to speed, Sarah,' says Damian, completely ignoring the prickly mood that's been created by Poutmouth Louisa. 'We're currently working on ideas that aren't just your bog standard "Moving to Benidorm" type shows – they're a bit dated and we want to find something a little more current to get the younger audiences back – whether that's through rethinking shows and ideas we already have or coming up with entirely new concepts. Ideally we'd like to target Channel 4 or MTV, but ITV2 or ITVBe could also work depending on what we come up with. Reality shows have changed dramatically over the last few years and we need to keep up and ultimately overtake.'

I nod to show that I'm listening, adding in a thoughtful frown for good measure. One thing I know a lot about is reality TV . . . in fact, if I were on *Mastermind* it would be my specialist subject.

'So, have you got any ideas you want to throw out there?' asks Louisa, her beady eyes looking at me expectantly.

'Erm . . .'

'Got anything in that shiny new notebook of yours?' she asks with a not-so-innocent shrug.

'This?' I stammer, flipping the beautiful pad in the air with a face that suggests it's actually a pile of dog crap. So far the only thing I've managed to write in it is my name and the date – nothing that's going to take the television word by storm and capture the imagination of millions.

'On her first day in the room?' Real Brett asks Louisa with a chortle. 'Give her a chance.'

I'm taken aback by the whole thing, so my eyes just flick between the pair.

'Joking, obviously,' Louisa shrugs, looking slightly embarrassed as she picks up her iPad and covers her face with it.

'All in your own time,' frowns Damian, bemused. 'Plus, for your own sanity, while you're in this room anything goes. No idea is too small or too big – you never know what could grow from a silly thought.'

'Nothing stifles your creative flow quicker than a questioning mind,' nods Real Brett while looking at Louisa.

'Right . . .' I nod, wondering whether I'm going to regret asking for the promotion in the first place.

'Just get brainstorming and flag up anything you think could really work. Now that we're all on the same page, let's reconvene next Monday morning and see where we're all at,' says Damian, while raising his shoulders as if what he's suggesting is a breeze and not something that's going to keep me up for the next six nights worrying.

And just like that, my first meeting in Development is over and I'm sat back at my desk whittling down the canapé options for our works Christmas do.

17

Seeing as our last few attempts at winning our title back have been appalling, we decide to forego the pub quiz night in favour of a pizza and film feast at ours instead. Mostly to give us all a break from being beaten by the dancing queens, but, obviously, this is also a little ruse to get the team together somewhere quieter so that certain topics (Carly being up the duff with our best mate's bubba) can be discussed without having to worry about eavesdroppers. Not that anyone there would be interested, but the group's reactions have the potential to be rather high-pitched and emotional.

Unsurprisingly, everyone was pretty chuffed to be meeting up away from the pub for a change.

Josh is first through the door for once, wanting to spend some alone time with Carly before the others arrive – they slink off to her bedroom until the flat buzzer rings twenty minutes later to tell us that Dan, Lexie and Natalia are standing on the doorstep.

You'd think it would be weird having Dan here with Lexie, seeing as it's the flat we once lived in together, but they've been over dozens of times in the past two years (thanks to my inability to ask the others over without including them), so they clearly don't mind. Living with Carly has meant lots of other memories have been created here . . . and not just of me weeping with heartbreak over Dan and his rejection.

The only time it did get a little strange was when Dan once helped himself to an orange squash during a visit, proving that he knew where everything was and that he still felt very much at home here.

I rearranged the kitchen cupboards when he'd left. He hasn't been able to help himself since.

The buzzer goes off to let us know the pizzas have arrived as soon as Alastair steps into the lounge.

'Well, how's that for timing,' he nods, looking happy that he doesn't have to wait to eat. I don't know what it is about Wednesday nights in particular, but the whole gang turn into hungry vultures – unable to function in a non-distracted manner until their tummies are full. We love our food.

'While we're all here, I have a little something to share,' says Carly, bringing in the boxes of pizza from the delivery guy and standing, holding them to ransom, in the doorway to the room.

Josh gasps, knowing what she's about to blurt, the others just looking bemused that their hot pizzas are at risk of getting cold.

'I'm pregnant and Josh is the dad,' she almost shouts, before whispering desperately to Josh, 'I'm sorry. There's no way I could've enjoyed these without getting that out first.'

Even though I knew the moment was coming, I must admit that even I'm a little shocked with the delivery – walking into a room of hungry adults, wafting deliciously smelling pizza in their faces and then dropping an almighty bombshell is a little untraditional.

Being able to watch their individual reactions, though, is quite beautiful.

'Wait ... Carly's the girl you've got pregnant?' asks

Alastair, getting up from the sofa that he's only just parked his butt on, the news making him spring to his feet.

'Seems so,' Josh smiles sheepishly with his hands in his pockets.

'Mate,' Alastair nods. 'I've been thinking you got a right wrong'un in trouble. This is epic.' He strides over to Josh and gives him a proper man hug, complete with overly enthusiastic patting on the back. 'You cheeky little fuckers.'

'I knew it! What did I tell you?' squeals Lexie to Dan.

'You guessed they'd had a cheeky snog at our engagement party – you didn't guess this,' smiles Dan, going over and joining the bromance between the boys before going to Carly, taking the pizzas from her, putting them on the coffee table and turning back with his arms wide open for a cheesy Dan hug.

Natalia's reaction is priceless. She's full on ugly-girl wailing on the sofa – to the point where Carly actually goes over to her to see if she's okay.

'This is amazing,' she sobs, laughing, wiping her dainty fingers across her soggy cheeks. 'I just really wasn't expecting it.'

'Neither were we,' grins Josh from across the room.

'It's so beautiful. You're growing a little miracle,' she laughs, placing her hand on Carly's stomach.

'Crazy,' Carly beams back, placing her hand over Natalia's and looking up at Josh.

I watch as the pair lock eyes and exchange a tender moment.

The sight brings tears to my eyes.

'Where are you going to live? Will you move into one

place?' Natalia asks with sudden panic, cutting in on the touching moment being shared.

Trust Natalia to think practically about the whole thing – I hadn't even thought about the idea of them living together, but they're a couple who are clearly in love and they're about to have a baby – it makes sense.

Although I've no idea where that would that leave me and our flat. I hope it won't mean I have to move too, though I guess that's what Gumtree's for. I can find another flatmate . . . I'm sure. I just have to hope they're not into anything weird – like veganism or trainspotting.

'We haven't properly talked about that yet. We have a few ideas but we're in no rush to do anything straight away,' says Josh, walking to Carly's side and rubbing the tops of her shoulders.

'It's still early days – you never know what could happen,' says Carly, pulling her lips together.

'Everything's okay though, yeah?' asks Dan, sounding concerned.

'We'll just be relieved when we get to the twelve-week mark and things are a bit safer,' Josh shrugs, leaning forward and kissing the top of Carly's head.

'I can't wait to have a scan. It still doesn't feel real at the moment,' she laughs.

'Know how you feel. It's quite a lot to take in,' puffs Alastair with a grin, draping his arm around my neck and pulling me in for a hug.

Carly and Josh might've felt as though becoming a couple in our group might've made things awkward – but the pair were so close anyway that their affectionate mannerisms with each other aren't completely new and surprising. In fact, it's rather gorgeously natural and has the whole group grinning wildly with a bizarre sense of what feels to me like pride.

'Oh my God – you're going to be pregnant at the wedding!' gasps Lexie, her head whipping round as she works out the months in her head. 'What about your bridesmaid's dress?'

Everyone tenses up, as though we've entered a spontaneous game of Musical Statues – I'm sure Alastair has even stopped breathing by my side. Silence falls on the room as Lexie's words make their way into my ears. Wedding. Carly. Bridesmaid. Dress.

Ohhh . . . I see.

I'm guessing Natalia is too.

Eurgh!

Of course Dan and Lexie would include the girls in their wedding party – I knew the boys were both ushers (Dan's brother is best man), so the girls getting involved too shouldn't be so surprising, should it?

They just should've told me.

'I'm sure we can get it altered or change the style,' Lexie mutters, going red as she looks down at her hands.

It occurs to me that she might have been feeling guilty about the whole thing (or at least a little uncomfortable) – and that's part of the reason why she gave me a present the other week, to soften the blow of this moment.

Well, it was a nice notebook – even if I'm still yet to write in it properly.

Bless her for trying.

With his arm still around me, Alastair's hand gently grips my shoulder and gives it a little squeeze.

'I'm sure you'll be able to sort something out,' I say with

a shrug and one of my best ever everything-is-fine grins, hoping to lift the air of suspense in the room.

'Pizza anyone?' asks Alastair, helping me out by moving towards our waiting dinner. He flips open the boxes and starts to offer them round the group.

Nothing breaks tension like food. Especially pizza.

'Anyone want a drink?' I quickly ask.

'Wine, please,' asks Natalia, still quietly sobbing on the sofa, although now looking even more worried.

'You need one,' Josh laughs. 'Beer, please.'

'Me too,' says Dan.

'Three,' says Alastair, picking up a slice of pepperoni pizza and cramming it into his mouth and turning to me with a wink.

'And I'm guessing wine for you Lexie, but something soft for you, Carly,' I say, turning to leave.

'I'll come help,' she says, following me into the kitchen.

'I'm so sorry,' Carly whimpers as soon as we're out of earshot – which isn't easy as our flat is particularly tiny – although I prefer to refer to it as cosy.

'It's not something you can say no to, darling. Unless you're a total bitch – which you're not.'

'But I should've told you.'

'Well . . . a heads up would've been nice,' I wink.

'She asked when I'd just done a test – my mind was all over the shop. I agreed and then haven't thought about it again since.'

'Hardly surprising with so much going on.'

'I'm sorry.'

'Don't be,' I say, giving her a hug. 'By the way – great announcement.'

Carly buries her head in her hands and laughs. 'What am I like?'

'Fuck!' Natalia mutters, scurrying into the room as though she is literally carrying her tail between her legs. 'Shit, shit, shit.'

Without saying anything else she buries herself into my arms and gives me a hug – it's her way of apologizing for being a total Judas.

I give her a squeeze back to let her know I understand.

'And you!' she says, turning to Carly with a sob. 'Come here.' She grabs hold of Carly by the wrist and pulls her into us, so that we're all huddled together.

18

The week ticks by with little inspiration for exciting new programmes for Red Brick Productions to produce – largely because Jonathan's kept me so busy with the Christmas party and personal tasks for his wife and daughter (I managed to bagsie the Beyoncé tickets through one of our directors who knows someone who owns a box at the O2, however clearing his wife of her M6 driving points is still an on-going saga with the DVLA), but mostly because I'm scared that anything I come up with is going to be crap and laughed at by people who actually know what they're doing. I'm not exactly keen on making myself look like an idiot, even if I am quite good at it.

So, instead of making loads of plans for the weekend, I decide to have a quiet one staying indoors and brainstorming. Above everything else, it gives me an excuse not to accept the invite over to Mum and Dad's for the weekend. Not that they minded – they were pretty impressed when I said I had to stay in and work.

On Saturday I sit staring at the blank pages of my book, willing and waiting for an idea to jump out and fill them. It's a tedious day that ends with me wanting to pull my eyeballs out and flush them down the loo so that I never have to see a piece of paper again (or see the look of disappointment on Damian's face when I go in on Monday morning and admit I have nothing to offer – and the look of satisfaction on Poutmouth's face when I confirm that I am indeed useless and probably only sent there as a spy – and the look of horror on my mum's face when I tell her I've been sacked for having little to no imagination). I believe this is what's known as 'development hell' – when the ideas just won't come and even thinking becomes an impossible mission. I've heard the expression bashed around the office a few times in the past and assumed it was just a term Louisa and Dominique made up for days when they'd been out the night before – but it turns out it's an actual, annoying, hellish, thing. At seven o'clock I decide to give up and join Carly and Natalia (she's here more weekends than she's not) on the sofa for a girlie night in of fab TV – *Strictly*, *The X Factor*, even a bit of *I'm A Celebrity . . . Get Me Out of Here*. It might not be particularly productive, but at least I'm not staring at a blank page debating pulling my eyes out.

Sunday morning is pretty much the same as the day before, with me sat on my bed thinking about thinking. So when Carly and Natalia knock on my bedroom door with a coffee, sausage rolls, some pickled onion monster munch and three Freddo frog chocolate bars, I welcome the distraction.

'*Four in a Bed* starts in a sec,' Carly winks, picking up the remote control and jumping into the middle of the bed, while Natalia pops the tray of goodies on the bed and scrambles in next to her.

The TV goes on and we watch as two of the four sets of B&B owners bicker over a used condom found in the rubbish bin at one of the properties. It's pretty disgusting. And riveting.

'Well, it was wrapped up,' shouts Carly, getting angry.

'Who goes through bins anyway?' I ask, shaking my head at the thought of it.

'Plus, he didn't need to sit there and unravel the whole flipping thing, did he? He must've known he wasn't going to find anything nice in there. I bet he planted it!' Natalia gasps.

I'm about to say something but the B&B owners are really going for each other and I don't want to miss a second of it – we sit in silence for the duration of the row and the rest of the show. Needless to say the team with the offending condom did not win – something Natalia's pretty miffed about.

'What happened to us?' Carly asks, once the end credits are rolling and Natalia's calmed down from the injustice the rubber johnny has delivered.

'What do you mean?' I ask.

'My life used to be full of adventure,' she moans, puffing out her cheeks.

'Erm, you've been having sneaky sex with Josh for the last year or so,' I laugh.

'Yeah, I think your life is still full of adventure,' Natalia says, eyeing up her tummy to further make our point.

The two of us cackle hysterically.

'Oh I know – a brand new adventure, blah blah blah,' Carly says, rolling her eyes at the pair of us. 'But gone are the days where I get high and dance the night away on beaches in Thailand without a care in the world. We've become grannies before our time.'

My head whips around to look at her as an idea starts to formulate in my brain.

'What? Why are you looking at me like that, you loon?'

'Out,' I shoo, getting up from the bed and brushing their legs away with my fingertips. 'Out, out, out!'

'You've got an idea?' asks Natalia, excitedly sliding off the bed and gathering up the mess our lunch has made.

'Yes, now OUT!' I yelp.

'Was it something I said?' asks Carly, taking her sweet arse time to move anywhere.

'Yes,' I nod.

'Oooooh!' she coos. 'Do I get a cut?'

'You can have my Freddo Frog,' I say, placing it in her hand and escorting her to the door.

'Good deal,' she nods as I shut her out of my room.

I pick up my gorgeous notebook and start to write out my plan.

19

On a warm summer's evening in Spain, I walk into an outdoor restaurant and speedily make my way across to the toilet – desperate for a pee. On arrival at the ladies I find that the cubicle walls are all made of mirrors. It's strange, as the rest of the place has an organic outdoorsy feel about it, echoing its position by the sea with wooden furniture, shells scattered everywhere and low candlelight, but I don't have time to think. I'm busting. I'll piss my pants if I don't go now.

I dash in, pull down my jeans and knickers and let out a huge groan of relief as the wee escapes. I didn't think I'd make it – it was touch and go for a minute.

Sitting there, on the toilet, I look out to the other people eating and drinking close by and notice they're glancing at me over their beer bottles and sniggering.

But how can they be?

I'm in a cubicle surrounded by walls . . .

Surely they can't see me . . .

But they can.

The walls are see-through.

Horrified, I glance up once more and see Dan's Uncle Andy at the bar talking to his Aunty Sally, both looking at me in disgust – their nostrils flaring and their lips curling.

I look at them with my jaw swung open, equally as surprised.

A motion to my left catches my eye – it's Natalia and Carly skipping past in matching pink chiffon floor-length gowns, looking like they belong in a mythical Shakespeare play with flowery garlands pinned into their hair. Following them, Josh and Alastair, each carrying hula-hoops and lit scented candles, grin as they cheer and holler through the crowd.

I can't hear exactly what they're saying but it sounds like a speech with jokes being set up and laughed at by the gathered crowd.

It's Dan and Lexie's wedding day, I realize with alarm.

And I've got my fanny out.

The people who aren't enthralled with what the boys are saying are actually just staring at me sat on the bog with my knickers around my ankles.

I shimmy around, trying not to flash my bits as I pull my clothes back up, but can hear laughter from my audience outside.

With my bum still out, my head whips back to the guests.

'Here she is, ladies and gents,' Alastair calls happily, his voice booming through the crowd. 'Our best friend, Sarah. This wouldn't be a celebration without her.'

I look at him aghast, trying to scream at him that now's not the time to draw attention to me, but he continues regardless.

'You might think it's strange that Dan's ex is here – but it would be stranger if she wasn't.'

'Hear hear,' echoes the crowd.

I pull a bizarre-looking smile at the faces in front of me in response, relieved when he continues talking to the crowd whilst walking off elsewhere and I can properly rearrange my clothes so that they're covering me up.

I stand upright and step out of the cubicle and spot James Corden sat on a bench talking to some of Dan's mates.

'Did you see what just happened?' I ask, unable to get over the humiliation.

He shrugs and raises his pint at me, before turning back to the conversation his friends are having.

I walk off in a huff and find myself wandering up some steps, where I stumble upon David Beckham and Justin Bieber chilling in a hot tub, staring out at the gorgeous view of the sea.

I literally shrug off my woes and clothes before climbing in to join them, closing my eyes and enjoying the warmth of the water.

Everything is still.

I'm engulfed with calm.

David and Justin leave.

I am alone.

Suddenly someone's lips are on mine, kissing me passionately. Hands are sliding over my body under the water, stroking and caressing.

I open my eyes to find Dream Brett's hazelnut eyes gazing at me lustfully as his perfectly white teeth nibble on my bottom lip.

I'm instantly on fire as a hot sensation of desire flushes through my body, wakening every last cell – making my whole body alert and ready.

I dive on him, pushing him back so that he's sitting on the other side of the tub, my hands running through his hair and pulling it slightly, making him moan.

I want him so much I feel dangerous. Powerful.

My lips find his.

My tongue finds his.

My body finds his – the desire mounting as we collide and slip with the water between us.

I kneel over him, straddling either side of his muscular legs, my hands working quickly to find him and slide him inside me.

I groan, my breathing erratic and loud thanks to the movement between my thighs . . .

I gasp as the well-known guitar riff wakes me up and pulls me away from my fun in the hot tub. Then I go as red as my crimson bedsheets as I realize I've had another naughty dream about my sort-of-work-colleague. Well, about Dream Brett. Although it's nice to know that Dream Brett hasn't wandered off into someone else's dreams (God knows I've missed him), I've now woken up desperately horny and deeply unsatisfied ... and am about to walk into a meeting with a guy that looks just like the one I've had sex in a hot tub with.

Oh life, how can you be so cruel?

I decide on a little skirt, tights and ankle boot combo – my dream tempting me to wear something sexier than normal. Plus, now that I'm in the Development meetings I really should be making more of an effort anyway, I reason.

'So my working title for this idea is *Grannies Go Gap*,' I say, kicking off my pitch in front of Damian, Louisa and Real Brett a few hours later – although trying my hardest to forget that the latter is even there.

'Grannies?' scoffs Louisa, adding in a little eye roll before looking at Damian as though the world's gone mad. 'Old people?'

'Yes,' I mumble.

'As in pensioners?'

'Shall we listen?' cuts in Real Brett – I must say, he's particularly good at shutting down her stroppy behaviour, even though he's new. He doesn't seem to be shy about it either – I guess that's down to having a good take on right and wrong and possessing a strong moral compass. Interesting to know he has that ... just like Dream Brett.

I wonder if he's good in bed like Dream Brett.

Focus, Sarah, focus!

Damian exhales loudly, bringing me back into the room. Oh fuck.

'Erm, would you rather something else instead?' I flap. 'Maybe it would be best if I talked about.. . .'

I flick through my notes frantically, feeling like a first-class tit – knowing that I have absolutely nothing else worth mentioning.

'I want to hear the Granny idea,' encourages Brett – his green eyes wide and keen as he nods enthusiastically.

Damian says nothing but looks at me expectantly – his eyebrows tilting upwards just a fraction.

Louisa looks like she's already bored. If Real Brett weren't here I imagine she'd be fake yawning to further her stance on the pitch I haven't even pitched yet.

'All right . . .' I exhale, calming the nerves that have exploded from my gut thanks to her input. 'So, *Grannies Go Gap* is different from any other show we've done where we're helping the elderly find some beautiful house on a remote island off the coast of Greece. Instead, we'd send them out to all the top spots for Gap Year students and young travellers. They'll basically become backpackers and travel the world – although we'd probably have to look into whether the bags actually have anything in them, we don't want anyone collapsing or worse – dying on us,' I stop myself knowing that I've gone off on a tangent and hit a bad note before I've really begun.

'Carry on,' says Damian, looking as though he wants to hear more – I take that as a good sign and plough on.

'We've all seen the stories in the papers of grandparents frequently feeling out of the loop when it comes to things like technology – it's a serious issue that was thrown into the limelight last year when an eighty-nine-year-old woman decided to end her life because she couldn't get to grips with how the world had changed so dramatically in recent years – she felt left behind in a world that had advanced beyond recognition. We know there are going to be loads of shows popping up about making things like the internet more accessible to the elderly – but what about making the world more accessible instead. I don't know about you guys, but my nan and granddad on my dad's side have only ever been to two countries – England and, on one occasion, France. When they were younger holidays were spent in Blackpool or on the Isle of Wight – they never travelled further than a few hours' drive from their home, let alone get on a plane and fly halfway around the world to walk up The Blue Mountains in Australia, dance in the streets of Rio de Janeiro or to elephant trek in Thailand. The younger generation has the world at their feet, and that's a fact that's largely taken for granted.

'I want *Grannies Go Gap* to be more than just showing a gran how to do her internet banking or open a Facebook account – it'll be about showing her a world that has only ever existed on the little black box in the corner of her living room.'

I pause for a moment and take a deep breath – astounded that the three of them have remained so quiet and interested, even Louisa.

'Too many people give up and think they're too old to go out there and grab whatever they want – but maybe this'll give other elderly folk some encouragement – maybe not to go to New Zealand and skydive, but at least to go off on holidays or do things out of their comfort zone.

'. . . And this shouldn't be a piss-take or like we're taking advantage of them in any way like some shows do. We would be genuinely giving them the chance to do some amazing things. I don't want people feeling sorry for them – although I'm guessing there'll be highly emotional moments within the programme. Maybe we could even find elderly folk who've had lifelong dreams to go to certain places and then take them there, rather than whisking them off for a whole year. We could have a play around and see what works best – a whole big adventure where our granny sees a few places, or individual trips to one spot where they see or do something specific . . . imagine waiting your whole lifetime to see the Niagara Falls and then marvelling over its beauty as you feel its spray lightly decorating your face . . . Anyway,' I breathe, glad to get my pitch out there in a coherent manner. 'That's where I'm at with the idea . . . Although, I'm happy to tweak and develop it. Obviously.'

Damian's eyebrows rocket up to his hairline as he expels a lungful of air whilst blowing a raspberry – I'm not sure he even caught a breath during my whole spiel. 'Well, I'll be honest, Sarah. I really wasn't expecting that.'

'In a good way?' I ask, because they're all looking at me really strangely now I've finished – Louisa doesn't look quite so Poutmouthy or bitchy and Real Brett is looking at me weirdly too – but then anything from him is weird when I'm used to gauging Dream Brett's reactions, not his.

'A very good way,' Damian nods, side-glancing at Louisa and Real Brett. 'I'd like you to develop this a little further – find case studies of old people who've never set foot outside of the UK. At some point Research can get involved when we're looking at locations and things, but for now find the old folk, find the popular Gap Year destinations and get a proper package of info together so that we can present it to Jonathan. Louisa and Brett can help you on this. Right, I've got a lunch meeting that I've got to get to, but this is great. Well done guys.'

'But I haven't told you my ideas yet,' says Louisa with a bewildered frown.

'Next time,' Damian offers, before walking out of the room.

Louisa throws a confused look at us before skulking after him.

'That was brilliant,' says Real Brett, winking at me. 'I've heard he can be a tough nut to crack, but you just smashed that.'

'Thank you,' I laugh, thoroughly pleased with myself.

My heart is still beating at a ridiculously fast pace, but the whole thing really couldn't have gone any better and was totally worth the week of sleepless nights and the mounting anxiety.

'Want to go grab a coffee later to celebrate?' Real Brett asks with a shy grin.

My eyes widen in response.

I'm stumped and in total shock – I wasn't expecting him to ask that at all.

Does he mean coffee like coffee-coffee on a date coffee, or just a coffee? Do I want a date coffee if that's what he means? Or is that weird when I've been dreaming of a different version of him entirely and this morning woke up from having jacuzzi sex with him?

I take too long answering and the air between us gets

uncomfortable – especially as I've had my mouth open as though I'm about to give a reply for the last thirty seconds, but with no sound coming out.

It's awful.

'Sorry – bad manners on my part,' he says, shaking his head as though he hasn't a clue what he was thinking by asking such a thing. 'Second week here and I'm already hitting on people. Terrible. You probably have a boyfriend. I shouldn't have . . . you know . . . assumed you didn't . . . Not that you look like you wouldn't have one. Oh crap. Sorry. I'll just . . .' and with that he shuffles through the door like a nervous and embarrassed little boy.

I feel terrible, and relieved, but mostly I feel terrible.

'Let me get this straight,' Carly says while she's stood over the stove throwing together a pasta sauce (literally throwing as she chucks in grated carrots and courgettes). 'Brett Last – the guy you've been fantasizing about for the last month – asked you out on what was clearly a date and you just didn't say anything?'

'Yep. Stood there gawping at him like a fucking twat.'

'You said nothing at all?' she asks, stirring the pot in front of her whilst shaking her head as though I've just done the stupidest thing *ever*.

'I was shocked. Plus I haven't been dreaming about this version of him, have I. He's differe . . .'

'He's real,' she says flatly.

'Exactly,' I nod, filling up the kettle and switching it on. She shakes her head at me.

'Yes, I know . . . it's pretty fucked up.'

'What's the worst that could've happened if you'd said

yes?' she asks, taking the chopping board and knife over to the sink and rinsing them.

'I'd become even more disappointed that he's not Dream Brett,' I nearly whisper.

'Ooh . . .' she says, turning back to me and screwing up her face. 'And what if he turns out to actually be a really nice guy?'

'That's possible . . .' I shrug.

'Think about it – there must've been something you liked about him all those years ago that's kept the memory of him stored away in that brain of yours for so long.'

'True. But I can't even look at him without getting irritated that he's not the other Brett – it's like someone's playing a huge trick on me.'

'They aren't and it's simple – one is real, one is not.'

'Ouch.'

'Sorry. Maybe you should give him a chance,' she shrugs, grabbing a tea towel and drying her hands. 'Or at the very least, not be such a dickhead to him.'

Carly is definitely a believer in tough love.

'Maybe you're right,' I mutter, getting a bag of fusilli from the cupboard and trying to stop myself getting into a petty strop over my inability to stop my dreams take over my feelings in real life – darn that sleep fairy. 'Anything new with you?'

'Nope.'

'Have you been to see the doctor yet?' I ask, pouring half the packet of pasta into a pan of boiling water and stirring it.

'Only to confirm I am actually pregnant – which I knew

anyway, but what's one more stick to pee on and a bit of blood being sucked out of my arm?' she giggles, squeezing some tomato purée into the sauce.

'Nice. No scans yet then?'

'Not until we get to twelve weeks – but it's all booked in for the beginning of January – although I think I'll actually be thirteen weeks by then. Just couldn't get an appointment,' she says, raising her eyebrows and sucking in air through gritted teeth. 'I can't wait to see him or her bouncing around inside me. I keep going on YouTube and looking at other people's scan videos.'

'That is strange.'

'I know, but I can't help it,' she says, bringing her hands to her face with embarrassment. 'It amazing to see what stage the little one is already at, you know?'

'So exciting . . . and real.'

'I know,' she winks. 'Petrifying, obviously, but seeing how brilliant everyone was when we told them and how sweet their reactions were – it's calmed me down and made me look forward to what's ahead rather than just seeing it as this huge thing hanging over me all the time. And Josh has been incredible, too.'

'Still can't get my head around that,' I laugh, my face distorting into an expression of disbelief. 'Eleven years of friendship and then one day you start seeing them differently. Just like that.'

'I can't even explain it, but we just fit,' she says, leaning against the kitchen counter, unable to stop herself from smiling. 'I know things got shit when he found out about the baby, but before that and ever since – I've never felt so safe and loved, you know?'

'You guys . . .' I gush, her smitten behaviour infectious. 'Who'd have thought it?'

'Certainly not me.' Pause. '*Definitely* not me.'

My phone starts ringing. I take it out of my back pocket to see who's calling.

'Mum,' I groan.

'Oh . . . have you spoken to her today?' Carly asks, avoiding eye contact with me.

'Not yet. I had planned to on the way home but then I morphed into a man-trampling bitch and forgot about it.'

'Oh . . . you might want to speak to her, then,' she says quickly, twisting her lips and scrunching up her nose.

'What? Why?' I ask, wondering what's going on.

'I forgot to tell you she called yesterday when you were in the bath – your phone was on the side in here and I picked it up.'

'That doesn't matter,' I shrug, confused, assuming she'd only been calling to check up on me and make sure I'd done my homework like a good girl and prepared properly for today. It's a good job I didn't talk to her, I reason, she'd only have made me more nervous.

'Yeah, but I picked up and started chatting. You know how she likes to ask questions . . . Next thing you know I'm telling her about me and Josh having a baby,' she says, bringing her hands to her face and blowing out her lips in a loud raspberry.

'Ah. I'm so sorry, Carly,' I say, relieved when the ringing stops and my mum's put through to my voicemail. 'What did the wicked witch say?' I ask.

I would feel bad about referring to my mum in such a negative light, but I'm well aware that she can have a vicious tongue at times and that she finds it difficult to keep control of it.

My phone starts ringing again.

'She was amazing, actually. Really sweet.'

'She was?' Pause. 'Are you sure it was *my* mum?'

'Answer,' Carly whispers.

'Mum!' I cry, picking up the call just before she gets cut off again.

'There you are. I thought you might be avoiding me,' she says – I imagine her eyebrows rising as she says it and her olive nostrils giving a wave as they flare.

'Sorry Mum, I was just cooking dinner with Carly,' I say, walking out of the kitchen and back into my room. She might've been lovely to Carly when she heard the news, but I'm expecting an ear-bashing of a reaction now – especially as she's had a whole twenty-four hours to mull it over and stew on it. Her daughter's best friends raising a bastard . . . whatever next!

'Ah, and how is she?' she asks with something bordering on compassion.

'Really good.'

'Good,' my mum repeats, with no hint of anything containing disgust or disappointment. If anything she sounds genuinely glad that Carly's doing well.

'What a shock,' I say, suddenly wanting to invite this conversation with my mum, seeing as she's not being very forthcoming with her opinion – something that, bizarrely, puts me on edge. It seems I must actually enjoy knowing exactly what she thinks on every single matter in my life (and anyone else's). 'You must've been surprised.'

'Hmm . . .' she says thoughtfully. 'Such a lovely couple, though. I've always liked Josh.'

'Yeah . . .' I find myself saying, wondering what her reaction would be if it were me getting knocked up by lovely Josh out of wedlock (or even a public relationship for that matter). Perhaps I'm being too hard on her.

'And how'd today go?' she asks, changing the subject.

'Really well! My boss wants me to develop my idea further,' I say, enjoying sharing *real* good news for a change – rather than an exaggerated truth, or a tale of half-truths.

'That's amazing news,' she shrieks for what must be the second time in two weeks, but also my whole adult life. It's a sound I could enjoy hearing a lot more.

'Thanks, Mum,' I mumble, feeling a bit bashful at this new emotion she's throwing my way in abundance.

'I'm so proud.'

Wow.

That single comment is enough to get my tear ducts working.

20

'What did you want to be when you grew up?' he asks, looking ahead at the road, his grip loose on the steering wheel in his hands.

'The Queen,' I answer straight away, it's not something I have to think about. 'You?'

'Tom Jones,' he replies, equally as quick.

'So it was really a question of who, rather than what for both of us,' I laugh.

'Exactly. There was something about that Welsh lothario that had me hooked. Still quite fascinated with him now,' he adds, brushing his fingers through his shaggy blonde hair.

'Total GILF.'

'Now that's gross,' he laughs, his face screwing up in mild disgust.

'True though,' I giggle, looking out the car window at the beautiful blue sky above.

'I used to have nightmares when I was younger – proper night terrors – and the only thing that used to calm me down was when Mum put his Greatest Hits on my walkman and let me fall back to sleep with my headphones on,' he admits.

'Hardly soothing.'

'It's not all about 'Sexbomb' – in fact, hardly any of it's like that. It's more soulful and moving.'

'I believe you,' I smile, enjoying the look on his face as he passionately talks about his idol – the way he licks his lips and squints his eyes, as though really focussing in on his love for Sir Tom.

I wish I loved something as much as that – I don't even think my *adoration of Kimmy K could compete – even though I'm currently sat wearing a tight white dress (showing off my pert boobs) which wouldn't look out of place in her wardrobe.*

'You should listen to one of his albums,' says Dream Brett, still championing his idol. 'Especially the old stuff. 'Without Love' has to be the most amazing song of all time. His passion and delivery are just out of this world.'

'I don't think I've ever heard it,' I say, mentally wading through the music collection in my brain but finding no Tom Jones archived in there at all.

'Really?' he asks in shock. 'It was huge. Elvis covered it the year before, but it was Tom's version that was the biggest hit in the charts.'

'You're really geeking out right now,' I laugh, reaching over and placing a hand on his arm. My fingers give a little squeeze.

'Ha. I really am,' he says, turning to me with a bashful smile. 'All I'm saying is, there's a reason why he's known as "The Voice" and why he's classed as a king to anyone who's Welsh.'

'You're not Welsh though, are you?'

'No . . . just love him,' he smiles with a shrug, looking a little embarrassed.

'And I love you too, boyo,' says a deep, gravelly Welsh voice from the back seat.

Dream Brett practically jumps in his seat with excitement.

The car is no longer forwards – we are no longer driving anywhere.

'Tom!' he squeals.

'All right, kid?' says Tom Jones in his trademark lilt, leaning forward in the seat and reaching out a hand for him to shake. 'How's it going?'

'Good,' Dream Brett says, taking his hand – delighted to have his god in the back seat of the car.

'Good, good,' Tom repeats before lifting a microphone to his lips.

The car disappears. Instead of sitting, we're on our feet, in a theatre with thousands of other people crammed in around us, watching Tom Jones strutting up and down the stage singing Lady Gaga's 'Do What You Want (with my body)', accompanied by a big band and a dozen singers.

The audience is hot, steamy and loving every thrust Tom makes in their direction, like a sex-crazed bunch of teenagers at a One Direction concert, even though they're all around my age.

Brett is behind me, his hands on my hips as we sway along to the beat. Side to side we rock, the heat of the room making our bodies sweat — that and the suggestive lyrics of the song.

I raise my hand in the air and close my eyes, feeling the music and atmosphere brush over me — making my nipples tingle.

Brett grabs my hand and spins me around to face him.

His mouth is on mine — kissing me passionately, his hands skimming my breasts before finding their way to my back and pulling me in closer.

We get lost in the crowd.

Lost in the music.

Lost in each other's touch.

I open my eyes as he opens his and see his cheeky smile grinning back at me.

I look down coyly, playing the sexy vixen he turns me into — but when my eyes next meet his, the hazelnut has morphed into green.

Green.

All I see is green.

That's not right.

I wake up with a frown on my face as my alarm goes off, although largely glad that I'm not about to see the fall-out of the new eye-colour in my dream state.

Is Dream Brett going to get replaced with Real Brett now? Is Dream Brett slowly going to fizzle out, leaving me with totally inappropriate dreams about a work colleague that I can't compartmentalize as someone completely different to the guy I'm hanging out with in my sleep?

Now, that would be awkward.

Correction.

That would be more awkward than the crazy situation I'm already in.

I don't want to give my subconscious any wild ideas about erasing Dream Brett, so I grab my phone to shut off the alarm, and look up Tom Jones on iTunes, downloading one of his greatest hits collections (there are many to choose from). My dad used to be a big fan, so I already know a lot of the songs on the album – I listen to them on repeat as I get ready for work.

In fact, I listen to it on shuffle for the whole journey into town and am still enjoying it when I get to my desk in the empty office.

I'm loving 'Burning Down the House' so much that I can't help but give a little dance as I wait for my computer to start up – my head flops along to the music as my shoulders jump around to the beat. There's something about songs like Tom's and others from his heyday that just set you free, removing all your inhibitions and almost liberating you in a wild way. God, I wish I were alive in the sixties or seventies when the sexual revolution took place – I can totally understand how music led the way to such a huge social release and guided youngsters into a carefree existence. I would've been a total groupie, along with the likes of Pamela Des Barres – and felt utterly cool being one.

'What are you listening to?' Real Brett shouts, as his grinning face pops up in front of me.

I yelp, jumping out of my seat in shock.

'What the – ' I manage, clutching my chest and feeling as though I'm on the verge of having a heart attack.

'Sorry, I didn't mean to startle you,' he says, guilt creeping across his face as his splayed hands move towards me, unsure whether to touch me or not. He decides not to, so they just linger awkwardly in the space between us.

'I didn't see you come in,' I breathe, whipping the headphones out of my ears and mentally knocking my head against my desk. I sit facing reception – I should've seen the doors open as Real Brett arrived.

'Oh, I was already here,' he muses, visibly relaxing a little now he can see he's not about to have to perform CPR on the drearily grey (and somehow spiky) office carpet.

'You were?' I frown.

'I was in the kitchen,' he says, gesturing towards it with his head. 'Making toast. You want some?'

'No, thanks,' I mumble.

'Really? I've brought in some of my nan's homemade raspberry jam. It's pretty amazing – she's won all sorts of local awards for it. You know, at fêtes and stuff. Nothing official.'

'No, I'm fine,' I sigh, although almost tempted by the jam.

I can't help but find the fact that he's brought his nan's concoction into work with him quite sweet and endearing – I can imagine Little Old Lady Last sending him home with a few jars, worrying that he's not getting a varied enough diet now that he doesn't live with his parents (or does he?), and making him promise to look after himself. Any guy who fusses over his grandparents and shows them a little bit of love (displaying that he has a real heart buried underneath any crappy laddishness) gets me in a flap – you can fake your existence to anyone but your elderly granny and grandpa. That's a fact.

This sort of behaviour never fails to make me go a little weak at the knees.

I don't want to be weak at the knees over Real Brett.

No thank you.

No.

I try to block out the spark of intrigue he's ignited in me – all of a sudden I want to know more about his family life, his sweet little old nan, and whether or not he's flown the nest and moved into his own pad.

I wonder if he takes his dirty washing home at the weekend.

Maybe his nan does it for him before she sends him off with food for the week.

Maybe he's an orphan.

Enough!

I don't want to know any of this stuff.

'You're early,' I note flatly.

'*You're* early,' he says with a cheeky shrug, his eyes glittering.

'I'm meant to be early,' I snap, realizing that since he's started we've been the first two people in the office almost every day. Perhaps I should go back to being late again and mooching in unnoticed ten minutes after everyone else with a takeaway coffee cup in my hand.

Darn this sudden urge to better myself.

Although, truth be told, there's something peaceful and calming about getting up that little bit earlier and arriving at the quiet office with time to gear myself up for the day ahead. Just a shame I've acquired regular company.

'So what made you get your groove on this morning?' he asks, lifting up my headphones without waiting for an answer and placing them to his ears. I glimpse down at my phone and see that 'Give a Little Love' is playing.

A lump forms in my throat as I wait for a reaction.

'Never had you down as a Tom Jones fan,' he says, nodding as he purses his lips – his eyebrows raising skywards as he listens.

I shrug, deciding not to share the reasons behind it being my soundtrack of choice this morning – or the fact that I've only owned a Tom Jones album for the past hour and fifteen minutes and have since morphed into a superfan. He might be in his mid-seventies, but man alive can he sing a good tune.

I watch Real Brett nibble on his bottom lip as he listens and find my own mouth open and pouting outwards in response – my lips edging their way closer to their desired landing spot. I suck them in and put my hand over my mouth – shushing them and their naughtily slutty behaviour.

Real Brett places the headphones back down onto my desk, but before he can comment we hear his breakfast spring up out of the toaster. He simultaneously grins and nods at my discarded headphones as he walks back to the kitchen.

It's a look I can't read, and that bothers me. Does the reaction mean that Real Brett likes Tom Jones too or that he finds it hilarious that a woman my age is listening to him? If he does like him, have I found a similarity between Real Brett and Dream Brett? And how does that make me feel about my newfound appreciation of Tom Jones?

I might be overthinking this whole thing . . . maybe. Besides, it makes no difference if he does love Sir Tom – they're two entirely different people . . . beings . . . spirits.

Oh bollocks.

Whatever they are, they're different.

I turn to my computer to get on with some work, just as Real Brett starts singing 'Sexbomb' in the kitchen. I can imagine him shaking his little hips as he butters his toast and spoons on his jam.

I do my best to block him and the image out.

'So, what are we up to today?' Real Brett asks as he stands in front of my desk and bites into his breakfast.

My tummy grumbles at the sight of the gooey red jam – complete with the pips. It really does look delicious.

'You sure you don't want some?' he asks, motioning towards the slice of heaven in his hand.

'Erm, no thanks,' I manage, reddening as I realize I've been salivating in his direction (and not for the first time).

'Not even a bite?'

His eyebrow raises just a fraction, making me wonder if that was a suggestive little remark on his behalf. Surely not . . . but was it?

'No,' I mumble, picking up my notebook and seeing what's on today's agenda. 'I actually have to do some bits for Jonathan and then the Christmas party . . .'

'Again? You spent all day yesterday doing that.'

'There's a lot to sort and it's only three weeks away,' I shrug.

'Must be riveting.'

'Yep . . .'

'Are we living it up at Hawksmoor or slumming it in Nandos?'

'Don't knock Nandos,' I say flatly.

'Clearly not . . . a fine eatery,' he nods, pursing his lips.

'Their wings are to die for.'

'As is their chilli nut mix. Good nuts are hard to come by.'

I find myself wondering if his talk of nuts is another sexual comment, but not a single flicker of amusement or recognition that it might be construed in that way crosses his face, so I imagine it's actually me with the filthy mind. It wouldn't be the first time I've found myself in that situation – when I was seventeen (and extremely sexually charged) Luke Green (the fittest boy in the year) asked me if I wanted to ride his horse the following Saturday. I turned up to the stables wearing a mini skirt, push-up bra and heels, only to find him mucking out in his wellies and dirtiest comfies. Turns out he actually meant for us to spend the day riding his horse Troy. Apparently I'd displayed an interest in his hobby a few weeks before (I'd have said anything to get him to look at me) and had since forgotten.

Oops.

'We've actually hired a spot in one of the function rooms of a hotel around the corner. It's a new place called The Nest,' I tell Real Brett in a self-impressed manner, pleased with the plans Jonathan, Julie and I have made. It's not often we all agree on the office parties – Jonathan prefers to do something cheap and cheerful, Julie likes anything where there's drink and loud music and I'm a tad more sophisticated with the whole thing – preferring the idea of it being on a par with the Oscars. I love seeing everyone in their finery sipping on bubbles and really celebrating the end of the year together. Usually my ideas are vetoed – but when I forwarded them both an email from The Nest telling us about their opening deals for the winter period they both jumped at the offer. It's a fab place too – they've really managed to blend the lavishness of a London hotel with the cosiness of home. I love it.

'A hotel?' Real Brett scoffs.

'Yeah?' I question, surprised by his disbelieving tone.

He raises his eyebrows and puffs out his cheeks before shoving another chunk of toast into his mouth and gnawing on it.

I manage to stop a snarl appearing on my face – I love to see a man enjoying his food, but I'd rather they didn't look so caveman-like doing so. At least he keeps his mouth closed, I guess.

'What's wrong with that?' I ask, wondering whether we've made a mistake.

'A work's do in a hotel?' he swallows. 'Hotel rooms to run off to . . . ?' he says, whilst nodding his head encouragingly, willing me to complete the rest of his thought. 'You're asking for trouble.'

A hot flush crosses from my cheeks down to my chest – even though I know he's not suggesting for a second that the two of us book ourselves into a room and drunkenly bonk all night, it's still a thought that shockingly enters my head and the space between us.

Not that I'd want to with Real Brett.

Obviously.

No thanks.

Right?

'This is Red Brick Productions – the closest we get to any drunken antics is Julie downing shots of tequila and insisting everyone strut their stuff on the dance floor. She might not look the sort – but she's got a seriously fierce twerk on her,' I state.

'And that's how it starts,' he laughs, his shoulders shaking as his head bows into his chest.

'Hmmm . . . I'll bear your concerns in mind, but I think it'll be fine.'

'Hopefully you won't be wishing you'd gone with the Nandos option,' he quips.

'Right,' I say in an authoritative tone before snatching up my notebook and putting an end to the conversation. 'I'd better get cracking with this, but it would be great if you could start looking into the top gap year destinations. Find out what the young travellers of today are getting up to. I'm going to phone up Age Wise a little later and see if they'll help us with case studies. I bet they have some wonderful characters that would be awesome for what we're looking to create – they might even let us put up a little advert on their site or something.'

'Do you think it'll be seen?'

'By grannies? Who knows – I'm sure some are quite computer savvy and the site is a place for them, so fingers crossed.'

'I guess,' he says, pursing his lips, seeming unconvinced and causing my belief in reaching out in this way to waver.

'We could always send a few tweets out about it, too,' I

suggest quickly. 'I'm sure people will nominate others they know if they think it could be for something life changing.'

'Sweet,' Real Brett nods. 'Anything else?'

'Not at the moment.'

'Great stuff.'

He nibbles on his bottom lip and looks down at the empty plate in his hand, before looking up and frowning towards the kitchen.

'You okay?' I ask – longing for him to bugger off back to his desk.

'Just wondering if I want some more toast . . .' he mumbles, his mouth screwing up with torment.

'Go for it,' I say decisively with much gusto – anything to get him out of my sight.

'Really?'

'Yep. Treat yourself.'

'But I've already had three slices . . .'

'Three?' I almost squeal.

That's a lot of toast and I wouldn't have thought he'd be the sort to gorge on so many carbs, not with his athletic physique.

Bet his nan would be proud.

'I had some before you arrived,' he clarifies.

'Oh.'

'It's the jam. Sucks me in,' he says guiltily.

'Your nan's jam?'

'Yeah.'

'I say have another slice. Your nan made it for you to enjoy – think how sad she'd feel if she thought you didn't love it. You owe it to her. It would be rude not to gobble it up.'

'I think I will,' he nods in agreement, rubbing his (no doubt) toned tummy hungrily as he ponders the thought of more going into it.

'And go on then, I'll have one too,' I shrug, making out as though I'm doing him a favour – although, clearly, I'm just being a greedy cow. Let's be frank, I've been wanting to munch on Brett's piece for the duration of this chat – I've even contemplated licking his plate as it had a discarded dollop of jammy goo on its rim this entire time. Luckily I do have an ounce of self-control somewhere in my being that has stopped me stooping to that absurd level of class and shamelessness. So far.

'Righto,' he grins, laughing as he plods off to fetch us our grub.

'Oh. My. God,' I groan a few minutes later when my teeth sink into the crunchy sweetness that is Real Brett's nan's raspberry jam spread on freshly cut buttered and toasted sourdough bread. 'This is delicious.'

'Told you.'

'I mean . . . seriously, fucking amazing.'

Real Brett pauses his own intake of heaven to grin at me. I grin back warmly.

No wonder he was eating it in such a feral way – this jams needs to be eaten at superfast speed, your tummy basically begs for its arrival in your gut as soon as your taste buds are pinged into applause.

'Don't suppose your nan has been confined to the UK her whole life and would consider being one of our case studies?' I ask in hope, as visions of dozens of jam jars lining up around my desk fill my head – I'd never have to or want to eat anything else ever again.

'Sadly not. Nan was well before her time in that department. Took off in her twenties to see the world.'

'Did she meet your granddad afterwards then?' I ask nonchalantly with a munch.

'Nope. Met him before . . . he asked her to marry him and then she absconded to India.'

'Wow. Bet he was gutted,' I chew.

'Not really. Her spontaneity was one of the things he adored about her.'

'Oh.' Pause. 'So what did he do to win her back?'

'Nothing. Just waited,' he smiles. 'Three years later she returned to England with an answer for him . . . and they've never spent a day apart since then.'

'Ever?'

'Ever,' he confirms.

'So romantic,' I sigh, feeling myself melt into the enchantment of it all.

'Very.'

'Does it run in the fam – '

'What you two gassing about?' interrupts Julie, using the journey from the front door to her desk to remove all of her outer garments. Once stripped, she gets a brush from the top drawer of her desk and quickly gives her hair a once-over before turning and smiling manically at us both.

'Family stuff,' I mutter, pulling myself together and snapping out of the trance Real Brett's wonderful grandparents have pulled me into. Note – I said his grandparents, not him.

'Ooh . . .' Julie replies distractedly, her eyes scanning the rest of the room.

'You okay, Julie?' I ask. It's not like her not to want to

be told every part of every conversation, no matter how big or small – she loves to know everything there is to know, whether it concerns her or not. It's part of her nosy mumsy quality.

'Oh yes. Absolutely,' she smiles, her cheeks blushing pink as she turns on her computer. 'Tea?'

'No thanks,' I frown, feeling as though I'm missing something as I watch her head towards the kitchen.

'Catch you later,' winks Real Brett, grabbing my empty plate from my desk and walking off with it.

My mind flicks back to the perfectness it once held.

I can't help but let out a sigh.

I'd have asked for another slice if he'd offered. Now I'm left wanton for more – WANTING. WANT-ING. Definitely not wanton.

No.

Not wanton.

Nope.

'Here you go,' Real Brett says after lunch, plonking a half-full jar of jam on my desk (its contents make it a half-*full* situation, definitely not half-*empty*).

'What's that for?'

'It's yours.'

'Huh?'

'You can have the rest of it,' he shrugs.

'What? Why?'

'Told Nan you enjoyed it so much,' he laughs, his eyes glistening at me. 'She called at lunch to see what I thought of this batch and was thrilled to hear I'm making new friends at work.' Cue blush and a roll of the eyes. 'She then told me I'd made a faux pas by not offering you the rest of this, seeing as you liked it so much.'

'She seems sweet.'

'Pushy,' he grins.

'Old people are,' I grin back. 'They've earned the right to get whatever they want.'

'Well this'll get her off my back,' he says, nudging the jar and moving back towards his desk.

'You could've just left it in the kitchen for everyone to use,' I call after him.

'And lie to my nan? She'd know. She always does,' he says, turning and smiling at me, continuing to shuffle backwards.

'What about you?'

'I'm hoping you'll still share it with me,' he says coyly, his eyebrows tilting skyward as a cheeky expression befalls his face, making him look at least five years younger and just the tiniest bit even more like Dream Brett.

'So I can't take it home?' I pout sadly, the thought of having to share it with everyone else in the office making me panic.

'You could.' Pause. 'I don't mind eating it there,' he winks, swivelling around and striding away from me.

The suggestive wink.

Now, there's no need to call me Sherlock fucking Holmes – that was most definitely a flirtation. A huge one.

And these are unquestionably butterflies in my tummy.

Fuck.

Major fuck fuck fuckity fuck.

Fuck.

*

216

'What if he doesn't actually have a nan and this is all a big ruse to get you to fancy him?' Carly asks as we make our way to the pub. We've decided to go back – despite having fun away from the place last week we're attached to our grubby little local and enjoy having the quiz to focus on, even if we don't always win.

'Would guys actually stoop to that level?' I ask, not sure anyone would bother to go that far just for a date with me.

'You never know,' she shrugs. 'I've heard of some doing worse.'

'Fair point,' I frown, mulling over her suspicions. 'I can imagine him now, stood outside work, pouring a jar of Essex's Wilkin & Sons' finest into a different jar, just on the off chance I'm a fan.'

'Weirder things have happened,' she muses, rubbing her tummy.

'Can you feel anything?'

'Not yet,' she says, screwing up her face in disappointment. 'Actually just feel a bit bloated – like I've had a mammoth curry session and need a big poo.'

'Sounds just as magical as they say in the films.'

'Oh definitely . . . shame they leave out the bit about you having to trump all the time as well.'

'And you're such a ladylike thing, too. I don't know how you're coping,' I say, opening the door to the pub for her.

'Exactly,' she laughs, walking through and heading straight to our group's favourite spot.

'You'll never guess who's started at my work,' I say to Alastair as soon as I sit down next to him. I'd been meaning to mention it to him the week before at our flat, but Carly's dramatic outburst pushed all thoughts of Real

Brett from my mind. I'm surprised I haven't thought about texting him about it – although I've been trying to convince myself that Dream Brett and Real Brett are two different people, and not wanted to blur that line with the truth, but I guess I knew I'd have to address the link with Alastair at some point – especially as I know Carly is dying to spill the beans and drop me in it.

'Who?'

'Brett Last,' I say, managing a smile at the blast from the past I'm giving.

'No way,' he says in surprise. 'Ned's mate?'

'Yeah! Him,' I nod.

'I've not seen him in years,' he says, looking bewildered at the connection. 'How is he?'

'Good, I think. I haven't really spoken to him much,' I lie, annoyingly feeling myself blush and trying to ignore Carly stifling giggles at the other end of the table.

'He's a great guy,' says Alastair with a nod.

'Seems it,' I shrug.

'I think he was the only one of Ned's mates that I genuinely liked. Shame they grew apart really. The others could be right tossers at times,' he says, squinting as he remembers. 'It's no wonder Ned had no qualms leaving them all behind.'

'How's he getting on?' Natalia asks, looking nicely relaxed as she breathes in her glass of wine. 'He's not been back over since the wedding.'

Unlike Real Brett, we were all invited to his intimate gathering in Leeds a few years ago – funny to think our paths would've crossed again then had they still been close.

'Great,' shrugs Alastair in response. 'Loving the sunshine Dubai brings.'

'I bet,' Natalia replies. 'You know my boss has been on about me doing some work over there? A load of the properties I'm working on here are actually just holiday homes for our clients to come over for a week here or there . . .'

'Oh, how the other half live,' Alastair smirks, rolling his eyes before winking at me.

'Tell me about it,' Natalia nods, curling up her top lip. 'But because they've loved working with us so much they've been talking about us doing up their main homes too – a total renovation. Big contracts. Huge.'

'Don't you dare leave us,' I grumble, reaching over and taking her hand in mine.

'Well, I'll probably just be shipping everything I source over there for someone else to take the glory – but a girl can dream.'

'And so she should,' nods Carly, tapping our friend's other hand in support.

'It's a totally different life out there,' Josh ponders, nodding his head. 'Maids, drivers – it's nuts. I'd love it.'

'Sadly your life is about to become as far from that as you can possibly think,' murmurs Carly, raising her eyebrows at him.

He widens his eyes in response before cracking into a smile and placing his hand on her tummy and giving it a little rub.

'You'll have to say hi to him for me,' Alastair says, looking back at me.

'Will do,' I chirp, knowing I probably won't.

'Who's that?' Dan asks, joining in the conversation as soon as he and Lexie walk in. If I thought he cared I'd assume his ears pricked up when he heard me talk about a guy. But I'm under no illusion there.

'Brett,' Alastair replies. 'Remember my brother's mate. Used to visit us.'

'Uni?' Lexie asks, managing to look interested. I've never really given it much thought before, but for someone coming into a group of established mates who already have a decade of memories together, it must be really boring when they always refer back to the 'good old days'.

'Oh yeah, I remember,' Dan nods. 'Top bloke. Had a really shitty black Corsa that they drove up in,' he remarks.

'That's it,' laughs Alastair at the memory.

'Is he driving something better now?' he asks me.

'I wouldn't know,' I say breezily, annoyed that he even knows who we're talking about, although aware that I'm being touchy and protective. Real Brett might not be Dream Brett but I'd still like to keep him to myself rather than have to share him with the dickwad stood next to me.

'Maybe you could bring him along here one week,' Alastair continues, his eyebrows rising with delight at his idea.

I must look as flummoxed as I feel, as he catches my expression and copies it.

'What?'

I swear he's smirking.

'Why would she do that?' asks Josh, from across the table.

'We never bring other people here,' I say, in agreement.

'She's working with him now,' Carly tells Dan and Lexie, giving them the missing piece of information.

'A new bloke in the office,' Lexie smiles widely. 'What's he like? Fit?'

'We're not at school,' Dan tuts under his breath as he turns away and walks towards the bar.

Lexie frowns at the back of his head before flashing a forced smile to the ground and following him.

It's a minuscule exchange, but it's awkward and unlike Dan to snap at Lexie.

My eye briefly catches Alastair's before he looks away uncomfortably. He shrugs his shoulders and with a bounce of his eyebrows he picks up his beer and takes a swig.

From the look I can tell he's surprised too, but isn't about to dwell on its significance.

No one else seems to have caught wind of the strange atmosphere at our end of the table; instead they've started debating our pub quiz guest policies.

'No strangers or work colleagues – it's the unspoken rule,' Josh continues, his hand moving from Carly's tummy to rest on her thigh.

'But he's an old friend of the group,' smirks Carly, placing her hand on top of Josh's.

'He is,' nods Alastair. 'And I seem to remember you going on about how much you loved him back in the day.'

'We always had fun when he came up with Ned,' nods Natalia with a mischievous smile – making me question why my brain couldn't place Brett so clearly when he first appeared in my dreams. I guess it's simply because he was in a setting I wasn't used to. Maybe if I'd stumbled upon him in a grotty pub in Leicester I'd have known instantly.

'He was pretty epic . . .' says Josh, looking like he's about to back down from his argument.

'Oh you *have* to bring him down so we can talk old times,' Carly grins at me.

'See if he can patch together some of our missing memories,' suggests Natalia, nodding to encourage the idea.

'But it's only a one-off,' states Josh firmly, letting us know that he's totally given in.

'Yes,' hisses Carly.

'Sounds fun,' I mutter, sending a death stare in her direction.

She notices but doesn't seem fazed in the slightest – if anything, she enjoys my discomfort.

Cheeky cow.

21

... *I'm drunk.*

Absolutely off-my-tits smashed.

Buried under a mound of purple pillows on a purple sofa, I'm struggling to function. My body is heavy and monged out and my eyes want to drift off to sleep even though they know they shouldn't at this precise moment as I'm out in public. I'm in a room filled with people, with a babble of activity and noise around me.

Looking across the room, I spy my friends all gathered on an oversized orange sofa, sipping on red wine while playing duck, duck, goose. It's Natalia's turn to bash on the heads of our friends. I watch with one eye slightly open as she teasingly walks behind them, causing them all to squirm and laugh, before finally choosing Alastair as her 'Goose'. He chases after her, catches her and throws her in the air, making her squeal in protest.

I close my eyes and chuckle, loving the weightless sensation the little movement causes in my zombified state.

My body gets knocked by someone slumping on the sofa next to me – I half open an eye to see Dan.

I audibly groan.

'You think you're the only one who's pissed at this situation?' he snaps under his breath.

'I'm the only one who's allowed to be,' I bark back, my eyes now awake and alert.

'How'd you work that one out?'

223

'You broke my heart?' I say, incredulous at his audacity to question his actions.

'And you don't think you broke mine?' he asks, visibly shocked, as though I'm being narrow-minded in my pain, that it's something I should share out and not hog all to myself. 'You think your disappointment as a partner didn't cause me to weep into my pillow at night while you snored open-mouthed next to me?'

'Fuck you,' I spit.

'You too.'

'Why can't you just bugger off? You've got the girl, why can't you just let me have my friends and live happily ever after with them?'

'Maybe they don't want that.'

Even in my dreams I know there's truth to that. My friends aren't pawns in our game of love and hatred. They're real people with their own thoughts and freewill – they're not either of ours to claim, although I wish they were. I wish I could bag them all up and whisk them off to some faraway land, away from Dan and Lexie.

'Why wasn't I good enough?' I whimper.

'It wasn't about you.'

'To me it was. To my heart there was only you and me, and you tossed me aside without even a second thought – on the first day Lexie entered your life.'

'She was different.'

'She was perfect.'

'She was fun.'

'I was fun once,' I bellow, suddenly annoyed that my entertaining side got snatched away by such an ungrateful twat. I was a hoot when we were together. I was always giggling and laughing – making him laugh until he cried. How can he say I wasn't fun? I was fun. I was the joker, his personal fucking clown.

224

'Debatable,' he scoffs, his eyes giving a little roll of agitation.

I see red, my eyes bulge out of my head like a character from Who Framed Roger Rabbit and steam gushes from my ears.

'What was that?' I snarl, daring him to say it again.

But I don't wait for a reply, instead I snatch the glass of red wine from his hand and chuck its contents in his face.

'What the . . . ?' he asks, shocked, wiping the liquid from his eyes.

He calmly grabs the glass in my hand and repeats the action on me.

Tit for tat, I realize as the red liquid runs down my face and seeps all over the big puffy white dress I'm wearing. The sight of it reminds me of all the dreams I'd collected of our future together. How I thought we'd buy our own place, get a puppy – get married, and live happily ever after with our two children in the suburbs.

That dream has been massacred, just like this dress – in my mind I'm like Uma Thurman in Kill Bill on her character's tragic wedding day and the image causes a fire to burn in my stomach.

I glare at Dan, my nostrils flaring at his wonderfully formed face and ridiculous good looks.

I roar, a sound that growls from deep within and scratches at my throat as it's released.

Snatching the pillows around Dan, I shred them to pieces with my razor-like nails, then I grab photoframes from the wall and crush them under my feet as I hurl them to the ground, snatching up chairs and flinging them across the room and into the walls.

I'm out of control.

I roar and roar and roar.

Snarling in an ugly, beastly manner while Dan cowers with his head in his hands, unable to even look at me and see the mess he's turned me into.

*

As music fills my room a cloud of confusion fills my brain. My head is heavy as I open my eyes and frown at the sunlit room.

I never want to be in a situation where I explode like that. I never want to feel so out of control and angry . . .

Funny that feeling of anger – it's popped up a few times in my dreams (like when I became The Hulk and slammed Alastair's canoe into the water) – that build-up of furious energy and raw madness that causes a blast of outrage to fly from the centre of my soul and smack into my victims . . .

I don't for one second think I'm going to succumb to those feelings and lash out at my nearest and dearest, but it's unnerving to know that rage is there within me, lying dormant.

If I think about it, I've got so much anger buried inside.

Anger at Jonathan for not valuing me sooner and seeing that I'm all kinds of epic, anger at my mum for making me feel like shit most of the time, anger at my mates for being Dan's mates too – and anger at Dan for still being in my fucking life.

Dan . . .

He is a large part of my simmering anger simply because I've left so many things unsaid and brushed his betrayal (mostly) under the carpet for the sake of others. Perhaps it's actually not healthy to bottle it all up like I have.

But what can I do about it now?

Talk to him?

Phone him and ask for a little closure chat, detailing all the ways in which he screwed me over and ruined the last two years of my life?

Seriously?

What kind of desperate person talks to her ex about how jaded she feels, knowing that he's fully moved on with someone else?

It's also worth noting that there's absolutely no way I'd be able to talk through it all (even now) without getting into some sort of state. Maybe not the furniture chucking, dirt-talking mess in my dream, but definitely a weeping, snotty and needy version of myself . . . I'd rather that side of me didn't come out to play in public.

But what can I do about this anger that's obviously stirring inside me? Will it all subside slightly when *Grannies Go Gap* is a stonking success and I'm given a promotion and make my mum prouder than ever? Well, that would be a start, I guess.

I'm not in the best of moods as I head out of the house. I grunt out my coffee order, barge my way through to a seat on the tube and land with a huff when I'm eventually at my desk.

But just as my disastrous mood looks like it's going to linger for the day, I open my emails and am struck with hope.

'I think I've found our first case study,' I grin at Real Brett a few minutes later as I stand next to his desk and wave around a piece of paper containing a printout of the email that's just arrived in my inbox.

'Tell me more,' he nods, sipping on a pint of milk as he pushes away from his desk, leans back in his chair and spreads his legs invitingly in my direction – an action I'm sure is only suggestive in my head and not intended by him to be anything other than him sitting comfortably.

'She seems quite sweet,' I say with a cough, scanning the

sheet in front of me and selecting which bits of information are best to share as I will my cheeks not to embarrass me. 'Her name is Ethel Snart and she lives on her own in the same house in Maida Vale that she's lived in for sixty-three years.'

'Hopefully she's redecorated a few times,' he muses.

'I'd like to think so,' I agree before swiftly moving on. 'She's eighty and married her late husband Samuel when she was just seventeen. They had five children – Joshua, Joseph, Jackie, Josie and Connie – and she now has twelve grandchildren and four great grandchildren.'

'Big family.'

'Yeah,' I nod, biting my lip. 'She says she's been getting computer lessons from one of her grandsons, which is how she found our little shout out on Age Wise – I told you that was a good idea.'

'You did,' he says, raising an eyebrow while putting his drink back down on his desk.

'What do you think?'

'Let's go see her and find out more.'

'Really?'

'Can't do any harm,' he shrugs. 'Want me to give her a call? I could see if she's free this afternoon,' he suggests, holding his hand out for the paper in my hand.

'That would be great,' I breathe, feeling triumphant that not only am I on the cusp of moving my idea forward but I'm also now able to delegate jobs to others.

Before I have a chance to walk away from his desk and head back to my own, Real Brett picks up his office phone and dials the number Ethel's left for us in her email.

'Ringing,' he tells me, putting his hand over the receiver.

I decide to stay put and listen to their exchange.

'Still ringing,' he frowns.

I never put him down as the impatient type. Although, I guess it's not him who I'm really thinking of, but rather adventurous, chivalrous, benevolent Dream Brett, who has yet to do anything seriously wrong – other than hiding from me in a rapeseed field.

I manage to suppress a longing sigh and focus on the task in hand – getting hold of my first courageous granny!

'Might take her a while to get to the ph – '

'Mrs Snart?' Real Brett asks interrupting me, his attention snapping back to the phone in his grasp. 'My name is Brett Last. I work at Red Brick Productions . . . a television production company. You emailed us about a show we're working on. Yes, that's the one . . .' he says, turning to me, his nostrils flaring and his eyes widening with amusement. 'Yes, you sent my colleague Sarah an email about yourself. We were wondering if we could come and visit you to hear more . . . Yes, me and Sarah, the lady you emailed . . . Would this afternoon suit at all? Fantastic . . . Yes, after two can work for us,' he says with a smile. 'Perfect, see you then.' He puts down the phone and lets out a chuckle. 'Now, she seems like a real character.'

'Really?' I ask, mirroring his excitement, thrilled that she's already making such a positive impression on us both and amazed at the change in my mood from this morning. 'And she's up for us going to hers today?'

'Yes, but not until after two,' he says with a serious look. 'There's a *Cagney and Lacey* re-run that she wants to watch before that.'

'Lives her life by the TV guide – now that's my kind of

woman,' I say, making him laugh. He clearly hasn't taken the comment quite as seriously as I meant it.

'Shame her grandson hasn't taught her how to use iPlayer yet – that'll be mind-blowing for her. She'd never leave the house then.'

'And that's the opposite of what we want, Mr Last!' I say, puffing air from my cheeks and walking back to my desk – adrenaline pumping through my veins at the excitement of my project potentially being brought to life by a little old lady in west London.

A few hours later, we leave the office together and head towards the tube, striding along Shaftesbury Avenue and down the steps of Piccadilly Station.

It's feels funny being out of the office and in the outside world alongside Real Brett – I'm so used to walking with Dream Brett that part of me feels it's beyond natural, as though it's something I've done dozens of times before without giving it too much thought. But the other part of me realizes that Real Brett is essentially a stranger and not someone I know very well at all (besides a few drunken nights in my very early twenties and some chats in the office about jam, Tom Jones and coffee). It's a weird tug of emotions in my head. Especially when I forget myself momentarily and look over expecting to see Dream Brett but see this older and more worn version instead. Still attractive, but different.

'Don't you think it's strange?' he asks, glancing up at me and catching me staring at him with the loving expression I'd intended for Dream Brett. Yikes. He definitely notices the look as he screws his lips inwards, as though he's trying to stifle a smile.

Bugger.

'What?' I ask, trying to hide my embarrassment.

'That I'm randomly working in your office after not seeing you for a decade or more.'

'Not given it much thought,' I lie.

'Really?' he asks, surprised, his face showing the faintest flicker of disappointment that I've brushed the whole thing off so dismissively. 'Of all the offices in London, I walk into yours. Weird.'

'I guess. It's a small world,' I shrug, my hand grabbing for my Oyster card in my coat pocket but clumsily dropping it on the dirty tiled floor beneath my feet as I pull it out.

'That's what they say,' Real Brett murmurs before touching in with his own Oyster card and walking through the barriers.

Without waiting for me, he strides towards the Bakerloo line, leaving me to fumble around trying to pick up the card I'd dropped and get through the machine – which annoyingly bleeps at me angrily because it knows I'm in a hurry and have already shown myself to be a complete tit. I wait a few seconds, try again, and then scurry after Real Brett once it opens for me, feeling like a comedy character from a slapstick film – the only thing missing is a limp and a cane.

A train arrives as soon as we get to the westbound platform. Without saying anything, we board and sit in the only two seats available – two side by side. We sit in silence, with Real Brett staring straight ahead.

With my hands placed on my knees, I scan the carriage and sigh expectantly.

Real Brett still says nothing. Instead, his eyes stay facing front while he sucks in his lips, and pulls them through his teeth slowly. It's a repetitive action – one that he alternates between his upper and lower lip – when one comes out the other goes in. I'm not sure whether it's something he's just doing without thinking to pass the time, or whether he's doing it on purpose to stop himself from talking to me.

I know I'm used to brushing him off and being a first-class idiot, but I oddly feel deflated at the thought of offending him – and I majorly feel as though I have, seeing as he's not being all jolly and in my face as usual like a Labrador puppy.

'So did you and Ned go to UCL together then?' I ask, wanting to erase the atmosphere filling the carriage.

'Yeah,' he nods.

'Did you live in the same halls?'

'Yeah.'

'Did you know each other before that?'

'Nope.'

'Right,' I sigh, irritated to be the one receiving one-word answers for a change. I much prefer it when he's buoyantly upbeat – at least that's readable.

'I mentioned you to Alastair last night – he said you should come down and join us for a pub quiz.' I wasn't going to say anything about Alastair, and I certainly wasn't planning on inviting him along, but that's what tense, unreadable situations do to me. They make me involuntarily act in ways I regret instantly. Agonizing silences make me want to leap in and fill them with whatever words spout out of my mouth first.

'Pub quiz?' he asks, pulling his mouth down at the sides as he mulls over the invite.

'Yeah.'

He nods but stays quiet.

Oh for God's sake this is tough.

'I wonder what she's going to be like,' I say, changing the subject after another humongous pause.

'Who?'

'Ethel.'

'We'll soon find out,' he shrugs, suddenly seeming not so excited about the whole thing.

He's not being moody or huffy – he's just being indifferent. I hate indifference with a passion. Especially when it's aimed at me. I much prefer being given something to work with – positive or negative. This is such hard work.

I decide to give up the anger-inducing task of trying to strike up conversation and watch the couple in front of me instead – keenly snogging each other's faces off without caring that they're in the presence of strangers.

Oh to be young, foolish and going at it with such ferocity on a Friday afternoon in broad daylight.

Eighteen minutes later, after I've ogled the inappropriate pashing more closely than is considered polite (well, sometimes you just can't ignore these things), we're ringing the doorbell of a small house in Maida Vale.

'Who is it?' asks an elderly voice behind the frosted glass.

'Brett and Sarah – we spoke on the phone this morning,' Real Brett replies.

'We did?' she asks, sounding confused.

'You emailed us,' I add cheerily, hoping this isn't about to fall flat on its face before we've even made it inside.

'Oh, on the world wide web – YES!' she cheers before

unchaining the lock on the door and opening it a fraction. Once she sees our faces smiling back at her she mirrors the expression before opening it fully.

Ethel is dressed in pale blue trousers and a pink cotton jumper, with the collar of her white blouse poking out and folded over the top along with a small pearl necklace. On her feet are dark blue corduroy slippers, which, I must say, look like the comfiest shoes in the world – I wouldn't mind a pair for slumming around the flat in.

She's every inch what you envisage when dreaming up an old lady with her kind wrinkled face, button nose, little gold-rimmed glasses hanging from her neck on a gold chain, and short grey hair set to perfection in the classic rollered style.

She's instantly likeable and I mentally fist pump the air – visually she's perfect for *Grannies Go Gap*.

'Well, come in, come in. You'll catch your death out there,' she ushers, closing the door behind us and putting the chain back across. 'You can put your shoes on this,' she says, pulling an immaculate Sainsbury's bag from her pocket, unfolding it and slowly bending over to place it in the corner of the hallway next to the stairs.

She looks up and beams at us both, her hands waving to prompt us into doing what we've been told.

We do.

'Can I get you both a tea?' she asks, walking us through to the living room and gesturing for us to take a seat.

'We don't want to put you out,' I say.

'Nonsense. I fancy one anyway.'

'Why don't I make it?' suggests Real Brett.

Ethel looks at him suspiciously, as though the idea of a

man in her kitchen making a brew is preposterously absurd. 'No . . . no, it's all right,' she says, fighting a frown that's trying to break through on her wrinkled forehead. 'Won't be a minute – kettle's already boiled.'

'Great,' I say, while sitting on the heavily patterned brown sofa. 'Just shout if you need a hand.'

Ethel nods before walking out.

Looking around the room I'm amazed at the amount of stuff in it – dozens of pictures of Ethel with the same bunch of people (some black and white, some in colour) at various different family celebrations adorn the walls and cover the retro seventies wallpaper. In some patches, though, the faded orange and brown flower design manages to peep through, giving a glimpse of what's lurking beneath from years gone by. More photos are displayed in a collection of different frames on the brick fireplace and the windowsill, occasionally masked by newer, unframed photos placed in front of them.

A large display cabinet is home to tons of teddy bears (no doubt given to Ethel by her grandchildren over the years – I used to give my own nan very similar ones on a yearly basis when she was alive) – china ornaments and official royal paraphernalia from various weddings and christenings. It's busy, but well kept and organized. Cluttered but clean.

Giving a golden glow to the room, hordes of orange fabric hang from both the large window at the front of the house and the French doors leading to the small but well-managed garden – I find myself wondering whether Ethel tends to it herself or whether her grandchildren help out in return for some pocket money.

Beneath my feet is a well-worn Axminster rug, set on top of a dark cream rustic weave carpet. It's all pretty ancient and characterful.

Beside the sofa that Real Brett and I perch on, is Ethel's armchair. A dark green recliner with a cream throw folded over the armrest. Next to it is a side table filled with everything Ethel could need during the day – the telephone, the current issue of *Radio Times* (opened on today's date with *Cagney and Lacey* circled in blue biro), the remote controls for the TV, DVD and video player, a box of tissues, glass of water, her glasses case and cleaner, spare glasses, packet of boiled sweets, packet of polos, her purse, and the latest addition – her laptop. Everything is in reaching distance and ready at her disposal.

'Looks like she didn't,' I whisper, widening my eyes at Real Brett.

'Didn't what?'

'Redecorate.'

His mouth twinges into a smile.

A smile that puts me at ease.

'Here we go,' Ethel coos, walking in with a tray loaded with tea and fruit shortcake biscuits.

'I'll get that,' offers Real Brett, leaping to his feet and taking it from her before placing it on the wooden coffee table in front of us.

'Thank you,' she smiles, making her way to her armchair. 'Big ones are yours and mine's in me cup. You can bring it over.'

Brett can't help but grin as he picks up Ethel's mug – the one claiming that she's the *World's Greatest Nan* – and places it on top of the coaster in front of her.

'So you emailed us,' I say, wanting to get the conversation started.

'Yes,' she nods, glimpsing proudly at her laptop – the device that's brought us here. 'I saw your article on Age Wise and thought I might as well get in touch.'

'And we're glad you did,' chimes in Real Brett, reaching over and opening the packet of biscuits and placing one in front of Ethel before taking one for himself. He really does have a sweet tooth.

'So, are you making a telly show?'

'Planning to,' I nod enthusiastically. 'It's in the early stages at the moment, we need to develop it all further, but we think you might be able to help us with that.'

'Me?'

'Yes.'

'All right, love,' she agrees, without hearing what that would actually entail.

'Do you mind if I record our conversation?' I ask, pulling out my iPhone and placing it between us on the arm rest of the sofa. 'No one else will listen to it, it's just to help me remember things later on.'

'Whatever helps . . . could do with one of those meself,' she chuckles to herself, picking up a tissue and cleaning her spare pair of glasses with it.

'Ethel,' I ask. 'When did you last go on holiday?'

'Now you're asking,' she replies, putting on the newly polished frames (ignoring the ones dangling from her neck) and looking up at the pictures on the walls as though scanning them for clues. 'Samuel died back in eighty-nine so it would've been a long time before that. We used to take the kids to the seaside and the like, you know.' Her face shows pride at the memory of her deceased husband.

I glance over to the pictures and my eyes land on one from their wedding day – both looking exceptionally young and startled at having their photo taken, with Samuel even blinking slightly at the flash. Nowadays we're all so click happy with our digital cameras and phones, we take dozens just to get 'the shot' (especially if you're Poutmouth Louisa looking to post the perfect selfie online), but I guess back then, when Ethel and Samuel got married, photos were still a novelty – with only a handful of them taken at one event. They didn't have the luxury of being able to see them back (and delete the unattractive ones) or an endless photostream – which is why Ethel's ended up with a less than perfect image from one of the most important days of her life.

'Did you go on honeymoon?' I ask.

'You could say that . . .' she sighs, still squinting at the walls. 'I got pregnant, you see. Me father practically marched me up the aisle and then sent us off to me aunt's on the Isle of Wight for the next nine months to hide the scandal.'

'Oh. I'm sorry to hear that.'

'Sorry? Don't be sorry. It might not have been planned, but it happened. Lucky for us we ended up quite liking each other – we certainly made the best of the situation, not like those youngsters you see these days divorcing whenever they have a lover's tiff or not even getting married at all. Oh the shame of it,' she tuts, viciously shaking her head. 'It wasn't easy, but we worked hard – both in our jobs and in our marriage. I was a very lucky lady. And him a lucky man,' she adds, raising her eyebrows at us.

'I've no doubt about that,' comments Real Brett, making her blush.

The exchange makes me smile.

'Not a day goes by that I don't think of him and miss him. We might've had a shaky, haphazard start, but in the end we were wrapped up in the hands of love,' she muses, clasping her hands together with a loud clap.

'We can tell – just look at the life you built together,' Brett says, motioning at the home around us.

Ethel dips her head in agreement, pride spilling from the smile that's formed on her lips at his praise.

'So, the seaside,' I start, wanting to keep the conversation on track – otherwise we'll be here for hours without learning a thing.

'Yes. Clacton, Frinton, Brighton, Margate – we even went as far as Cornwall one year. Stayed in a B and B overlooking the sea. We loved a beach,' she beams with enthusiasm.

'And you never fancied going abroad?'

'There were so many of us. It wasn't something we'd have been able to afford, you see,' she tells us, reminiscing. 'Plus, I don't know about you two, but I don't really fancy me chances in a chunk of metal floating in the sky. Makes no sense,' she gasps.

'Couldn't agree more,' chimes in Brett, wearing a faux frightened face to amuse her.

I flash him a warning look.

'Although, obviously planes are, er, totally safe. Just the science that still boggles me. Doesn't stop me jetting off on holiday though,' he grins.

'Mmm . . .' Ethel grunts, suddenly seeming like her mind has wandered off elsewhere as she picks up her *Radio Times* and taps her nails against it absentmindedly.

'What makes you think you'd like to travel and get on a plane now, then?' I ask, attempting to pull her back to the conversation we're in the middle of, wanting to keep her mind in the present.

Ethel turns to me with a frown. 'I think there's more to life than this,' she says, gesturing around to the room we're sitting in. 'Has to be.'

Her response surprises me. Yes, it's apparent she spends her days sat in her comfortable chair watching re-runs of her favourite TV shows and now, thanks to her grandson, searching 'the world wide web', but she's evidently had a great life. She's surrounded by the memories of it – each significant moment is marked and treasured in the home she's built for her and her family.

'More than what?' I ask, unable to resist pulling more meaning from the words she uttered.

She stares at me, her expression telling me I should know the answer to that already.

'This empty home. Every day I do the same thing. I sit here and watch me programmes, I get me brass and china from the cupboards and polish it all, I hoover – make meself a bacon sandwich in the morning and a Heinz tomato soup at lunchtime – a roast in the evening if I can be bothered . . . it's the same. Every day,' she says, giving a big sigh. 'Do you know what I've been doing since Samuel died?'

'No . . .' I say, intrigued as to where this is headed.

'Waiting.'

'For what?' asks Real Brett from my side, swallowing hard, seeming as though he doesn't want to hear the honest answer this sweet old lady might be about to give.

'To die.'

I'm not one for morbid chats – I'm never sure how to navigate my way around the topic, and seemingly Real Brett feels equally uncomfortable. We both sit there, sipping on our teas, unsure how to respond and allowing Ethel to continue her admission.

'Don't want to be all doom and gloom – but that's what I've been doing. Watching the seconds slowly tick by,' she admits, looking down at the gold watch on her wrist. 'My life stopped when Samuel's did – and I know he'd hate me saying that. But life lost its purpose. I made us a happy home life, and then, all of a sudden, there was no one here to share it with. I still don't know what me purpose is outside this room – perhaps I've fulfilled it already in me lifetime with me kids and that, but I think there's more to life than sitting in here on me tod waiting for the Grim Reaper,' she chuckles, removing her glasses and rubbing at her eyes. 'I've wasted enough time for now. I'd be happy if I popped me clogs tomorrow – I've had a good run – but until I do I'd like to have one more adventure.'

My heart simultaneously bleeds and soars. It bleeds for Ethel's loneliness and emptiness – despite once having a home filled with family, but it soars for the corner she's turned and how perfectly she fits into the show I'm trying to create.

'And if you could go anywhere in the world or see anything, what would you choose?' I ask her, as Real Brett stands and offers her another of her own biscuits before sitting down and dunking one in his tea.

'You know, I saw that Denise Van Outen lady on the telly with Lorraine the other week talking about how she climbed some mountain some years back and then went on to see The Great Wall in China . . .'

My brain works quickly to decipher through the hundreds of articles I've read on the Mail Online over the years. 'Yes, she climbed Kilimanjaro with Gary Barlow, Cheryl Cole, Alesha Dixon and a whole bunch of other celebs for Comic Relief, then climbed the Great Wall of China,' I nod, enthusiastically. Both trips were quite a while back, but we all know how they like to rehash old ground in interviews – I'm pretty sure she even found her way to Machu Picchu at some point.

'Well, I quite fancy that meself.'

'Kilimanjaro?' I ask with a squeak, wondering what the insurance would be like for something as strenuous as that. I'm pretty sure some of the celebs suffered from altitude sickness and were given serious medical attention. From what I remember reading, it was quite a strenuous climb even for those gym-obsessed celebs.

'Don't be daft – have you seen how slow I am?' Ethel tuts, rolling her eyes at Real Brett, as though I'm barking for even suggesting it.

Real Brett politely manages to curb a laugh, but I still feel him shifting in his seat beside me.

'I want to go see The Great Wall,' concludes Ethel with a decisive nod.

'Oh,' I voice.

'What?' she asks.

'Nothing,' I shrug, wondering how we'd be able to get around the issue of there being millions of steps for her to climb up and down. Suddenly my idea of getting old folk to see the magical sights the world has to offer doesn't seem quite so straightforward. In fact, I'm beginning to sense a great big hole of disaster looming within the pitch as I ponder over just how physically able the old folk I find are actually going to be. It's certainly something I'm going to have to give a lot of thought to – especially as insuring something like this isn't going to be straightforward.

'I've looked it up,' Ethel says, refocusing my brain as she reaches over to her laptop and brings the screen to life. 'This place has wheelchair access – not that I'm in one yet, mind,' she says, looking past me and talking to Real Brett. 'But I do know my limits.'

I move off the sofa and crouch beside her seat, the faint smell of urine hitting me and tickling the hairs up my nostrils, taking me by surprise.

'The Badaling Great Wall,' I read, impressed that she's already done her homework and relieved at the prospect of such places being accessible to all.

'What is it about there that makes you want to go so much?' asks Brett from the sofa, nibbling on a fresh biscuit – I'm sure it's his fourth already.

'Nice to be in the presence of something older than meself,' she cackles before becoming sombre and letting out a big sigh. 'Did you know you can see it from the moon?' she asks, looking at us both expectantly with this little nugget of information that holds the key to her dreams.

We both look at her in surprise – on my part this is something I hadn't actually known before, but I'm not entirely sure whether this is new information for Real Brett or whether he's gawping in disbelief at Ethel just to humour her.

'If you can see it from the moon,' Ethel continues. 'Then you must be able to see it from up in the heavens. Now, I know my Samuel is up there – that's a given, he was a kind old fool in his day so I can't see him going down to hell, even though I did get pregnant before we got hitched,' she says, shaking her head at the thought. 'No. He's up there. I know it. And I want to go somewhere I know he can *see* me.'

And there it is, I smile to myself – my hook. The piece of her story that's going to melt the hearts of millions across the country – little old lady goes to The Great Wall of China to grab the attention of her dead husband who she's felt lost without, but has now regained the strength and courage to explore the world's beauty, if only to feel closer to him.

I know I'd be weeping on my sofa at such a tragically romantic tale.

'That's beautiful,' I sigh, unable to stop a smile appearing on my face.

A loud bang interrupts the moment and makes me jump so high that I end up scrabbling on my knees in the middle of the room.

'Nan?' calls a voice. 'You there?'

'Sammy,' she grins in surprise, getting up and walking to the door.

I put my hand to my chest and take a deep breath as I get up to my feet.

'Nice work,' winks Real Brett.

'Right?' I puff – nodding and waving a fist in the air. I resist the urge for a celebratory dance. Ethel is perfect for *Grannies Go Gap*.

'This is my grandson,' calls Ethel, returning with a man in tow.

I was expecting her grandson to be some sort of nerdy computer geek in his teens with glasses and bad acne, but instead, in walks an absolute god of a human being. Tall, shaggy dark hair, juicily kissable lips and the most piercing grey eyes I've ever seen.

I practically melt on the spot at the sight of his suited buff body.

'Hello, I'm Sam,' he says, his lips pursing in confusion as he shakes Real Brett's hand before holding his hand out for mine.

'You're the one who put your nan online?' asks Real Brett.

'Bought me me laptop,' nods Ethel, looping her hand through his arm.

'She wanted to get on Facebook and see what we're all up to,' smiles Sam, looking down at her. 'There's a lot of us. It's a good way for her to keep tabs – although now she's on it we can't seem to get her off. She's addicted. Comments on everything.'

'Nice,' grins Real Brett, patting him on the back. Showing no signs of being bothered by the arrival of this beautiful specimen.

Okay, I might be slightly exaggerating on the whole Adonis thing – he is incredibly good looking, but the fact that he spends time with his nan and has helped her live in the twenty-first century makes him a whole lot more appealing. It's that fact alone (helped along by his mild attractiveness) that makes me wish he'd rip my clothes off and make love on the retro rug beneath my feet right this second.

On reflection, I think that might be the sexual frustration talking . . .

'So, who are you guys?' he asks, thankfully cutting my crazy imagination off, as his eyes flicker suspiciously between the two of us. 'If you're selling something then she's really not interested . . .'

'No!' I practically scream, horrified that he assumes we're taking advantage of Ethel and turning crimson at my sordid imaginings. 'Ethel emailed us.'

'She did?'

'We're from Red Brick Productions,' explains Brett. 'Sarah wrote a post for Age Wise sharing details of a TV show we want to pilot and Ethel got in touch.'

'Really?' he asks, looking at her with a chuffed expression on his face.

'I did it all meself,' nods Ethel. 'Remembered everything you taught me – even put me name in the subject box.

The pair exchange a smile that is utterly adorable. I might be running ahead of myself here – but I sincerely hope Sammy comes as part of the deal if we get Ethel to The Great Wall. Maybe he could even come with us.

'We just came to meet your nan and hear more about why she'd like to take part,' I say, still grinning at the pair of them.

'Oh right. So you're researching?'

'Exactly,' nods Real Brett.

'And what's the show? She's not signing herself up for something like *TOWIE*, is she? You're not wanting her to be the new Nanny Pat, are you?'

'No,' I declare.

'She does make a good sausage plait if you need her to

make one, though,' he admits under his breath, winking at Ethel.

'I do,' she nods.

'But we don't,' confirms Real Brett.

'Oh,' ponders Ethel, before her eyes light up in delight at a new thought. 'Will Nanny Pat be on your show, though? She's old. Not as old as me, mind.'

'I don't think she will be . . .' I say, trying to let her down gently and utterly confused as to why we're talking about the Essex Gran. 'It's a very different sort of programme,' I reason.

'Shame. I like her,' Ethel said sadly, 'Great show.'

Even though we obviously weren't coming here to audition Ethel for it, I can't help but feel sorry for her that we're unable to make her *TOWIE* wishes happen for her – she seems so disappointed.

'You'd have been great on it,' whispers Sam.

'Back to the reason we're here, though,' says Real Brett, widening his eyes at me and willing us to get back on track. 'Sarah?'

'Yes,' I say, snapping back into action and realizing we have to win Sam around to the idea if Ethel's to take part. I feel as though I'm back in Damian's office about to give the pitch again. 'It's an idea I've recently created – which is why it's in the early stages and why we need to have someone like your nan as a case study – but the general idea of it is that we take people of your nan's generation, who've never left the UK, and give them the experiences that are currently being enjoyed by people in their late teens, early twenties, who've decided to take a gap year and travel the world.'

'Like going to some rave in Thailand and getting off your tits?' he scoffs.

'Samuel!' gasps Ethel.

His tone and language in front of us all stops me in my tracks. I'm no saint – I'm aware I've got a mouth like a sewer at times – but there's a time and a place. Swearing in front of my elders (especially my mum and grandparents) is definitely a no-no. His attractiveness instantly drops from mild to zero, even if he is attentive and kind to Ethel.

'Not quite the angle we were thinking of,' smirks Real Brett, taking over in a friendly manner, unfazed by his outburst. 'This is more about giving them the chance to see a part of the world that has, for whatever reason, been out of their reach – but that they have a passion to see. It's inspirational entertainment, rather than drunken debauchery in some eighteen-to-thirties clubbing resort.'

Sam places his hands into his trouser pockets as he cocks his head to one side and nods, mulling over the information we've shared.

When he's not looking, Real Brett turns to me and gives me a cheeky little wink – reassuring me that this is going to end well and that we're going to bag our first case study by the time we leave this seventies-infused room.

'I told them I want to go to China,' declares Ethel to no one in particular.

'She wants to see the wall,' I add for Sam's benefit, taking a swig of my warm tea.

'And you'd just take her there? Just like that?'

'Well there'll be a whole process to go along with it,' coughs Real Brett. 'Obviously the main point of the show is to document Ethel's first journey abroad.'

'Let her see what it's like thirty thousand feet in the air,' I add, grinning widely at Ethel as I say the words.

'Not sure what I'll make of that bit,' Ethel scowls, scrunching up her nose.

'Nan – you've done it before.'

'What?'

'What's that?' I ask, my ears starting to burn along with my crimson face.

'Been on a plane,' he says, frowning at Ethel. 'You've been on a plane, Nan.'

'Really?' I swallow. 'Where to? Ireland? Scotland? Manchester?' My voice squeaks with each suggestion, willing one of them to be correct so that Ethel is still eligible for the show – but the bigger Sam's grimace grows I realize that's becoming increasingly unlikely.

'We went to Florida for Sharon's birthday.'

Oh shit.

'Sharon?' asks Ethel.

'My sister, your granddaughter,' Sam says with a hint of annoyance. 'We went to Disney World for her thirtieth. Remember? Big family trip with all the little ones.'

'We did?'

'Nan, there's a picture of us all in front of the castle up here,' he exclaims with exasperation as he points to a frame neither Real Brett nor I had seen looming above the TV.

'Am I in that?' she asks softly, as the reality starts to seep through.

'Yes. You had a great time,' he reminds her. 'But you didn't think much of the food.'

'All burgers and French fries,' she nods with disgust, suddenly remembering. 'A bunch of crap.'

'Yes. That's what you said then,' he laughs. 'And Aunty Jackie took you to Jersey a few years ago, remember? And you went to Tenerife with Aunt Corrie, Uncle Mick and the kids. Actually, Nan, you've been on more holidays than most of my mates.'

Ethel doesn't say anything. Instead she sits back in her armchair and bites her lip, looking worried.

'It's all right, Nan,' Sam says quietly. 'We all forget things sometimes. It's no big deal.'

He looks at us both with a sorrowful look in his eyes.

I'm guessing this isn't the first time Ethel's found herself in a forgetful situation, although it feels like quite a huge chunk of her life to have a sudden mental block about. She thought she'd been sitting here quietly, uncared for, while life continued without her – but in actual fact she'd been having the time of her life in The Magical Kingdom as the family she'd spent decades pouring love into fussed around her.

How sad for her to forget those happy memories and replace them with nothing but emptiness.

'They were going to take me to China,' Ethel whimpers, staring at the laptop on her side table that's taunting her with images of grandeur that we won't be able to take her to see.

The whole thing is so awkward it makes me want to cry.

'Sorry about this,' Sam says to the two of us, visibly embarrassed.

'It's fine,' I say kindly. I can't help but feel for Ethel. Sod *Grannies Go Gap*, it's horrible to see someone as lovely as her so confused as memories meanly decide to play hide and seek with her.

'It's been a pleasure to meet you, Ethel, regardless,' says Real Brett, going to her and placing a hand over hers. 'Sounds like you've already had some amazing adventures.'

'It does, doesn't it,' she sighs, her free hand gripping the top of his as she squints and looks into his eyes, searching them for kindness – which he gives, making me feel a wave of gratitude towards him.

'And you know, Disney World is pretty huge,' he says, lowering his voice. 'I've no doubt Samuel would've seen you and all the family stood around having your photos taken with Mickey Mouse.'

'I hope not,' she grumbles, her face screwing up at the thought. 'They made me wear those stupid ears – and the water made me hair go all fluffy. I looked a right state.'

'You looked great, Nan,' Sam says, rolling his eyes at her comment. 'Women, hey? Always fishing for compliments.'

None of us laugh as Ethel's delightful grandson becomes more unattractive by the second. What a pig.

Real Brett gets to his feet, and sighs.

'Right, I'm guessing these two have to get back to searching for their next TV star,' Sam says with a hint of mockery, looking at me and Real Brett while raising his hand up towards the door.

'Yes!' I start, picking up my coat and belongings and throwing Ethel a sympathetic smile.

She ignores me, and instead gets up and walks past us both to the wall of photos and memories. With a sad face she looks at each of them more closely, her face showing glimpses of either recognition of the moment captured or complete befuddlement – as though it might as well be someone else in the picture. It's heartbreaking to watch.

Real Brett tugs on my hand to stop me from staring, but the moment is so tragic it's difficult to walk away from. Quietly we go to the hallway and collect our shoes from the immaculate Sainsbury's bag Ethel had laid out for us when we first arrived.

'Thank God I turned up when I did,' exhales Sam in bewilderment, watching us as we put on our footwear, before opening the front door for us to leave.

'Yeah . . .' is all I can manage to muster up in reply.

'Bye, Ethel,' calls Real Brett.

She doesn't respond.

The door is shut on us as soon as we're through it.

I exhale loudly as we start the short walk to the station – feeling every kind of crappy.

'You okay?' Real Brett asks.

I shrug my shoulders in reply.

'Not a great start,' he admits, sucking in his bottom lip.

'Doesn't it make you want to send her to China anyway?' I ask, somehow hoping it's a possibility. 'Pretend she's never been to those places and film her regardless?'

'What, lie?'

'Maybe,' I mumble.

'I'd love to,' says Real Brett, leaning into me and giving my elbow a slight nudge with his. 'But can you imagine the fallout if the press found out the delightful show you created, that's meant to be about enlightenment and discovery – no matter your age, is actually all staged? It would be awful and would send out the opposite message.'

'True,' I huff sadly, gutted that we can't make it work for dear Ethel.

'Sweet lady, though,' he nods.

'It's made me think. I don't think someone so old could realistically be up to doing more than the one destination. I know I said about them having this whole big excursion like they're on a gap year but I think that would be too much. Perhaps it's best to limit it like I said we might in my pitch . . .' I mumble, unable to remove the frown that's invaded my forehead.

'Wow . . .'

'What?'

'One knock and you're out?'

'I'm not dissing the whole idea, I just think it needs to be refined and worked on.'

'I hear what you're saying, and I think it might be something you tailor to each of our cast – but, let's wait to find them first. They aren't all going to be like Ethel,' he says shaking his head. 'I know ninety-year-olds who are out and about like they're in their teens. It's just about finding the right people to take part.'

'Maybe . . .' I mumble, putting my hands in my pockets and feeling like a sulky teenager who's not had things go her way.

Not for the first time, I wish Real Brett were Dream Brett. I'd do anything for a little comfort right now – for him to grab me by the waist and snuggle me into his strong chest while I grumpily brood over our encounter with Ethel, my worries about the task I'm taking on and my feeling that it's something I'm incapable of pulling off.

'When are your quiz nights, then?' Real Brett asks, cutting into my woes while looking down at his perfectly polished black leather shoes as they hit the concrete slabs of the pavement beneath our feet.

'The *pub* quiz?' I ask, unable to stop a slight high-pitched squeak from entering my voice.

'Yeah . . .'

'Wednesdays. In a little place near Bethnal Green,' I offer, feeling my nostrils flare as I reluctantly relay the information.

'Oh, right.'

'You don't have to come,' I shrug as I shake my head – trying my best to put him off, without making it seem like I'm rudely revoking the invite I gave him less than an hour ago. 'It's probably a trek or whatever.'

'No, no . . . I love a good pub quiz,' he says with a decisive nod. 'I'll come. I'll see when I'm free.'

'Great,' I say, hoping I sound a little happier with his answer than I'm actually feeling.

Carly is going to piss her pants when I tell her he's coming. Hopefully not literally . . . I mean, I hear pregnant ladies can do that. I love her, but that's something I do not need or want to see.

Unless she's being a totally cheeky cow, then it would serve her right.

22

'Okay, round two,' I say to Real Brett when he arrives the following Monday morning.

I couldn't actually sleep over the weekend because I'd started worrying about whether anyone would message in who fit the criteria we were looking for in a case study. So, this morning, I got up far earlier than normal, wandered to The Barge Café and sat inside nursing a latte, before dawdling into Soho. I arrived a whole hour earlier than necessary and have since been scrolling through the dozen (yes, that's twelve) emails that had arrived with *Grannies Go Gap* in the subject box. Albeit most of them were just from complete chancers who were looking for a freebie holiday – one lady was in her thirties and I'm pretty sure the photo she'd sent in was of her on a sun lounger somewhere abroad with a cocktail in her hand (she clearly thought it was some kind of competition), but one (one is better than none – for now) caught my attention immediately.

'This time it's come directly from Age Wise, so I'm hoping there won't be any confusion,' I say, my mind with Ethel as I look down at the piece of paper in my hand that I've already read several times over.

'Carry on,' Real Brett says with a smile, finding his way out of his coat as he listens.

'Julian is seventy-eight and lives in an old people's home in Kent.'

'Old people's home?' he interrupts, his face tensing, clearly worried that we're about to suffer from a repeat performance of last week.

'Yes, but he's totally able and capable, apparently. Just didn't know what to do with himself when his wife died a couple of years ago, so he checked himself into a local home.'

'No family?'

'One son, but he moved to America in the nineties – Julian didn't fancy going there and he didn't fancy coming back here.'

'So sad,' Real Brett frowns. 'I couldn't imagine doing that with my dad.'

'No . . .' I agree.

I decide not to share that my mum would be a different story, I couldn't cope with spending every day with her and having her in my home picking out all my failures, but my dad . . . Well, it's highly unlikely I'd let him go into a home if it wasn't absolutely necessary.

'I couldn't let him down like that,' Real Brett adds.

'Well, it sounds like Julian rather enjoys being there,' I say, wanting to dispel Real Brett's doubts of the place that's apparently given our next candidate a new lease of life.

'Really?'

'Makes sense,' I brood with a smirk. 'Most homes are filled with old women – any guys in there are hugely out-numbered.'

'As close to the old "if I were the last guy on earth" scenario as anyone's ever going to get,' he laughs.

'Exactly,' I say, laughing along with him. 'Apparently, he

loves being the centre of everyone's attention and really brightens up the place.'

'Want to go meet him?' Real Brett asks, taking off his beanie hat, gently shaking his head and running his fingers through his short hair so that it's swept back away from his face. 'See if there's more to his popularity than the fact he's the only male in the place?'

'Definitely,' I nod without hesitation, turning my back on Real Brett and busying myself with Jonathan's diary.

I did not find the way he just whipped his hair around mesmerizing at all.

Not even in the slightest.

Although I might've forgotten to breathe as I watched.

That afternoon as I ring the doorbell of Bramble House in Welling, I can't help but take an audible deep breath as unexpected nerves start to build. I thought finding people to fly around the world to far-off locations was going to be the easy part in all this, but having met Ethel and realizing that my target cast might come with a list of problems (both mental and physical) that I hadn't even thought about, my confidence is starting to wane.

'I've got a good feeling about this one,' whispers Real Brett, nodding at the door.

I've no idea whether this is something he truly believes or whether he's spinning me some upbeat line, like I saw him do with Ethel about Walt Disney World being seen from space, but either way it helps relax me the teeny tiniest of fractions and I find myself grateful that he's there by my side and that I'm not having to do all this with Poutmouth Louisa instead.

Who'd have thought I'd ever find myself expressing that . . . gratitude for Real Brett.

Huh.

'You must be Sarah,' beams a skinny girl in her twenties as she opens the door. She doesn't look like she should work in a care home for the elderly. She's top to toe in baggy black clothing, has blood red hair and has seriously overdone it with the kohl eyeliner. Nonetheless, her smile is infectious and it's clear to see she's a sweetheart despite her gothic-inspired exterior.

'Fiona?' I ask.

She nods in reply. 'I'm the one you spoke to earlier on the phone.'

'Great. This is my colleague Brett,' I say, narrowly avoiding calling him by the full name I've given him, and watch as they exchange a formal handshake.

'Want to come through?' she asks, letting us in before closing the door behind us and securing it with several bolts and locks.

'Wow,' says Real Brett under his breath.

'Worse than it looks,' she says, rolling her eyes mercifully. 'A few of the guests here get a little confused at times and tend to want to venture outside late at night. It's best we find them trying to pick the locks here than wandering lost outside in their nighties and rollers.'

'Fair point,' grumbles Real Brett.

'Does he know we're here?' I ask, moving our attention back to the reason we've come – keen to see if Julian is going to live up to the mountain of expectation that I've placed on him in the few hours I've known of his existence.

'Of course, I couldn't just spring something like this on him. Not that he'd have minded,' she winks. 'He's just helping clear up after lunch.'

We walk into the dining room to find Julian flamboyantly waltzing around the room to classical music and twirling between the groups of tables while picking up empty bowls and stacking them on a trolley as though he's one of the staff and not one of the inmates.

And he's not alone.

Seven women are still sat at their tables sipping on cups of tea whilst watching him. He is, without doubt, their entertainment.

'Julian?' calls Fiona, cutting into his performance and grabbing his attention. 'This is Sarah – the lady we talked about, and Brett – he works with her.'

'Oh!' says the dancing man, dropping his arms and lowering his heels, seemingly startled at being cut short.

Julian puts down the last of the bowls on the trolley and strides over, straightening out his gingham flat cap as he approaches. He is shorter than average (although that could be down to his age – has it actually been scientifically proven that people shrink as they get older or is that just a myth?), has a head full of white hair, a nose that looks like it's never stopped growing (complete with wispy hairs to match those sprouting from his ears) and a twinkle in his sparkling blue eyes that explains why he's everybody's friend. Even before he opens his mouth to speak I know that I've fallen utterly in love with him and want to adopt him as my new granddad.

'Lovely to meet you both. I'm Julian,' he says with a nod and a fancy flurry of his hands.

'We guessed,' I grin, feeling like a little girl entranced by his wonderful persona.

'Want to sit down in here and talk?' asks Fiona. 'I can grab you some tea and biscuits. Won't be a second.'

'Great,' I say to the back of her flaming head as she walks straight out without waiting for an answer.

'Sit, sit, sit,' beckons Julian, pulling out a chair for me and willing Real Brett to do the same for himself. 'Annabell from Age Wise called me yesterday and asked if she could put me forward for this – I've never done anything like it before,' he admits, adding a grave tone to his voice – although I think it's more for theatricality than to express his own concerns.

'Neither have I,' I whisper, unable to wipe the grin from my face. 'This is actually the first programme I've ever developed. I've no idea what I'm doing.'

'New for us both then,' he says, raising his eyebrows before looking at Real Brett expectantly.

'I have done this before and I do know what I'm doing,' he confesses.

'Well someone has to,' Julian replies with a shrug, winking at me.

'Before we get started,' I say, taking a deep breath. 'I just need to ask you one question which you must answer truthfully.'

'I'll do my best . . .'

'Have you ever been outside the UK?'

'No.'

'Are you sure? You've never been on a plane?' I ask in the slowest and most coherent manner I can muster without it bordering on patronizing or rude.

'No,' he says adamantly. 'Flo had a thing about planes.'

'Flo?' asks Real Brett, allowing Julian the chance to open up on his own without us prodding him too much.

'My wife,' Julian says without a flicker of emotion other than delight at uttering her name. 'A fine woman who insisted we kept our feet firmly on the ground at all times.'

'So you've never holidayed in France or gone on a Mediterranean cruise?' I question further.

'Wish I had – those things look great. But no, no we never did any of that. Flo had relatives in Scotland so we used to go up there whenever we got the chance – immerse ourselves in the Highland fling.'

'You're quite the dancer then?' asks Real Brett.

'Oh, yes. We met through our love of dance. Blackpool ballroom in the summer of 1955,' he remembers, closing his eyes and returning to that moment as though he's in a Hollywood film about to leap into a black and white flashback of that important day as they enchantingly waltz around the dance floor. 'We were both competing.'

'So you were both professional dancers?' I gasp, instantly loving the romantic visions that it triggers off in my imagination of floaty fabric sashaying from elegant bodies as they glide around the majestically lit dance floor.

'Well, I could show that Craig Revel-Horwood a thing or two, that's for sure,' he says under his breath before giving a cheeky wink.

'Didn't you travel the world with that, then?' asks Real Brett.

'Could've done. Should've, I guess. I'd worked hard to get to Blackpool and that was meant to be the start of everything – but Flo had an elderly mum back at home who she didn't want to leave and I didn't want to leave Flo. So I didn't,' he pauses. 'I followed Flo, the love of my dreams, up to Scotland, where she cared for her mother and I worked as a porter in a hospital. We stayed up there until her mum passed – then we moved down here.'

'Didn't you ever regret not continuing with your dancing?' I ask, wondering how it would feel to work so hard for something and then just give it up one day because I'd met someone I liked the look of. I don't know if I could ever be so selfless – maybe that's why I'm doomed to a life of being referred to as the jilted ex.

'Regret? There was nothing to regret,' says Julian, shaking his head vigorously.

'Really?'

'Absolutely. I'd sooner pirouette my girl around our living-room and receive her full love and attention than perform for some know-it-all judge in a penguin suit,' he declares.

'Nicely put,' smirks Real Brett, raising his eyebrows at me before nodding in agreement with Julian.

'I want to show you something. Do you want to come up to my room?' Julian asks, looking directly at me.

I look at Real Brett, unsure whether it's entirely appropriate to go into a pensioner's room.

Just as he catches my eye, Julian cuts in.

'Don't worry, you're allowed. There's no rules about girls being in my room,' he winks. 'They think we're too old for that . . .'

I blush as a laughing Julian leads us up a set of stairs (I resist getting too excited about this meaning he's fit enough to tackle them), down a long corridor and into a room that's probably the size of my bedroom at the flat. Not large enough to swing a cat (why would you ever want to), but spacious enough to make you feel like you're not existing in a box.

Nevertheless, the sight of it seizes my heart.

What strikes me immediately is the stark contrast between Ethel's home and Julian's room in the care home. Ethel had every possession surrounding her in a place that was undoubtedly hers – filled with memories of the decades past (even though she failed to recall a large chunk of them). But here, Julian has a small wardrobe for his clothes – one dresser to keep and display his treasured items, a single bed and a bedside table. It's stark, barren and lacking in any sort of personality or warmth.

It's not Julian.

It's a room in a home, waiting for its current inhabitant to move on to whatever comes next before it can be filled once more with a newcomer preparing for their last days to be spent in that same room, sleeping in that same bed.

I wonder how many occupants that bed has had since being here . . .

I can't help but feel sad at the thought of a lifetime of living being whittled down to this.

'Here's what I wanted to show you,' Julian says, grabbing something from his bedside table and holding it out for us to look at. 'A picture of my Flo. My girl.'

It's a black and white picture of a young woman in a polka dot swimsuit, holding a Mr Whippy ice-cream in her hand. She's grinning at the person taking the picture, which I'm assuming is Julian, rather than at the camera lens and her eyes are doe-like – filled with youthful love and admiration. Written on the back in pencil, Julian has inscribed, 'My girl Flo, September '55'.

'Isn't she a beauty?' Julian beams, turning the picture back to himself so that he can have another look. 'And what a body.'

I sneak a glance at Real Brett and see him watching Julian in awe. It's not just me our new friend has enthralled.

'Seriously,' says Julian, shaking his head in disbelief. 'How on earth could I ever regret *that*.'

Quite.

When he takes the picture to his lips and kisses it, I have to dig my fingernails into my palms to stop myself from crying.

What a lovely man.

'If you could go anywhere in the world,' asks Real Brett. 'Where would be your top choice?'

Julian puffs out his lips and blows a raspberry as he puts the picture of Flo back on his bedside table, his empty hands finding his pockets as his heels rock forward and back.

'You know, I *should* say to go visit my son in America – he lives in New York. Got some important job over there. No idea where he got his brains from . . .' he shrugs, tapping his head while simultaneously knocking on the wooden door of his wardrobe – trying to emulate the sound of his skull being nothing but an empty shell.

Real Brett guffaws beside me, clearly taken by Julian's humour.

'I've not seen him in a few years,' he admits, winking at Real Brett through the sad admission.

'Well, I guess you seeing him again would be nice,' I

say, squirming slightly at the thought of the show becoming more of a *Surprise Surprise* segment where people get reunited with long-lost family instead of the inspirational thrill-seeking show I'd loosely intended.

'But,' Julian says, wistfully. 'I don't think many of these young travellers go to America, do they?'

'Some do,' shrugs Real Brett.

'Hmmm . . . Well Patrick's not like me and his mother, he's not a performer and he'd hate taking part in anything like this,' he says, pulling a face to express his disdain. 'So why waste the ticket?'

'Really?' I ask, not wanting to change his mind but intrigued to hear more about this unusual family dynamic.

'I can pop and see him on the way back . . .' he says, seemingly enjoying the thought. 'I could be a seasoned traveller by then. It would give me something to talk to him about. He's always been quite the jetsetter, has Patrick.'

There's a tinge of sadness to his admission, so this time I decide to leave it there and not prod further. I'm sure we'll find out more in good time.

'So, not New York – for now,' I say.

'No,' he confirms, shaking his head.

'Then where?' asks Real Brett, smirking at Julian. 'The world is literally your oyster.'

Julian puffs out a lungful of air and looks around his lacklustre room.

'Anywhere,' he says courageously. 'Everywhere,' he adds, the cheeky sparkle in his eyes returning as he boldly opens up a world of possibilities.

'You know what, Julian,' I say, elated to have found such

a wonderfully characterful man. 'I think we might just be able to make that happen.'

The three of us stand grinning at each other – knowing that we're on the cusp of an epic adventure.

23

I wake up to the sun shining through the gap in my curtains, spreading a thick strip of light across the room and on to my face. I lie there looking at the way the light bounces through the space, feeling calm and serene.

Turning on to my side, I'm aware of my skin sliding across the coolness of my silk sheets. I'm naked. Totally naked. Not like me – I prefer to wear a baggy old t-shirt and a pair of comfy knickers (Bridget Jones style) to bed, just in case something happens. Not entirely sure what I'm waiting for (a fire, burglar, my mum turning up unannounced), but it's nice to know I wouldn't have my foof and baps out if anything did.

So, my nakedness.

I look to the floor and see a pile of discarded clothes – an actual mound of clothes, some belonging to me and some belonging to . . . who?

A whistling in the kitchen causes me to hold my breath before my body dissolves and relaxes at the sound.

I groan and shimmy my bottom around, loving the sensation it sends through me of naughty sexiness as the sheets glide over my bare breasts and stomach. I've blatantly woken from a night full of satisfying sex as I feel glowing and wonderful.

'Coffee?' Dream Brett offers, his voice low and gravelly as he comes through my bedroom door bum first – although, sadly, it's covered up in a pair of white Calvin Klein boxers, I still manage to admire its peachiness.

As he turns to face me I let out a sigh at the sight of his face. He looks deliciously dishevelled with his hair ruffled, creased-up face and the morning shadow of rough stubble on his face.

'Thank you,' I smile, delicately holding the sheets across my body as I reach up for the mug.

'Actually,' Dream Brett says, taking the coffee back from me and placing our mugs together on the bedside table. 'I want to do this first.'

Joining me on the bed, he straddles me and cradles my head in his big, manly hands. Leaning over me, his hazelnut eyes twinkle as they gaze into mine.

We stay like that for a moment or two and I'm in heaven – enjoying the comfortable feeling of being utterly exposed, loving being able to admire every little fault and flaw on his perfect face – from the little wrinkles around his eyes to the tiny, almost invisible, scar below his right eye.

And he inspects me.

I glimmer at his scrutiny, knowing he won't falter or wane at what he might find, knowing that every mark and blemish has a story to tell.

When he's seen enough, he strokes his thumbs across my cheeks, his face lowering as his mouth finds mine for a soft, loving kiss.

'Hmm . . .' he groans.

I let out a chuckle as a fuzzy feeling invades my head.

'That's a fucking great way to start the day,' he murmurs, placing both arms around my shoulders and pulling me into his chest, holding me tightly.

I feel secure, safe and loved . . .

I feel important.

Suddenly we're up, dressed and out of the flat – looking like the perfect couple as we hold hands and walk along the sunny canal towards the station in our warm winter coats.

As we pass The Barge Café, Dream Brett drapes his arm around my shoulder and brings my body into his.

'Our special place,' he says, his lips talking into my hair and making my scalp tickle. 'I've been wondering – what was your first impression of me?'

'When?' I ask.

'When you saw me sitting in there.'

'I was just grateful you weren't reading porn like the schoolboys next to you,' I smile.

'Atrocious behaviour,' he chuckles after a playful tut. 'But seriously . . . ?'

'Well, I'm here, aren't I?' I laugh, cuddling into him.

'True.' Pause. 'I felt like it was meant to be. That we'd been drawn back together for a reason.'

'Really?' I ask, taken aback by the sentiment in his words.

'Chance encounters don't just happen for no reason,' he shrugs. 'There's always some greater purpose behind them. People come into our lives because they're meant to – they usually leave when they're meant to too, but what does it mean when they come back?'

'That they should've stayed away the first time?'

'Or that they were never meant to leave?' he asks slowly. 'Food for thought.'

'Yeah . . . I sigh.

When I open my eyes, my first thought is of Real Brett, not Dream Brett, and that terrifies and excites me all at once – I'm not sure how I feel about my dream feelings spinning into truth, or about how the line between reality and make-believe seems to be blurring with the two men merging into one romantic catch.

Do people really enter our lives for a reason? Is that

what I believe? If so, why have I been dealt the heart-breaking situation I've found myself in with Dan. Surely he's served his purpose now (it was probably to break my soul into a million pieces so that I could claw my way back into society and find a desire to live life to the max – that's what it would be in a film, anyway). Isn't he meant to have buggered off again by now? Or is Real Brett here to repair the damage and make me see how beautiful opening up your heart to someone can be?

Destiny.

Fate.

Meant to be.

Written in the stars . . .

I'm not sure I believe any of it, and I'm doubly unsure over whether I need any guy swooping in to give me life lessons. I'm still hurting from the last wound, why would I open my heart for another so willingly?

It's a thought I ponder as I shower, blowdry my hair and get dressed into the same blue swing dress I wore for my interview a few weeks ago.

'Are you going to your quiz tonight?' Real Brett asks later that morning as he settles a coffee on Julie's and my desks.

Since learning which buttons to press on the machine (and that a cup should always be placed beneath the spout to collect the boiling brown liquid as it falls), Real Brett has taken it upon himself to become our personal refresher boy, bringing us drinks every few hours. It's a kind gesture, and one that would be awkward if I were the only one benefitting from it – but seeing as Julie is being treated too (a fact she loves), I choose to just enjoy each new drinks arrival rather than question it, even if it does give him licence to open up a conversation several times a day.

When Real Brett questions my evening plans, Julie looks up at me, grinning behind him – her eyes dancing with delight, obviously sensing a little bit of office gossip on the horizon.

'Erm, that's the plan,' I say trying to ignore her as she performs a little celebratory jig with her arms. I make a mental note to correct her later on before nonsense gets whispered around about the two of us.

'And who's on the team?' he asks.

'Alastair, obviously. And then Carly, Josh, Natalia, Dan and Lexie.'

'As in Dan your ex?' he asks with a bemused frown.

'I said we still saw each other,' I shrug, feeling my cheeks redden a little bit at the unusual set-up.

'And I take it Lexie is . . .'

'The perfect one he left me for and is subsequently marrying in a few months' time,' I confirm, finishing his sentence for him in case he couldn't quite fit the pieces of the fragmented puzzle together.

Julie dramatically flings her head forward on her desk, in mock despair at my tragic situation – ironic, as I feel like doing the same on a daily basis.

'Nice,' Real Brett responds, pursing his lips and looking baffled. 'Anything else I should know?'

'Carly's pregnant with Josh's baby.'

'What?' shrieks Julie, her head pinging back up like a jack-in-the-box.

'Oh yeah . . .' I say, sheepishly, realizing too late that I've just announced their bun-in-the-oven news to my co-workers, even though Carly and Josh are trying to keep it between close friends and family for now.

'Wow . . .' Real Brett says, clearly not having expected that reply.

In hindsight his question might actually not have been a question but more of a remark on the delightful circumstances of my friendship group.

Ah well.

'I didn't even know they were a couple,' Julie gasps, reeling from the news, looking like I've just told her that Cheryl Cole is actually Simon Cowell and Louis Walsh's lovechild.

'Neither did we,' I say flatly, not wanting to discuss the topic that I shouldn't have mentioned anyway.

'Well . . .' she breathes.

'Obviously don't say anything, though,' I say with a panic.

'My lips are sealed,' he winks.

'And mine,' says Julie, pretending to zip across her mouth.

If only that gesture could actually keep her from opening her huge gob, I think, knowing that it's never stopped her before.

Real Brett glances back over his shoulder at Julie having a flap, before turning to me.

'And we're going to Bethnal Green?' he asks.

'That's right,' I nod, wondering if he's thinking about changing his mind now that he's learnt more about my wacky friends and the unique relationships we share – he probably thinks we're a right bunch of bed-hoppers.

'Well, why don't I come with you after work?' he asks

casually. 'We could even stop for a drink on the way and mull over our plan for Julian.'

'I'd love to, but . . .' I say, not able to find an excuse quickly enough – my brain stranding me and leaving me to stare at him with my mouth wide open like a confused fish instead. We do have to work out the details of where we're going to send our new friend, and then work on pitching the idea to others in the company, but the whole thing sounds more like a cheeky date than a casual brainstorming session and I'm still not certain I want that – despite what my dreams might be trying to tell me.

'Right,' Real Brett nods, unable to contain a smirk at my awkward response as he slowly puts his hand to his chest and bangs on it a couple of times. 'Shot down twice. I'll try not to be offended.'

I can't help but laugh.

He *was* after a cheeky date.

'I've got loads to do here,' I shrug, gesturing towards my desk while tapping my pen against my luxurious notebook.

'Oh . . .' he says, his bottom lip pouting out. 'Christmas party admin?'

'Something like that,' I nod, although I'm fairly on top of all that if I'm honest. I just know that if I say I've got to do anything on *Grannies Go Gap* he'll offer to help or suggest we do it together . . . and I'd rather not have to worm my way out of that one too.

'Actually, I should probably work on a few bits here anyway . . .' he muses, rubbing his chin and looking around the office.

'There we go then,' I smile, picking up my coffee and taking a gulp.

'We'll both stay late to work and leave together a bit later. We can just head straight to see your bunch together,' he nods decisively before turning on his heels and heading back to his desk.

I stare at the back of his head in shock, trying to block out the laughter that's coming from Julie's desk, and the fact I can see her shoulders shaking in my peripheral vision.

What I really wanted to do was slink off home and freshen up before heading to the pub later with my mates. Now, as if it's not bad enough that Real Brett is coming along for an evening with them, I'm now going to have to stay at the office for an extra hour or so to stop me looking like a complete bitch.

Argh.

What a pain in the arse.

Even though I've been on the single scene (punch me now because I hate that term) for the last two years, I've never really dated. I've had encounters, but never in that time have I had to walk into where my friends are gathered with a guy in tow. Which is why I feel my face blush and my insides curdle aggressively as I walk into the pub with Real Brett by my side.

It's not a date.

He's not my boyfriend.

We are not romantically linked in any way.

Not really — even though I have a million romantic moments surging through my heart with someone that looks and seems a whole lot like him, all of which he's totally unaware of.

It feels weird, especially as I decided not to tell any of them that he was coming with me. I think I was still living in the hope that he'd change his mind or remember some important poetry recital he had to go to (or something equally as riveting). Of course, I could've warned them when we left the office and made our way over, but by then I was feeling quite sick about the whole thing and didn't want to make a huge deal of it. I figured this was the most casual way of turning up with our old fleeting friend and my current work colleague who my subconscious mind had turned into my boyfriend before he re-entered our lives.

When worded like that, I've no idea why I'd have an issue with it.

Alastair and the boys greet him as they would an old friend (because he is an old friend to a certain degree) – with man hugs and slaps on the back, although seeing Dan welcome him so warmly causes my nostrils to do a little dance of revulsion. Natalia coyly glances up from her iPhone long enough to throw a surprised little wave and a wink in his direction before looking back at her screen, and Lexie sweetly kisses him on both cheeks – happy to meet an old friend of Dan's.

Carly (I'm thinking about changing her name to Cheeky Cow Carly) just sits and grins at me while these exchanges occur, as though she's on the verge of giddy giggles. She manages to suppress the urge when it's her turn to greet Real Brett with a friendly hug and the obligatory 'It's been a long time' chat, but when diverting her attention back to me she mouths the words, 'Space sex'.

My eyes widen in horror, although all that seems to do

is make Cheeky Cow Carly's giggles escape with great ferocity.

Josh turns to her and looks confused, but luckily the others don't seem to pick up on it.

I shrug at Josh and pretend not to have a clue what she's laughing at (hoping he'll put it down to her crazy preggo hormones) before leaving Real Brett with the others and dragging my cackling mess of a friend to the loo.

'What the fuck are you doing?' I whisper loudly in the way that only women on the verge of losing it can get away with.

''I'm so sorry,' she manages, grabbing her sides – the laughter clearly causing them to split. 'I just forgot how fit he was and it caught me off guard.'

I frown and prod her shoulder.

'Ouch!' she says rubbing her shoulder through her laughter.

'Stop taking the piss.'

'I'm not!' she squeals. 'I thought you said he hadn't aged well. I was expecting this wrinkled old man with a potbelly to walk in – but instead that hunk arrived.'

'He's totally changed!' I hiss.

'That's what you told me,' she nods, her arms flailing around dramatically between our two bodies. 'I don't see it. He's not aged any more than us or the guys have. In fact, he's gone from boy to man. Face it, he's just an extremely fit guy who you've been having rude dreams about.'

'They're not all rude,' I say in a high-pitched squeak, defending my nightly excursions – not wanting to spoil their complicated beauty with her lewd attitude towards them.

'Really?' she asks, arching an eyebrow in my direction.

'No.'

'Either way,' she says, trying to gain control of herself. 'You've been dreaming of *that* dude . . . if I were you I'd be lying horizontal every spare minute of the day and lapping up that space travel.'

'Whatever,' I say, slightly miffed that she doesn't see what I do. But then she is pregnant and delirious. Who knows what's going on in that brain of hers.

After more hissing (from me) and giggling (from her), I manage to calm Carly down enough for her to be allowed back with the group – but only on the condition that she promises not to have any more giddy outbursts that might lead to explanations/lies having to be made up. God knows I'm crap at them, especially when put on the spot.

When we walk out of the ladies we see that our nemesis group of high-kicking performers have already arrived, and that they're unknowingly being scowled at by our gaggle of friends in the corner.

'The competition,' I explain to Real Brett, sitting down in the only spare seat at the table, which happens to be the one right next to him. I'm grateful for the large glass of red that's been placed there for me to guzzle on.

'I thought that might be the case,' he grins, his eyes dancing between my friends who already have their game faces on, ready for war. A playful smile creeps up on to his lips. 'You guys take this really seriously.'

'It's a serious battle,' says Natalia, her eyes widening at him. 'Don't mock it.'

'I wouldn't dream of it,' he smirks, bashfully looking down at his beer before bringing it to his lips.

Call me nuts, but their little exchange sends a flush of

green envy through me – something that's laughable seeing as I'm being so hot and cold with my own feelings towards Real Brett. I find myself trying to cast my mind back to our nights out in Leicester – did Natalia and Real Brett have a thing back then? I don't think they did, but I was already busy bed-hopping with Dan at that time, so I would've missed the whole thing if they did.

Before I have a chance to stew over my newly acquired jealous streak and the possible past liaisons of Real Brett and Natalia, Ian announces that the quiz is about to start.

'We've got this,' nods Dan around the table, flashing one of his mega-watt smiles as his fist pumps at the air. 'The time is ours!'

The group starts making a collection of nervous noises and team morale-boosting chant-like grunts in response.

I join in.

Real Brett throws his head back and laughs, rhythmically bashing his knees with his fists nervously.

'You ready Bretty boy?' Josh barks like a sergeant across the table.

'Yes, sir,' Real Brett booms, pulling back his shoulders and sitting tall and alert.

Alastair beats at his chest like the alpha male in a shrewdness of apes, egging the rest of us on.

'Aaaaaah,' Josh cheers, like he's on a rugby pitch about to aggressively tackle the opposition.

We all join in, forming an ascending collection of war cries and animalistic wailing, ignoring the stares we're attracting from the rest of the pub.

Real Brett leans in to me, his bodyweight resting against my right side.

I look up to see him smiling down at me and find myself smiling back – I can't help myself.

'Thank God you know this lot,' I laugh, enjoying the madness of my friends and the energy that our crazy fighting chorus has given me.

'Know?' asks Josh with a guffaw, his eyes playfully manic. 'He's one of us, Sar!'

In response Real Brett rises from his chair and roars like a beast – the others in our group joining in like insane buffoons, although I spot Lexie looking a little petrified at first and have to stop myself from laughing.

'Erm, when you're ready to start . . .' says Ian nervously into the microphone, avoiding eye contact like we're strangers – even though he has seen us in his pub almost every Wednesday night for the past few years.

Laughter erupts from our table to such a level that tears stream from eyeballs and Carly finds it difficult to breathe.

Ian licks his lips and wanders behind the bar to pull himself a pint, perhaps deciding that tonight's quiz is going to be a rowdy one and that he's going to need a little helping hand to get through it.

'Do you think our losing streak has gone to our heads?' I ask.

'Seems that way,' smirks Real Brett with an amused frown. 'I thought you guys were wild a decade ago and that you'd seriously tamed down with all this quiz chat. Seems I was wrong.'

'It's enthralling stuff. You'll see,' says Alastair, grabbing the pen and paper and writing out our team name – ready to start. 'Ned's going to love that we're together.'

'How is he? I haven't spoken to him in so long,' admits

Real Brett with a tinge of sadness at the mention of his old friend.

'You know what he's like – gets a girl and forgets the lot of us,' winks Alastair with a grin. 'But at least this one is his wife.'

'Well, tell him I said hello,' he says brightly.

'He's coming back in a few months actually. We should hook up then.'

'Really? He's coming back?'

'A flying visit for these two,' Alastair says, sticking his chin out in Dan and Lexie's direction.

'Oh. Your wedding?' Real Brett asks, shuffling in his seat.

'Not that the invites have gone out yet,' says Dan, much to Lexie's horror.

'Seriously?' she mutters.

'People will probably get all the details via text at this rate,' Dan laughs.

'I posted out all the save the dates today,' she nudges him, rightfully annoyed that Dan seems oblivious to the amount of effort required to organize a wedding, especially in a three-month time span – they've really taken on an obscene amount of stress what with that and moving house. No wonder they've been bickering. The cracks are normally hidden behind a glossy exterior that leaves me feeling inferior and flawed. I wonder if they're regretting leaving themselves such a short time to plan everything.

Even though I don't care about Dan's feelings, I can't help but feel sorry for Lexie.

'I'm sure you've got it all under control,' I appease.

Lexie looks up and gives me a smile of thanks.

'Question one,' booms Ian, finally getting the quiz underway now that we've calmed down and he's quenched his thirst with a beer.

Our heads gather forwards, huddling over the sheet of paper in Alastair's care, ready for battle.

With our team united to full force for the first time in weeks, and with Real Brett's knowledge thrown into the mix too (he's surprisingly quite up-to-date with current affairs), we plough through this week's questions with ease, feeling confident when we hand over our answer sheet.

'I've got a good feeling about this,' declares Josh to the group, shaking his fist animatedly.

'Don't jinx us,' says Natalia, rolling her eyes before grabbing her phone. I don't know how she miraculously manages to stay off the blooming device for the duration of the quiz each week. Although it's never too far from her gaze, and she's always ready to pick it up as soon as the quiz is finished and people have dispersed to the bar or loo. I'm relieved to see this trait hasn't changed in the presence of Real Brett – she's clearly not interested. Perhaps I imagined their exchange earlier . . .

Hold on. Did I say relieved? I meant intrigued . . . Meh.

'So when are you two getting married?' Real Brett turns and asks Dan.

I throw a glance in his direction, wondering why he's bringing up the topic when he's aware of the history, and see his mouth twitch.

'Valentine's Day next year,' Dan says, with an excited smile that makes me want to punch him in the face.

'Not long, then,' says Real Brett.

'No. Mate, you should come,' Dan offers suddenly, his forehead wrinkling upwards to emphasize his invitation.

'But . . .' voices Lexie, before taking a deep breath, biting her lip and holding in her thought.

'What's up?' asks Dan, seeming a little annoyed at her objection.

'Nothing,' Lexie mumbles at him. 'It's just space, you know.'

'It's all right. I totally understand,' says Real Brett graciously, holding his hands out in front of him to let her know it's not an issue.

'What? No,' stammers Dan, his face screwing up in protest. 'What about Sarah's plus one?'

'What's that?' I ask, my ears pricking up. 'I didn't realize we were all getting plus ones.'

'No, not everyone is,' says Lexie, side-glancing at Dan with annoyance, clearly not wanting to talk about it here in front of everyone. 'I just thought you might like a date seeing as these lot are going to be part of the wedding party and away performing their different roles. Not that you have to stay away or anything like that. You're welcome to be with the girls as much as you like –' she babbles on, unable to stop the words pouring from her mouth and on the verge of suggesting things I know she'll regret. No matter how friendly our circumstances are now, who wants someone's ex loitering around with their bridesmaids on their wedding day?

No one.

'Lexie,' I say, stopping her. 'Seriously, don't worry about me. I don't need a plus one. I'll be fine.'

I manage to stop myself from saying that I know most of Dan's family anyway and won't be on my own – but I think pointing out, yet again, that I have a history with his family and that I've spent many Christmases and holidays with them isn't necessary. She doesn't need another reminder.

'Brett should totally be your plus one,' says Carly to my left.

I know she's grinning before I even turn to glare at her with the deathliest death stare I can muster.

'Well, who else would you take?' she asks innocently, with a meek little raise of her shoulders to highlight her point further. 'At least Brett knows you guys and has a history,' she says to Dan and Lexie, rallying them into her way of thinking.

'Weddings are so boring when you don't know the couple,' adds Natalia, not even looking up from her phone.

'That's true,' nods Dan. 'There you go, problem solved.'

'Only if Sarah doesn't mind,' argues Lexie, who seems to be the only person at this table talking sense.

'Why would she mind?' asks Carly. 'He's the perfect plus one.'

'What's this? You coming to their wedding?' asks Alastair with excitement, patting Real Brett on the back before leaning across the table to pick up his wallet. 'That's awesome.'

'Well, I don't know if – '

'You'll get to see Ned,' Alastair sings, cutting Real Brett off and heading back to Josh at the bar.

'And face it, Sar, you'll find it near impossible to talk

anyone else into it,' nods Carly. 'Especially as it's on Valentine's Day.'

'Thanks,' I mutter, thrilled that my friend is declaring my love life to be pathetic to both my ex and sort of dream lover.

'You'd be doing her a favour,' she continues, looking at Real Brett.

'Er, I think that's pushing it a bit too far,' I stammer, ready to drag her pregnant arse back to the loo for another chat.

'Possibly, but will you accept the task of putting up with her for a whole day?' she asks Real Brett.

'We'll see,' he frowns with a shrug. 'I'll go help with the drinks.'

He picks up his empty glass and makes his way to join Alastair and Josh at the bar.

'I'll come,' says Dan, gathering the rest of the empties on the table along with the empty crisp packets, before carrying them over.

'I'm going to pop to the loo,' says Lexie, before leaving me with Carly and a distracted Natalia.

'Great,' I say, rolling my eyes. 'Thanks bitchface. You've made me look really desperate.'

'You are.'

'Nice,' mutters Natalia on my behalf.

'Worst part about having your friends set you up with someone in front of you? Watching them say no,' I say, squishing the palms of my hands into the sockets of my eyes.

'He didn't say no,' she tuts.

'He did,' I say flatly.

'It was practically a yes,' chips in Natalia, with a feeble shrug.

'Were you even listening?'

'I'm a woman. I multitask ... especially when it suits me,' she winks. 'And stop protesting so much. I could think of worse people to be forced into spending time with. I don't remember him being so hot.'

At that Carly lets out another cackle.

One guy – three very different accounts of his looks: I think he's aged, Carly thinks he looks exactly the same as he did before, and Natalia think he's hotter than her memory can offer ... a gentle reminder that life makes us all view beauty in very different ways. Unless it's George Clooney, Brad Pitt, Billy Buskin, Ryan Gosling, Leonardo DiCaprio or that bloke who's just joined the cast of *EastEnders* ... they're fitter than fit and there's no denying their looks.

'Seriously,' Natalia continues. 'I had to pick up my phone and shove it in my face just to stop myself from staring at him inappropriately.'

'Right? And this madam is totally looking a gift horse in the mouth,' shrieks Carly, waving her hand in my face.

'I'm not.'

'Are.'

'I just don't want to feel like he's being forced into spending the most romantic day of the year with me,' I argue.

'But I beg of you, think of the babies you'd make,' swoons Natalia.

'What?' I squeal.

'Think of your mother's happiness,' adds Carly.

And with that they cackle in unison.

'You're such losers,' I mumble into my near-empty glass, feeling like I'm nearing a full-on sulk.

'And that's why you love us,' replies Carly, pouring some wine into it.

'Cheers to that,' laughs Natalia, raising her glass to mine and chinking them together.

I take a big gulp and scowl at them both, making them laugh again.

'Ooh, have you heard from Max? How's Andrea?' asks Natalia.

'She's huge and restless apparently,' I say, repeating what my brother texted me earlier in the day.

'Isn't her due date soon?' asks Carly, subtly placing a hand on her tummy and thinking of her own growing baby.

'Yep, on Sunday – so anything could happen now.'

'Exciting times Aunty Sarah,' grins Natalia.

'God, that sounds so grown up,' I reply, taking a gulp of my wine.

'It was going to happen at some point,' she replies, pursing her lips.

'Ladies and gentlemen,' calls Ian over the microphone, making everyone dash back to their seats speedily. 'For the second time this month we have a tie-breaker situation.'

'Ooooooh . . .' cheers the room with much commotion.

'And, for the second time this month, it's between "Rehomed from Leicester" and "The High-kick-flyers".'

'Get in,' mutters Josh, clearly forgetting our fate the last time this happened.

'I'm staying quiet for this one,' whispers Lexie, baring her teeth at the memory.

'Right, you ready folks?' asks Ian. 'Here we go . . . Many

people mistakenly think "It's Not Unusual' was Tom Jones' debut single, but it was in fact his second. What was the first?"

'That's not a tie-breaker question,' huffs Dan, looking around at Ian, as though he's about to protest.

'Shh,' I whisper, unable to hide my excitement at knowing the answer.

But before I can reach over for the pen to write it down, I see Real Brett whisper to Alastair, and him writing down 'Chills and Fever'. It's what I would've said . . . and something only people who are fans (or have spent a lot of time Googling Sir Tom) would know.

A link.

A connection.

A feeling of elation in my chest.

We give in our answer.

We win.

There's uproar from the opposition at the nature of the tie-breaker question not being the usual 'closest person wins' type answer – that they weren't in with a chance from the start due to their lack of knowledge in the Tom Jones Trivia department.

Ian waves off their complaints.

We cheer, hug and whoop, then let the opposition order themselves a free round on us – we might act like we despise them, but quiz night certainly got a lot more fun since they started coming along.

'Thanks for having me,' says Real Brett, getting up from his seat and putting on his coat.

'Thank you!' smirks Josh, ecstatic to have finally won a game again.

'You're not going already, are you?' cries Carly to Real Brett, her face aghast that he's leaving, probably because she's been looking forward to winding me up in front of him a bit more.

'Early start,' he replies apologetically.

'We owe you one,' nods Alastair.

'It was nothing. Just something I knew,' he shrugs, before side glancing at me.

As a knowing look is exchanged between us, my breath swells in my throat at the sight of his startling green eyes. Other than to observe their colour, I'd never really looked at them before and had missed not only the sparkle in them, but their wholesome quality that matches the kindness and openness of their owner.

'I think Sarah probably knew the answer anyway,' he continues, gazing at me, the corner of his lips twitching up into a smile.

I find myself mirroring the expression.

'Not likely,' remarks Dan, butting in on the moment. 'Her music collection is filled with boybands from the noughties and a bit of classical Mozart to please her mum.'

'And when was the last time you checked? Perhaps her taste has changed,' Real Brett fires, pulling his gloves from his pocket and slapping them together.

I watch as Dan looks up at him and gawps speechlessly.

'Probably right,' he frowns, turning to an unaware Lexie and rubbing her back affectionately.

'So good to see you mate', says Alastair, coming around the table to give Real Brett a pat on the back, leading into a man hug. 'You'll have to come back and play again some time.'

'Yes! You might be our lucky charm!' says Josh, already thinking about the next win.

'Oh dear – the fate of our pub quiz future success now rests on your shoulders,' mocks Natalia.

Real Brett laughs and holds his hand in the air as he swivels on the spot and makes for the exit. 'See you all soon, maybe.'

'At the wedding,' shouts Carly.

He waves his hand in response.

Once I've stopped staring at the empty space that he's left in his wake, I turn back to the table to pick up my glass and find Carly staring at me with a big grin on her face.

'Yeah . . . he's so not your type,' she mouths.

Cue cackle.

24

The next morning I wander into work with an almighty spring in my step – bar the fact that my friends tried setting us up, I thoroughly enjoyed having Real Brett out with us and am glad he came along. I was wrong to dread spending more time with him. Perhaps there's a reason my dreams decided to pick him for a recurring lead role and not some other random guy from my past.

I cheerily skip (yes, I actually skip like a little girl) through the office doors and spot him already sat at his desk, staring at his computer screen while munching on some toast and slurping on a pint of milk.

'So you are a Tom Jones fan,' I say, heading straight to his desk and performing my winter ritual of delayering myself of clothes.

He arches an eyebrow at me. 'Guilty as charged.'

'Is that more of your nan's jam?' I ask, while taking off my orange cardigan, spying a touch of red on his last piece of toast as he rams it in his mouth and guzzles it down with a mouthful of the white stuff.

'No, I gave that to you,' he says, frowning at the memory. 'Now I'm having to suffer the shortcomings of this crap from the corner shop while I wait for you to start sharing.'

'I took it home.'

'Exactly,' he smiles, looking back to his computer screen. 'I'm still waiting for an invite.'

A bashful smile pings on my face as he says it. 'And there I was thinking I'd imagined your forward behaviour.'

'Not that forward then, clearly,' he smiles cheekily, his sparkling green eyes back on me. 'I'll have to work on it. Thanks for the tip.'

'Pleasure,' I laugh, turning away from him to dump my many layers of discarded outer garments and black leather shoulder bag on to my desk.

'So tell me, what's the deal with you two?' he asks my back, the tone of his voice changing from flirty to inquisitive.

'Huh?' I ask, turning back.

'You and Dan?' There's a waver of nerves in his voice now, as though he's questioning whatever thought pattern had led him to start this thread of the conversation.

I look at him confused and bewildered. 'What? There's no deal.'

'No loitering feelings?'

'Definitely not,' I reply boldly, finding that I am repulsed at the thought.

'Right,' Real Brett says, his eyebrows shooting skyward in surprise.

'Why'd you ask that?'

'It's nothing. I just thought I picked up on something, but I'm clearly wrong.'

'What?' I ask, intrigued as to why the first guy I've taken with me to see my friends (albeit in a non-romantic capacity) has concluded that there are dodgy goings-on with the guy who inconsiderately broke my heart.

'The way he invited me to the wedding – as your date – was weird,' he reasons, while barely looking at me. 'I mean, it's nice to be asked, but I've not seen you guys in years. Felt like I might be being used in some way.'

'You were – as my guardian,' I laugh. 'Ex-girlfriends don't usually get invited to things like this. There's probably a small part of his brain that wonders whether I'm finally going to call him out for being such a shit.'

'Wow.'

'Well . . . he was.'

'You also held your breath throughout the whole discussion.'

'Did I?' I ask, genuinely surprised to hear that as I was completely oblivious to the action my body must automatically perform on my behalf. Although, on reflection, I'm certain I was more worried about what was going to come out of Carly's mouth than Dan's. Not that I can say that to Real Brett, of course. Not without running the risk of revealing far more than I should.

'Yes,' he nods. 'Well, when you weren't practically begging them to take back the offer.'

'I did not do that,' I laugh, horrified that he'd seen through my shocked reaction. 'I was caught off guard.'

'You and me both.'

'Ha. Sorry about that.'

'I know you don't have a boyfriend as such,' continues Real Brett with a sigh. 'But there's certainly someone – which is why you've knocked me back a few times.'

'Oh is *that* why?' I laugh.

He bites his lip and grins back at me. 'Can't be anything else.'

I tilt my head in response and break eye contact, suddenly feeling shy.

'But your relationship status is complicated,' he decides.

'So either you've got an imaginary boyfriend or you're dating someone you shouldn't.'

I look at him agog. Not because he thinks there might be some hidden feelings between me and Dan, but because he's almost hit the nail square on the head.

I, at twenty-nine years old, have an imaginary boyfriend – a boyfriend who I've shared a plethora of adventures with, but only in the creative mind space of my dreams.

Oh the shame of it.

I laugh hysterically at the realization.

To Real Brett it must sound like a genuine case of the giggles, but in reality I'm on the verge of tears. It's a tragic tale of events.

'I guess I put two and two together . . .' he offers, seeming apologetic.

'Clearly,' I say, getting a grip of myself and becoming calmer. 'I can categorically say that there are no hidden feelings between me and my ex – I'm not entirely sure what you picked up on there. Actually, it's a bit worrying that you thought that. And also, I do not have a boyfriend.'

'Oh crap.'

'What now?' I almost shriek.

'I figured you having a complicated relationship status was the reason for you knocking me back twice . . . turns out you don't fancy me and I was just being rejected.'

'You got me,' I mock. 'At least you know now.'

'Ouch,' he says, rubbing his chest. 'You've got a real nice way with words.'

I smile to reassure him that I'm joking and only going along with his playful banter. I'm relieved when it's returned.

'You don't need to come along as my date,' I say, letting

him off the hook. 'Despite what they might think I'm totally okay about the whole thing. I really don't need someone to hold my hand and check I'm all right every five minutes.'

'Or to stop you running up the aisle and declaring your unwavering love for Dan?'

'Exactly.'

'Or starting a food fight with the wedding cake?'

'Only if it's fruitcake – I hate fruitcake,' I reason.

'Or tripping up the bride as she walks past you?'

'More likely to do it to the groom,' I nod.

'Or throwing a hissy fit when you're not allowed in all the photos?'

'I'm sure I'll have to be in at least one.'

'Or telling his nan about the time you had sex in her pantry?'

'How'd you know about that?' I jokingly gasp aghast.

'Or getting really drunk and streaking across the dance-floor during the first dance?'

'Ah, is that one really not allowed? Because I've been practising all sorts of moves.'

'I'm sure we can negotiate on that one – it would be too funny to stop.'

'Oh God. Maybe I do need a chaperone,' I sigh.

Real Brett nods. 'Well, we'll see.'

'How was the quiz?' calls Julie, as she waddles through the door carrying a dark green overnight bag.

'Great,' I say, wandering back to my desk, deciding it's time to switch my computer on and get going.

I can't stand around talking all day.

No matter how much I'd love to.

*

Ten minutes later Jonathan arrives carrying a gym bag and looking incredibly pleased with himself.

'Morning,' he booms as he strides past Julie and I, giving us both a wink.

'Morning,' we call.

'Oh Sarah,' he says, poking his head back out through the door of his office. 'Grab a coffee and Brett if you would.'

Three minutes later I place a coffee in front of Jonathan and am about to walk back out the door to my desk when he stops me. 'You can stay actually, Sarah.'

'Really?' I query, confused as I look at Real Brett and Jonathan.

'Take a seat,' my boss encourages hastily.

I quickly sit next to Real Brett.

'Now, I had a meeting last night with Derek and Damian to discuss the company and any future projects that might be on the horizon,' he says, resting his hands on the top of his rounded tummy in the same way I've seen Andrea do whilst heavily pregnant. 'Sarah, your pitch came up.'

'Oh?' I ask, feeling my cheeks redden. 'You mean my *Grannies Go Gap* idea . . .'

'That's the one,' he nods. 'I know you two are looking into case studies for this. How far have you got?'

'We've found a great elderly guy,' I say, looking at Real Brett and feeling comforted when he sends an encouraging nod in my direction.

'A man? But isn't this about grannies?'

'Yes, that's what the title suggests,' reasons Real Brett for us. 'But Julian is such a character, we'd be foolish not to include him among any women we find.'

'Also, I've been thinking,' I add. 'This is something that I've not run past Damian or Brett yet, but I was thinking about changing the concept slightly so that the cast stay together for the duration of the show – like a group of mates on a gap year. It might strike more of a comparison to what eighteen-year-olds do so freely without thinking of how amazing it is that they can travel around the world and go on these types of adventures together.'

'It would obviously help to make the whole thing more concise and easier to navigate if we're following one group, too,' nods Real Brett.

'Exactly,' I nod back. 'They'd each have their own stories to share and moment to tell them, but it might make the whole thing feel a little more organic and fluid.'

'Great work,' booms Jonathan. 'That's what being in Development is about – taking your idea and expanding – not feeling like you have to stick rigidly to your initial thought. Brilliant, Sarah.'

'Thanks . . .' I mumble, embarrassed.

'What I really want to hear about is your time scale. When can you see this all happening? Could we get this off the ground soon?'

'Soon? How soon?'

'Early part of next year?' he suggests in a way that's not really a suggestion but a request.

'But, we're only just sorting out the case study to see if it could actually be something good – we haven't even met with the research team yet to talk it all through,' I panic.

'Welcome to television,' barks Jonathan enthusiastically. 'We're like a kitchen in a top London restaurant. Some dishes are left to ferment, marinade or mature while others are sped through and served piping hot – needing to be gobbled up instantly.'

'Right . . .' I say, nodding along to his food-based analogy.

'This needs to be gobbled up now while the topic is current and on people's minds,' he clarifies, as Julie walks into the room and puts another cup of coffee in front of him before smiling eagerly at Real Brett and me as she turns to leave.

'I see.'

'Plus, let's not beat around the bush here – we're talking old folk. We don't want one of our key characters to pop off and leave us up shit creek.'

'Quite,' agrees Real Brett, visibly struggling to keep a straight face at Jonathan's sensitivity on the matter and choice of language.

'So, Julian, is it?' Jonathan asks, checking to see he's got his name correct. 'Where were you thinking of sending him and his new friends?'

'We're not entirely sure yet, but maybe Australia – from the research I've done I think it's still the top location for British travellers. Probably because there's no language barrier there.'

'Good for us when negotiating and planning, too – God knows we've had some disasters when language gets in the way,' he shares with an intake of breath before blowing out his cheeks. 'Right – let's settle on there then. Look into all the gap year spots around the country – choose where you want to go and how long for. I'll get Siobhan from Research to look into this too. You two can go on a recce with her in January, that'll get the ball rolling.'

'January?'

'New year, new project,' he nods passionately.

'That's so soon,' I flap at his plan. 'I haven't got the time to organize all this when I'm doing the Christmas party too.'

'Sarah, how many times have you asked if you can come along on trips?'

'Erm, a lot,' I stop, my cheeks burning at the reminder, embarrassed that my first thought is the office party, which is in just twelve days' time.

'Exactly,' he nods. 'Julie can handle the bloody party arrangements. Now, stop questioning it and go away and make it happen.'

He doesn't need to tell us twice, we scurry out of the door with huge panicked grins on our faces.

'Fuck,' Real Brett whispers.

'Fuuuuuuuck,' I say, echoing his nervous excitement. 'How on earth did that just happen?'

'It's a great idea, that's how,' praises Real Brett, making me blush.

'Well in principle. Now we've got to find a few grannies to make our collection complete and send them on the trip of a lifetime.'

'Then let's get cracking.'

'Yes, I'll phone Age Wise and put some more feelers out through social media encouraging people to nominate candidates they might know for a life-changing opportunity. In the meantime you look into Australia, and then we can get together later today to brainstorm for Julian's trip,' I say in a decisive manner that makes Real Brett grin at me.

'On it, chief, or should I say chef?' he winks.

'Only Jonathan,' I say, shaking my head and rolling my eyes.

'Just a thought – might be worth checking with Julian if he has any mates in his new home that are in the same position as him.'

'God, I'm sure all of them would flock to travel halfway around the world to spend time with him.'

'Who wouldn't?' he asks seriously. 'It would be good to see an already existing friendship pairing in there.'

'I'll phone Fiona and talk to her about it.'

'Great,' Real Brett smiles, nudging my elbow repeatedly in excitement before wandering off to his desk. 'See you in the boardroom later.'

'Yep,' I nod, pulling out the chair at my desk and plonking myself on it.

As I grab my notebook I see my phone screen flash, telling me that Mum's calling. She rarely calls me during work hours – probably because she hates the thought of me nattering nonsense when I could be working hard and bettering myself – so I resist the temptation of letting her ring through to voicemail, too intrigued as to why she's calling.

'Mum?' I say, picking up.

'Ooh, darling, you're there,' she says, sounding happy to have a call answered on her first attempt for once.

I instantly feel guilty.

'Have you got your save the date?'

'From Dan and Lexie?' I ask, immediately dreading where this conversation is heading and feeling less guilty for not picking up all those other times.

'Yes.'

'The post hadn't arrived before I left for work, Mum.'

'Of course. Well, they're very nice,' she says smugly, confirming what I'd just feared.

'You've been invited,' I say, managing to hide my shock, annoyed that Dan didn't think to tell me that my hellish mother had been invited.

'Well, Pat did mention it the other day.'

'Ah,' I say, envisaging the scene when Pat and Terry (Dan's parents) would've sent Lexie a huge guest list of their own friends. I can imagine Dan throwing a strop about Mum's inclusion (if he bothered looking at the guest list) and Pat putting her foot down, seeing as they've offered to pay for the majority of the wedding (such a double-edged sword but one they had to deal with seeing as they'd just moved into their dream home).

I've no idea what Pat's playing at by inviting my parents, or why the two women still speak.

'All happening very quickly, isn't it,' Mum digs. 'Not another one of your friends unexpectedly expecting?'

She might've been friendly over Carly and Josh's situation, but if Dan and Lexie were to be in the same boat she'd clearly have a field day over the matter – Golden Boy Dan who was too good for her daughter is forced to run Lexie up the aisle in a bid to make an honest woman of her.

I'm almost sorry to burst her gloating bubble.

'Mum, they just don't want a big lead-up and for the whole thing to be drawn out.'

'Hmm . . .' she replies despondently, clearly preferring her own scenario.

Great, that's all I need to add to what's no doubt going to be a spiffingly lah-de-dah day – my mother there casting her judgement over everything. I've no doubt she'll struggle to keep those thoughts to herself, too. She's bound to offend someone. There go my chances of getting ridiculously drunk and zoning out, now I'm going to be on edge the whole day.

'Have you heard from Max, Mum?' I ask, attempting to change the subject.

'Max? Oh, I'd be the last to hear if the baby was on its way. They wouldn't want me there fussing,' she replies accurately. 'You know, I can't help thinking that this wedding is going to be a shambles – three months to plan? I took longer to plan your dad's sixtieth.'

With the conversation swivelled back round to the impending doom of next Valentine's Day, I listen quietly for a further five minutes as she rabbits on with her speculations and expectations.

As soon as I manage to hang up (not an easy task when she's fired up on a topic – even if she knows I am at work), I call Carly.

'My mum's been invited to the flipping wedding!' I spit as soon as she cheerily picks up.

'Ah. I did wonder about that. I think all of our parents might be actually – if that makes you feel any better.'

'Not really.'

'Sorry,' she groans. 'It could be worse.'

'How?'

'Fair point. I don't even have the energy to come up with a funny scenario. You win, this is going to be awful . . . but at least your dream lover will be there.'

'Oh fuck.'

My tired friend then cackles down the line with such force that I put the phone down on her and head to the loo for a breather.

Coming out of the cubicle (from a one, not two), I spot Poutmouth Louisa reapplying her lips in the mirror.

'Hey,' she smarms, flashing a suspiciously kind smile in my direction.

'Morning,' I reply, washing my hands in the sink next to her.

'I heard Jonathan called you into his office earlier,' she says, looking at my reflection in front of her before turning her attention to hers and pouting out her perfectly glossed lips.

'Yeah, to talk about *Grannies Go Gap*,' I say, not at all surprised at how quickly the news has spread around the office – it's taken less than twenty minutes for Louisa to hear.

'Amazing feeling to see your idea take off, isn't it?' she asks in a benevolent tone that I'm not used to hearing from her – not lately, anyway.

'It's not sunk in yet,' I admit. 'Feels quite surreal.'

'Oh, I totally get that,' she says, pursing her lips and frowning at me. 'If there's anything I can do – just let me know. I'm on your team, after all.'

'Thanks,' I say, unable to stop a laugh coming out. It's absurd that I've been put in this position of power.

Louisa smiles at me and squints her eyes in the way I've seen her do in her millions of selfies – almost like she's smouldering at me.

She wants something from me, I realize.

'Siobhan said Australia might be on the cards.'

I nod in reply.

'You know my ex lives over there?'

'Ah,' I say, as the reason for this calculated collision in the toilets falls into place in my mind.

'He moved back a couple of weeks ago. I was devastated,' she declares with a sigh. 'Cried. Like, loads.'

'Sorry to hear that . . .'

'Well, he's only my ex because of the distance, you know. We knew it just wouldn't work, so we thought finishing things would be the kindest thing on us both. I still love him so much,' she says, her puppy dog eyes glazing over with a teary shine. 'It would be awesome to see him again.'

'I bet,' I say, realizing this is why she's talking to me.

'I'd love to be part of the recce team – or over there helping with the show in any way I can. I'm really good with old people, you know.'

'Thanks,' I manage to say without laughing. Given the fact that she was appalled at my idea initially when she found out it was centred around the elderly, I can't imagine she actually is. It's blatantly transparent that she's just looking for a free flight to Oz so she can have a good pashing session with her ex. 'I think Brett and me will be okay though. For now,' I add, not wanting to be unkind – and covering my back in case she does end up coming. No good making enemies. Damn my sensible side – the feisty part just wants to call her out for being a dick. Oh the internal struggle.

Her face falls instantly over my reluctance to roll out a red carpet and welcome her on the team.

'Really? You're happy with Brett? He seems a bit of a drip – are you sure he's going to be up to getting things done.'

'I think so,' I smile. 'But you never know – we might all have to go out for filming. Take on an old person each.'

303

'Fun,' she says, her cheeks barely able to lift at the thought.

She turns on her heels and storms out of the loo.

25

Despite the disruption of Dan and Lexie's wedding invites arriving and having emotional blackmail fired at me in the bogs, I end up having a productive day. Age Wise manage to put us in touch with five further possible travellers and a collection of tweets have sent out a flurry of excitement and intrigue, meaning we now have a further ten old people as potentials. On top of that the last half of the afternoon is spent in the boardroom with Real Brett looking through *Lonely Planet*s and *Rough Guide*s – dreaming up the perfect excursion that will make great TV, both visually and emotionally.

Before we know it, it's half six and most of the office have left for the evening.

'Wow, is it that late already?' I ask, looking at my phone.

'Time flies when you're living in travel books,' he grins.

'Nice to be thinking about somewhere hot and sunny,' I agree. 'We should probably stop for tonight, though. Before we end up staying here all night.'

'Good plan,' he nods, closing the books and placing them in a neat pile on the shelf behind us.

'Come on, then,' he says, opening the door for me. We both walk back into the main area of the office and over to our desks.

'What are you doing tonight?' I ask Real Brett as I grab

my colourful scarf and loop it around my neck, throw on my coat and do up the buttons.

'Nothing much. You?' he asks as he shuts down his computer.

'Nothing either,' I shrug, popping my moleskin note-book into my bag, happy with the progress we've made. I thought it was a great idea to start with – but now it's fucking epic.

'Oh. No plans,' he answers, pursing his lips, before looking at me expectantly.

'What?' I laugh.

'Well, just to give me a heads up here and to save me looking like an absolute twat, again – if I were to hypo-thetically ask you to maybe accompany me to the pub or to provide me with some company at dinner tonight – just so I'm not eating on my own like a loser, would I be shot down again? Or would I have better odds of a successful and less awkward response this time?'

'Just hypothetically?' I ask.

'For now,' he nods, raising his left eyebrow a fraction as he pulls on his dark grey coat and buries his hands in its pockets.

I can't help but smile at him for being cute and for not being put off after my appalling response the first time, and the second – heaven loves a trier, as my nan would say.

'I guess it depends what sort of food you were after,' I shrug. 'I'm not into anything poncy or formal.'

'Oh, definitely not. I wouldn't want anything like that,' he says, scrunching up his face and shaking his head as if the idea of us going somewhere lavish were absurd. 'I was only thinking Wagamamas . . .'

I can't help but laugh. 'In that case I would hypothet-ically be tempted if you were to ask me to join you,' I smirk. I can never resist a Wagas – even walking past and not going in seems like a trial some days – that chicken katsu curry just calls out to me, demanding I go inside and stuff it into my face as quickly as possible.

'Great,' he says, nodding thoughtfully, looking around at the rest of the empty room.

'Shall we, then?' I ask with a grin as I motion towards the door, not bothering to wait for him to offer for the third time.

'Let's,' he says with a decisive nod.

We giggle our way out of the office and along the streets of Soho until we get to Wagamama on Lexington Street.

'Ladies first,' he says, opening the door when we get to the restaurant.

'Thank you,' I mutter, walking through and heading down the stairs into the seating area.

If we were anywhere but the casual setting of Wagamama I'd start having regrets about agreeing to go to dinner as soon as we arrived in any sort of date-like-setting, but thanks to its dining style of long banquet tables (you're basically sat side-by-side with strangers) it feels less intim-idating than it could. Especially when we're wedged in between a chaotic family of six and two girls in their early twenties who've obviously not seen each other in a while and have a lot to catch up on ('Did you know Shelley's been having it off with Johnny's dad for the last six months?' 'What, no way . . .'). Non-stop noise comes from either side, leaving any quiet moment between the two of us almost unnoticeable.

Neither of us bothers to turn over our menus, something I can't help smirking over.

'Not looking?' I ask.

'Already know what I'm having.'

'Me too.'

'Katsu?' he says with an eyebrow raised.

'Standard go-to dish,' I nod.

'Me too – it feels wrong coming here and having anything else.'

'Couldn't agree more,' I laugh – thrilled that he's not about to go for some healthy option and make me feel uncomfortable about going for a dirty curry. I've started to refuse coming here with Natalia for that very reason – she usually opts for a chicken salad and I can't deal with eating my katsu while feeling guilty. Takes all the fun out of it and makes me feel like a fat beast.

'Oh. My. God – don't look now but Bryan Cranston is sat to your right,' he mutters under his breath, while playing with the chopsticks that have been placed on the table.

'Who?' I ask, recognizing the name but not able to pinpoint where from.

'*Breaking Bad*'s Walter White . . .' he whispers, trying to be inconspicuous while talking out of the side of his mouth. 'Heisenberg.'

'No way! Seriously?' I gasp, tensing up and trying to resist whipping my head around to have a good old gawp.

Carly and I were obsessed with *Breaking Bad*. The boys banged on about its brilliance for ages and we thought it was going to be laddy and crap so didn't listen to them or bother watching it – even though they brought round the first series on boxset to tempt us. It sat on the side in our living room, unwatched, for a couple of years. Then one Sunday the only thing worth watching on TV was reruns of MTV's *Catfish* or some crappy black and white films, so we decided to give in to the boy's recommendations and see what all the fuss was about . . . we watched six episodes that day and whizzed through the rest of the series so that we were finally up-to-date before the finale aired.

Mind.

Blown.

Best ending ever.

'I'm so fucking excited right now,' he grins, drumming his legs with his hands.

'Me too.'

'I am not in danger, I am the danger,' he says – giving his best Walter White impression.

It's pretty good.

'I am the one who knocks,' I mimic back, trying to sound low and gravelly.

I'm awful but Real Brett is polite enough to laugh.

'I'm going to look,' I say quietly.

'Aaah . . .' Real Brett silently screams – his mouth opening as wide as Wallace's from *Wallace and Grommit*.

I try my best to look casual as I turn my head to the right – sweeping my eyes across the décor of the room as though I'm taking in the finer details of the usually simplistic Wagamama white walls and observing what the owners have done with the underground space – looking up to the street level with enthusiastic interest. I do so until I can't take it any more – I look down and there he is. Bryan Cranston sat talking to a female companion while tucking into some sort of noodle soup and a bowl of chilli edamame.

Fuck!

'Get your phone out – you could totally get a cheeky selfie with him in the background from where you're sat,' Brett says, his face animatedly excited.

'I hate selfies,' I state, my mind flicking to the amount of time I've spent ranting and cringing at Poutmouth Louisa for being a walking advocate for the current craze . . . photos used to be about capturing the image in front of you and recording the memory of a beautiful moment in time forever – now it's used to take a picture of yourself (taken from a stupid angle to get those cheek bones to appear and your double chins to disappear), and gloat on Facebook about how hot you look. It's a throwaway image that says nothing special . . .

'It's Heisenberg,' he says, rolling his eyes at my stubbornness. 'Pass it here and I'll take it then.'

'Fair enough,' I giggle, not really having to be talked into it too much. After all, this *is* an important, noteworthy moment that should be documented and posted on both Twitter and Facebook via Instagram (it's worth using the filters on this occasion – especially as I've been at work all day and look like crap personified). I reach down to my bag and pull out my phone. I click the main button to open the camera app, but before I do that, the screen lights up to let me know I've missed five calls from Carly, and have a voicemail.

'Sorry – I'll be right back,' I say, stepping away from Walter White and Real Brett. Pressing play, I lift the phone to my ear and take a deep breath, trying to ignore the feeling brewing in my gut, screaming at me that something's wrong. Why else would she have called so many times? She always mocks people who repeatedly call – not trusting that the person they're wanting to speak to would see that they've tried to call and phone back when they're able to talk. Let's face it, we all have our mobiles on us ninety-nine per cent of the time (we're in the shower for the other one per cent, or, if we're lucky, having sex) so although we can't necessarily tend to it every second of the day, we're still aware of activity flashing away on the crafty device.

'Sarah,' Carly sobs – ugly, needy and panicked.

I'm whacked by a block of ice.

Every part of my being goes cold.

'I don't know what to do . . . There's blood. Lots of it. Josh isn't here. I can't get hold of him. I don't know what to do. I think . . . I think . . . oh God . . . Fuck.'

Sobbing is all I hear until the message ends ten seconds later.

'Shit,' I mutter, trying not to panic, and drastically failing as I look at the phone in my hands.

'I need to go,' I blurt at Real Brett once I'm back at the table. I reach for my bag and put on my coat, all the while battling over what I should do – calling Carly back being the most obvious starting point, but I know I have to leave before I can do that. I need to go home.

'What? But we've not even ordered,' he says, standing up and putting his hands in his pockets as though it's his fault that I'm running out on him and our night of katsu delight.

'My friend . . . Carly,' I start, but can't finish. I wave my phone at him instead.

'Are you okay?' he asks, his green eyes searching mine, a frown of concern knitting above his brows before his face opens up with understanding – clearly jumping to the right conclusion. 'Oh fuck. Is she okay? Can I help at all?'

I shake my head as my bottom lip starts to tremble.

This is ridiculous. I really should just call Carly back before I get so upset.

'I've got to go. Sorry Real Brett,' I mumble, kicking myself for my slip up as I scurry away from the table, up the wooden stairs and out into the cold dark night.

'Sarah?' Carly says quietly, as soon as my hands have stopped shaking enough for me to regain the ability to press the dial button on my phone.

I'm surprised by her tone – so different to the panic in her voicemail that was left twenty minutes earlier.

'Everything's okay!' I state relieved, allowing myself to feel hopeful.

'No. No it's not,' she whispers.

'Oh Carly . . .'

'Mmm . . .'

Silence.

'Is there anything I can do?'

'Just come home? Can you? I don't want to be on my own.'

'Already on my way.' I say, sprinting to the tube.

'Have you spoken to Carly?' Josh asks when I'm out of the Underground and have signal on my phone once more.

'Yes, nearly home now,' I say as I lightly jog (it's all I can manage thanks to my appalling fitness level) towards the flat. 'Where are you?'

'I drove back up home to see Mum and Dad. I wish I hadn't. I wish I was there with her,' he sighs. 'I should be back in a few hours.'

'Are you okay to drive?' I ask. He sounds distraught at being anywhere other than by Carly's side.

'I have to be. I have to be there.'

'Just take your time and don't worry . . . We'll see you when we see you,' I say, trying to muster up some encouragement, calmness or hope, but failing dramatically – I just sound like a total twat instead.

I'm not looking forward to walking into our flat and into the devastation that could be waiting for me. Obviously I want to be there for Carly and help her through whatever is happening, but I'd do anything not to be doing so alone. I think about calling Natalia, or Alastair, as back-up or extra support, but realize it's not my place to do so. Carly called me to be there for her. Perhaps she, rather understandably, doesn't want to see our other mates right now. She must be shit scared.

'Sarah?' Josh asks softly from the other end of the line.

'Yes?'

'Tell her I love her,' he implores. 'I really do. I mean it.'

'I will do,' I say before hanging up, trying to swallow the lump that gathered in my throat from hearing the desperation in his voice.

When I get home I find Carly sat in our tiny hallway staring into space. She barely turns to acknowledge me when I walk through the door, but seconds later her head bows into her knees as she lets out a meek sigh.

'Oh darling . . .' I muster, walking to her and joining her on the floor.

She bites her lip and glimpses across at me, her face ashen with confusion.

'It's gone. Just like that,' she says, her eyes wide and unblinking.

'Are you sure?'

She nods.

'Shouldn't we go to the doctors, though?'

'Why?'

'Just to check?'

'It's definitely gone,' she says slowly and adamantly. 'I'm empty. Deflated.'

I nod, trying to understand what she's going through, knowing that all I can really do for her right now is to be there and listen.

'It was horrible.' She screws up her face at the thought of it. 'I saw my baby,' she says quietly, wanting to voice the memory of the sight feared by so many. 'It looked sort of like a baby too. I wasn't expecting that – I thought it would still be a gloopy lump of cells and tissue – but that was him or her. Our little creation. The little helpless being I've been so afraid of.'

'What did you do with . . . ?' I ask, not knowing what to call her lost baby. 'The doctor might want to see what . . . you know.'

'I flushed it down the loo . . .' Pause. Realization. 'I flushed my baby down the loo.'

'Don't think of it like that.'

'I did though. I was in shock. I wiped and it was all there and – '

Looking down at the hands she's held up, she stops herself. Not because it's gory and information she'd be

314

embarrassed to share – but because the image is clearly reforming before her.

The memory too rancid and cruel to forget so quickly.

She bites down hard on her bottom lip to rein herself back to reality, to regain control. When she talks again she is calm. 'I sat and stared at it for ages, unsure what to do – telling myself, blindly hoping, that it might not be what I knew it was. What I could see it was.'

I can feel my heart in my chest as I listen, hating feeling so inept and clumsy in my friendship – wishing I could take away the distress she must be feeling but working her hardest to suppress.

'I hate calling it an it,' she muses, continuing as though in conversation with herself. 'There would've been a heart-beat by now, you know – it was a living thing already. It wasn't an it.'

'It was your baby.'

'Yeah . . .' she says sadly. 'It was.'

She takes a deep breath before moving to lie across the floor in a foetal position, using my lap as her pillow. I can't help but run my fingers through her hair. In some feeble way I hope the soft touch might give her some comfort, but really I know it's more of an action for myself – to make me feel like I'm actually *doing* something to help lessen her burden, to console her and take the pain away.

She looks different. Older. Silently broken. Nothing like the strong and feisty ladette I've grown up with over the last decade.

'I knew it was coming,' she says, her quiet voice wavering just a sliver of a fraction. 'I woke up this morning and something didn't feel right. It was my boobs. My boobs told me this would happen. As soon as I found out I was pregnant they turned into these huge squidgy mounds of flesh – I couldn't stop touching them. They weren't hard or painful, they were just fuller and different. It blew my mind that my body was intuitively reacting to my growing baby so quickly. Today when I woke up, they were back to normal.' She pauses. 'It was already happening. I was already losing my baby. I've had cramps too – but I'd read up. Mild cramps are normal . . . the thing is, where do you draw the line between mild cramps and cramps? It's all so ambiguous.'

'I bet.'

'I've been on Google a lot,' she half laughs. ' And on every one of the pregnancy apps Josh made me down-load to keep us posted on our little one's growth and development. Unsurprisingly none of them really cover this outcome.'

'Probably don't want to worry people unnecessarily.'

'Yeah. Bit morbid.'

'Yeah,' I agree.

Pause.

'I should probably delete them now.'

'Have you spoken to Josh?' I ask. It seems like an appro-priate time to bring him up, seeing as she's mentioned him.

'I can't . . .' she says flatly, her face turning into my thighs. I wonder if she's crying.

'Why not?' I ask softly.

'I'm scared to. This little being was the start of some-thing crazy and new for us. It cemented us together and gave us a joint purpose, forcing us to stop hiding what was happening between us, make huge decisions and act. It made it all real. What do we have now?'

'You still have each other.'

'Do we?' she squeaks.

'He's your best friend.'

'But I failed him. I failed us. I failed our baby.'

'Oh darling, no you didn't.'

'I did. I knew this was going to happen. I knew it. I knew I was going to fuck it up.'

The disappointment in her voice is heartbreaking.

'This isn't your fault, my love.'

'Isn't it?'

'No.'

'That's debatable,' she sighs. 'It doesn't feel that way.'

'I know, but you mustn't think like that. It won't help,' I sigh. 'How do you feel? Physically. Are you in any pain?'

'It's like the worst period ever, but the pain barely resonates. It's nothing in comparison to the pain in my heart,' she says, her hand moving from her tummy up to rub her chest. 'I'm surprised I feel like this. I didn't know I wanted a baby so badly.'

'I don't think any of us know what we really want until we're put in a situation or have something snatched away from us. Maybe life is more about reacting rather than acting . . .'

'Deep.'

'I'm quite the philosopher,' I reply.

Silence takes over then. I think for a long while about what I could say to make her feel better, or to lighten the mood – but I come up with nothing. My brain fails me and instead I become conscious of my thinking and can only think about me thinking.

I'm useless. She should've phoned someone else.

'Do you think I deserved this?' she utters suddenly, breaking into my pathetic musings.

'How could you possibly?' I ask, trying to understand her thought pattern.

'I worried. Thought I didn't want it and worried about how I'd cope. I should've embraced it straight away.'

'I think a lot of women probably have the same fear but don't say it. I bet it's quite a taboo to have a moment of panic . . . although it seems standard for men to have a wobble.'

'You don't think I wished it upon myself, then? That somehow I made it happen? That I'm to blame?' she asks, all the while her tone steady and measured.

'No, darling,' I reply with a punch in my voice, letting her know that in no way do I think she deserves to be put through this torture. 'No, I don't.'

I hold on to her a little tighter, wishing I could take away the thoughts that'll haunt her for as long as she allows them to. Thoughts that are natural, heartbreaking and unjust.

My poor friend.

I'm lying in Carly's bed a few hours later when the bedroom door opens and I see Josh stopping to catch his breath in the doorway, before walking into the dark room.

'Baby?' he whispers.

'Josh?' she whimpers, not budging from her balled position in bed.

'Come here,' he breathes, going to her.

His strong arms find their way around her body, clutching on to her tightly in his strong embrace.

The bed shakes with their joint sobs.

Their joint loss.

Slowly, I manoeuvre myself from the bed and their private moment, and leave the room unnoticed.

I go to my own bed and weep for them.

26

I feel groggy when I wake up a few hours later, unable to open my eyes thanks to my throbbing headache. It takes a few seconds for this uncomfortable feeling to lift before the events of last night painfully creep in.

Oh shit.

My poor friend.

For a moment I imagine that it was all just a dream – or a nightmare. God knows I'm used to those being majorly fucked up at the moment. Although my heart isn't up to thinking about my nightly escapades with my imaginary lover. Instead it's with the couple next door who've had their own hearts ripped out and trampled on unfairly.

Oh life, what the hell are you playing at?

I drag myself from my bed and sneak into the bathroom, getting ready for work quickly and quietly – wanting to get out of the flat without disturbing Carly or Josh, who could probably do with a few more hours' sleep. I can't imagine how confused and hurt they will be feeling when they wake up, I can't even begin to imagine their heartache.

My phone rings and vibrates across my bedside table, and I run to get it before it wakes the others.

It's Natalia.

'Sar?' she sniffs.

'Hey . . .' I whisper.

'Has she?'

'Yeah,' I sigh.

'Oh, fuck.'

'It's been awful.'

'Our poor little lamb,' she chokes, beginning to sob.

'How did you know?'

'She left me a voicemail. I was out with my bosses and forgot to listen to it when I got in.'

'Oh . . .' I groan, thinking back to the horrendous voicemail Carly had left me.

'I should've listened to it.'

'Nat, you weren't to know,' I say, sitting on my bed, hating that she's feeling awful and wishing I'd have called her. If Nat had seen us both try to reach her she'd have known something was up.

'I should've been there.'

'Don't beat yourself up, it wouldn't have made a difference.'

'I know, but . . .' she takes a deep breath. 'I could've just hugged her.'

I listen as more sobs escape and feel helpless.

'How is she?'

'She's been better. Josh is here now and I think that'll help.'

'How's he?'

'The same.'

'Fuck.'

We sit in silence for a moment, both wrapped up in our own thoughts. Unable to put into words how we feel about the situation and finding it impossible to verbalize our sorrow for our friends' heartbreak.

'I love you,' Natalia eventually says.

'I love you, too,' I whisper.

'I'll call you later.'

'Okay, love,' I say, putting down the phone before sitting there and staring at the blank screen.

Taking a deep breath, I scribble out a note for Carly and Josh, telling them I love them, and then leave it on the kitchen worktop before tiptoeing out of the front door, breathing out a sigh as I walk away from our home and make my way to the station.

My phone vibrates in my pocket – I grab it and see it's my brother.

'Max,' I croak, picking up the phone, surprised to hear how awful I sound now that I've spoken above a whisper for the first time today – the emotion of last night gripping my throat so tightly that my voice is on lockdown.

'Morning, Aunty Sarah,' he yells gaily, his voice booming down the phone line.

'Ouch,' I moan, the noise bashing against my aching head. 'Morning to you, too.'

I hear a snigger on the line.

'Wait! What?' I scream stopping on the pavement, suddenly hearing what he's said. 'The baby's here?'

'Yes, little Mavis Rose is here. She arrived about twenty minutes ago,' he says, choking up.

'Oh my God!' I scream, continuing on my walk to the Underground. Even though we've all been waiting for the little one's arrival for the past nine months, I can't help but feel shocked that the day's actually arrived. 'I love the name! What's she like?'

'She's so tiny and beautiful,' he gushes.

'Who does she look like, you or Andrea?'

'Dad actually.'

'Dad?' I scoff.

'A pretty version,' he states, his voice telling me he's wearing a ridiculously goofy new-dad grin. 'I'm in awe of her. She's perfect.'

'So you're already wrapped around her little finger?'

'Happily so,' he laughs.

'And how's Andrea? How was it all?'

'I can't even tell you how amazing she was. I've never seen anything like it.'

'Did you watch, then?'

'Of course I did. It was the craziest sight I've ever seen – I still can't get my head around it,' he says in a high-pitched voice.

I can't help but laugh at the thought of my brother witnessing his child being brought into the world. He's always been so squeamish, so I'm surprised to hear he hadn't fainted and stayed horizontal while Andrea did all the hard work.

'Have you told Mum and Dad yet?'

'Thought I'd call you first – otherwise Mum would've put Dad on and called you herself.'

'Ha! I've no doubt she would,' I laugh, a tear streaming down my face as I think of their reactions when they hear the news that they've been made grandparents overnight. 'Are you okay though?'

'Yes. Better than yes.'

'When can I come meet her?' I ask.

'As soon as you like. We'll be here for the rest of the day, at least,' he says. 'I'd better go call them now, but, Sarah, life is so fucking incredible.'

'It is,' I say, my voice catching in my throat as I say it.

I'm outside The Barge Café by the time Max hangs up. I stop and sit on one of their benches as a whirlwind of emotions gets the better of me. I weep a mixture of happy and sad tears. Happy ones for my brother and Andrea for the safe arrival of Mavis Rose and the life they've started together, and sad ones for my gorgeous friends who've had their new life snatched away from them. The two scenarios are worlds apart, and I can't help but feel awful for them happening so close together. When I feel happy for Max, I see the look of anguish on Carly's face and hear the sound of the gut-wrenching duet of sobs that leaked through the walls of her bedroom throughout the night.

Unable to stop myself, I bury my face in my arms and let a tirade of tears fall, not caring that I might draw attention to myself, not even thinking about passers-by.

I'm full on sobbing when I feel a hand on my shoulder and an arm reach around, pulling me into an embrace.

It's only when I smell the familiar scent of Issey Miyake that I realize it's Dan.

I instantly feel myself stiffen.

'Sorry,' I sniff, unable to stop my sobs or steady my breathing, as I try to pull away and wipe the tears from my face.

'Shh,' he says, pulling me tighter into him so that my head is on his chest.

I don't fight to wriggle free from the hold that I once knew so well; instead I take warmth from it, and feel myself slowly melting into it, letting him comfort me.

'You okay?' he whispers, once my breathing has slowed down.

I exhale in reply, and break away from him so that my body is no longer against his, although I let him take hold of my hands and cradle them.

'I've heard,' he says quietly, his blue eyes pained. 'Josh phoned me last night when he was on his way back – think he needed someone to talk to while he was driving, to keep him calm.'

'You spoke the whole way?' I sniff, rubbing my nose with the back of my hand.

'We got cut off a few times,' he shrugs, pulling a tissue out of the pocket of his hoodie and handing it to me.

'Thanks. You're not on your way to work?' I ask, noticing his jogging bottoms and trainers.

'No. Didn't really feel up to it today . . . thought I'd go for a run instead.'

'Right,' I nod.

He lets out a big sigh and readjusts his beanie hat with one hand, the other grabbing hold of mine again.

'Poor Carly and Josh,' I mumble, my thoughts staying with them.

'How were they last night?'

'Awful. I feel so bad for them,' I say, shaking my head at the memory. 'I just wish I could make it all disappear for them. Yes. Okay. We all knew they were going to have a struggle on their hands and that it wasn't exactly the picture perfect set-up – but they would've made it work. I know they would've.'

'He wasn't at his parents last night,' Dan says, biting his lip, wanting to tell me whatever he knows, but feeling guilty for doing so.

'Where was he, then?'

'At her parents' house, asking for permission to marry her,' he says sadly.

'Shit,' I say, holding back a fresh stream of tears.

'Yeah. How's that for a come-down of emotions.'

'Imagine him driving home, thinking he was going to, and then . . .' I say, unable to finish the sentence, weeping at the thought of our cuddly Josh when he received that devastating call from Carly.

'Yeah.'

'That's just awful.'

'Me and Lexie went through the same thing,' Dan says quietly, swallowing hard, suddenly developing a dry mouth from starting up this thread of conversation.

'Yeah?' I say, feeling myself tense up and not really wanting to know more.

'Only Josh knew about it. It was right after we – you know.'

'Split up,' I reply flatly, saying the words for him – watching as a young mum power walks past us behind her Bugaboo pram.

'Yeah' he says, following my gaze before looking down at the ground. 'We hadn't even been together long and things were still awful between you and me.'

'They were never awful.'

'Only because you boxed away all your feelings and pretended it wasn't happening,' he says calmly, his brow gently knitting together at the memory.

'I never did that,' I lie, causing Dan to shake his head at me.

'Lexie was only six weeks gone when it happened,' he says after a pause, looking up at me. 'And, although I felt awful about her and the baby – I felt worse about the fact that I didn't know her. That I found it difficult to talk to her about what I was feeling.' He looks down at our hands and covers the tops of mine with his. 'All I actually wanted to do was pick up the phone and call you,' he says quietly.

'Me?'

'You knew me. You'd know to just let me speak when I was ready, to let me stew in my own misery for a little bit. She didn't know me. She wanted to talk about everything and send our prayers up into the sky on a fucking paper lantern,' he says, jokingly huffing at the thought, although unable to hide his pain.

'She'd have been hurting too,' I say.

'I know, and worse than me. It killed me that I didn't know her well enough to take that hurt away.'

'Well, you know her well enough now,' I say, offering a sad smile, not entirely sure what to do with this new information about a time that wounded me so badly, but feeling my barriers drop as a result of his honesty.

'I'm sorry I was such a shit to you, Sarah.'

'You weren't,' I lie again.

Dan raises his eyebrows at me in response.

'Okay, you were.'

'Cheers,' he nods and half-laughs. 'I'd have made it right, I'd have tried – only that all happened and I got sidetracked.'

'It's understandable,' I shrug. 'It's in the past now.'

'But it's not. Is it,' he whispers, his fingertips stroking the top of my hand, stirring a tenderness between us that's been buried for the last two years.

'What do you mean?' I croak, suddenly realizing this is the first time I've been alone with Dan since he broke my heart – and not entirely sure how I feel about it. Part of me wants to run away, but the other wants me to stay and listen to whatever he feels he has to share – and he knows that. He's got me as his audience, so he pounces, while he's got the chance.

'I want you to stop hiding everything that's bubbling away inside of you. I want you to give me all the abuse I deserve. I want us to be – '

'To be what?' I shrug, exhaling a quick breath. 'We are all we can be.'

'But I need you to forgive – '

'Dan,' I say, stopping him, not wanting to go there, not wanting this to turn into a big dramatic chat where I pour my heart out and cry ugly girl tears to someone who'll run back to their future wife as though nothing's changed. But I'm also nervous of the anger that's mounted inside me, and that it's going to charge at him like the monster I've been becoming in my dreams.

I don't want to become that irrational beast.

'But I need you to forgive me,' he tries again. 'There's always this thing, this uncomfortable, unspoken thing – yes, you're all lovely and bubbly on the surface, but you forget that I know you.'

'You knew me,' I correct him. 'You knew me and you decided to leave me.'

'But I want my friend back,' he begs.

'I'm still here, aren't I?'

'I know it's awkward. I know I'm a shit for loving someone else and not hiding that fact.'

'You shouldn't have to hide it,' I tut.

'But I hurt you. I see it. I notice you watching and it's like a dagger in my heart. A constant reminder of what I did to you.'

'Dan, please,' I say, squeezing his hand, wincing as I watch the agony on his face.

'I just don't know what I can do to make it right.'

I take a deep breath, exhaling slowly as I think about our past, present and future.

'Just love the girl you left me for with all your heart and never hurt her,' I say, managing some kind of a smile. 'Never let her go. Then I'll know what you put me through was all worthwhile.'

Dan hangs his head, raises my hands to his lips and kisses them before clutching them to his heart.

This time I lean forward and give him a hug.

We sit there in an embrace for a few moments and I feel my anger wane. A huge part of me will always love the guy in my arms. Yes, he's a total twat at times and has done some heinous things to me, but he's also someone that I cared for for a very long time and who I shared so much with. Seeing as he's going to be in my life, whether I like it or not, I should probably let myself see the good again, rather than recoil in horror whenever he's near.

Just being there with him, in this less hostile manner, causes a literal weight to be lifted. I could say I wished we'd talked months ago about our situation, but I don't think I was ready to hear it then. Now I am. Now I know that if I open my heart again, it won't be sadly longing for Dan's affection, instead it's moving forward.

'I can't believe we're having this chat today,' he exhales,

breaking away from our hug and rubbing his hands along his cheeks. 'I was an emotional wreck already.'

'Same,' I say, wiping my face once more, breathing out a puff of air as I think about everything that's happened in the past twelve hours. 'I'd better get going.'

'You heading into work?' he asks, looking surprised.

I nod. 'Carly's got Josh there with her today. Wanted to give those guys some space.'

'You could always come over to mine if you don't fancy going in? Lexie would understand if you wanted somewhere to go,' he adds, letting me know it's not a scandalous offer.

'Actually, I think keeping busy will do me good. Plus it's manic there,' I say, standing, not entirely sure that the setting of their happy home is where I'd like to be today either – even if we have just patched up our troubled friendship.

'Of course. Well, I'm going to go for a run and continue to skive,' he says, also getting to his feet.

'Right, well you have fun,' I say.

We stand awkwardly, looking at one another, unsure how to say goodbye.

'Thank you,' he says, gently pulling me close, softly giving me a kiss on the cheek.

I close my eyes and receive his love.

I squeeze his hand and turn on my heels before the tender gesture makes me burst into tears.

'I've been wondering where you'd got to,' says Jonathan when I eventually get to the office half an hour later than normal.

'Oh, I'm sorry,' I say, turning from my desk to face him.

I must look awful because his expression suddenly changes to one of fear – probably worried I'm about to ugly-girl wail in the office and cause a scene, meaning he'd have to bumble around trying to offer some sort of awkward comfort.

'Ah, no problem. I'll be in here,' he mutters, widening his eyes at Julie before turning back into his office, removing himself from the situation.

'You okay, love?' asks Julie, looking concerned.

'Not really. Rough night.' Pause. 'Carly,' I say in way of explanation.

She instantly gets it and offers a sympathetic look. 'I'm sorry to hear that.'

'Boardroom?' Real Brett swiftly asks/suggests/guides as he walks past with a coffee in his hand.

'Erm,' I sound, looking at my desk.

'I've got the Christmas stuff sorted, don't you worry,' says Julie, almost reading my mind. 'Jonathan's mentioned about booking a few rooms for people as treats – you and me included – so I'll get on to that and see if anyone else wants in.'

'Nice,' I mutter in a daze, as I retrieve the notebook from my bag and follow Real Brett.

'Thought you might want to hibernate in here today,' he says, pulling out a chair for me to sit in and handing me the cup of coffee.

'Thanks.'

'And before it plagues you, I guess we should address the elephant in the room.'

'What's that?' I ask, getting ready for him to talk about Carly and what happened last night.

'Yes, I did stay after you left and I did eat a katsu. I even had some salted edamame . . . and duck gyoza. Just don't judge.'

I smile at him before making my face serious again. 'I see. Well, that's disappointing, Brett.'

'Thought it was best to be honest.'

'You're right.'

'Actually, I also had the chilli prawns,' he adds guiltily, biting on his bottom lip.

'Wow, quite a feast,' I smile, wondering how he manages to keep in such great shape with his questionable diet. I eat a single slice of cake and instantly put on a stone, whereas he seems to constantly stuff his face with treats.

'And I know what else you're wondering. You're wondering whether I managed to get a selfie with Walter White. Well, no. With you there it would've been fun, but on my own it was geekish.'

'Oh damn, you missed out on your chance.'

'I thought about it, but some dude got in there before me and was a total blow-out, doing impressions to the poor guy's face – at least we did ours behind his back,' he says incredulously. 'Thought it was best to leave it because I would've undoubtedly been a total fangirl slash moron.'

I know what he's doing. He's being extra light and breezy to distract me from my thoughts. I admire him for doing it, considering he's only known me for a few weeks.

'Thank you,' I say.

'What for? Not getting the picture? That would've seriously earned me some credit with the boys at rugby.'

'No . . . for being sweet.'

'You mean my natural self?'

'Yes . . . if that's what it is.'

'There's only one Brett Last. Well, actually – it's a common name. There's probably loads of us,' he shrugs, looking bashful as he goes to the shelf and pulls down the pile of travel guidebooks we'd been searching through the day before. 'Time to disappear to somewhere new . . .'

I grab the *Rough Guide to Melbourne* and turn to the page I'd left it on the previous night. 'On another note, I became an aunty today,' I tell him, part of me wanting the world to know that a very special little lady has arrived and feeling extremely proud of my brother and sister-in-law. 'My brother's wife had a little girl called Mavis Rose.'

'Well how's that for juxtaposition?'

'Tell me about it.'

'When are you going to go meet her?'

'Today at some point,' I smile, feeling the stirring of mixed emotions in my gut that have been gurgling away all morning.

'Why don't you go now?' he asks with a shrug.

'I couldn't do that.'

'We've got ten people we want to meet to see if they're right for the project. If I book some appointments in this afternoon we can say we're both there. I don't mind doing them on my own – providing you trust my judgement.'

'Erm . . .'

'I'll film them so that you can watch it all back,' he offers with a smile, letting me know that he's not too offended that I'm sceptical over his ability to interview old people without me.

I sigh, not knowing what to do.

'What's wrong?'

'Nothing,' I shrug, not wanting to tell someone I barely know how I'm feeling.

'Right . . .' he nods, licking his lips and pursing them together. 'My sister has a little baby. A boy, called Matthew. I was going through some really shitty things when he was born, but I met him and it blew everything else out of the water . . . it won't make things better for Carly, but you'll be amazed at the magnitude of the love you feel pouring out of you when you meet Mavis Rose.'

'I just keep thinking about Carly and what she'll be feeling today. I'd feel guilty having that rush of love when I know what a state she's in,' I answer truthfully.

'I get that,' he nods, offering a sympathetic smile. 'It's a horrible situation all round. However, Carly and Josh? They'll probably have other children – they've got a whole future together to decide exactly what it is that they want. But your niece? Well, she's here now, and she's waiting to meet her aunty.'

'Oh fuck,' I mutter as my eyes start leaking for the hundredth time today.

27

Her tiny button nose is what makes me adore her instantly.

Her ickle mouth, lips and chin make me want to kiss her continuously.

Her fragility and the fact that she weighs next to nothing make me want to protect her for evermore against the brutality of the world she's yet to discover.

Her dainty fingers, when all of hers wrap around one of mine and tightly squeeze, make me love her with everything that I am.

And when she opens her eyes . . .

I am floored.

My love is limitless.

My love knows no bounds.

'She's perfect,' I say repeatedly, meaning it every time the words come out of my mouth.

'Isn't she just,' coos my mum, coming over and sneaking another peak at her granddaughter.

'She really does look like Dad, though,' I laugh, screwing my face up at Andrea, who's in her nightie, resting in the hospital bed. She looks fantastic, as though she hadn't been in labour throughout the night. Her honey-streaked brown hair is tied back in a scrunchie and her make-up-free skin looks flawless. She smiles over at us looking serene and in love.

Love.

The room is filled with it.

'Can you believe you made this?' I ask her.

'It all feels so surreal,' she says, shaking her head.

With Dad and Max out of the room fetching coffees, we persuade Andrea to close her eyes and rest while we talk quietly next to her, cuddling Mavis Rose.

'Nice of Jonathan to give you the time off,' Mum says, as she strokes her granddaughter's face and chuckles when she yawns. I've never seen her like this – all gooey and warm. 'He's been working you hard.'

'Yeah,' I agree, deciding not to tell her that I'm effectively skiving off work.

'Is it all coming together, though?'

'Seems to be,' I nod.

'How's Carly?'

'Not good,' I say, looking down at Mavis and holding on to the miracle of life a little tighter. 'She lost the baby last night.'

Mum doesn't say anything, but she puts her arm around my shoulder as we continue to look down at the bundle in my arms.

I stay at Mum and Dad's over the weekend. We go to visit Max, Andrea and Mavis Rose, watch a lot of zombie TV (not *The X Factor* – they still can't stand it) and then Mum and I go on long walks together (Dad stays at home because his knee's continuing to play up), and just take in the Kent countryside. Surprisingly I don't feel like killing Mum at the end of it. She doesn't push, prod, moan or rile in the way I usually expect from her. Instead she's strong, silent and present – which is just what I need. Someone to just be there for me without loading all their own thoughts and feelings on to me.

I check in with Carly and Josh every so often to see how they are. They're coping, they say – which I believe as I even hear laughter during one call, which reassures me that their hearts are on their way to healing somewhat.

The following week whizzes by in a blur as the final full week before Christmas means we have to cram in as much planning as possible before everywhere closes for the holidays. We have met several old people – Real Brett interviewed a cracking old Welsh lady called Gwyn who had him in stitches during their whole encounter (it was fun to watch back), so we went to visit her together and confirmed her for the trip, as well as shortlisting four others who are all on board for leaving late February for their trip of a lifetime when finalized. We've phoned around to various Australian locations from Sydney to Whitsunday, Melbourne to The Great Barrier Reef and Perth to Adelaide – plus we've added New Zealand as a possibility, depending on what we find when we head out there for the recce. It's been non stop and I breathe a sigh of relief when the 22nd of December rolls around and it's the final day at work *and* the day of the Christmas party – which doesn't really count as a working day as I'm sure pretty sure there's going to be drinking over lunchtime as well as an afternoon of fooling around thanks to the aforementioned lunchtime drinks.

Unsurprisingly there's quite a buzz surrounding tonight's bash as a few people have realized they can get as wasted and debauched as they like, knowing they've not got to face anyone else in the office for another two weeks. Well, it is meant to be a chance for them to let their hair down and I know a fair few of them are going to grab that opportunity by the horns and pour as many free drinks down their gullets as they can manage – which I'm sure shot-pusher Julie will encourage.

Jonathan calls us in at the start of the day to see how we've managed to get on with our plans. Even though we've cc'd him in on all the important emails, as his PA, I know most of those have been left unopened in his inbox or just skimmed through. Luckily we've not needed his input seeing as Damian has kept a close eye on the project, happy with how we've been progressing.

'Everything organized?' he asks, jamming a creamy chocolate éclair into his mouth, which makes my mouth water hungrily.

'We think so,' I nod.

'And when do you leave?'

'We leave for Oz on the ninth for three weeks,' I say with a nod, swallowing hard at the thought of being away for so long and also spending that much time with Real Brett. He's been a real sweetheart over the past week and a real friend – but being together in such close proximity for that long has certainly given me something to think about when I can't sleep at night. 'There's lots to see and sort through.'

'Yes,' Jonathan agrees, not giving the slightest grumble that we're going to be away from the office for that length of time. 'It's best all the technical stuff gets sorted before you're out there with the OAPs and camera crews, et cetera. People get huffy when they have to wait, and the costs start rising quickly. Plus, the heat over there – that's what you'll be up against. It'll be a busy three weeks.'

'We're still not sure about New Zealand yet,' Real Brett informs him. 'We've made contact with a few different companies and tour groups over there, but we'll know more once we've seen a bit of Australia.'

'Yes, yes,' Jonathan nods, licking cream off his fingers before wiping his wet hands on his trousers to dry them.

Somehow I manage to resist screwing up my face in disgust at the sight.

'You two both seem to know what you're doing. A great project to end the year on. What a wonderful team you make,' he says, standing up and extending the hand he's just sucked cream off out for a handshake.

I go along with it, all the while trying not to vomit, thrilled when he finally lets us out of the room.

'Kitchen?' Real Brett mutters in my ear.

'To fumigate my hand? Oh, yes please!' I grimace, as we charge through the office and into the little kitchen area.

'Me first,' he says snatching up the soap and rubbing it between his hands, lathering it up so that his hands are white and foamy.

'My turn, my turn,' I quietly squeal with a giggle, shaking my offending hand out to the side.

'Ahhhh . . .' Real Brett groans, stamping his feet and continuing to friction burn the soap.

'You're hogging it,' I moan like a petulant child. 'It's my turn!' I say, playfully grabbing at his hands and trying to extract the white bar.

My attempt fails. Instead, it slides from Real Brett's slippery grasp, ricochets off my foot and flies underneath the kitchen cabinet beside us.

'Fuck!'

'Ha!' Real Brett smugly laughs, swirling his creamy hands in my face.

Without thinking, I grab his hands and run mine all over them, so that the soap covers my hands too. As my fingers glide between his and our palms meet, my mind flashes to my bedtime encounter with Dream Brett – in the hot tub that David Beckham and Justin Bieber sat in before Dream Brett and I had crazy wet sex in it.

I look up to see Real Brett's green eyes sparkling in my direction and realize I have a sudden urge to kiss him.

My face gets all flustered as I gasp in shock and whip my hands away.

'You okay?' he asks.

'Me? Yeah, yeah . . . hate germs,' I mumble, running the tap and washing off the soapy bubbles from my arms, feeling like an absolute moron as I shake them off and go back out to my desk.

28

I get ready for the evening in my own room at the hotel – a lovely treat for Julie and me, from Jonathan and Derek, for all the help we've given them this year. I'd rather have had the money as a nice little bonus for the work I've pulled off in Development, but I know I shouldn't be such a cheeky bitch and that I should be thankful for the gesture – especially as the hotel room is all kinds of epic.

'What have you decided to wear?' asks Carly as she lounges on the lavish white sheets of the humongous bed in my enormous room.

I called her as soon as I got here and, seeing as she only works up the road, she decided to come check it out. I've been amazed at her strength. Sure, I still see the glimmer of sadness in her eyes when she's looking thoughtfully off into a world of her own, but she seems brighter eighty per cent of the time – and she appears to have stopped crying . . . at least in front of me.

'It's got to be the black number,' I say to her, opening the wardrobe and pulling out a slinky floor-length gown.

'Eurgh,' she groans, flinging herself into the piles of pillows placed on the bed.

'What? Is it awful?'

'It's fucking amazing,' she cries. 'It's just totally unfair that I'd look like a total goth if I tried that with my blonde hair. I bet you look stunning in it though with your dark mane and eyes.'

I flash her a cheeky smile because, for once, I know I do. I look hot . . . shit hot! The way the material cascades down and around my curves makes me feel sexier than ever – and the dainty, barely there straps give the illusion that my body is doing all the work to keep this dress on – but that it might just slip off with ease if I wanted it to. The dress might cover up ninety per cent of my body, but it really brings my sex appeal up to a whole new level.

'You're going to sleep with Brett!' Carly exclaims, her jaw dropping as though the thought has just entered her head.

'What? No I'm not!' I exclaim.

'You're smirking – you so are.'

'Carly!'

'Okay, fine,' she says walking around the bed and standing by my side to inspect the dress a little closer. 'Oh this hem is lovely . . .' she mumbles, bending down to touch what I'm sure is a normal seam with nothing special, before whipping out a hand and stroking my smooth leg. 'I knew it!' she yells.

'What?' I ask, running away from her with a squeal.

'You've shaved your legs! Girls only shave their legs if they're going to have sex. It's a fact.'

'Carly, I can't remember the last time I had sex – if that were the rule then I'd be like a chimp by now.'

'But you've also put cream on them.'

'They were dry,' I shrug, willing my cheeks not to redden.

'It's the expensive smelly stuff you asked for last Christmas.'

'I'm allowed to treat myself,' I whine.

'Fine,' she huffs, crossing her arms and scrutinizing me with her eyes. 'Show us your foof.'

'What?!' I laugh, pulling the gorgeous white hotel bath-robe around me a little tighter.

'You definitely wouldn't bother shaving that unless you were hoping for some action,' she decides, lunging for me, her hands grabbing at the white material.

'Carly, get off!' I scream, slapping her hands away.

'Show me your foof,' she demands, continuing to reach for my clothes.

'No, you twat.'

'I want to see it.'

'No.'

'Why?'

'Because . . . because I look like a pubic hair model from the seventies. It's a proper bush down there. Big. Bushy . . . nasty. A forest! Can barely see through the trees.'

'You fucking liar,' she giggles, as we grapple around on the floor and slap each other some more before coming to a breathless giggling mess of a heap in the middle of the room.

'You're nuts,' I breathe, closing my eyes and wiping the laughter tears from my face – thank God I hadn't started putting on my make-up yet, it would've been totally ruined.

With my hands preoccupied, Carly laughs and whips open my robe, catching a good view of my freshly shaved bikini line.

'I knew it!' she shrieks.

'You bitch,' I laugh in shock, pulling the material back around me.

'You're gonna get some, you're gonna get some,' she sings, while waving her arms and shaking her hips around in a way that I hope is not how she performs in the bedroom.

'It doesn't mean we're going to have sex,' I exclaim.

'It means you'd like to.'

'It means that if we were to be totally unprofessional and ended up making the most of this fucking amazing room then at least I would be prepared.'

'Slut,' she grins.

'It would be such a bad idea though,' I groan, hating myself for thinking through the matter logically and wondering whether the champagne at lunch might've gone to my head for the thought to even be in there anyway.

'Why?'

'Because, we're going to Australia together for three whole weeks. Imagine if it's really shit sex and horribly awkward – we're then going to have to pretend it didn't happen and the whole thing would be so embarrassing.'

'That could happen. Or it could be mind-blowingly good and you could spend that whole three weeks doing more of the same.'

'Carly!' I say, giving her arm a slap.

'Don't act like the thought hadn't crossed your mind.'

'It could just be really disappointing and awful.'

'Because you're used to having space sex?' she asks smugly, raising both her eyebrows at me. 'Babe, everything is going to be shit compared to that – you just have to face facts there.'

'Thanks.'

'It's the truth. You're rusty and he's not the guy you've

344

been fantasizing about. Doesn't mean it can't be orgasmic, though,' she grins.

'It won't happen . . . it really shouldn't.'

Before Carly can retort with a reply there's a loud banging from above and the sound of distant groaning.

'Well, looks like someone's getting it,' she shrugs. 'Now, what's on the room service menu? I'm starving.'

Over the next hour, Carly sits on the bed (wearing the other white dressing gown she's found in the wardrobe) and eats her burger and fries while watching me get ready. When my make-up is as near to perfect as it's going to be (it's drastically flawed, but it's a smudgy black eye look so I think I'll get away with it), I put on my dress and step into my heels.

'Holy shit!' Carly gawps when I walk out of the bathroom. 'I'm so glad Josh can't see you right now – he totally picked the wrong friend to shag. I need to take a picture.'

She grabs her phone and starts clicking.

'Stand over here,' she bosses, while I walk around and pose like a model, grabbing on to the chair, table and bed – using them all as my props as I giggle my way across the room. 'So stunning.'

'Thanks,' I gush, feeling giddy. 'Right, I'd better get downstairs and check everything's ready for everyone – I'd planned to do it before people started arriving but someone's made getting ready a task and a half.'

'Or you spent too long shaving your fanny hair into a heart shape and lost track of the time?' she suggests with a cheeky grin.

'Ha-de-ha,' I say, rolling my eyes at her while chucking a pillow in her direction.

She catches it and hugs it to her chest.

'Are you going to stay here?' I ask. 'You're more than welcome to – I'm going to be downstairs anyway.'

'Only for a bit,' she sighs, stuffing a chip into her mouth – her face screwing up when she realizes it's cold. 'Josh is going to come pick me up and we're going to head back to ours.'

'Nice.'

'God, this has been fun,' she says, sliding the room service tray away from her and climbing into the bed. 'Feel like I haven't laughed like that in ages.'

'You foof hunter!'

'You should totally pitch that as a new TV show,' she gasps.

'Bye, Carly,' I sing, giving her a kiss on the forehead, grabbing my bag and walking out of the door.

I'm not even at the lift before my phone bleeps, telling me I have a new Facebook notification 'Carly Pearson has added a photo of you'. I click on the link to see it's one of me from minutes ago – laughing while holding on to the chair, my shoulders forward, highlighting my collarbones and giving a great view of my ample cleavage. 'A beauty, inside and out,' is what she's written alongside it.

'Love you,' I comment, to which she replies with a big red heart.

I'm delighted when I see the function room. Battered brown leather sofas have been moved to the edges of the room, all gathered in groups for people to sit on, with miniature twinkly Christmas trees used as the centrepieces for each of the wooden coffee tables placed amongst them. Along the bar

346

there's a garland of holly and ivy – stuffed with festive choc-olates and sweets for people to pick and nibble at while waiting to be served. Above the makeshift black and white dance floor, in the centre of the room, is a collection of beautiful arrangements made out of mistletoe – far more pleasing on the eye than haphazardly sticking springs of the stuff up here and there, which is what Jonathan suggested doing when Julie insisted we needed the kiss-inducing twigs. The room is dark, atmospheric and subtly festive.

I love it.

Watching my colleagues already lapping up the party I'd planned for them, I reach for a celebratory glass of cham-pagne from the waiter stood at the entrance greeting all the guests, and breathe a sigh of relief that it's all come together so seamlessly and without any drama.

'Wow,' I hear from behind me as soon as the glass touches my lips.

I turn to see Real Brett walking in, looking unbelievably fit in a dark green velvet blazer over black trousers and shiny black patent shoes.

'I did good,' I nod, gesturing around the room.

'On both counts,' he says, his eyes looking me up and down. 'You look sensational.'

Suddenly I feel very naked, and sexily so. I look down in what I hope is a demure manner (move over Marilyn), failing to hide a smile at his praise.

'Well . . . thank you. You look pretty suave yourself.'

He nods his head to accept the compliment.

'Brett, where's your drink?' gasps Julie, galloping over, grabbing him by the arm and giving it a squeeze. 'Ooh, haven't you two scrubbed up well.'

'So have you,' Real Brett smiles, looking down at her heavily beaded pink dress and matching kitten heels – she still looks mumsy, but at least now she looks like a mum at a wedding.

'She's quite the minx, aren't you, Julie,' I tease.

Come on,' she says, tugging on Real Brett's blazer and looping her arm through his. 'Let's get to the bar. Time to start the party.'

'Here she comes,' I laugh. 'Shot-pusher Julie.'

'God help us all,' replies Real Brett with a look of panic as Julie whisks him off.

I grin at them as they go, laughing as he reaches an arm out to me as though he needs saving.

'I'll see you in a bit,' I whisper, flashing him a wink.

Turning back to look at the room, I spot Poutmouth Louisa living up to her name – holding her iPhone high in the air and doing her best duck impression whilst opening her eyes as wide as possible (stopping the moment before her forehead would crease up – that would not be a good look). She's dressed in a tiny neon orange bandeau body-con dress, and is wearing the highest and brightest electric blue shoes I've ever seen. Hanging off her arm, rather appropriately, is a dark red bag in the shape of giant lips.

We look like we should be at completely different events.

She spots me watching and smiles. 'Great work.'

'Thanks.'

'How are the plans coming along for Oz?' she asks, tottering over and sipping on her champagne.

'Really good. I think we're on top of it all,' I nod politely – still irked from our conversation in the loos at work. I've managed to largely avoid her ever since.

'Good, good,' she smarms, her eyes narrowing slightly. 'Such a shame you didn't want me on the recce with you.'

'It's not that I didn't want you there,' I say, rolling my eyes.

'It's okay,' she stops me, looking over at Julie and Real Brett at the bar downing shots together. 'I totally understand why . . .'

'It's not like that.'

'Isn't it? I mean, I'd probably do the same thing if given the opportunity to spend three weeks away from the office with a hot bloke.'

'You said you thought he was a drip.'

'Did I? Must've changed my mind,' she says slowly, pouting her lips at me.

'Louisa, give it a rest. It was all Jonathan. He's the one who pushed all this forward.'

'Hmm . . .' she sounds. 'Officially you're still just his PA though, right?'

'Well, yeah . . .'

'So who's going to be looking after him when you go away? It's a long time to be absent from the office.'

'Julie, I guess,' I say, realizing it's not actually been addressed with me, although I'm sure Jonathan would've spoken to her about it and cleared it with Derek.

'Gosh. I wonder if she minds . . .' Louisa says. 'It's a lot to take on.'

'She's not said anything.'

'No, I expect she hasn't,' she sings, widening her eyes and looking over at Julie as though she's finding the situation amusing.

'She'd say if she wasn't happy,' I say firmly.

349

'I'm sure she would. Well, well done. You've done really well for yourself,' she says without a hint of sincerity before strutting off to chat to Siobhan from Research.

I'm dumbfounded at her audacity to be such a cow on such a lovely evening – and the fact that she suddenly thinks Real Brett is attractive.

How dare she.

Bitch.

I'm frowning at her pert behind when Julie grabs me by the hand, 'Let's dance!', she yells, dragging me and Real Brett along with her. We look at each other with worried faces as we nervously side-jig to the cheesy music being played.

The dance floor is empty when I'm thrown on it. However, all it takes is a bit of 'Dancing Queen', 'Don't Stop Me Now' and 'Sex on Fire' for people to get off their backsides (or to step away from the bar) and join us in making questionable shapes and shaking our booties. Then, as hit after hit plays, cheers of appreciation rise at the start of each song – keeping us on our feet as we belt out the tunes and boogie away.

Julie disappears soon after getting us there, no doubt to rally more victims on to her fun train, so Real Brett and I stick together. When 'I'm Still Standing' plays we partner up as though we're on *Strictly*, shimmying our torsos and showing off with our wildest jazz hands, as we side kick and jump around.

It's fun.

We're fun.

Gone are the awkward side-stepping and the goofy shapes, we're now working the room as though we're in

White Christmas, performing a lavish musical number. He holds me close in a manly embrace with his strong arms around my waist and twirls me round, spins me on the spot and guides me through the space.

The room is loud and boisterous, festive and joyous.

We're gay and spritely, happy and bouncy.

I feel fantastic and giddy, free and light.

Fuck Poutmouth, I tell myself. Fuck her. She's not going to ruin tonight for me.

And she doesn't.

I'm every inch the old-school Hollywood movie star and, as the hours tick by, loving every second of it.

'Drink?' Real Brett asks, suddenly stopping us mid-flow before taking my hand and filling it with a glass from a waiter who magically pops up with a tray of refreshments.

'Have you finished that pot of jam yet?' Real Brett asks, leaning into me so that I can hear him.

With his mouth so close to my ear, his breath rushes past my neck and causes a tingling feeling to run all the way across my chest and down to my toes, the endorphins causing my brain to pleasantly shiver in my skull.

'I've got a bit left,' I tell him, my lips tingling.

'So, you've probably got just enough left for the morning,' he comments with an intake of breath, looking concerned. 'Well, what a pickle . . . you promised you'd share it with me.'

'I did, didn't I?'

'Yes. Looks like I'll be coming home with you tonight then . . .'

'Actually, I'm not going home tonight,' I say, enjoying the flirt.

'Oh?'

'Jonathan's booked me a room here . . .'

He hides his reaction well, but I notice the flash of a smirk before he pulls his poker face. 'God, and there I was talking about employees taking advantage of the fact we're in a hotel and getting up to scandalous behaviour.'

'Thankfully I'm not like that.'

'You're a real lady.'

'Just like you're a real gent,' I grin, my lips feeling bigger than ever as his green eyes cheekily sparkle as he stares at them.

His gaze remains there as his hand softly skims my bum before pressing into the small of my back. His tongue pokes out of his mouth a fraction, enough to wet his lips.

I mimic the action, my breathing becoming lighter as it rises to my chest.

He starts to lean forward.

I stop breathing.

He edges closer, still transfixed by my lips.

They tingle with desire.

His eyes flick up to mine so quickly that I gasp in shock.

He stops.

I swallow and hesitantly nibble at my bottom lip before deciding to remove the barely fifteen centimetres remaining between us.

Slow.

Teasing.

Wanton.

I.

Will.

Kiss.

Real.

Bre –

'What the fuck do you think you're doing?'

Our eyes widen at each other at the outburst, wondering what's happening – the space between us growing wider as we move apart.

The commotion has caused the music in the room to be stopped, those on the dance floor have been halted mid-flow, those gossiping in the corners have been cut short.

The party has ceased.

The faces in the room all turn to one another in perplexed shock and a hint of excitement as we each try to locate the owner of the booming voice that's exploded into our quaint and drunken little office party.

'I said, what the FUCK do you think you're doing?'

I know the voice, I've heard it before, but in that moment my brain can't quite place it.

'Get the fuck off her!' the voice snaps. 'Now!'

Heads whip round again, but this time the source is found and it doesn't take a genius to work out the target of the fury.

Dianne, Jonathan's wife, is stood holding open the door to an unused cloakroom – behind which Jonathan and Julie look like shocked children with their hands behind their backs and heads bowed. Their pallid faces, dishevelled clothes and sorrowful body language help the room to fill in the blanks.

There's a gasp, followed by muttering and then shuffling, as people move to get a better view.

It's a pitiful sight.

The room is silent and expectant. Waiting for more.

'I'm sorry,' snivels Julie, unable to raise her gaze higher than Dianne's expensive Jimmy Choos.

'Who even ARE you?' asks Dianne, not waiting for a response. 'What on earth would he want with YOU?'

'You know who she is,' barks Jonathan. 'She's Derek's –'

'Oh shut the fuck up, Jonathan. For once just shut it. If you were going to play away I'd have rather you'd done it with a cheap bit of skirt like your own secretary – not someone who dresses like your mother and isn't much to look at,' she spits.

Real Brett reaches over and takes my hand in his.

Julie bursts into tears.

'Dianne!' Jonathan hisses, going to put his hand on Julie's shoulder before thinking better of it.

'What?' Dianne asks, calmly. 'I'm sorry, was that unkind? God rest your mother, Jonathan. I shouldn't have compared her to THAT. At least she had class.'

'Stop it,' Julie sobs.

'Stop it? I haven't even begun.'

I've heard Dianne lose it before on the phone to me, I've seen her when she's come into the office and had a diva tantrum over me not getting her coffee order right, I've watched her throw a plate of dinner at Jonathan because he couldn't get her an invite to the royal wedding. When she says she's not even begun, I believe her.

'Dianne, I'm warning you –'

'Warning me, Jonathan? What are you going to do? Divorce me, darling?' she gasps, pretending to be shocked or upset at the thought of it.

'Why are you here?'

'Why didn't you tell me about it? Surely the WIFE of the boss should be invited to the Christmas bash. Isn't that the perk of being the wife at home – getting to put on a pretty designer dress once in a blue moon and making small talk with your minions? Isn't that one of my roles?'

'Partners weren't invited,' Julie mumbles feebly, as though that justifies the whole thing.

'And who's idea was that? Yours?'

'No, I – ' Julie stammers.

It was mine, I realize – one I'd simply made because I hate being reminded of just how desperately single I am, and that, at the time of planning this, my only potential boyfriend was a fabrication of my dreams.

'Was that your plan? To eliminate me from the equation so you could make your move?'

'I didn't plan – '

'Oh, you didn't plan to kiss my husband. Is that why his cock was in your filthy mouth when I first opened the door?'

My jaw drops.

The room takes a collective sharp gasp.

I will Julie to walk away and remove herself from the situation, but she doesn't. She stands there, accepting this humiliation as her punishment for having it off with the boss.

'Is that the kind of woman you want, Jonathan? Is it?' she barks, letting him know that silence is not an option.

'No, no – of course not.'

Julie winces at his response.

'You have a daughter! What will she think?'

'You can't tell her,' Jonathan grovels.

'Did he tell you he'd leave me for you?' she asks Julie.

355

Julie remains silent but looks up at Jonathan, visibly willing him to speak.

'No point looking at him. He'd say anything to get a quick shag or blowie. Shame on you for falling for it,' she snarls. 'What kind of a woman does that? How could you possibly stoop so low – a lady of your age? Do you have no self-respect? No dignity? No pride? Are you that much of a common whore that you need to gallivant in hidden nooks –'

'That's enough,' I hear myself mutter as I feel my body moving towards the drama. 'Come on, Julie,' I say, side stepping around the bat-shit-crazy wife to retrieve the office mum from the naughty step.

'YOU!' Dianne rages at me, clearly recognizing me as Jonathan's worthless PA, aka the cheap piece of skirt. 'Where do you think you're taking her?'

'Away from you,' I reply curtly, wrapping my arms around Julie and pulling her away from the spot she seems glued to.

'Are you going to go after her, Jonathan? Start your new life with the slut on her knees?'

'Of course not,' we hear him say as we make our way through our gathered work colleagues and out of the function room.

'Air. I need air,' Julie gasps, running for the front door of the hotel and out into the frosty December night.

'Julie,' I call, going after her.

A hand stops me.

'Wrap her in this,' Real Brett says, giving me his blazer. 'I'll go get her a drink,' he adds, striding back to the bar purposefully.

When I find Julie, tucked in the doorway of one of the delivery entrances, she's shivering manically from a mixture of the freezing cold and shock.

'I don't even know how it happened,' she sobs, her teeth chattering together.

'When did it start?' I ask, unable to help myself as I throw Real Brett's blazer over her shoulders and rub up and down her arms to warm her up.

'Years ago,' she mumbles with a whine. 'When he first tried it on I told him I was flattered but happily married. Then, once Brian left – turns out we weren't so happily married – he tried again and I was glad of the attention. Happy that *someone* wanted me.'

'Oh Julie . . .'

'It was harder before, but when I started doing some of your work and looking after Jonathan things became easier – it gave us more of an excuse. No one would question us spending time together if I was directly working for him too.'

'No wonder he was so keen for me to spend as much time as I liked out in Oz with Brett.'

'Sorry,' she sighs. 'God, I don't know how he can stand her. She's a bitch.'

I raise my eyebrows in agreement.

'*I'm* such a bitch.'

'No you're not. Just a bit . . . foolish.'

'Thanks,' she mumbles, stamping her feet to tread out the cold.

I do the same – my pretty dress wasn't made for standing on street corners in frosty weather and my toes are quickly turning to ice.

'Here you go, ladies,' whispers Real Brett as he hands out two shot glasses.

'Shots?'

He shrugs in reply as Julie snatches one of them and throws it down the hatch before grabbing the other and knocking it back in the same hasty manner.

'Thanks,' she says, handing the glasses back and bending over to put her hands on her knees. 'What do I do now?'

We both look at her and each other helplessly. I can't even imagine how she must be feeling.

'Why don't we go up to your room? You can get into some warm clothes and I'll make you a tea or something,' I suggest.

'Oh, I can't go back in there,' she groans, standing up and shaking her head adamantly. 'I can't stay in that room, I don't even want to look at it.'

'Why not?'

'His stuff's in there,' she says, looking down at the floor shamefully. 'He was in there with me earlier.'

Real Brett takes in an audible breath at the confession, before blowing it out, causing his lips to raspberry.

My mind goes back to the couple Carly and I overheard bonking earlier – never in a million years had I suspected it would be Julie and Jonathan.

'Well, you can't stay out here all night,' I say.

'Why not? Because I'd catch my death? Pneumonia seems a pretty good option to me right now,' Julie says glumly.

'Don't be daft,' Real Brett says, elbowing her gently. 'I know it seems like the worst thing in the world to happen but it'll all sort itself out. It always does.'

'Yeah?' she asks. 'You think so?'

We smile encouragingly in reply.

'Usually I'd agree with you, but I just don't see how that can happen here,' she says quietly.

'I think it'll all seem a bit clearer in the morning after some sleep,' I reply. 'We've all had a lot to drink.'

'Why don't we get you home?' suggests Real Brett.

'But my stuff . . .'

'We can sort all of that out,' I tell her. 'Or do you want me to come home with you now?'

'No,' she says anxiously, sucking on her bottom lip as she considers it. 'I think I'm better off on my own tonight.'

'Are you sure?' I ask, looking behind me as I hear Poutmouth Louisa stepping out of the hotel with a couple of guys from Accounts – all clearly talking about what they've just witnessed as they chug on their free drinks and light up cigarettes.

Julie looks past me and steps back into the crevice of the doorway, shielding herself from their sight.

'Yes. Just get me into a taxi. Please,' she pleads. 'Oh, my bag . . .'

'We'll grab all your stuff and I'll drop it over to you tonight,' Real Brett tells her.

'Do you have your keys?' I ask, thinking practically.

'There's a spare one under the mat. I just need money for a cab . . .'

While Real Brett gets his wallet from his back pocket and fishes out twenty pounds Julie hands me her room key.

'Thank you so much for this,' she says, fresh tears streaming down as Real Brett hails a taxi for her.

'Don't worry,' I say. 'Please call me if you need anything. Okay?'

'Thanks.'

'I'll be over soon with your stuff. We'll be as quick as we can,' says Real Brett, opening the car door and helping Julie inside. He closes the door and I wave sorrowfully as she leaves.

'Shit!' mutters Real Brett under his breath. 'This is crazy.'

'Tell me about it.'

Fifteen minutes later we're back down in the hotel lobby and Real Brett is carrying Julie's belongings – it didn't take us too long to gather it all, although the sight of Jonathan's discarded underwear beside the unmade bed will stay with me for a long time.

'Are you sure you're okay to do this?' I ask, handing him a piece of paper with Julie's address written on it.

'Of course,' he shrugs.

'Will you come back after?'

'I think I'll stay with her for a bit – just to check she's all right. This is heavy shit.'

'I would come but I need to oversee things here,' I say guiltily. 'Just in case any more drama unfolds.'

'I thought you said nothing happened at Red Brick.'

'Well, that's what I thought. Didn't realize I'd been so blind to what was going on right in front of me,' I admit, starting to question every time I saw Julie go into Jonathan's room for a meeting or when he'd come back in a cheery mood after a working lunch. 'This is not how I pictured tonight going,' I admit, saying a firm goodbye to my fleeting thoughts of a steamy night of passion with the guy stood in front of me who, on reflection, is actually quite dreamy.

'No, me neither,' he says, firmly grabbing my jaw in his

hand and gently pulling it towards his, his lips landing on mine.

I breathe him in.

'Enjoy the rest of your night and Merry Christmas. See you in January,' he winks, pulling away from me and walking out of the hotel.

Oh, how I swoon!

29

Christmas comes and goes, thankfully without any drama. I spend the shortest amount of time possible out in Tunbridge Wells with my parents and stay there for Christmas Eve, Christmas Day and Boxing Day. I would've spent less time there if I could, maybe just popped in for the Christmas dinner before making a swift exit, but a major downside to being single at this time of year (as well as the lack of sex, companionship and presents) is that I don't really have a valid excuse to be anywhere else other than in my old bedroom in my family home. My parents are highly accepting of this fact, especially as Max and Andrea have the excuse of wanting to be in their new home with Mavis Rose and don't come at all.

Luckily for me I'm not the only one who finds too much time with their family difficult. The gang, minus Dan and Lexie (who are with his parents this year – he is the golden child of the family and therefore loves going home), all reconvene back in the big smoke of London at the earliest opportunity. We mooch. We eat. We drink a gallon load of wine and eat a shit load of cheese. In fact, I stuff my face with cheese in the hope that it'll bring on some dreams because I find myself in serious need of some Brett time. Dream Brett, Real Brett, Any Brett – because Any Brett in my dreams is better than No Brett . . . and that's the void which I seem to have entered. I realize I've not dreamt of him since he was adamant that him coming back into my life (albeit via dream form) meant something. Ironic that he should then disappear on me.

The cheese doesn't help. Obviously it gives me the strangest and trippiest dreams I've ever experienced, but sadly there's no Dream Brett, just lots of clowns looming in my face and being eaten by sharks wearing goggles and snorkels.

I'm devastated, not to mention extremely petrified at where my dreams have taken me instead.

Following our lip-smack at the dramatic works party, I do hear from Real Brett. He sends a few texts during the time off, from his family skiing holiday (couldn't think of anything worse, even if me and my mum are on better terms now), but they're mostly polite and cordial – none telling me that he wants to rip my clothes off, but perhaps he's waiting to tell me in person . . . or in Oz! Either way, I try not to get disheartened by his reluctance to even mention our quick kiss. After all, I know he's been flirting with me and I'm pretty sure that's not all been in my head – although I am starting to doubt myself.

With regards to the office saga I'm returning to work none the wiser. I tried emailing Jonathan over the festive period but, from looking at his inbox, I know he wasn't checking them. I also tried calling him but he didn't pick up. When I phoned Julie, it continuously went straight to voicemail. Whilst I'm sure one of them would've been living in denial and pretending *it* never happened (if his wife let him), I know the other would've been stewing in her misery and having an awful time of it.

Half of me is dreading returning to work and seeing the

fallout, the other can't wait to get there and lay down the final plans for the Australia trip before flying to Sydney in just a few days' time.

I'm up early (surprisingly difficult after having a two-week snooze-fest) and, thanks to a major pampering session, looking my best – there was no way I could follow up my gorgeous black party dress with a baggy Disney jumper over some jeans. No, my mum would be proud if she saw me in my red skater dress, thick black tights and ankle boots. I really have made an effort and am feeling great for it despite all the yuletide overindulgence.

I feel positively filmic as I stride by the frosty canal, glide my way through the Underground and float into the office.

I know that my happy cloud is going to be burst to smithereens as soon as I see Julie's desk completely empty and Derek and Poutmouth Louisa sat in Jonathan's office, with her pouting along to whatever it is Jonathan's saying.

When Jonathan spots me at my desk he opens and closes his mouth like a clueless goldfish, before shaking his head and continuing with their meeting.

When Real Brett walks in five minutes later, I'm spying on their conversation from the kitchen with a huge frown on my face.

'Happy New Year,' he grins before mirroring my frown and looking into Jonathan's office. 'What's going on?'

'God knows, but I think I'm about to find out,' I say as I spot Jonathan standing from his chair and looking out at my empty desk.

'You're here,' he says, noticing Real Brett. 'Would be good to talk to you both. Come in.'

I take an almighty deep breath before following Real Brett.

Poutmouth Louisa looks up at us innocently when we enter the room, and Derek barely acknowledges us other than to send a nonspecific wave in our direction.

'Welcome back,' Poutmouth says, giving a solemn smile, as though she's really sad about whatever it is that's about to happen. 'I hope you both had excellent Christmases.'

'Yes, thanks,' nods Real Brett brightly, although refraining to ask the question back.

I ignore her entirely and remain silent, keeping my eyes on Jonathan as he heads back into his seat.

'I trust the break has done you both good,' he says, shuffling awkwardly in his seat before looking at us gravely. 'I'm not willing to make a big deal of this, so I'll just tell you exactly what's happening and we can stay professional about it. Julie's left. Her possessions have been packed up and sent to her home, she will not be coming back to the office,' he says flatly, his face showing not a flicker of emotion or embarrassment for his accountability in the matter.

Whilst I'm incredibly sad to see her go, it's hardly surprising given that she's been publicly humiliated in front of all of her work colleagues for something that the boss instigated.

'And there lies the problem,' he sighs, glancing at Derek before continuing. 'The coming weeks are going to be extremely tough as we interview for someone to fill the position and then train them up to the standard we require and have come to expect. To be a single PA down is not a position we relish being in, and, unfortunately, being two PAs down is just not feasible.'

'What are you saying?' I ask, my jaw clenching at what's to come.

'You're not going on the recce.'

'What!'

'I can't give you the time away from the office – three weeks, possibly more?' he asks, as though the thought is absurd. 'Come on, Sarah – you know that it's highly impractical for you to leave the office right now.'

'But the recce?' I stammer, too stunned at his decision to react quickly and come up with an alternative solution that doesn't involve me being left behind. 'We're meant to be leaving this Saturday!'

'And that will still be happening,' he nods. 'It's not ideal, but I've spoken to Louisa and she's graciously agreed to step in and go along with Brett.'

I bet she has, I think to myself as I feel my temper start to rise at the injustice.

'But it's Sarah's project,' argues Real Brett, thankfully put out by this new arrangement and not thrilled that he's going to be spending those three weeks with Poutmouth instead. 'She should be there.'

'Yes, but she's not actually a part of the Development team,' points out Poutmouth with a coy smile that makes me want to punch her in the face. 'It would probably be quicker with me anyway.'

'Well, there is that too,' nods Jonathan. 'Louisa knows how to dot the i's and cross the t's.'

'That's shit,' I murmur, my mouth wide open in shock. 'That's utterly shit.'

'Now Sarah,' Jonathan warns, visibly getting flustered that I've not immediately complied and then gone off to fetch him a coffee and pastry. 'I'm not saying that you won't be out there for the actual filming. But, I can't excuse you from the office right now, given the shift in staff.'

'I'll keep you updated,' purrs Poutmouth, her face looking increasingly satisfied the more agitated I get. 'I'll even send you a nice postcard.'

I resist the urge to fly across the room and rugby tackle her to the ground like the ninja warrior I suddenly feel I've become. Instead I stand up, glare at Jonathan and exit the room.

'I'll go,' I hear Real Brett mutter as he runs after me, takes me by the arm and leads me to the boardroom.

'I don't believe that,' I hiss as soon as he's shut the door. 'He's the one who's been having a bonkathon with his employee and I'm the one who gets punished for it. What an absolute bellend.'

'I know, I know. But stay calm,' Real Brett says, grabbing me firmly by the shoulders and anchoring me to the spot.

'Calm? How can I just stay calm? It's not fair.'

'No, I agree. It's totally unethical, but . . .'

'But what?' I stammer.

'I don't know,' he says helplessly. 'The matter's been taken out of our hands. I don't think there's much we can do about it.'

'I could quit!' I say boldly. 'I could walk in there and tell him to go fuck himself and leave him and his shitty job behind.'

'You could. But then you walk away from your project, too,' he says matter-of-factly, moving his face close enough to mine so that I'm forced to look at him. 'I think that's something you should take time to mull over. At the

367

moment it's still yours,' he reasons, his eyes imploring me to locate my rational-thinking-head and screw it back on.

'It doesn't feel like it,' I whine, just like a child. 'He's taken it off me.'

'No he hasn't. Don't let your hard work go to waste,' he whispers, his hand moving from my shoulder to my neck. 'You'll be out there for the filming.'

'He hasn't guaranteed that.'

'You will be.'

'Do you really believe he won't suddenly change his mind about that too?' I ask, staring at him with a distressed look on my face – my eyes heavy and miserable. 'Five days, Brett. He's taken me off this five days before we're meant to be leaving – after I've poured so much into it. How cold can one guy be? Nobody should trust a single word that comes out of his mouth. We saw what he did to Julie.'

'Sarah, I believe you've got to fight for what you think is right, I really do. But for now, you've just got to sit tight and not blow this up into something that can't be backtracked,' he sighs, before pulling in his bottom lip and sucking on it – his face looking just as weary and miffed as mine as he releases me from his grasp and puts his hands on his hips. 'Use the time while we're faffing over lighting and sound control to make the show even better. Make it impossible for Jonathan not to give you the promotion you deserve.'

'Do you really think I'll get one?'

'He'd be foolish not to.'

'And what if he doesn't?' I ask, knowing that it's a possibility.

'Only you can answer that one,' he says, offering an encouraging wink and sympathetic smile all at once.

I hate the uncertainty of the whole thing, but decide he's right – I shouldn't act rashly. I've got to think carefully about what I want from my future at Red Brick and whether I want to jeopardize what I've worked hard to achieve. When I asked Jonathan for a promotion all those weeks ago I was looking to ignite a passion within me and to prove my self-worth. I'd achieved that just by coming up with the pitch and then developing it further. Jonathan's seen that, I've seen that. If I am on the cusp of getting somewhere within the company, then I'd be stupid to walk away now . . . right?

I'm deflated, punctured and mournful when I eventually return to my desk.

I don't say a word to anyone for the rest of the day.

Not even Real Brett.

I deliver Jonathan's coffee and apricot Danish in silence – calmly hoping he chokes on it.

'What the actual fuck?' asks Carly when she gets home and I fill her in on the wonderful news, her jaw falling so low I'm worried she'll never be able to pick it up again. 'Please tell me you're joking.'

'Nope,' I confirm, my miserable head against my pillow while I hibernate in my bed, feeling sorry for myself. 'I'm not going to Oz in five days' time. Instead I'll be here training someone up to be a skivvy to ungrateful bastards.'

'Oh shit!' Her voice punches, as she sits on my bed.

'Yep.'

'What are you going to do?'

'Not tell my mum for a start.' I say with certainty.

'How are you going to do that?'

'Turn my phone off.' I shrug, pulling the duvet into myself. 'I'll say we're somewhere with really bad reception and email her every now and then saying I'm in an internet café.'

'You don't think she'd be suspicious? There are phone lines in Oz, you're not going to the middle of nowhere.'

'She doesn't know that. I'll tell her we're going somewhere really remote. If anything that'll impress her,' I say, enjoying my plan. 'And hey, not having to get an ear-bashing from her for three whole weeks could be my silver lining to the whole disastrous thing.'

'She's not that bad,' Carly says, raising her eyebrows at me and telling me off for being mean about the woman who brought me into the world.

'No, I know. She's not,' I admit, actually feeling bad seeing as Mum's been great with me over the past few weeks. 'But she's only *just* told me she's proud of me. *Now*, Carly, after twenty-nine years. Do I really want her taking that back and telling me she knew I was a waste of space after all?'

'She wouldn't say that,' Carly tuts. 'She'd probably storm into Jonathan's office and smack his bum at the ordeal he's putting you through, though.'

'Maybe I should tell her then,' I joke.

'And Louisa's going instead?'

'Yep. How fucking brilliant is that?' I shrill, starting to put on a stupid accent while waving my arms in the air theatrically, 'Oh yes, so Sarah can't come but here you go Brett – ogle Louisa in a bikini for long enough and you'll forget she even existed.'

'He wouldn't do that,' Carly frowns. 'He seems like a nice guy.'

'They all seem nice until they're faced with temptation. Then they're quick to jump ship and act like arseholes. Face facts – if Mark Owen could do it then none of us are safe.'

Carly gasps through her teeth. 'Still not over that betrayal,' she mutters.

'Ditto.'

'Oh Sarah . . .' she sighs, joining me in the bed. 'This is really crap.'

'I know.'

'And when will Brett be back?'

'Should be the 30th of January if they don't go to New Zealand,' I say, knowing the itinerary that I helped put together, and have dreamt of for the last month, by heart.

'Then perhaps that's your silver lining?' she says, widening her eyes at me in delight.

'What?'

'You'll still have your date for the wedding . . .'

Cue lots of smirking and sniggering from my Cheeky Cow friend.

30

With Julie gone and me playing PA for the two bosses in the company I become snowed under at work fairly quickly – especially when all the other offices around London and beyond return from their Christmas breaks and start phoning or emailing in. The only positive is that because I'm doing everything on my own I'm not asked to do anything non-work related – which means I don't have to talk to Jonathan's bitch of a wife Dianne. God knows what I'd say if she phoned in. I'd probably say something awful and get fired . . . or hang up on her to stop myself saying something awful and still get fired. Fingers crossed she'll realize she can reach Jonathan on his mobile and then decide to hire her own PA instead of harassing his – although I'd feel sorry for the poor soul who takes on that job.

Unfortunately my chaotic workload doesn't mean that I'm not aware of the meetings still going on in the boardroom without me. I have been invited along by Real Brett, but with no one to hold the fort for Jonathan and Derek's needs, I can't go in – even though it is only sixteen steps from my desk and I can hear almost everything they say as they talk of all their plans for the trip I organized.

My blood nearly boils over one morning when I hear Poutmouth squealing over her lack of wardrobe for the hot weather – I even hear her proclaim that if she doesn't have any luck sourcing summer clothes out of season then she'll have to spend the duration of the three weeks in her bikini (of which she has plenty).

Cue lots of laughter at her own 'joke'.

I've no idea what Real Brett's reaction was as he was sat with his back to me at the time, but I can just imagine the look of sheer delight on his face at the thought of it.

Even though I really don't want them going on the trip without me, I'd rather they just left so that I could forget about them and immerse myself in dreary January in London.

I huff and puff my way through the week – wishing it could be over. Especially as Real Brett takes a step back from talking to me so much – or maybe I take a step back from him because I'm still walking around carrying a ball of anger in my tummy and hating everyone in the office – even the innocent bystanders. Him kissing me at the Christmas party seems like a world away as I find myself wondering if perhaps it was just a 'caught in the moment thing' and that maybe we only ever talked because we were working together. Maybe the fact that I was the subject of his flirtatious ways was simply down to convenience.

My paranoia isn't helped by us both being busier than usual. Seeing as I'm flooded with skivvy duties and he's only days away from a huge trip, time slips away and robs us of the times in the day that we would usually spend together. Even the mornings seem rushed – especially as Poutmouth has started to appear around the same time as us, apparently desperate to get on top of all their plans during the last few days.

I am wretchedly unhappy.

This week is the worst I've had to endure during the whole eight years of being with the company, and I'm relieved when Friday rolls around and it's almost over so that I can go straight home, hibernate in my room for two days, watch repeats of *The Desperate Housewives of New Jersey* (much more dramatic than the one set in Beverly Hills), and eat lots of crap. It's a far cry from the visions I'd previously had of me this weekend – sat on the beach in sunny Sydney sipping on a cocktail and munching on watermelon while perving on Real Brett in his swimming shorts – but a weekend of feeling sorry for myself is certainly what I feel like I need. I'm quite looking forward to letting myself shamelessly mope over the ordeal.

The night before they fly off on their big recceing adventure, Real Brett comes over to me as I'm sending off an email to a recruitment agent called Tor (a task Julie used to take care of), saying thank you for putting Mark forward for the position (he was successful and starting a week on Monday).

'I can't tell you how much I wish it were you coming with me,' he moans, his knees cracking as he crouches down next to me and rests his chin on my desk, looking glum.

A smile creeps across my lips at the admission – and there I was thinking he'd gone cold on me.

'It sounded like you've been having a wonderful time in there,' I say casually, nodding towards the boardroom as I tick sending the email to Tor off the to-do list in my notebook.

'Really?' he asks, surprised at my assumption. 'I've hardly managed to say a word. She's so self-absorbed. I've never known anyone to talk about themselves so much. It's relentless.'

'At least you won't run out of conversation, then,' I quip, enjoying his description of Poutmouth and letting it reassure me.

'Conversation? Aren't they usually two-sided things?'

'You'll cope,' I say, sighing lightly as I look back at my computer screen. 'I'm not about to start feeling sorry for you, Brett. You're off to Oz while I'm going to be sat here watching Jonathan stuff food in his mouth and then spray it all over me while he gives me an endless list of boring and unfulfilling tasks to do – at least he won't be shaking my hand with his saliva-riddled hands any time soon, though – probably worried I'll bite it off if tempted.'

He laughs. 'Want to come grab a Wagas?'

He leans his shoulder on mine, trying to tempt me.

'Oh, you know – I'd love to,' I say, looking at him and breathing an apologetic sigh. 'But – I'm off to spend the weekend with Mavis Rose. Heading straight there once I finish work. Sorry.'

'No . . . I should've asked sooner,' he sighs sadly.

'Yeah,' I mumble, happy that he's accepted the lie, although suddenly sad that he hasn't questioned it as an excuse as he'd previously done – we're a funny breed us girls, always unhappy whatever the outcome.

'Feels like I've not seen you this week,' he grumbles, his green eyes wide and lugubrious as they look over at me.

'Yeah, it has felt like that,' I admit, glad to know I'm not the only one who's felt estranged. 'A busy week. Everything look good with you guys, though? You looking forward to it?'

'Hmmm . . .' he groans, acting as though his trip is going to be a complete ball-ache – something I'm sure he's only doing to make me feel better. Because, let's face it, if we were going together we'd be giddy with excitement right now and singing Men at Work's 'Down Under' while jumping around the office pretending to be kangaroos without a second thought.

I push back my chair and take a copy of the new guy Mark's CV into Derek's office, leaving it on his desk – just so he can remind himself exactly who's going to be working for him instead of Julie. Mark seemed nice from the brief chat I had with him while ushering him in and out of his interview, but he's certainly not going to have as big an impact on the office as his predecessor did.

When I get back to my desk Real Brett is on his feet, putting on his coat.

'I've decided something,' he says thoughtfully, wearing a frown. 'And I don't want you changing my mind here.' Pause. 'But you can finish the jam off.'

'Really?'

'I can get Nan to make us some more,' he winks.

'That's good, because her last batch is no more.'

'You ate it without me?' he asks, his jaw dropping as he tries not to laugh.

'Look, I've just been grounded in London – I think I deserved it.'

'Fair dos,' he winks. 'I will miss you, you know.'

'I'd miss me too,' I say, my dodge of an emotional goodbye making him smile.

'Well – be good while I'm away,' he says, loitering around my desk.

'As if I'd be anything else.'

He lunges for me then, his arms spreading around me and giving me a hug. 'I really am sorry you're not coming. I wish there was something I could've done to change that.'

With a kiss on the cheek and a further squeeze, he releases me, turns and leaves.

I stand, looking after him, and feel totally bummed at the situation as I stop myself from bawling my eyes out.

Five minutes later, once I've composed myself, I grab my red moleskin notebook from my desk and pop it in my bag, put on my coat and head out of the door – still thinking of Real Brett as I leave.

I wonder why I lied to him about seeing Max and my family tonight, and why I impulsively ducked out of spending time with him.

I'm embarrassed, I realize, sadly. Embarrassed that Jonathan thought so little of me to strip me of something he knows I've worked hard for, and humiliated that Real Brett saw him do it.

Even though Real Brett was right in telling me not to act without thinking in the heat of the moment, I'm ashamed that I slid back into the role of Jonathan's doting PA so quickly. That I was there making him coffee, replying to his emails and booking his car in for an MOT the very afternoon that he trampled all over my loyalty.

Do I really have no self-respect? No dignity?

Do I really place my own fulfilment so low down on my scale of priorities? After all, it's not the first time I've put someone else's needs and happiness before my own. I did the same with Dan all those years ago.

Perhaps I'm someone that people take for a pushover.

A total mug.

Mum's completely right about people like me being totally undesirable.

Well, I'm sick of being that person. I no longer want to make things easier for everyone else just to keep the peace. Fuck that. Sometimes in life you have to stop and say to yourself, 'You know what? Now's my time to be selfish . . .'

Well, now's *my* time to be a little selfish and make my life about me.

I walk home with great gusto and feel fully charged when I get back to our little flat.

Saturday morning I wake up happier than ever, which is surprising seeing as I should've been thirty thousand feet in the air at that very moment. I rebuff my plans for a weekend hiding under my bedsheets watching crappy TV – instead I pull out my moleskin notebook and flick through my initial pitch notes for *Grannies Go Gap*. I loved brainstorming for that and developing my tiny idea into something worth watching, that viewers would connect with. I'm not prepared to settle for being someone's unappreciated PA when I loved doing something else so much.

Continuing to flick through my notes, I stumble across a page that's not written by me, but by Real Brett. He must've written it while I walked away from my desk the night before.

'All our dreams can come true, if we have the courage to pursue them.' Walt Disney.

I take a deep breath.
I turn to a blank page.
I start conjuring up new creative ideas and scribble them down.

31

When I walk into Jonathan's office on Monday morning carrying his coffee and the requested pain au chocolat, I feel confidently ready for action. The last time I asked to be considered for a promotion I felt timid and shy, nervous of being rejected and laughed at for my audacity to dream bigger than my current role. But this time, I've done it. I've created, I've developed – I have a show that's currently being recce'd (albeit without me) on the other side of the world, and have proved that I've got what it takes to do the job.

This time I have self-belief.

This time I know my self-worth.

'Jonathan?' I ask, putting his treats down on his desk.

'Yes Sarah?' he answers without even looking up as he grabs his sweet roll from the plate and jabs it in his pie-hole.

'I was just wondering what the plans are moving forward?' I say, my voice as steady and calm as I feel.

'In what way?' he asks, flakes of croissant spraying over his desk.

'Well, will you be getting someone in to cover me? When I go to Oz?'

It's bold, it's brazen. It's necessary.

'Erm. I see . . . well it's a tricky situation, you see,' he coughs, taking a moment to swallow his food.

'Oh?'

'Well, no one's left the Development team — there's no position to move you to yet. I can't just magic one up. And, the fact of the matter is you are my PA. I can't have you swanning off when we're so busy. Your job requires you to be here.'

'I see,' I say, giving him an understanding nod.

'Don't be too despondent,' he sighs, in a way that is just that.

'No, of course not. I totally understand your point,' I nod. 'I'll just get back to my desk. Unless there's anything you need?'

'Oh, wonderful, thank you Sarah. Couple of biscuits if there's any going spare. That would be fabulous,' he says, stuffing the remainder of the food on his plate in his face.

'Certainly, Jonathan,' I say, turning and leaving his office.

I find two chocolate bourbons to accompany what I've already taken in and efficiently deliver them with a smile on my face.

When I'm back at my desk I email recruitment agent Tor about getting a new job, as I am now in absolutely no doubt that I need a fresh start somewhere new, in a place where I'm going to be valued and taken seriously.

Tor emails back within five minutes, telling me that there are already a few jobs out there that might suit me and asking if she can put me forward for them.

I say yes straight away.

I then stand up from my chair and leave my desk. Walking tall and full of self-belief, I head towards Jonathan's office. I don't want to stay here a moment longer than necessary now that I've made the decision. Yes, I realize I've got nowhere to go yet — but I will.

Walking in, I'm surprised to find Jonathan at his desk, slurping on his coffee and reading rugby player Gareth Thomas' autobiography – so much for being manically busy and needing me around.

'Jonathan, could I have a word? If you're not too busy?'

'Yes, of course. Come in, sit down,' he says without even a hint of embarrassment as he dog-ears the page he's on and rests his hands on top of the closed book.

'I'm sure this won't come as a complete shock given recent events, but I'm afraid I'm handing in my resignation,' I say, wanting to laugh as the words come out of my mouth – shocked that I'm seeing this through and making the change.

'What? But you just said you understood . . .'

'Yes, and I do. I understand that there's no room for me here to do what I want and that if I want to further my career I have to move on.'

'And you're sure?' he bumbles.

'Very sure.'

'But your project?'

'Oh, it is my project now?' I say, my face one of amused bewilderment. 'I thought I was just your PA?'

'That's not what I meant. That's not what I was saying,' he stammers.

'It was, Jonathan. Regardless of whether I stayed or not I wouldn't actually be a part of that show – so I'm happy leaving it in the capable and kind hands of Brett while I contribute my ideas somewhere else.'

'But, Sarah . . .'

'Yes?' I answer.

He sighs.

'Very well. I'm actually sorry we couldn't make this work.'

'So am I,' I respond, leaving the room.

It's a slight lie. Although I am sad not to be seeing my *Grannies Go Gap* idea come into fruition, I know a fresh start somewhere else is exactly what I need. If anything, Jonathan's done me a favour by not fully seeing my potential.

My only regret is that I might not be here when Real Brett comes back, depending on whether they extend their trip to include New Zealand too.

I try not to let the thought dampen my independent-women-moment that's worthy of a few finger clicks and some questionable head flicking.

For the rest of the week, as Tor successfully lines me up with some last-minute job interviews, Jonathan graciously lets me out of the office, knowing that I'll make up the workload and have even set about finding my own replacement to make things easier for him – well, I am still his PA.

By the end of the following week I've magically bagsied a job in another production company a few streets away. As soon as Tor sent me over the job description I knew I was right for the role – especially as it's with the people who made *Four in a Bed*, *Gogglebox* and many other reality TV shows that I've spent hours of my life watching.

It wasn't an easy interview process, but Tor's feedback was that they loved my passion for their genre of shows and thought I'd bring great ideas to the table. They were gutted that they couldn't nab *Grannies Go Gap* from Red Brick, but I think knowing I was going to jump ship without it anyway made them realize I was serious about the role and my future in Development. Having slashed their own Development team a decade ago, they understood how difficult it was waiting to be bumped up.

When Tor phones me with the good news I'm flabbergasted. I sit at my desk for a whole five minutes wondering if I'm dreaming the whole thing – although the chance would be a fine thing, seeing as my dreams seem to have vanished, taking Dream Brett with them.

32

There have only been a handful of times in my life when I've had to phone Mum and confess to some sort of naughty behaviour – like when I drove home from uni one Saturday morning stupidly tired from an all-night party and got pulled over by the police (they'd been driving behind me for ten minutes and noticed I had my windscreen wipers on full, even though it was a scorching hot sunny day). Although I passed the breathalyser test (I'd responsibly stopped drinking at midnight), I was in no fit state to drive and the nice policemen made my parents pick me up from Milton Keynes. They weren't impressed. Then there was the time I was caught stealing chocolate from Budgens by my friend's mum (luckily not the shop staff), who then made me phone Mum and tell her what I'd been doing. And finally there was the time I'd played truant from school and went to Brighton with my friends. After getting too enthralled by the two-pence machine I got separated from everyone in the arcades and my friend Laura Ponsford wandered off with my purse. With no clue as to where I was or how to get home, I panicked. Thankfully I managed to phone them with the handful of two-pence pieces that I'd won, although their stony faces when they came to collect me will never be lost from my memory. Even Max was pissed off with me because them making the drive to Brighton meant that he had to miss a karate lesson. It was a shit night, to be honest.

So, although on this occasion I know I'm calling with good news and that she'll eventually be pleased with/for me, I firstly have to tell her that I've withheld the truth and never left the country. As you can imagine, my straight-talking mum doesn't appreciate being lied to and I'm anxious as hell when I call her.

'Hello?' she welcomes, answering the house phone in her poshest voice.

'Hi, Mum.'

'Sarah, darling? I wasn't expecting to hear from you until you got back,' she says, seeming surprised and impressed that I've made the effort to call home.

'Yeah . . .' For a second I waver and wonder whether there's any need to tell the truth at all.

'Where are you now? What time is it there?'

'I'm not in Australia, Mum, and I've quit my job,' I say – quick, clean and to the point – killing the lie and setting my conscience free.

'Oh fuck.'

'Yep,' I say, not even surprised that my mum has dropped the F-bomb. Clearly the apple didn't fall very far from the tree, despite how prim and proper she might seem. Well, I had to get it from somewhere.

'What happened? What did you do?'

'Long story short?' I ask, not waiting long enough for her to reply. 'Jonathan was having an affair with Julie. Jonathan sacked Julie. Jonathan stopped me from going to Australia so that I could stay and make him coffee. Jonathan then said he couldn't guarantee a promotion. So I left.'

'Wait,' she responds, her mind clearly ticking away as she breaks down my quick ramble. 'Why did you ask for another promotion?'

Oh crap, I forgot that white lie.

'I didn't actually get one before,' I mumble, screwing up my face as I say it and wait for her response.

'What?'

'Well I did. I was in all the meetings Mum, and contributing – my idea *is* being made and there are still people out in Australia recceing for it – it's just that I wasn't getting paid for the work I was doing alongside looking after Jonathan.'

'So he basically gave you a hobby?'

'Sort of . . . just so he could hide his affair with Julie.'

'I see. Well it sounds very *Jeremy Kyle*.' Pause. 'What now? Have you signed on for dole money?'

'No, Mum,' I say, amazed at her tactfulness. 'I'm not claiming benefits.'

'Thank goodness,' she exhales. 'I was worried there. You hear of all these people scrounging from the state and I'd never let a daughter of mine . . .'

'I've got a new job,' I say, cutting her tirade short. 'I start next Monday.'

'Already? Oh God. Doing what?'

I've no idea what she expects from me, but from the tone of exasperation in her voice I'm guessing she's already presumed that I've turned to pole dancing – or prostitution.

'Working for another television company. In Development this time.'

'No.' Pause. 'Really?'

'Yes,' I say.

'And this time you're not lying? This is an actual job that you're being paid money for?'

'Yes,' I confirm. 'Good money too.'

'Well, I'm relieved. You don't need a boss like that. Onwards and upwards,' she sighs, neglecting to congratulate me. 'Actually dear, I'm glad you phoned. We have some rather unfortunate news.'

'Oh?'

'Well, we were all set to go to Dan's wedding but Dad went to the GP about his knee back in December and it turns out he needs a little operation on it.'

'What? Why didn't you tell me?'

'Oh, don't be silly,' she says, shrugging me off. 'Nothing major. We didn't want to worry you seeing as you were going out of the country – we were going to wait until you got back and tell you then. Anyway – the letter's come through from the hospital and it's scheduled for the Wednesday before the wedding. He's not going to be back up on his feet in time and I don't really want to travel all that way without him.'

'Oh no,' I say, genuinely concerned for my dad but quite delighted that they won't be at the wedding – that'll give me something less to worry about.

'Ghastly timing.'

'Yes, but Dad's health comes first,' I say.

'Obviously, darling,' she says flippantly. 'Although I want to hear about every single detail of the day – you must take photos. The official invites came through and I noticed the reception is being held in Pat's back garden. Well . . . I'm not sure what I think of that. Are they using a tent?'

'You mean a marquee? No Mum, they're just going to chuck all their guests outside in the middle of February.'

'Well I don't know, do I?' she tuts.

When I eventually get off the phone I walk into Carly's room, who's getting ready for a date night with Josh. Thanks to them ducking and diving around London keeping their relationship secret, and then Carly feeling ill whilst pregnant, they never really got to go out and enjoy each other's company without worrying – so tonight they're off for a date on the river. It's all very romantic and it's now my turn to lounge and watch her get ready for a change. I jump on her bed as she's finishing off her make-up on the floor.

'How'd that go?' she asks, looking at me in the mirror, before sucking in her cheeks and applying her blusher.

'Better than I expected.'

'See, she's never as bad as you think she is.'

'I think she's getting soft as she gets older,' I say.

'So, next on the list – when are you going to tell Brett?' she asks, turning to me.

'I already have,' I admit.

I hadn't wanted to tell Real Brett about leaving the company until I had another job to move on to. Just leaving with no solid plan seemed a little skittish and worrisome – I wanted to wait until my future looked promising and full of potential. Gosh, maybe my mum's views and morals have seeped in somewhere, because those words could've popped right out of her mouth.

'Whoa,' sounds Carly. 'When?'

'Right after I got the news,' I smirk.

'And?' she asks, raising her eyebrows at me.

'What?'

'Has he replied?'

'No . . . but when I next went on Facebook Louisa had posted a few dozen pics of them out at some beach party looking really drunk and dancing together.'

'Esssssshh . . .' she sounds, turning back to the mirror and picking up her lip balm.

'Yeah. My thoughts exactly,' I groan, rolling my eyes.

'It might not mean . . .'

'Hmm . . . it might not, in fact it probably doesn't – but it doesn't look like he's missing me too much right now,' I shrug, trying not to let the situation tempt me into becoming a bunny-boiling loon.

'You never know. Have you heard from him at all while he's been over there?'

'Not really. Only to let me know they'd got there and met the tour guide.'

'Well, he is in the middle of nowhere,' she says running her fingers along her lips.

'No he's fucking not,' I moan at her for using the exact excuse I was going to give my mother when she didn't hear from me for three weeks. 'He's in Australia – there's phone signal in every place they're staying. I've checked.'

As if by magic my phone pings to tell me I have an email – it's from Real Brett. Bizarrely I feel nervous as I click on it.

WOW WOW WOW! So chuffed for you. Now you'll never have to make coffee again. ;-) Look forward to celebrating with you when I'm back. x

P.S. She's doing my nut in.

I feel myself physically gush at my phone and laugh out loud.

'What? Who's that?' asks Carly, glaring at me in the mirror.

When I don't reply she turns to me, a big grin on her face.

'YES!!!'

I find myself stalking Poutmouth's Facebook page for the next few days, but thankfully find no further pictures of Real Brett – just the standard ones of her pouting in the sunshine. I'm guessing there's more to the pictures she took than I'd fleetingly thought. She was probably trying to make her ex jealous as I've not seen her post a single picture of him since being over there. Or she could be trying to make me jealous – which I wouldn't put past her.

I've no idea how, but I'm pretty sure she was behind Jonathan and Julie's exposé at the Christmas party – someone had clearly spoken to Dianne and pointed her in their direction, and, as far as I can see, the only person set to gain from the whole thing was Poutmouth. She'd have wanted to rock the boat somehow and scupper my chances of Oz . . . She's a total witch and I'm glad to be seeing the back of her. I'm just sad that Julian and my gorgeous elderly folk are going to have to put up with her while on their big excursion. Although, at least I know they'll have Real Brett.

Just as I'm about to leave the office of Red Brick for the very last time after four weeks of wrapping up loose ends and handing over my job to Jonathan's next skivvy, I find myself going over to Real Brett's desk, scribbling a note and leaving it in his drawer to find on his return from New Zealand (yes, sadly their trip got extended). It reads:

'No more half measures.' Breaking Bad

I smile at the quote, sigh at the office I'm hoping never to walk into again, turn on my heels and leave to meet my nicer work colleagues and my gorgeous besties in the pub for a very drunken 'So long, farewell' drink.

33

I get lost in the whirlwind of my new job. New office, new people, new names to remember – I hardly stop at all during the first week. I want to totally absorb myself in my new surroundings and forget all the negativity I've been wading through lately.

However, on Monday morning, on the first day in my new job, at eight thirty-two, just as I sit at my desk with a coffee I've brought in with me from The Barge Café, I get an email.

> Wow, mornings are dull here without you. Want some toast?
> I've got fresh jam! ;-) x

I smile at my screen.

It's also Real Brett's first day in the office since landing back from New Zealand at the weekend and it warms my heart that the first thing he's done is contact me.

> Yes please! Don't scrimp on the good stuff, though. I want a
> decent sized portion. x

> Size doesn't matter, Sarah – it's what you do with it that counts.
> You should know that. x

I receive similar emails around the same time over the next couple of days. None of them saying much, just having a little flirt about nothing extraordinary, but still – they each make my face crack into a grin and are a lovely note to start the day on.

Tuesday:

Fun fact: when Twister was first introduced in 1966, it was denounced by critics as 'sex in a box'.

Wow, I didn't know that . . . Thanks Brett.

Want a game? ;-) x

Wednesday:

Fun fact: otters sleep holding hands . . .

he writes, along with a Youtube link to a video of a pair of otters doing just that.

That's so cute.

I'm glad you think that . . . because I sleep like an otter.

Cheese . . .

Best you know from the start. I'm very snuggly. x

I think of the dreams spent lying in Dream Brett's arms and find myself sighing longingly at the screen . . .

'So, are you going to remind him about the weekend?' Carly asks on our way to the pub for our final quiz night before the wedding – the last one before our group contains a married 'grown-up' couple.

'I've thought about it – but I don't want to push it.'

'Why not?' she asks as we sidestep around a gaggle of teenage boys outside Londis who've gathered to look at their mate's new bike and glug on cans of Dr Pepper.

'It's on Valentine's Day so it's hardly a day that's going to pass him by unnoticed. He'll know it's coming up. I just don't want him to feel like he has to come . . . I don't want to force him there.'

'That's ridiculous.'

'No it's not.'

'It is. How's he meant to know where to go or any of the details? He's your plus one.'

'He's not my plus one,' I protest, pulling my coat around me a little tighter. 'That's just what Dan and Lexie have called it so that she doesn't get into a flap about the numbers.'

'Babe, he's your plus one,' she grins, throwing her arms around my waist and resting her head on my shoulder. 'You're meant to at least pass on the details and see if he wants to be lumbered with your company for the day.'

'Thanks,' I reply with an eye roll, tapping her cheek.

'He might have a date anyway,' she shrugs, lifting her head and screwing up her face as though she's not bothered about the whole thing suddenly.

'Oi,' I say, slapping her on the arm.

'What?' she asks innocently.

'Don't you play that reverse psychology thing on me, bitch . . .'

She starts cackling then and squeezes into me. 'God, you're hard to manipulate.'

Walking into the pub, we see all of our mates already gathered with drinks, crisps and nuts that are waiting to be consumed.

'Are we late?' I ask, looking at my watch.

'No, only just got here,' says Alastair, standing up and giving each of us a hug. 'Got you both a drink each.'

'Very organized, Alastair, that's what I like to see.'

Once hellos and hugs are out of the way I'm relieved to perch my butt down into a seat and grab for my large glass of red — it's become my must-have drink over the winter months.

'Is everything coming together?' I ask Dan as he sits down opposite me — surprising myself when I don't feel my body stiffen or my jaw clench.

He nods in response and puffs out his cheeks. 'We've spent the last few nights wrapping up the favours. I'm exhausted.'

'Exhausted?' laughs Lexie in disbelief. 'That's not even the start of it — we've got the place cards to go yet and the seating plan to finalize — and even then we'll still have a million more jobs to master over the next few days.'

'I'm surprised you've been allowed out,' laughs Josh.

'Nearly wasn't, mate,' Dan admits, rolling his eyes cheekily.

'All those little touches are worth the extra effort, though,' says Natalia, her eyes wide and sincere. 'They really make the difference.'

'At least I know you'll appreciate the time I've spent painstakingly tying delicate little bows,' he says to her.

'Mate,' Alastair says, shaking his head at the fact that his best friend has become so emasculated.

Thankfully Lexie laughs along with the rest of us.

Dan throws his arm around her shoulder and pulls her into him. 'You know there's nothing I'd rather do,' he says, lowering his voice.

'Oh, don't worry. I know that,' she giggles. 'Actually, if it's okay with you all – I'd like to say a few words,' she squeaks, shuffling forward in her chair.

Dan gives her a questioning look, clearly in the dark about what she's about to say or do. The rest of us just sit quietly as we sip on our drinks and munch on our snacks – we're a contentedly captivated audience. Even Natalia puts her phone in her bag earlier than normal to avoid being distracted by a client calling with a pillow dilemma.

'Right . . . I know I'm probably not going to see all of you before the wedding, so I wanted to use this last time of us all being together to say thank you,' she says, her eyes glistening. 'I thought it was going to be tough joining a bunch of people who'd been friends for years and shared so much together, but you all made it easy from the get go. From day one I've felt nothing but welcomed, even though there might've been cause to hate me.'

She looks up at me then with a pensive look and a nibble on her bottom lip, which is wobbling with emotion.

I wink slowly at her – and hope the look conveys enough.

She looks down at her glass of wine and takes a deep breath.

Dan reaches under the table and takes her hand, something I'm grateful for.

'You might've been introduced to me back then as friends of Dan's, but I'm so happy that each and every one of you is now a friend of mine too. I know we're going to make lots more memories together – and I promise to never turn into the nagging wife.'

'Unless it's necessary,' interjects Carly. 'Got to give yourself a bit of movement there so you can keep him in check.'

'Was almost looking like the perfect marriage there, man,' laughs Josh, his arm moving around Carly.

'Knew it was too good to be true,' sighs Dan, turning to Lexie and flashing her one of his mega-watt smiles. 'Not that I mind in the slightest, of course.'

Alastair gives a little fanfare as he slowly lifts his arm skyward, his hand forming into a thumbs-up sign, before dramatically slamming the single digit down on to the table in front of us.

Dan turns bright red with embarrassment as the rest of us laugh around him.

'Let's toast,' I say, raising my glass in the air, smiling happily for the duo sat in front of me. 'To being happily under the thumb.'

'Happily under the thumb,' the table choruses together before we all swig from our glasses.

Dan catches my eye and bows his head, throwing a pensive smile of thanks in my direction.

Thursday:

Fun fact: Leonardo da Vinci could write with one hand and draw with the other at the same time . . . Who says us guys can't multitask?

Are there any tasks you can do at the same time?

I reply, wondering where he's heading with this one.

Only rude ones. ;-)

Friday:

Fun/disturbing fact: twenty per cent of office coffee mugs
contain faecal matter.

I've just spat out my coffee.

Good job . . .

My hands loiter above the keys, wondering if I should
say anything about the wedding that's two days away.
Before I really have a chance to mull it over, my new colleague Debbie (she's my age, super cute and all kinds of
amazing – nothing like Poutmouth) comes over for a catch
up. The morning slips away along with my working lunch
and the afternoon and, if I'm totally honest, I don't have
a chance to think about Real Brett for the rest of the day.

After a manic (but hugely enjoyable) week, I breathe a
happy sigh as I wrap myself up in my winter warmers and
step into the dark, cold London night.

'I thought I might find you here,' a familiar voice says in
my ear.

'Brett,' I grin, turning round and, without thinking,
throwing my arms around him – either I've missed him
more than I've realized or I'm in a much brighter place
than I was before and giddily loose with my PDAs. 'What
are you doing here?'

'I've come to give you this,' he says, pulling a small

399

cardboard box from behind his back. 'You look lovely, by the way,' he adds, looking down at my new black dress, tights and heels combo – I went out and bought lots of new clothes to go with my new job. In fact, I went a bit credit-card crazy, so it's good to know it's money well spent.

'Thank you,' I smile, taking the gift from him and wiggle it slightly. 'What is it?'

'Open it,' he shrugs.

I lift the lid and pull out a mug with *World's Greatest Nan* written on it. 'Whaaaaat?' I giggle, looking bewildered at the mug that's identical to the one we saw Ethel using when we went to visit her.

'After today's fun fact I didn't think you'd be wanting to drink out of any old mug lying around the office, so thought I'd get you your own.'

'I'm not a nan,' I point out, pursing my lips at him.

'No, but I thought it would make you smile every time you used it.'

I do just that as I hug him once more, pulling him tightly against me.

'Thank you.'

'It's nothing . . .' Pause. 'So, what do you think? Want to try Wagas again?'

'I'm meant to be going home to a microwave dinner and a nice long soak in the bath . . . but sod it. Yes. Let's,' I say, looping my arm through his as we walk through Soho, feeling my cheeks blush every time he looks over at me to talk.

'Well, I've got to ask,' I say, when we're eventually sat down at the wooden benches and have ordered an obscene amount of food for just two people. 'How was it?'

400

'Honestly?'

'Yes . . .' I say with a squirm, part of me hoping he's going to say he hated the whole thing and wishes he didn't have to go back over there for filming.

'It wasn't what I thought it was going to be – but then, I had thought that you were going to be out there,' he says, his brow rising with disappointment.

'Well. You and me both.'

'I'd have enjoyed that much, much more,' he tells me, his green eyes dancing in my direction as our knees flirtingly touch underneath the table.

I try to hide a smile but it doesn't work as all I can think about is the fact that our legs are touching and that I can feel the heat of him through my tights and his trousers. It's a simple, little, thing – but it makes my breathing lighten and rise to my chest.

'Was Louisa a nightmare?' I ask, ignoring my voice as it catches.

'To be honest, I thought she was going to be a lot worse than she was. She got savagely duped by her ex over there so I don't think she was quite up to being the bitch we know her to be.'

'Why? What happened?'

'She went over to surprise him at the address she had for him but he wasn't there. It was his family home, so it's not like he gave her a fake address or anything, but apparently he'd moved out and into his girlfriend's place a long time ago.'

'Whaaaat?!' I ask as my jaw drops.

'Yep,' he nods, matter-of-factly, almost as though he's enjoying delivering the gossip even though he feels bad for her. 'Turns out he'd been dating and living with this girl for years but just came over here for a few months working or something. Needless to say he'd never told either of the women about the other one and had simply left Louisa in London and carried on with his old life in Oz.'

'Playa's gonna play,' I say like some rude girl before slapping myself around the cheeks and burying my face in my hands.

'Are we ignoring you just said that?' he laughs.

'Please,' I squeak, bright red.

He laughs again, leaning forward and placing a hand on one of my shoulders, giving it a reassuring squeeze to let me know he doesn't think I'm a total twat. Not a *total* one . . .

'Anyway, Lou was quite cut up about the whole thing and spent the rest of the trip crying or taking selfies – mostly to show him what he's missing out on,' he frowns. 'You know what you girls are like.'

'That's crap,' I say sadly, ignoring the fact that he's just called Poutmouth 'Lou' and that he's just bracketed me with her – he knows I don't do selfies!

'Yeah, it wasn't the best time to have a relationship drama – I think she regretted ever going over there . . . the rest of it was good, though, and obviously Oz and New Zealand are amazing. I just know it would've been a very different experience with you there,' he says, his knee knocking against mine slowly so that our legs gently bash together.

In response my foot arches in my heeled shoes, causing my shin to skim up his calf.

My head spins at another moment of having my breath

snatched from my throat as my happy endorphins send a surge of orgasmic waves to my head.

I'm given a few seconds to compose myself as the waiter arrives with a random mixture of our food – perhaps the oddest thing about the restaurant is that they just bring the food over whenever it's ready, dish by dish. It's nice in the sense that you don't know what's going to come out next – but I did once stuff my face with katsu and edamame, and then tried to squeeze in some gyoza that arrived ten minutes later, even though I was full to the brim.

'So,' Real Brett says, munching on a mushroom onigiri. 'What's new your end?'

'What isn't new?' I ask with a smile.

'Well, rumour has it you had Jonathan in quite a mess.'

'Did he cry?'

'I can't confirm that.'

'Or deny?' I ask, raising my eyebrows at him playfully.

'He looked quite embarrassed when he had to tell me, Lou and Siobhan about it when we got back.'

'Good,' I nod, hating the thought of them all in a debrief meeting with him.

'Idiot,' he shrugs. 'Him. Not you.'

'Obviously.'

'So how's the new job?'

'I love it,' I gush.

'Brilliant. They're lucky to have you.'

'Thank you,' I say, popping an edamame pod in my mouth and then feeling self-conscious as I slowly pull on it and suck out the beans. I've never realized how rude and suggestive the whole debacle is – definitely on par with eating a banana (which I've never been able to do in public without thinking about giving head and subsequently blushing my way through the snack).

'So, what I really want to know,' he says, oblivious to my inner thoughts as the waiter comes out with our chicken katsu curries and a fork and spoon – correctly assuming we're not going to faff around with the chopsticks laid out for us. 'Yes, so, what I really want to know is . . . what are the plans for the wedding this weekend?'

'You don't need to come to that,' I blush, shrugging as I spoon some breaded chicken and rice in my mouth and then quickly shoving in some water because it's too hot.

'I'm your plus one.'

'Well, yes . . .' I stammer, coughing on my food. 'But it's not exactly going to be – '

'I was invited.'

'You said you weren't sure if you could make it,' I flounder, delighted that he's remembered but panicked in case he's only coming because he was put on the spot and not because he actually wants to.

'I said, "We'll see" . . .' Pause. 'I saw and I'm free.'

'Are you sure?'

'Please don't leave me all alone on Valentine's Day,' he pleads, pretending to be distressed. 'This is my only hope of it not turning into yet another lonely affair as I eat icecream and sob while watching *About Time*.'

'Oh that is sad . . .'

'Exactly,' he nods, dragging down the edges of his lips with his fingers to highlight the sad face he's pulling. His mouth cracks into a grin and mine responds with one equally as goofy and ridiculous.

'Well, in that case – if it's actually a favour to you . . .'

'It is. I'm a total charity case,' he reasons.

'Fine – you can come.'

'Thank you – you're a life saver,' he winks.

'We're leaving tomorrow at midday,' I smile.

'And we're staying . . . ?'

'Ha! I'm staying in a little B&B down the road from Dan's.'

'I'll squeeze in.'

'Oh, will you now?' I say, amused by his choice of words.

'Oh fuck, I didn't mean it like that,' he moans, the tops of his cheeks pinking.

'Are you seriously going to blush over that after all the innuendos you've been flying my way over the last three months?'

'I don't know what you're talking about,' he laughs, innocently spooning some food into his mouth.

'Yeah . . .' I say, rolling my eyes at him before going back to talk about the weekend's plans. 'The wedding obviously isn't until Sunday, so tomorrow night us lot are going to a local Indian restaurant for a buffet.'

'Lovely,' he comments with a minuscule frown.

'It's his favourite,' I tell him, wondering if he's not an Indian food lover, or whether he thinks Dan should be doing something more boisterous the night before his wedding.

'Nice,' he nods.

'It'll be great. I think the boys have organized a funny little quiz for him – our way to send him off into married life,' I say, my hands flying into the air and causing my elbows to bash into the waiter as he brings out our chilli squid — thankfully the last dish to be delivered as I'm almost fit to pop.

'Maybe I'll leave you guys to it tomorrow night and get the train up first thing on Sunday,' he says, once the commotion with the waiter is over and the plate is calmly placed on the table.

'You don't have to do that,' I tell him, not wanting him to feel like he's not welcome.

'No, no . . . I think I should,' he shrugs. 'It sounds like a special moment for your group.'

'You sure?'

'Yeah.'

I pull a questioning face in his direction. 'What is it?'

'I just don't understand how you're not weirded out by the whole thing,' Real Brett says with contemplation.

'What? With Dan?' I ask, my eyes popping out of my head as I blow a pondering raspberry at his admission. 'It is what it is, I guess.'

'Really? I think if my ex was getting married in two days' time and I had to go along and watch it I'd be pretty messed up in the head right about now.'

'Yeah . . . the line has been drawn, though,' I shrug. 'It's not as if I still have lingering feelings or think of Dan as anything other than an ex who's a friend. Thinking of him in any other way just freaks me out,' I comment, picking up a piece of squid and placing it in my mouth.

'Glad to hear it.'

'Actually,' I chew. 'I think I'd feel shittier if I knew my mates were there celebrating all together and I was missing out . . .'

'Even at your ex's wedding?'

'Yep.'

'Girls are strange.'

'Couldn't agree more,' I smile. 'Plus, I now have an amazing date who's going to look after me and keep me entertained the whole day.'

'That's me,' he winks, making me laugh.

'You'd better not disappoint.'

'Pressure's on,' he smiles.

I've missed Brett and our exchanges – something that's been highlighted by the fact that I've had NO Brett for company for a whole month after weeks of having Real Brett and Dream Brett soaking up both my waking and sleeping hours. There's been a Brett void, and I'm so thrilled, relaxed and happy to have the huge crater of emptiness filled at last.

Therefore, I'm sad when we come to the end of the meal and it's time to say goodbye.

'Well, I guess I'll see you at the church,' he smiles, putting his phone back into his pocket now that I've typed in the address.

'I'll be the one in the big white dress,' I joke. 'It's huge and fluffy, you won't be able to miss me.'

'Nice, I'll look out for you,' he nods, leaning forwards and giving me a soft kiss on the cheek – pulling away slowly and stopping just a few inches from my face.

I actually feel giddy, mischievous, magical stuff oozing out of me as I look into his beautiful sparkly eyes – unable to stop myself as I glance down longingly at his lips.

He notices the look and breaks out into a grin. 'I'll see you Sunday,' he whispers with a wink, standing tall and walking away.

Just as I start melting on the spot my phone starts ringing in my pocket.

Mum.

'Hi, Mum,' I breathe, picking up while still gazing longingly in the direction that Real Brett's walked in. 'How's Dad?'

'Oh he's fine – they've really dosed him up on painkillers so he can't feel a thing.'

'That's good,' I say with a sigh, starting to make my way towards the tube.

'And how are you? How's your first week been?'

'Amazing. They're so great there.'

'I'm so pleased,' she says. 'I've been telling everyone about Jonathan's appalling behaviour towards you.'

'Oh Mum . . .'

'No, I have. I don't know how you remained so loyal to him for so long.'

'Neither do I,' I reply – although feeling like everything's actually fallen into place at the right time.

'You're a good girl,' Mum continues, sounding like she's on a roll. 'It's not easy changing jobs in the current climate but you courageously went forth and made it all happen. Such a brave move. You should be really proud of yourself.'

'Thanks, Mum,' I say, smiling at her words. 'I am.'

'Good,' she punches. 'Now who's this date you're taking to the wedding?'

'What date?' I laugh, surprised at the sudden switch in conversation.

'Don't you play that card with me, madam – Carly mentioned someone called Brett and Pat's just confirmed that his name's on the seating plan.'

408

'Why'd you call Dan's mum?' I ask.

'To show support and check how everything's going, obviously,' she tuts. 'Sounds like utter chaos there. The tent is up but the flowers have been a total disaster – all still in little buds. But that's beside the point. Who's Brett? You didn't tell me you were dating someone.'

'I'm not.'

'Then who is he?' she demands.

I can't help but giggle.

'Just a guy from work,' I answer, stopping outside the tube station and preparing myself for the Spanish Inquisition.

34

Two days later I'm standing behind a tree wearing a light blue Karen Millen bodycon dress (I totally self-indulged for the occasion) with the Manolo Blahniks Mum and Dad bought me (who cares if I can't walk, at least I'll look good), watching as the wedding congregation joyously heads into the church.

I'm hiding (actually hiding) as I see Alastair and Josh with Dan's old school friends and extended family, all greeting each other with beaming smiles. For the first time since accepting the invite to come along, I find myself hit with nerves.

I'm totally fine with the fact that it's Dan and Lexie's wedding day, but what has shaken me is the thought of going into that building when I know so many of the familiar faces will be wondering why on earth I'm there. Dan's elderly grandparents are going to be so confused when they see my face – and you can bet others will assume I've not been invited and have just come along to cause trouble.

I might've just got to grips with relationship dynamics within our group – but that doesn't mean everyone else is going to know that we still hang out together and consider ourselves friends.

I take a deep breath and exhale slowly – hating the fact that everyone else is in the wedding party.

'Going in?' a low, gravelly voice asks behind me.

'God, I can't tell you how close I've come to leaving,' I say, turning to find Real Brett in a dark grey suit, sat on a wooden bench behind me.

'How long have you been there?'

'Long enough to know it's a good job I'm here,' he says, raising his eyebrows at me.

'You were right – this is weird,' I sigh.

'And you were right,' he says, standing up, striding over and placing his warm hand on my bare arm. 'You have an amazing date who'll take care of you all day.'

'Promise?' I groan, sticking out my bottom lip like a child.

'Absolutely,' he says, leaning down and kissing the top of my head – a gesture that makes the butterflies that have been already going batshit crazy in my tummy go totally berserk.

'Please don't let me streak and ruin the first dance,' I mumble into his jacket.

'Such a shame, but I promise,' he grins, spinning me around and guiding me away from the tree and up towards the church entrance. 'Private show later?'

'If you're lucky.'

'Well here's hoping.'

'Guys!' Josh calls, once he stops talking to Dan's Uncle Andy and Aunt Sally, and has ushered them inside. He gives Real Brett a man hug before wrapping his arms around me and really giving me a squeeze. This is, without doubt, the perfect occasion for such an epic hug. 'All right?'

I wink in reply.

'Fancy seeing you two here,' Alastair joins in, slapping Real Brett on the back before draping an arm around my shoulder and looking down at my choice of outfit. 'You look beautiful today, Sarah.'

'Don't I always?' I ask, impressed with myself that I've been able to joke around, even though my body feels like it's about to self-combust.

'True story,' he laughs.

I hold my breath as we walk into the church and I spot Dan at the altar – a sight I don't mind admitting I had thought about seeing for the majority of my twenties (it's always the romantic bit in all the great filmic wedding scenes).

I feel nothing.

Well, I feel something – I mean, it's Dan stood at the altar on his wedding day, and I'm not made of stone – but it's not enough to make me weep down the aisle in despair or even throw secret daggers in his direction.

Turning to the man by my side, I take hold of his hand, knowing I'm truly grateful to have him here with me on a day that could've been a total nightmare. I feel fine and far removed from the lost girl I was only a few months ago, knowing that I've moved forwards in more ways than one.

Once the service begins, I smile at Natalia and Carly walking up the aisle in their pale pink bridesmaid dresses, sigh with happiness at the sight of the gorgeous bride Lexie (who looks like a magical angel in her exquisite ivory fishtail dress with heavy-detailed beaded waistband) and her dad as they pass us by, and cheer when the bride and groom kiss for the first time as husband and wife.

All the while, my hand is in his.

*

Once the service is over we walk outside and linger under a huge oak tree as other guests stream out of the church and wait for further instructions – all the while bombarding the new Mr and Mrs Tipper with their best wishes. I haven't had a chance to grab them to congratulate them yet, although we have the whole day ahead of us, so there's no rush.

'Did you see me trip?' asks Carly as soon as she sees us, her hands gripping hold of the fabric of her dress and holding it up – exposing her white legs and pretty silver heels.

'No, when?' I ask.

'Hello Brett,' she puffs, dropping the material and reaching up to give him a hug before continuing with her dramatic account. 'Just before I sat down. I tripped on my own fucking foot. Josh and Alastair saw it and then got the giggles every time they looked at me during the service.'

'Oh babe . . .' I smile, knowing she'll be really embarrassed.

'We didn't see a thing,' winks Real Brett.

'Are you still going on about that?' asks Natalia, coming over and putting her arm around my waist and leaning her head on my shoulder.

'It was fucking embarrassing,' she whispers.

'That was the funniest thing I've ever seen,' cracks up Alastair as he and Josh join us.

'It was the look on your face. Pure fear,' says Josh, bursting out laughing as he mimics her expression.

'Oh shut up,' Carly grumbles.

'It was pure class,' smiles Alastair. 'I hope the videographer caught it.'

'If you two don't stop I'm going to cry,' she pouts, her eyes already wet and ready to gush.

'Don't listen to those meanies,' I say, taking her hand and pulling her into a huddle with me and Natalia.

'I didn't even notice,' whispers Natalia, putting an arm around her.

'Brett!' someone calls from the gathered crowd we're loitering on the edge of.

'Ned!' he replies, his face breaking out into a huge smile as he opens his arms and walks over to his long-lost mate to give him a heartfelt manly hug. 'It's been so long!'

'Too long, man,' agrees Ned, who is almost identical to Alastair – although he doesn't have the fabulous man bun or tattoos. He's basically Alastair without the East London vibe – more business-like and clean cut.

Having bumped into Ned at the B and B, I know he was really excited to see Brett again – it's lovely to see the two having a good natter, especially as I know how deflated Brett was about them losing touch.

'Dan and Lexie have asked for you guys to head round for a quick picture,' says a young female striding over, who I'm guessing is the photographer's assistant. Everyone else seems to already know her – no doubt from having their photos taken as they got ready earlier.

'Great,' says Josh. 'Who are you after?'

'Everyone in "Rehomed From Leicester"?'

'Oh . . .' I say. 'You guys go – you're in the wedding party.'

'Don't be daft,' says Natalia, leading me by the elbow, totally ignoring my protest.

'But they might want a picture of you guys without me

in it,' I hiss, looking back at Real Brett, who is still with Ned.

'They'll have plenty of them,' she whispers back. 'This one is about us . . .'

We walk around to the side of the church as Dan and Lexie are having their last couple shot taken. They're beaming with so much love and happiness that it's almost impossible not to grin back at them and be soaked up in their joy.

There's a lot of whooping and laughter as we all mingle together and get giddy in the moment.

'Congratulations,' I grin, hugging Lexie and giving Dan a kiss on the cheek.

'Thank you so much,' says Dan, wearing a smile to beat all the other mega-watt smiles he's worn before.

'I can't believe we're married!' squeaks Lexie, jumping on the spot.

'Neither can we!' jokes Alastair, making us all laugh.

'If you'd all like to gather around the bride and groom, that would be marvellous,' says the male photographer, holding his camera up to his face.

We do as he says. Josh and Carly hug next to Dan, while us remaining three stand next to the bride, all grinning manically while the photographer clicks away.

'Lovely – now everyone turn to each other and laugh.'

We all look at each other with confused expressions at being told to conjure up this fake reaction out of thin air.

'Just think about something funny,' he encourages further with a shrug.

'Look, there's "The fucking High-kick-flyers",' exclaims Alastair, pointing past us all towards the rest of the guests.

We all gasp in horror and turn to look with huge frowns on our faces.

'Huh?' asks Carly.

'Where?' asks Lexie.

'Were they invited?' gasps Natalia.

'I'll tell them to leave,' frowns Dan.

'Those fuckers,' exclaims Josh.

We see nothing.

As Alastair starts howling we slowly realize he's been pulling our legs and fabricated the whole thing. We all crease up with laughter – getting the giggles at how gullible we've all been.

As tears stream down my face I look at my bunch of crazy-arse friends and fall in love with each and every one of them a little bit more – even Dan and Lexie.

Love really does make the world go round – and that's any type of love, not just the romantic kind.

I breathe a sigh of relief as soon as I check the seating plan and see that our bunch (minus the bride and groom, but plus Ned and his wife) are sat together – I was dreading the thought of sitting with strangers and being asked how I know the happy couple ('Er, well I used to date Dan,' is a bit of an icky sentence and one I'm sure would be greeted with horror).

We joke, we laugh, we get competitive over the table quiz (we win), we drink and we are very, very, very merry . . .

I have a lovely day.

One of the best.

Stuffed to the brim with delicious food (we had posh fish and chips and a trio of chocolate cake magic for dessert), I head to the toilet. On the way back I take a little detour and wander up the lit garden path running alongside the marquee, finding myself perching on a wooden bench that's been decorated with roses.

I sit there for a few moments and enjoy the stillness of my mind.

It doesn't feel like I'm there any time at all when I hear footsteps coming towards me. I'm about to get up and join the others when I realize it's Real Brett.

'Hey,' he smiles, taking off his suit jacket and placing it over my shoulders.

'Thank you,' I sigh, enjoying the warmth of his body as he sits down next to me.

'You okay?'

'Even better than that.'

'Really?'

'Absolutely,' I beam, leaning my head on his shoulder and gazing at the night sky above us. 'Tell me something, what did you think when you saw me in the office that day?'

'What, other than being totally confused and thinking I'd been transported back into some weird alternative universe?' he chuckles, his legs shuffling beneath us.

'I guess . . .'

'I wondered whether it was someone's way of giving me a second chance.'

'Second chance?' I muse, looking up at him.

'Yep.' Pause. 'With you.'

'Oh . . . ? And why would you have needed one of those?' I ask coyly.

'Because I was too chicken when we were younger to act on whatever it was I was feeling.'

'What?' I ask, completely surprised by his answer.

'What yourself,' he chuckles, brushing a finger under my chin and lifting my jaw out of its gawping position. 'I'm surprised Alastair never said anything.'

'Why would he?'

'Because I was always getting Ned to ask about you, to see if you were dating anyone. We were just talking about it actually.'

'You were?'

He nods and pulls his bottom lip through his teeth. 'Once I found out about you and Dan, though, I figured that was that . . . I even stopped heading up with Ned.'

'Why?' I ask, pulling a confused face as I remember his sudden absence and how Ned starting coming up on his own.

He shrugs and turns red. 'So, in answer to your question – when I saw you on that first day I wondered if you'd ever be able to live up to the memory of you that I'd built up. You'd become like this phantom dream-like goddess in my head – '

'Oh shit,' I blurt. 'I stood no chance of living up to that.'

'Is that what you actually think? You couldn't be further from the truth.'

'Oh shut up,' I whine, slapping him playfully on the arm at his nonsense talk that's nonetheless making me blush and winning me over. 'As if I could live up to some dream version of myself.'

My words stop me.

I gawp at him.

Whilst I've been having nightly dreams about him, he's been having daydreams about me . . .

'It's nice to think we were brought back into each other's lives for a reason, isn't it?' he says. 'Like it was meant to be.'

My mind whizzes back to the romantic stroll with Dream Brett, where he said those exact words.

I'm left in no doubt that dreams are powerful devices. Whether we believe that they are our brain's ways of clearing out the debris polluting our brain, our imagination's way of running free when our brain isn't in use in our busy lives or a portal to future events – they move us. Subtly or dramatically, they cause a shift to occur – making us wake up with new thoughts and feelings.

Sometimes frightening us away from the darkness that we need clarity on, sometimes pushing us towards the light.

They're guides to what could be and what we can achieve when our inhibitions are removed, but it's up to us to take from them what we wish – we can ignore them, or we can act on them.

After months of dreaming about Brett – the beautiful, funny, manly, goofy piece of perfection to my right, I decide to act on them.

I pounce on him. My lips are on his before he can say another word.

Acknowledgements

A huge thank you to the following awesomely cool folk:

Hannah Ferguson – there's a reason I always put you first in these things and that's become you're the one I send emails of self-doubt to and possibly drive insane. You're amazingly kind, thoughtful and encouraging and I couldn't ask for a better agent. Thanks for believing in me!

To everyone at The Marsh Agency and Hardman & Swainson, for making everything easy and for talking about my books even though we've never officially met.

Team Penguin! Maxine Hitchcock, Kimberley Atkins, Celine Kelly (although you're no longer actually in the office I'll include you in the team), Katie Sheldrake, Hattie Adam-Smith (welcome to the team), Beatrix McIntyre, Fiona Brown, the sales team and everyone in the Penguin building who's ever been nice to me.

To everyone on Twitter, Facebook, YouTube and Tumblr who has messaged me lovely things – I hope you realize how much those words spur me to keep doing this!

My lovely friends – I've not hung out with you all in so long because I've been writing this book (that's dedication). PLEASE can we go eat cake now?!

My wonderful family – Mum, Dad, Giorgie, Mario, Debbie B, Chickpea, Bob and Carrie! You're all superb and I love you dearly. Thanks for being so understanding, loyal and for always bringing dinner when you come over.

Debbie Fletcher – this book would not have happened without you looking after Buzz. Thank you for pouring so much love into your grandson – it really helps to ease off the mummy guilt knowing he's having so much fun with you and Bob.

Tom and Buzz, my two dudes. You are my world and everything I've ever dreamt of having in my life. My love for you knows absolutely no bounds. Long may the love and laughter continue!

'Warm and romantic, this charming read will
certainly brighten up your day'

Closer

Billy and Me

'A gorgeous, gloriously romantic read with
buckets of charm – I absolutely loved it!'
Jill Mansell

Giovanna Fletcher

The gorgeously romantic story of one small-town
girl and the world's most famous movie star . . .

The perfect romantic
short story to warm you up
this Christmas!

'A heartbreakingly beautiful story about friendship and unrequited love. I was totally and utterly captivated'

Paige Toon

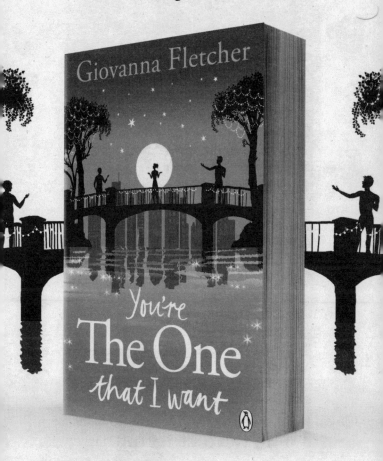

Giovanna Fletcher

You're
The One
that I want

It's Maddy's wedding day but has she made
the right choice between the groom and
his best man . . . ?

The gorgeously romantic sequel to
Billy and Me

The charming sequel to
Billy and Me

Giovanna
Fletcher

*Always
with
Love*

Los Angeles to Rosefont Hill: 5,241 miles.
Can their love last the distance?